The Undertaker's Daughter

by

M. Culler

The Undertaker's Daughter

Cover Art by *Rae Monet, Inc.*

The Wild Rose Press, Inc.
PO Box 708
Adams Basin, NY 14410-0708
Visit us at www.thewildrosepress.com

Publishing History
First Edition, 2023
Trade Paperback ISBN 978-1-5092-4655-7
Digital ISBN 978-1-5092-4656-4

Published in the United States of America

"All my life, I've been given the ability to converse with those who've passed away but not yet passed on. Lavinia is not able to be free. I do not believe she willingly chooses to stay. Other spirits seem mildly confused, transient. Lavinia doesn't even speak to me. She… transplants me into the thoughts that bind her here. Terrifying, miserable thoughts." Charlotte gave a desperate shudder, then steeled herself. "Dr. Everly, I want Lavinia and myself to find peace and some measure of freedom. I believe that solving her murder would help us both. If you wish to assist me in such an endeavor, I should be very grateful, but—" She took a deep breath. "If not, I shall undertake the matter myself." She thrust her chin forward in determination, something her auntie Molly had also told her was unbecoming in a woman, either making them look willful or saucy.

****

James' eyes flickered to the side, catching the iron in her tone, hidden under quite delicate features, a small, shapely nose and beautifully shaped lips that were thin and grim at the moment. "You're quite right," he admitted with a sigh.

Charlotte nearly fell over. "I am? That is, yes. I am. Although you made a good point, too. We shall have to be very discreet."

Dedication

To my beloved husband, Phil, who makes my dreams
come true.
To my children, who cheer me on.
To Harry, Becky, Rachelle, Judy, Shannon, Jen, Laura,
Evan, and dozens of my writing brothers and sisters
who pushed me all the way.
To my grandmother, Gladys Felice, who knew I could
do it.
To my parents, who don't like spooky stuff, but will
read this because they love me.
Soli Deo Gloria.

Historical Notes

While the setting for this series is inspired by Victorian-era London, including the tragic Whitechapel Murders, this is a fictional universe. Some of the practices described in the medical and funereal arts are actually true, though they may seem shocking today. For example, prior to the American Civil War, embalming was a practice rarely used. Bodies were typically "laid-out" at home until taken directly for burial. The death of a loved one meant contacting many different entities. Funerals were only attended by the immediate family in many cases. The idea of a "funeral director" who would take charge of all the preparations was unheard of in the mid-1800s. (Until Mr. Harkness came along…)

Additionally, short, serialized fiction, such as detective stories, were popularized during the Victorian era in the United Kingdom. Known as penny dreadfuls, the term typically referred to a story published in weekly parts of 8 to 16 pages, each costing one penny. *The Undertaker's Daughter* was originally released as three shorter works. Perhaps they were *pound* dreadfuls?

Historical "inaccuracies" are deliberate fictional twists and tweaks made by the author for reasons of the plot.

Part One:

Dearly Departed

Chapter One

Harkness and Sons stood apart from any other building in the crowded corner of its East London dwelling place. It was as if fate had decided to protect the surrounding citizens from rubbing shoulders with death's earthly representatives.

Oh, it was all too true that death and the East End were no strangers. Her squalid yards and overflowing doss houses meant nightly contributions to the body merchants who would take the poor and unfortunate inhabitants to their final destination, not one of the overflowing and foul city churchyards, but to large baskets outside of hospitals and anatomy clinics where porters would collect them in the morning. Aspiring surgeons would spend days dissecting and breaking down a body, faces wrapped in camphor-soaked cloths to block the stench. When flesh was properly separated from bone, everything was sewn up in sturdy cotton sheets and buried in a giant pit on the far reaches of the hospital grounds.

Not so for the clients of Harkness and Sons. Reginald Harkness, Proprietor, Undertaker, and Director of Funeral Services, had a state-of-the-art facility for the dearly departed. No more calling for the undertaker, the coffin-maker, the shroud-maker, the feather-wavers, and the funeral carriage as separate entities. Harkness and Sons would supply all the services required for one fee, a one-stop shopping experience for the recently bereaved.

Unfortunately, Mr. Reginald Harkness, a distinguished man with an appropriately sympathetic face, was also a *one-man* operation. He was the only remaining son of Harkness and Sons, a reputable firm of undertakers since His Majesty George III's time. Fathers and sons had kept the business going, but now it seemed that its doors would be shuttered when Mr. Harkness joined his clientele.

No daughter of his would run the family business—even if she seemed oddly keen to do so.

****

"Charlotte! Charlotte?" Reginald poked his head into the kitchen. Clean. No smells of cooking. He sighed. "Charlotte, are you—" The brassy pealing of the bell from the back garden made Reginald abandon the search for his daughter.

Most women, certainly women with a clever mind like Charlotte's, should have been pursuing studies suitable to her sex, perhaps art, music, or sewing. The business made a good income, enough to help the girl set up her own shop. She could find employment as a seamstress or perhaps a milliner? A florist would have been ideal as he would have loved to supply flowers for the funeral carriages as well.

He had no illusions that Charlotte, even though she was radiantly beautiful to his proud paternal eyes, would easily find a husband. Who would come to pay her court here, with coffins in the small showroom that had once been his late wife's parlor and open-sided carriages coming to the back gate instead of lovesick boys with bouquets?

Speaking of carriages, Mr. Bartlesby was just coming to collect the coffin and shroud for the late Mr. Samuels. "Charlotte."

"Yes, Father?" A sweet face with wide blue eyes and curling golden hair arranged in a mass of pins atop her head poked around the door from the "laying-out" room.

Mr. Harkness jumped. "What are you doing in there?"

"Keeping Mrs. Perkins company until the vicar comes to collect her this afternoon."

"Charlotte, I've told you—"

"I know the spirit has gone on, Father, but imagine what it must've been like, to live ever so long and then to be taken ill so quickly and that mean landlady unwilling to leave her lie until the gravediggers could prepare a space in the churchyard. The cheek."

Her father rolled his eyes heavenward. "Charlotte, a lady mustn't say things like that."

An impish grin crossed her face. "At least I didn't say blo—"

"Dear me. Listen, Mr. Bartlesby is here, and I must go collect the late Mr. Samuels. The vicar won't come until after tea. If he's early, give him a cup of tea and a biscuit—"

"We're out of biscuits."

"Then be useful and *bake* some biscuits, finish sewing those shrouds I've been reminding you about for a week, and take some money to the flower stalls and get the usual." He swiftly kissed her cheek, jamming his black silk top hat on his head. "You forgot to steam the brim." One side of the brim had lost some of its elegant curl.

5

"Yes, Father, I will." Charlotte ducked her head to kiss his cheek in return, mindful not to knock the hat askew.

"Thank you. And Charlotte?"

"Yes?"

"For heaven's sake, don't let the vicar catch you 'chatting' to the dearly departed."

As her father hurried away, Charlotte sighed. "It's not my fault. It's not like I *start* the conversations. I'm simply too polite to ignore them."

****

Charlotte rolled out shortbread biscuits. They were easy to make and her father's favorite. She was debating whether to run to the flower stalls in the market or put the leg of mutton in for supper.

"When Mr. Perkins worked for Smithfield, we had such lovely chops and all the tripe you could ask for, calves' feet, too. But cruel to the beasts, they were."

Charlotte sighed. Mrs. Perkins was a very chatty soul—literally. "Isn't he waiting for you?"

"Oh, I imagine so, dear, but you were so kind to come and settle me down when I found m'self all discombobulated, neither being here or there, you might say. A nice light hand with the dough you've got. Make someone a good wife."

"Thank you." It was no point in arguing with the gregarious and nebulous voice inside her head. She was not the marrying kind. She was the kind that was one step away from a permanent spot in an asylum, or at least the Yorkshire Dales.

The Yorkshire Dales were where her mother's sister, her aunt Kate, lived with her strapping farmer husband and their three enormous sons. To her father's way of thinking, the place radiated wholesomeness, clean air, sound bodies, and sound minds. It was the latter he believed Charlotte was lacking.

"I'm not mad, you know," Charlotte muttered.

"Are you talking to yourself? Sign of being touched in the head," Mrs. Perkins tutted.

"I'm not touched. You're here, aren't you?"

"I seem to be. S'pose it's because I haven't been properly buried. Do you think that's why?"

She slid the biscuits into the black-leaded oven and shut the door with a bang. Charlotte wished she could answer in the affirmative, but it hadn't been the case. Her mother had died years ago now, and she still heard her voice sometimes, felt her presence like a fleeting shaft of sun when passing by a window on a bright day. Her governess, whom she'd called Auntie Molly, had died four years ago and never made a peep or an appearance.

"I think that's why," Mrs. Perkins continued. *"Makes sense, don't it? That must be why there's ghosts at places where wars were fought, haunting the battlefields. Some like as never got buried the proper way."*

"Then why do they think the Tower is haunted? The executed were buried." Charlotte was beginning to feel cross. Most of the spirits who decided to speak to her needed a simple nudge, a little kind explanation. You've passed away. Your soul must go on. Yes, the body is in good hands, my father is the best in the business. But some… She fetched her hat and shawl with a sigh. "I'm going to go out as soon as the biscuits are baked."

"What? And waste all that good fire you've got going? Mutton ought to be roasted long and slow, dearie."

"I'll build another fire up." Impatience crept over Charlotte.

"Must be nice for them's that can."

Charlotte turned toward the direction of the nebulous presence, feeling its location rather than being able to see the owner of the scolding matronly voice. Mrs. Perkins' tone held quiet disapproval.

Charlotte told herself that was the bulk of her troubles.

I can't please anyone, alive or dead.

She was quite relieved to leave the house and hurry through the damp, chill air to the flower stalls. Mrs. Perkins hadn't realized that she could follow her and that was a bit of a relief.

****

"Hello, Miss Harkness." Bob doffed his flat, rather stained cap.

"Hello, Miss Harkness, how's your father keeping?" His wife shuffled forward, a smile on her round, ruddy face.

"Hello, Bob. Hello, Mary. He's busy today. What have you got?"

"Mums and daisies, mainly, miss. It's the season, miss, losing the summer flowers."

"I imagine. Winter is a busy season for us, too. Consumption. So much worse in winter." Charlotte made conversation with Bob and his wife, loading her basket with flowers, buying them out, and feeling a bit guilty about it.

"You could do them fake flowers like they have on hats?" Mary suggested.

"I might have to, but they cost a lot more." Charlotte, for all the flaws her father gently assured her she possessed, was very clever with money.

"Well, you'll charge it back to the customers, won't you?"

"I suppose we'd have to. Although I was thinking we could do pine and holly. That would look nice, surely?"

"I suppose it would, miss."

Charlotte looked at the slate by the wooden cart filled with baskets and surrounded with barrels, now fairly empty. She counted out the coins quickly and passed them to Bob, who made notes in a scrawl that must've meant something to him, though it was indecipherable to her.

"And an apple for you and one for your father," Mary insisted, pressing them on top of the flowers.

"That's very kind, thank you."

"You could get a few more and make up a nice apple tart for your father," Bob hinted.

"Bob," Mary scolded. "Pushy devil."

Charlotte smiled and shook her head. "I've made his favorite shortbreads and I have to get on. The vicar will be coming after tea. I need to get the mutton in the oven."

"Ahh, pretty girl, she cooks, and she's good with figures. Mark my words, Miss Charlotte, you'll be needing your *wedding* flowers by the summer."

Charlotte laughed and waved. Bob and Mary were a devoted little couple, both with plump faces and weather-beaten hands, both missing a few teeth, and wearing the same worn brown coats no matter the weather. While Charlotte and her father lived near Tower Field, in a more prosperous area, she had gathered that Mary and Bob lived farther afield from the market, a long way down the Whitechapel High Street, right before

St. Clementia's. St. Clementia's was a tiny, unadorned church that was the last bastion of respectability before squalor, opium dens, and houses of low character took over beyond the main road. The deeper you went, the worse it got. When Mary had suffered a bad fall in January, Charlotte had been all for taking them a meat pie. Her father had nearly needed to be outfitted for a coffin of his own.

A lady must never, ever, *ever* venture past St. Clementia's at night, unescorted, or at all, he had thundered, idly shredding January's *Undertaker's Gazette* in his distress.

Why he'd bothered with mentioning night or unaccompanied when he was going to add "at all" was beyond her. He didn't much care for Charlotte pointing that out, either.

"Mind your reticule and basket, Miss Charlotte." Mary always reminded her of this when she turned to leave, her voice a wary whisper, eyes roving through the crowded market. Today was no exception. "Are you heading straight home?"

"I'll be careful, Mary, and yes." Charlotte's smile was strained. Heaven only knew what girls ten years her junior were doing on London streets, selling flowers, fish, fruits, or something else, walking alone day or night, living alone, like old Mrs. Perkins. To say nothing of the boys!

But she was a "lady" of good family and respectable status, hovering around the upper bit of middle-class, she supposed. As she hurried home, keeping her eyes properly averted, she couldn't help but wonder. Was it for her protection as a person or the protection of her reputation that she mustn't venture too far from the main

10

streets in the better parts of the city?

"Both, little bird," her mother's voice seemed to breathe against her ear.

****

"Ohhh. Oh, you mustn't say such wicked things." Lavinia Everly giggled and fluttered dark black lashes that framed laughing brown eyes.

"But I must when you encourage me so." Her companion bent his head, his dark, curling locks combed in the latest rakish style. They tumbled forward, hiding his mischievous eyes. His lips flicked the soft skin of her ear and watched her shiver. Something in him shuddered, too. Disgust. Desire.

It was a constant struggle for supremacy.

Just like her, just like a woman. She shied away from his touch on her neck, his hand pulling her too intimately close, and yet if he should treat her with cold reserve, she was cloying and clinging, a leech upon his elbow.

Yes, women were all the same, vines choking the flowers, pretending to be so helpless when really they were the devils who would ensnare unsuspecting men. Like Lavinia did now, shuddering from his touch like a shrinking violet, but urging him with squeezes on his arm as the cab rambled over the cobbles.

A wave of fog rolled in, carrying a sepulchral stench and a metallic taste on the tongue. Outside, the driver coughed violently, startling Lavinia into speech.

"Why, where are we?" She craned her neck and drew back with a gasp. "Oh. Oh my. This is the place you wished to bring me?"

"You wouldn't be allowed in my rooms, and your mother won't have me 'round, now that she knows my prospects are bleak," he informed her bitterly. Anger flared again. *She wanted to meet but can't be seen with me in public. What did she expect me to do?*

"Why, you'll keep us fine. Mother's got money; I'm sure Father left us plenty," Lavinia said complacently.

Another dead father. His own had passed. Hardly been cold before his mother married again, a florid-faced man with a title, a baronet with a decent estate. She promptly bore him a son to pass the title on to as well. This ensured that he, the unwanted stepson, would have nothing but his late father's legacy, whatever was left that his mother hadn't spent in catching her second husband's eye.

With an angry rap, he bade the driver stop and handed Lavinia down from the carriage with a whirl of skirts and nervous giggles.

"Can't we go to *your* mother's home? Oh, no, I suppose it is too far for a night's journey. But I must be back soon. Mother doesn't know I've left, you know."

"No?" The blackness behind his eyes suddenly ticked up a notch.

"I told her I'd gone to bed with a headache. She found your last letter to me, and she and I had such a row."

"Thank heavens I didn't sign it."

"Oh, but you did." Lavinia sighed dreamily. "Not with your true name, but still. *Love*, Jack. How deliciously scandalous it is, our clandestine meetings, secretly posting letters, using an assumed name lest Mama intercept them…"

He said nothing, taking her arm and looking above the doors for a house that had a large lantern swinging from an iron hook. Any one would do.

"Is this where you stay when you come to the city?" Lavinia's voice was a tiny squeak.

"Fourpence gets you in," he said shortly, steering past leering drunkards and beggars. He pushed her roughly through the pile of refuse and filth outside the battered doorway. She let out a little squeak and all but fell into the dark hall.

A beggar's hand grabbed his pocket. Darting a glance at his floundering companion, he made a quick decision. A violent punch sent the man's head cracking into the exterior wall with a sickening crushing sound. Was it the wood or his skull?

"No matter," he muttered.

"Want a room?"

Lavinia shrieked as if someone had stabbed her with a hatpin. He rolled his eyes and dropped money into the outstretched palm of a very dirty and wizened old crone, her face barely visible over layers of lice-ridden blankets.

"All the way in the back. On the right. Out in the morn by ten or pays again!"

"Yes." He curtly nodded and steered Lavinia ahead of him.

The houses of Registered Common Lodging were usually all the same, a den for thieves and whores, or worse. They didn't care for the cleanliness if they were saved from a night in jail or a night freezing to death in the elements. The government officers who were supposed to be stamping out the filth, disease, and crime of the London slums rarely came to inspect the worst premises. If they did, they could usually be bought off for a song.

As he opened the door, he saw a stripped bed, a

chamber pot that was mercifully empty, and a three-legged stool.

"Oh! Oh, we can't stay here," Lavinia hissed, her voice quaking with fear. "I saw a mouse."

"You'll see a rat in a minute." He laughed. "Come now, you wanted to be alone with me. Implored me so sweetly in your letter. How did you post that?"

"Mama has not been well. The doctor came round last week, and I sent it with Sadie, the maid."

"She didn't think it was odd?"

"Sadie can't read. She wouldn't think it odd if she could; the poor thing can barely think at all!" She laughed as if she'd said something very clever.

"Hm. But she can clean and cook and dress her lady in fincry?" He kissed her gloved hand.

Lavinia hesitated, letting his lips linger as her eyes closed. He knew Lavinia was aware of his eyes on her. She lit up under his attention. She took off her hat, carefully setting it on the stool with a swish of her hips, letting her long ebony hair fall free. "What brains does one need for cooking and cleaning?" she simpered.

"Let's see *your* talents then."

"You've heard me sing and play the pianoforte."

"Very lovely it was, too. But what else have you got to offer a man?" *What else, but what you think I want, a chance to rut inside you like some filthy beast…*

Maybe you're right, Lavinia. We'll see.

"We… mustn't."

"Mustn't do what?" he led, stealing a kiss from her paling lips.

"I want to go home!" Lavinia pushed him off with a pout.

"Fine. Go home. There's the door."

"I can't—I can't go alone."

"Then stay."

"Take me home right now."

Look at her, giving orders, so haughty, her dainty nose in the air when she's not looking down at you, that is. Worst kind of woman. The blackness raged. It fell. *Let her escape. Escape yourself.*

"As you wish." He retrieved her hat and held it out to her with a flourish.

"Wait." Lavinia bit her lip, nervously twisting the ornate piece of silk and ribbon he presented to her. "I… I know you wouldn't do anything wrong. It's only that meeting in a place like this seems so sinful!"

He held his tongue for a moment, then smiled. "Deceiving your mother isn't?"

"Don't talk me round in circles, you confuse me so," she said peevishly.

"Temper, temper." He leaned as near as he had in the coach, his arm stealing around her waist.

"Ohhh." Her eyes melted as they looked up at him. One moment so innocent, the next saucy. "Kiss it better?"

His lips met hers, and the shudders took him over as he gripped her arms hard, fingers grasping hard enough to bruise.

Maybe he'd be satisfied to hurt her just a little.

****

"Charlotte?"

"Yes? One moment, Father." She concentrated hard on her sewing. That was the trouble with white shrouds. One drop of blood and the whole thing was spoiled. She had very little patience for hand-sewing and would have preferred to use their recently acquired sewing machine if this last bit mustn't be ruched up to cover the head. Charlotte was glad that for all her father's prudence with finances, he didn't make her sew her own dresses but always gave her a generous allowance for clothing and linens. "There. That's seven done. Do you think I need to do more?"

Her father scratched his chin. "Well. I talked to the vicar yesterday after he came to collect Mrs. Perkins. The members of the parish ladies' guild are raising funds for the elderly and infirm to help them eke out the winter. Still, anyone who doesn't survive it..."

Charlotte's eyes lit up. "Oh, Father! A sort of contract?"

"I'm pleased with the idea myself. But hearing my bright-eyed, pink-cheeked daughter say such things gives me pause. Charlotte, a lady ought not to—"

Charlotte turned the topic back to business, a skill she had mastered. "A lady ought to support her father in his endeavors. After all, a father's fortunes are his daughter's favors, is that not so?"

He sighed. "Indeed, and now that Kensley Green has opened up outside the city for burials, I've made arrangements with Mr. Pottsgrove, the property manager. He'll be sending referrals our way."

In spite of her father's reservations, Charlotte watched a smile spread across his face as he discussed his plans with her. Charlotte rushed from her sewing and hugged him, patting his hand eagerly. It was the sort of thing her mother would have done when he set up to improve the place, offering more services under one roof. "Mother would be so proud of you."

His smile vanished. "Charlotte, leave the sewing for now. Another seven would be welcome, just in case. I heard rumors that the pump on Bethnal Circle has been contaminated with the fever, and you know what that means."

She nodded gravely. "If the city won't see to it soon, we'll be dealing with that as well as the consumption and cold-related deaths this winter."

He nodded in return, the gravity on his face taking a different direction. "A girl shouldn't know so much about death."

"Oh, Father. Not this *again*."

"No, I'm serious. You're twenty-four, and you're very clever. You could turn your hand to so many things. Now, I know you want to help the family business. What about if we hire a storefront in the High Street? A flower shop. Mr. Mungabee is getting older and will want to retire soon. Those two in the market you're so fond of, Rob and Maudie—"

"Bob and Mary," she corrected automatically.

"They could help you with supply. We need the flowers, after all. You'd be helping provide those two some security. They're getting on in years," he led.

Charlotte's lips thinned. Yes, indeed, her father was a brilliant man. He knew just how to make her consider it, even for a moment.

The moment passed. "I prefer to help you on the premises. There's a lot to do that you would have to hire help for if you didn't have me. I'm a good savings, Father."

"No one could deny it."

She knew *he* couldn't deny it, which is why this discussion, which had happened every few months for the last four years, never arrived at a successful conclusion.

"You'd have to buy shrouds and hire an assistant to greet the funeral carriages and coffin-makers when you're out."

Her father made a noncommittal noise. "True."

Charlotte added to the list silently. She had a calm and cheerful demeanor. She smiled comfortingly and never seemed to feel squeamish. Perhaps that was the problem. If she'd ever been truly afraid or ill around the bodies that rarely ended up staying on the premises for more than a few hours, perhaps she wouldn't be so content to stay here, and she would be receptive to her father's attempts to get her away from Harkness and Sons, away from death.

"Charlotte. You're a great help to me. But it isn't fair to you to spend all of your time here, among the dead and the funeral furnishings."

"Why?"

"What?"

"Why isn't it fair? There's a sort of grace and dignity among those who've passed. They have lived their lives, good or evil, and they're finished. Only the Almighty has to deal with them now. Nothing they can do will change—"

"Nothing they can do? They're dead. There's nothing they do. Full stop."

She flushed. Her father's eyes narrowed suspiciously. Heat rose to her face, leaving her fingers cold. She hated lying to him. Lying was a sin. But being locked away when she wasn't insane would be a sin, too, wouldn't it?

"Are you hearing things again?" he whispered.

"I hear you plainly, Father."

"That's not what I mean. You said you were keeping

Mrs. Perkins company. Oh, dear Lord, Charlotte, were you 'hearing' her, not simply being your incorrigible self?"

"Lots of people carry on conversations with what's around them, Father." This was not technically a lie. "I cannot tell you how often Auntie Molly used to argue with the oven. I hear you muttering insults at your waistcoat at least once a week, but it's not at fault when you find it snug." She abruptly got up. "Speaking of snug, Mary and Bob sent us two apples. Shall I bake them with cloves or try to make a small tart, just for the two of us?"

He followed her into the kitchen. "It's not madness to mutter an odd word or two to an uncooperative button or an oven that takes too long to get hot. It's madness if you think the oven is talking back."

"I've never heard a peep out of the oven. Now, I think I'll try that tart after all. We have just a bit of lard left."

Someone rapped on the front door. Her father's shoulders sagged. Charlotte knew that her father wanted to press her further, but he was clever enough to know there was no need. Her evasiveness would be enough to tell him his suspicions were correct.

****

Reginald trudged toward the door, heart heavy.

His poor, dutiful daughter was deluded.

Or perhaps it was some strange female malady, hysteria from spending too much time alone. It wasn't his fault that she had no siblings. If Prudence hadn't passed… "Oh, Pru. I wish you'd help her get over this," he sighed to himself as he hurried to open the door and deal with yet another unexpected client.

As he listened patiently to a suddenly bereaved widow, he realized that his business was surely the most predictable and the most uncertain of all. Death visited everyone. It was capricious about how, when, and why. It was simply too much for a woman, especially a woman like Charlotte, with her wit and waspish tongue. Throw in her penchant for hearing voices from beyond the grave? He blamed himself.

Oh, Prudence, what did I do wrong? Should I have sent her away? I couldn't have borne it.

But I must now.

****

Charlotte brought two cups of tea and two biscuits to her father and his guest, a working-class woman judging by her dress and shoes. Her father was providing price options in his gentlemanly way. She knew with almost total certainty that the woman would pick the two-pound funeral. It was probably all she could afford.

"I want my Ned to have the very best. I want the mutes. Feather-wavers." She had a defiant set to her chin as if daring Mr. Harkness to argue with her. "An open-sided carriage with flowers, lots of 'em, white ones."

"Erm. Yes. That will of course run into some money. The mutes are tuppence each. The open-sided carriage is part of our services. White flowers, now... Hm. Charlotte?"

"Daisies and yellow mums. Would your Ned have liked that?"

The woman looked at her with grateful, red-rimmed eyes. "Bless you, miss, I think he would. He said yellow was a cheery color."

"I'll make up a nice long strand to ring both sides of the coffin. Then a nice spray on top. Understated, but very elegant. Too showy might make Ned feel a little bit of a prig, don't you think?"

Another nod, another grateful glance. "That might be so. Yes, I'm sure that's so."

"He wouldn't want you to go all out on his last expenses, not out of proportion." Charlotte smoothed her skirts and sat down beside her. "Mrs.—?"

"Bailey."

"Mrs. Bailey, Ned would worry himself sick if he knew you were spending all of your savings on the funeral. What about the rent and everything to follow?"

"I'm going to live with my married daughter in Bolton. But you've a point. There's the fares to consider and the last month paying, not to mention the doctor's bill, not that he did any good, mind you." She dabbed at her eyes with a crumpled bit of cotton edged in tattered lace.

"The two-pound funeral will be quite a nice showing and with the mutes and feather-wavers that will bring it to two pounds and sixpence," Mr. Harkness jumped in. "Have you fixed the time for the services?"

Charlotte unobtrusively shrank away, back to the kitchen where she'd start weaving the daisies and mums into long strings, white thread and green stems. She could hear her father making arrangements about picking up the body the morning of the services. Fortunately, Mr. Bartlesby, their coach driver, always helped her father carry in the coffins and carry them out if there were no strong relatives of the deceased.

He really ought to have a son. Or even a son-in-law, I suppose. Although that would mean finding a man who was both interested in undertaking and in her.

"That may be nearly impossible," she lamented to

the basket of daisies on the table.

****

When Mrs. Bailey left, Mr. Harkness found Charlotte diligently weaving flowers by lamplight. "Dear, you should go to bed. You could work on that tomorrow."

"Just let me finish this last bunch, Father."

"They do look lovely. You see, you have such a talent for it! You—erm—you could do very well with a flower shop of your own. You know we're much respected in the trade. You needn't work exclusively for our family, there would be dozens in the area who would want your services. Nor would it be confined to funerals. Weddings, Charlotte. Husbands celebrating birthdays. Young men paying calls. One might even decide to stop in to catch sight of something much more lovely than the bouquets." He rested a fond hand on the mass of falling curls.

Charlotte looked up at him with a smile. "That's a fine idea, Father. I'm not sure I'd enjoy that, though. I would like to stay on here, stay with you. You know… it's not that women don't already assist, Father. Usually, a local woman has already laid out the body when you arrive. It's rarely a man."

"I don't think they're affected by it in the same manner." His genial smile turned sad. "What about studies? You can read and write better than half the lads I went to school with. You're far better in maths. There's talk of some new ladies' college in Cheltenham. You're only twenty-four. That's not too late to attend, I'm sure."

"And what would I do when I've completed my studies? They won't let a woman study medicine. They surely won't let me study embalming—though heaven

22

knows I could do it better than half the undertakers today."

"Charlotte!"

But she warmed to the subject, abandoning her flowers and pacing the kitchen. "Would you have me enter domestic service, become a ladies' maid or a housekeeper? I've dressed myself and managed this house nicely since Auntie Molly passed. I suppose I could be a governess to some other little girls who won't get to choose a career, either!"

"Career? My darling girl, your career is written in the Bible, to be a helpmeet! A wife and mother."

"Or a judge like Deborah, or a tentmaker like Priscilla, or a seller of purple like Lydia?"

"Well… well! Sell cloth if you like. Make dresses. Whatever you wish." Mr. Harkness enthused. "Better to make dresses rather than… Erm."

"Commune with the dead?" Charlotte supplied.

"Well. Yes."

"I wish you to change the shingle over our doorpost, Father. Harkness and Daughter."

Her father's relief departed abruptly. Cold calm replaced it. "No."

"You said whatever I wish. I wish to stay with you and help you!"

"No, I said."

"Mother helped you."

"A fat lot of good she did, dying on us and turning you funny, these visions and voices and—" A look of horror bloomed on his face. "Oh. Charlotte, I am sorry. I never meant…"

"Yes, you did." The laughing eyes were hard and the normally smiling, sweet face as stiff as those he prepared for the grave. "She didn't turn me funny. She's dead, Father. The dead have no control in this world. Sometimes the soul speaks on, that's all. I'm not 'funny in the head.' You all but admitted I'm as clever as most of the men in your class at school. It's not funny for a woman to want to continue the family business she's grown up around."

She took the small lamp from the table and carried it carefully up the backstairs to the drafty upstairs rooms. Her hand cradled the tall, smoke-stained lamp chimney from the sudden gusts of air as she swished up the passage.

Mr. Harkness hurried up after her, leaving the lamps burning below. "It's not funny. No, it isn't, you're quite right. But there's no future in it."

"Almost one hundred years, Father! Don't tell me we couldn't go one hundred more. You're already far more advanced than any other undertaker in London, save maybe the ones in Kensington and Mayfair, but they have the means to—"

"There you go. Proving you could handle this business." Harkness didn't sound proud, he sounded aggrieved.

Charlotte gave her father a startled, half-hopeful look. He'd never said those words before. "I could?"

"You could. You could do it all, even the things not fit for a woman to do. I have no doubt you could embalm the most foul of corpses while chatting cheerily about what to serve at the funeral luncheon. Perhaps you'd expand our services to offer ready-made hampers for the mourners."

"Oh. That's a thought, Father."

"No! Charlotte, it's not a thought at all. It would be

different if you were born a boy. But you weren't and therefore hard truths must be spoken. Let's say that you take over the business. Who will come to you? Which clients?"

"Progressive-minded ones. Women like Mrs. Bailey, possibly. They'll respect a woman's efforts." *Or would they doubt a woman's skill?*

"Who will help you nail the coffin wood together, do the fittings and the carrying? You can't drive a coach."

"I could learn those things. I could hire help."

"Which men would work for a woman? Where would your profits go?" he demanded.

"I'm certain that someone in the whole of Stepney, or even farther afield, somewhere in Whitechapel, Limehouse, or Bromley, there are two honest men who could heft a wooden box."

Mr. Harkness looked heavenward. "I was too easy on you. I let you read as much as you liked, whatever you could get your hands on, including *The Undertaker's Gazette*, including *The Modern Embalmer's Guide*. I've been a blind fool."

"Father, don't be so hard on yourself."

He turned his gaze to her. "You've answered every challenge I've set you. What happens when you wish to retire?"

Silence.

"You'll sell it to one of those honest men? You'll toss away all those generations of the family business? Because you won't have a child of your own like this, Charlotte. You won't find a husband. You won't wed. No one sees you."

"I see people all the time."

25

"Ah, yes. The vicars and coach drivers, the men in market stalls, the butcher, the grocer, and an occasional widower."

"I'm sorry the annual Undertakers' Ball hasn't seen fit to incorporate a coming-out party for the unfortunate daughters of the dead-mongers." Her tone was biting and bitter. *Unsuitable behavior for a woman, I'm sure, to show so much spirit.*

"Yes, there's little for you here," her father said slowly, deliberately. "The summer in London is a place of ills and infestations."

Charlotte stepped back, caught off guard by this sudden change of topic. "I suppose it is. Bodies must be buried or embalmed awfully quickly. Perhaps we could look into having the icehouse further insulated?"

"A good thought. Yes, I'll do that. I think that your Aunt Kate would love you to pay her a visit. The air is so bracing up there. It would do you good."

"I see. It will get me away from home? You?"

"Oh no! No, I want you here. Dearest, don't you know how sad and lonely I would have been? I've been selfish long enough, hiding you down here in the shadows and shrouds. You deserve a holiday. Maybe you'll love it."

Maybe I'll magically fall in love with a farmer who wants a wife to help spread manure and birth calves. "Summer is such a busy season."

"All our seasons are busy."

"Death doesn't take holidays. Will you go with me?" Charlotte turned the wick up on the lamp. Her room was small and narrow, simple. She was hardly ever in it. It was a comforting place, dark brown curtains, a red blanket, an old daguerreotype of her mother, and a sketch of Auntie Molly, and books. Books on shelves and stacks of books next to the pile of knitting on her rocking chair. Right now, there was no comfort. Her father, her dearest friend, wanted her to leave. His reasons didn't matter.

"Someone has to mind this place." He laughed weakly. "But a few months away won't matter much. We'll be together again before you know it. Unless, of course, you find you love it up there. Those boys of Kate's, they'll be such good company. Her letters are always full of their tricks, the scamps. Oh, and the Women's Institute and the Parish Ladies Auxiliary... I'm sure they have fun doing"—he groped for words— "all sorts of things!"

"I'm sure they do." Her voice was sad as she sank into the chair beside her bed. She'd never been one to faint or be overcome by the vapors, to fan herself and weakly demand smelling salts. Right now, the weight of her father's forced cheer and the sad smile was smothering her. For the first time ever, she wished her father would simply leave her alone. She wished she had a proper friend to talk to, not just him. He was so clearly against everything she had to say about this, no matter what it was.

"You might find a nice young farmer," he hinted.

"I might find a nice young undertaker here. One interested in joining the family business." The words sprang out of her mouth without thought. She'd met a wide variety of the men in her father's trade, but she hadn't found a single one engaging or attractive. They didn't speak to her like a person, more like a standard reminder of exercising their manners. A dignified and mournful sounding, "Good evening, Miss Harkness," or

27

"Is your father in, Miss Harkness?" had been the extent of their interactions.

Mr. Harkness had been lovingly tracing the frame around his late wife's likeness. Now he lifted his head in surprise. "Yes. Yes, I suppose that could happen."

"Some of these mortuary families are quite large, aren't they?"

"Mr. Parson of Parson and Parson has six children, four of them boys. I believe a few of them are eligible."

"Well…" Charlotte stared at her tightly clasped hands as they rested in her lap. "In some cases, in some of those larger families, perhaps one of the sons would rather strike out on his own, be the head of the business, an opportunity that wouldn't afford itself to all of the sons at once."

"True. Gideon and Danvers, now Mr. Danvers has a son about your age. Peter? You've met Peter?"

"I'm sure I have." She wasn't sure at all. Her heart was pressing into her ribs far harder than her corset stays. *I don't love these men. I certainly don't love Peter Danvers, whoever he is! But I love it here. I love the work, I love my father… Many a princess marries for political unions, not for love. I suppose I shall be Queen of the Funeral Directors, forging an alliance between two noble houses. Harkness and Danvers sounds acceptable. Not as good as Harkness and Sons. Or Harkness and Daughter, for that matter.*

This is madness, not hearing the soul's echo. To marry a man you don't know if you can stand, simply to stay with the father who by every right should keep you in his home all of your days, if you don't wish to leave his side.

"Have I been a good daughter?" Charlotte asked

suddenly, her voice hoarse.

Her father carefully moved her books and knitting, sitting on the footstool as his knees creaked in protest. "The very best of all daughters. Or sons. The very best." He kissed her hand, white at the knuckles, even in the dim light. "No man could ask for better. That's why I only want the very best for you. I want you to be loved and cherished. Healthy and whole. Not alone."

"You're not that old, Father," Charlotte murmured thoughtfully. "You needn't be alone. You're only forty-eight. Many a man has a son later in life. Why, King Henry VIII was only a few years younger than you. Perhaps Harkness and Sons could still—"

"Now, hush. It is unseemly that a girl should give her father such advice." He drew back, flustered. "Furthermore, in my heart and my mind, there is none who can compare to your mother. I want no other."

"A love match," Charlotte murmured, nodding.

His spine stiffened. "Yes. A love match. Ah, your mother was strong, just like you. She had your blue-eyed glare that could make a king cower." He laughed, a short morose bark. "She would give it to me now if she could hear this conversation."

Charlotte imagined she would. What would her mother say if she knew her only daughter, her dumpling, her dear little sparrow, was calmly considering making a match for the sake of saving the family business? Unlike her father, who could but wonder, Charlotte might soon find out.

"I'd like you to find a love match, Charlotte. Your mother would have wanted that as well."

"She wants me to be happy."

"Wants. Not wanted." Reginald's eyes closed

briefly. "Yes."

"Being here makes me happy." Charlotte rose, helping her father rise as well, smothering a smile as his back clicked and groaned in perfect unison with his knees. "Now, the next time you see Peter Danvers, you must ask him to tea."

"Are you sure?"

"It needn't be him." Her shoulders rose and fell in resignation. "Feel free to ask someone else instead."

"Dear? This idea of happiness, it is tied to love, at least in some small part. An unhappy marriage…" He trailed off ominously.

"Now then, Father, how can you know it wouldn't be perfect bliss? I've barely met him. It's up to the gentleman to inquire after a lady's interest. He might not take to me."

Mr. Harkness clucked his tongue. "Any man with eyes would take to you, and that is partly the trouble. Any man might wish for your hand. If you take the first offer, any offer, it could end badly."

"There's no pleasing you!" Charlotte laughed and kissed his cheek. "You're going gray with worry that I'll be an old maid, meanwhile you're utterly panicked in case Peter Danvers proposes on sight. What do you want, Father?" she demanded in playful exasperation.

"What do I want? Honestly? A cold mutton sandwich."

With a sigh, she led him back to the kitchen. "I'll finish the wreath for Ned Bailey while you finish a sandwich and what's left of that apple tart."

Chapter Two

Lavinia couldn't tell him. She put her pen down, cheeks hot with shame and worry. She'd behaved so horribly the other night, breathing uneasily in his ear as he moved against her, pinning her to the wall. His hands moved over her, causing a thrill of lust. Lust gave way to dread when he pulled himself away from her. She was still fully clothed and so was he, but he seemed to be making uncomfortable adjustments in a place where her eyes weren't meant to linger. Her neck was sore where his teeth clamped down and held on, lips bruised from ferocious kisses.

She'd managed to get back into her house that night without issue, going through Cook's door. The next morning, she felt hot and itchy. Perhaps she'd picked up something from that foul little room? She became uneasy and nervous, so nervous that even her mother, who barely seemed to recall she still had a child living at home, mentioned it. Lavinia hastily claimed a headache and spent the day in her room.

She relived the good moments, the womanly way he made her feel, the attention he gave her, the thrill of going to places she knew she didn't belong. The cab ride home, clinging close to him, his arm tight around her shoulders, was silent. In the silence, she dreamed about what would happen in a few years, or months, when he could prove himself to her mother. Or perhaps they'd elope, shock the city, and live a gay, continental lifestyle abroad.

She relived the bad moments. Whenever she tried to speak, he roughly shook her, forcing her against the wall. His angry eyes. The way he could barely seem to look at her as his hands moved over her clothing, ignoring her startled gasp. How his voice had the mocking edge. Well, why shouldn't it? She knew nothing about the ways of men and women when they were alone together, and it was clear that he did.

That night's events became a hazy tangle until she worried she'd dreamed it all.

It was a long, tedious day, with her discomfort growing, physically and mentally.

The next day passed the same way, only worse.

A horrid suspicion preyed on her mind. "It can't be. I couldn't be."

Trying to compose herself, she decided to ask the one person she knew intimately who actually had children of her own.

Her mother.

Her mother was no help, of course.

Lavinia tried to ask the question burning in her mind in a delicate, vague way that wouldn't arouse suspicion. Wary of being overheard, she waited until her mother had given the servants their orders and sent them out and about the town to run errands. The only other soul in the house was Cook, but the kitchen was far from her mother's sitting room.

"Mother? How old were you when you met Father?"

A dreamy look crossed her mother's features as she sipped a tiny glass of dark blackcurrant liquid. "Seventeen. Of course, we didn't marry until much later.

He was twenty-five when we met at Aunt Eleanor's presentation dinner. Such a dashing figure. Everyone thought Aunt Eleanor fancied him, but of course, she was besotted with one of my father's friends, a young bookkeeper with ginger whiskers." Her mother laughed as if this tale was the height of comedy.

Lavinia laughed politely even as her stomach heaved and rolled. "When did James come along?"

Her mother's smile vanished. "A few years after we were married. Yes, right around our second anniversary. Splendid baby. Flaxen curls. Dimples."

"How did you tell Father?"

"Tell him what?"

"That—that you were going to have James."

Her mother's face closed over completely. "Married couples have ways of knowing these things, dear."

"How did *you* know?"

From closed to open, the ugliness and anger fairly flew across her mother's features, bold and unmistakable. "This discussion is a product of your unhealthy curiosity! You're thinking of that shameful cad, Jack. A common, dirty, nasty name, *Jack*. Writing to a lady of your station and asking to meet you. *Meet* you! Heaven only knows but that you might've gone had I not intercepted that letter."

Lavinia pressed her lips together silently. Since her father died two years ago, her mother had been more and more given to these bouts of hysteria, calm and giggling one minute and shouting the next. Her health deteriorated and she spent hours a day in her room, mixing patent medicines and tinctures, hooked up to various health machines like Dr. Smith's Liver Rejuvenator and Skin Firmer. Lavinia was sure that her grandmother hadn't rebuffed her mother this way.

She tried to keep the tremble from her voice as she pressed on, "It's not improper curiosity, Mama. I'm nineteen."

"You've only been out for one Season, and part of that you missed thanks to that bout of fever. Only a girl on the eve of her wedding need ask such things. You're far too young to marry."

"You wouldn't say that if *Jack* had a title and money!" Lavinia tossed her head proudly. It wasn't as if he were poor. He simply wasn't wealthy. Besides, his work would surely keep them well enough, not to mention the money that Papa must have left to settle on her at maturity or her marriage, whichever came first.

If her mother heard the emphasis on the suitor's name, she ignored it. "So he hasn't? Just as I thought. All the more reason why such a conversation is unnecessary. I'll speak to you on matters of motherhood once you have a husband."

"But Mama—"

"I wish to hear no more about it! If you keep carrying on so, word will spread and your first Season, pitiful as it was, will be your last. No one will invite you to have so much as a licorice drop in the park, let alone attend a weekend party or a night at the theater. Go to your room and reflect."

"Mother, please!"

"*Go*, Lavinia." Her mother's hand trembled so that her afternoon cordial spilled everywhere, including the hand-woven lace on her sleeves. Her eyes were positively alight with fury as she looked at the wine-colored stain spreading over white lace.

Lavinia fled.

****

Another fretful day.

Another fearful night.

The pen and paper lay untouched on her dainty writing desk, a grim reminder of all the questions festering in her mind and the growing worry.

Growing.

Her mother was asleep, and the house was silent. The servants had gone home, and Cook was in her little room by the kitchen. James could help her. Her brother was a physician but training to be a surgeon. He could tell her anything she wished to know about the human body, she was certain. But he wouldn't be home until the end of the term, early in December.

What if things happened sooner? She knew it took months. It had only been a few days, and she was already getting fatter in the waist.

Growing. Growing panic.

"Oh, think. *Think*!" The girl whispered to herself, lip between her teeth as she paced her pretty bedroom, idly arranging hairpins, combs, and hat boxes, then flipping through the contents of the ornately carved wardrobe. She passed her desk and considered pushing the stiff sheet of stationery under a pile of her old books, meant to educate her enough to be engaging and interesting, but not so much as to intimidate a future husband.

Suddenly, all she could think of was the dire warnings of her former governess, Miss Potts. Miss Potts was a woman with an iron rod in place of a spine, a narrow, pinched face, who unfailingly wore her hair in a severe bun. Miss Potts' words were chasing themselves round in her brain until she made herself quite sick.

"Lavinia, in a few years' time, you will be presented

at court, then you'll be going from party to party, ball to ball. This is not all gaiety. It is a measure of your deportment and your lady-like behavior—don't slouch, Lavinia. Now, you must never allow a man to kiss you until after you're wed, nowhere but your wrist or your cheek, and only the cheek if he is a very dear, old friend of the family or a very little boy."

Lavinia recalled asking why not, innocent curiosity as a fourteen-year-old girl who had only recently had the need to learn about such secret things as feminine napkins and belts to keep them in place. Her governess turned an ashen color and hastily replied that such improper kisses led to disease and babies.

"If ever he should touch your lips or anywhere else for that matter, rest assured that there is every possibility that you will bring shame and disgrace upon yourself and your entire household." Miss Potts had made that declaration in a ghastly whisper, almost a threat.

Lavinia had been horrified and remembered making her voice match Miss Potts', equally terrified and shocked. *"I'll never do such a thing. Never, ever!"*

"Oh, never, never," she echoed the words now, hot tears spilling down her cheeks. How had her handsome "Jack" wormed through all of Miss Potts' teachings? "Never" had vanished when he made her feel so desperate for his touch, so desperate to be wanted by him, so angry at her mother for keeping them apart. His kisses seemed almost angry, too.

Yes. That must be it. His anger wasn't at her. The anger was masking his desperation and frustration that they were forced to meet in secret.

Lavinia's breathing slowed as she nodded resolutely. She could ask him. She'd have to ask him or at the very least inform him of her suspicions. Would he be dreadfully angry? Done with her? Would they have to marry in secret and leave Mama and James forever? She felt quite faint. That was one of the symptoms, she was certain.

There was only one way to find out, of course. Her shaking fingers grasped the pen and tried again.

My Dearest Jack,

I must see you as soon as you are able. It's terribly urgent. Write back in the usual manner.

Love always,

Lavinia

Chapter Three

"Everly!"

Dr. James Everly found himself shaken awake by the grave-looking Sir Henry William Lawrence, one of the deans. The normally perfectly attired, austere man was wearing a dressing gown and long nightshirt, his bony feet halfway out of flopping slippers.

What in the world have I done?

The last time a dean had bothered to come into the Halls of Residence was when Percival fforbes-Wellington had tried to carry a cadaver to the third floor and dropped it, creating one memorable mess.

"Everly, wake up and get dressed."

"Sir! Of course, Sir Lawrence. Why, sir?"

"Your mother has sent a coach to collect you." The dean looked around furtively. "It's very early in the morning. Your mother is a very generous benefactor to our school."

James nodded, utterly bewildered. If his mother decided to donate a pipe organ and personally re-slate the roof in her finest frock, it had no bearing on the hour or the cab. Not that his sleep-addled mind could work out, at any rate. "What, sir? Is she ill?"

"She begged all discretion, Everly. Please pack as if you were going home for the term."

"But my exams! Sir, anatomy finishes in three weeks. If I don't qualify this term, I'll have to take the course all over."

"I shall personally arrange a private examination, or I shall allow you to come in just for the practical dissections, provided you pass the written work I will send you."

James froze. The last time anyone had shown such kindness and blind disregard for rules and tradition had been when he was in his last year at the Royal College of Physicians. It was the famous Dr. William Hargrove who had come to him with news that his mother wanted him at home urgently. His father had passed suddenly, most likely owing to a ruptured internal organ, perhaps the appendix. It was that news that made him decide he wasn't content with being a physician but wanted to go beyond that and apply to the Royal College of Surgeons.

"Your mother is fine at present." The dean suddenly seemed to be aware of his state of dress. He harrumphed and his mustache bristled as he pulled the dressing down more tightly around his portly frame. "The coach is at the East Gate. I'll send the date for your examinations by wire."

"Yes, sir. But..."

"Her message is simple, Everly. James is urgently needed at home, be discreet. We'll have to say you were taken ill. Your home is not that far, is it?"

"No, sir." Could it be his uncle? His uncle had managed the business alone since his father's death, though his cousins were keen to enter the family business as well.

Lavinia. Lavinia had a horrible bout of fever last year, losing some of her hair and far too much weight, missing most of her grand first Season. She was never very strong and had become rather frail and pale with a weak constitution and nervous disposition after his father's passing.

The dean nudged his arm as he stood, transfixed by his own worries. "Haste, man! We'll arrange for you to take them in my office, if necessary. All except the dissection lab. I don't know what we'll do about that, but perhaps you'll be back before long. If not, I suppose we'll arrange it with Middlesex." He referred to the busy hospital where many of the anatomy clinics took place.

"Right. Yes, sir. Perhaps I needn't pack?" James said hopefully.

The dean paused in the doorway. "She said you're to come home for the term. Pack accordingly."

As soon as the door shut, James was a blur. He didn't bother to sweep back the sandy locks that were dangling into his eyes, nor did he bother with socks. He dumped all the contents of his bureau and wardrobe in his trunk, used a belt to bind all his textbooks together, and pulled on his greatcoat.

Two confused-looking porters were standing outside the door to his room. "Dr. Everly?"

"Yes, take these down to the coach by the East Gate. I'll be along presently." He let them enter and drag the trunk out between them, puffing slightly. What else did he need? There was too much to take in his arms and his leather satchel.

Thompson. He knew his mother had said to be discreet, but Thompson was a decent fellow and held the rooms across from him at the RC of S. He hurried across the hall and rapped lightly on the door.

No answer.

Too early for most people not working the wharves, market stalls, or fields. Thompson must still be asleep or not yet managed to sneak in after a night carousing. He'd nearly gotten sent down for that trick earlier in the term. "Blast it." No time. He ran back to his own room and dashed off a note, asking his friend to keep an eye on his room and its contents, assuring him he hoped to be back in a few days.

Lavinia was probably just ill. Seriously ill, that is, and his mother was so prone to hysteria after his father's death. That was it.

That must be it.

****

"Charlotte, look!" Mr. Harkness was practically dancing a jig.

"What is it?" She hastily slid *The Mortician's Reference Book* back into the shelf and left her father's cozy office. If it were up to him, he'd have all his clients sitting on orange boxes. She was the one who had persuaded him to have a fire in the grate when clients came, she who had insisted on three comfortable wing-back chairs around the desk and always a plate of biscuits or a pot of tea at his beck and call.

Why make death so unpleasant, after all?

"Harkness and Sons is being mentioned in the December issue of *The Undertaker's Gazette*!"

"But it's still November!"

"Only just. Here's an advance issue. Old Mr. Parson of Parson and Parson is a consulting editor, and he slipped me a copy this morning." Her father preened, buffing his nails with pardonable pride on his neatly pressed gray waistcoat.

Charlotte tugged the thin sheets of newsprint from his hand and looked at the front page. "*Modernizing the Model Funeral*." She read the article's title aloud.

"Read on."

She cleared her throat and read, eyes widening. " 'Harkness and Sons is a standard-bearer. Mr. Reginald Harkness is more than an undertaker, he's a funeral director.' Oh, Father! A *funeral director*."

"I know. The term sounds downright regal if you ask me."

"Me, too! Oh, we must celebrate. I know, I'll tell the butcher we don't want the usual today. We'll get a ham."

"A ham? For just the two of us?"

"It will keep. Ham pie, ham sandwiches."

"Yes. Yes, I suppose. We could also invite Mr. Parson and his sons 'round for tea. Or Peter Danvers. You could make ham sandwiches and… what else does one have at nice teas?"

"Watercress and boiled eggs. Scones and things." Charlotte tried to warm to the idea.

"Can we get watercress this late in the year?"

"I could make a ham and leek pie. We have leeks in the cellar."

"Yes, yes. Still, the ham is rather an unneeded expense, and coal is dearer and dearer these days."

"With an article like this, Father? Business will soar." Her pulse quickened. "You know, no one would see us in the back garden. You could teach me to hammer the wood together, couldn't you?"

"What?"

"What about the ladies who come in?"

"*What*?" Mr. Harkness' eyes opened so wide that his thin wire-framed reading spectacles lost their perch on his nose.

"Well, of course I can understand why you wouldn't want me to help embalm the male bodies, but the females—"

"Good heavens, girl. We've discussed all of this."

"I know, I know. Wouldn't it be sensible, though, to be able to help my future husband in his work?" Charlotte handed back the newspaper with the dangling carrot attached.

"Mr. Parson or Mr. Danvers, or whomever you marry in the trade—*if* that's what happens—will undoubtedly prefer a wife who doesn't show an interest in that particular side of things. Do please content yourself with the sewing and the flower arranging. Such things are fitting. The other matters are not and are going to put off any prospective suitors, in *any* trade!" He stomped past her and shut the door on the embalming room with a bang.

Charlotte was numb as she watched her father storm away. She and her father had always been very close, a darling daughter and doting father, made more dependent on one another first by her mother's death long ago and then by the loss of practical, kindly Auntie Molly, their housekeeper-cum-governess. She could recall shocking and stupefying the poor man on a daily basis. Making him so angry that he called her *girl*, not Charlotte or some other fond endearment? That had happened only a handful of times, but each one was stuck in her mind like an ax-blade in kindling.

She remembered the first time it had happened like it was moments ago, not more than a decade.

****

"Father? Mama wishes you would see the doctor. She's ever so worried about you." A little girl, her hair in one long braid with wings of golden frizz escaping along the sides, had snuck out into the scruffy back

garden that was little more than a series of cramped outbuildings.

"Charlotte, pet, please don't bring up your whims and fancies now." Her father was pale and sweating as he hauled a huge block of ice into the icehouse with thick iron tongs.

"She loves you so, but she says don't join her just yet. She's worried about her little bird being all alone. I'm worried, too."

A patient man, her father. Rarely cross. His voice, used to speaking to the recently bereaved, rarely rose above a well-modulated murmur. Suddenly, his patience had fled, his face had mottled in anger, grief, and frustration. He dropped the block of ice, no, threw it so that it splintered into four or five jagged chunks on the clean sawdust. "You watch your tongue, my girl, and say no more about your mother to me!" he'd roared.

She'd fled to her room, heart hammering, feeling suddenly very lost and alone.

****

Charlotte reminded herself that she was a grown woman now, of marriageable age. There was really no reason her heart should still hammer at her father's anger, she rationalized.

It did no good.

Her black shoes with their single row of polished buttons up the ankle squeaked as she ran up to her room, curled into her rocking chair, and tried not to cry. She hadn't felt like this, even after her mother passed away.

"I'm with you still, my little bird," her mother's voice caressed her brow, like a soothing hand to a fevered face.

"Mother... I shan't be sent away. Doesn't he love

me enough to keep me as I am… even if I'm not quite right in the head?" Charlotte murmured the words into the pillow she'd dragged into her lap.

"Not quite right? As bright as a new copper."

"I know I'm not meant to hear them. Hear you."

"Practice not listening." Her mother's voice held a note of amusement. "Pretend it's your poor father who's talking."

Charlotte didn't find the thought humorous. Not listen to what she could so plainly hear? Why lie? How was that the Christian thing to do, when hearing voices of those passed was not of her own doing, beyond her control? She'd never prayed for this ability, was never tempted to use it as some perverse power. It wasn't madness, nor some work of the devil.

It had started so innocently, a grieving girl hearing her mother's voice…

****

Nineteen years ago…

It spread through the street. Houses were shuttered. Noises of sickness were heard if you lingered too long outside. Her father and her grandfather had been busy for weeks, and then suddenly, work stopped. Charlotte remembered the day her mother hastily took the Harkness and Sons shingle from the swinging iron chains outside the door.

Her mother nursed all of them, her husband, father-in-law, and little Charlotte, who was by the far the worst, only five at the time.

It was sad but not shocking that her old grandfather, already sixty (quite an accomplishment for his day and age) passed suddenly from the disease. Charlotte's father seemed to recover and feel relief that his family had been further spared.

Of course, her mother, the busy nurse, had managed to hide her growing illness until she collapsed and was taken in a matter of days. Her father lost his relief and stoicism. There was no time to send for Aunt Kate and her husband. They wouldn't have risked coming to the city in the middle of an outbreak, anyway, not with their infant son.

No, her mother must be taken and buried at once, as soon as possible, before the infection passed from dead to living and sickened someone else. The grieving widower feared it could be Charlotte, all he had left in the world. She wouldn't survive another bout of the disease. If she fell, too? He'd be utterly alone.

For her own good, Charlotte was confined to her room with the door locked and the window shuttered. The first was because Mr. Harkness knew it was wrong to leave her alone but was too fearful to trust anyone else, all the neighbors being sick themselves. The second reason was to keep out the sun that hurt her feverish eyes.

"A bad business, Mr. Harkness. Prudence was a blessing to all she met."

When Charlotte heard those words coming from outside the house, she found strength she didn't know she had. Her legs were shaking, and her head was pounding, but she managed to scramble out of her bed and get the heavy wooden shutters pushed apart in time to peep into the back garden.

Her father, gaunt and pale, walked with the vicar behind Mr. Bartlesby, who was driving the open-sided carriage pulled by a single horse. She could see a box with a simple spray of flowers inside.

My mother is in that box.

No. My mother's body is in the box, but the soul is not. The soul is in the happy land, far, far away. Her voice was still raspy, but she tried singing the words her mother so often sang. "There is a happy land, far, far away, where saints in glory stand—"

Another voice was suddenly passing under the words, a soft, sad contrast to the child's brave song. Charlotte's singing died abruptly as she heard a gentle whisper of, *"Goodbye, my little bird. How I wish I could stay with you longer."*

Her response had been automatic and relieved, "Then do, Mama, please!"

It had made a grieving child happy. It was a comfort. Mama stayed.

When Father came home, quiet and exhausted, he was so happy to find Charlotte smiling and sleepy. "Mama sang to me while you were out," she informed him with a yawn.

"I expect she did." He kissed her pale white brow.

****

"He didn't hate it at first. He was happy I had some sort of comfort," Charlotte muttered, again opening the shutters. *Perhaps I'm too old for such comforts?*

"Death doesn't seem very fearsome to me. But being alone... But being cut off from parts of myself..." Charlotte clutched her head, then shook it vigorously. "No. No, I won't, I won't turn into one of those girls who sits and cries." She abruptly turned from the window. Her mother's presence was gone.

"Laundry to see to. Tonight's supper. The ham. Yes, I'll still get the ham, and that'll cheer Father up. I'll write out an invitation to Mr. Parson and his sons for Sunday tea. Perhaps one of the Parson boys will be clever and sweet with a handsome face and charming conversation."

Perhaps one of them would be hideous, covered in boils, and sharp-tongued, but actually like her just as she was. Maybe he would ask her what the dead were saying instead of threatening to send her far from home if she admitted she could hear them. Maybe he would hand her the paper at night instead of snatching the best bits away as unfit for a woman's delicate sensibilities. Perhaps he would discuss Ruysch and Burggraeve's methods on preserving the dead with her, proud that she'd read their treatises, instead of scolding her for her interest.

"I'd rather have the ugly one."

****

"It's an ugly business, ma'am. Tragic."

"Your superiors informed you not to speak of it," Mrs. Everly spoke sharply, eyes tiny slits in a red, puffy face.

"No, ma'am. Only saying, ma'am, that it's tragic." Though her eyes practically disappeared in her tear-swollen face, Police Constable Gill's skin sizzled from a single look. Clearly, Mrs. Everly was used to having things just as she wanted them. Deviations from her plan would not be tolerated.

"She fell into the river. She was walking too close and slipped on an icy patch. It was a simple accident. Is that clear?"

P.C. Gill scratched his sandy mustache with a worried hand. He was no detective, but even he could spot holes in that story. Firstly, why would a well-bred lady like Lavinia Everly have ventured out alone at night, unescorted? Secondly, even if she had, why in the world would a lady in dainty shoes and a fine frock go tripping along the very edge of the Thames, near enough to "slip" to a watery death, in the dead of night where no one would have seen or heard her fall and come to her rescue? Thirdly, what icy patches? This week had been wet, cold, and foggy, but no snow or ice yet. "Not to question you, ma'am, but—"

"Then do not. I have made a generous donation to the Metropolitan Police Force, directly to your chief inspector, with the clear understanding that it will be reported exactly thus if it must be reported at all. And thus it *shall* be or you will be dismissed. *Instantly.*"

The mustache bristled alarmingly. "But… the body, that is, Miss Everly—hrm." Gill broke off. Even if the old snob was threatening him, he had a heart, didn't he? It was hard to talk to a lady about these things, 'specially a grieving one. "I mean to say, ma'am, that this was clearly *not* an accident."

****

Mrs. Everly choked back a sob. She'd been sobbing since dawn, blaming herself and dreading what would come after the news broke. The scandal! Lavinia's tawdry lapse of judgement exposed, brought to light, and aired repeatedly across every table in the home counties. Lavinia's death would be the topic of horrified, scandalized whispers at every opera intermission and every ball this Season. Her husband must be turning in his grave that his dear, innocent daughter, barely nineteen, should have snuck out of the house and run afoul of some—

The sobs transformed into a low snarling hiss that no well-bred woman should ever make. "Your superiors have agreed to report it as an accident and not to speak to the papers. I've sent for my son, James. He's just changing from his travels, but I've informed him of Lavinia's 'accident.' I'll also instruct him that for matters of privacy, the funeral shall be a private affair. Your superiors informed me that they would choose a less-fashionable, yet still respectable undertaker who will handle the matter with all due discretion. When the arrangements are made, you'll inform us."

"*I* can't be the one, ma'am, no. A relative has to make the arrangements direct."

"Make an exception."

Gill drew himself up. He clearly felt this was crossing a line on top of a line. "Certainly, ma'am. We can have her put in the prisoners' field at Newgate, where they put those poor souls who die as guests of Her Majesty with no relations—if that's where you'd like your daughter's final resting place to be."

Mrs. Everly paled. Lavinia's body, buried in some low pit, side by side, surrounded by, and walked over by murderers and common criminals? James would understand an accident, he would understand her shying from discussing Lavinia's death, but he'd never, *ever* blindly accept that his sister was being put to rest behind the walls of Newgate Prison. She simply *couldn't* let James know the sordid details. James, her pride and joy, top of his class, a physician, a man with his star in the ascent. Not to mention, he was her family's last hope for respectability and her only chance that one day she would again lose herself in the happy prattle of afternoon calls and strolls in the park, all of this behind her.

"I'll have to bring you some other papers to sign, Mrs. Everly. I don't know that it's ever been done that the police bury the victim, not the murderer, in the prison yard!"

The word "murderer" galvanized her. Blind terror seized her as she heard James' door shut upstairs. "One doesn't need to view the body when making the arrangements, does one?" she whispered, praying the answer was no.

"Well... strictly speaking, kin ought to identify the body. But we found her calling cards and the letter addressed to her in her reticule and the identity was initially confirmed by the detective who called this morning, based on the photographs you showed him."

"Yes, yes." She nodded impatiently. It had all been a blur, Cook waking her in frightened confusion, the sickening dread of confirming Lavinia's bed was empty and hadn't been slept in, and finally letting in the imposing detective who showed her items she recognized instantly, Lavinia's new reticule, her new hat, one of her earrings. He didn't need to ask to see photographs. Lavinia was rather vain, and she loved the newfangled things so. They were all over the house.

"Normally, one would need to see the body in person. For identification, you understand."

"He said I needn't, not a lady of my station, a mother. Oh, *please hurry*!" She could have shaken this imbecile. "Will my son have to see her today, or won't he?"

"I suppose given these circumstances, he won't have to." The woman almost toppled with relief. "But he might *want* to, being as it's his sister—"

Lips thinned, face white. "Twenty pounds."

****

Twenty pounds for him? Or the branch? Either way, they were already hushing up this foul thing for reasons of respectability. It didn't sit right with him, the higher-ups being willing to close the case, make it go away without an investigation of any sort. But he wasn't in charge, and he didn't want to be back to the night patrol in Canary Wharf, or worse, get sacked outright.

Gill nodded reluctantly, eyes resting on the photograph on top of the piano. It showed a fair-haired man with his raven-haired sister, both beaming. The detective in charge had already made use of a photograph. What's sauce for the goose... "Right then, Mrs. Everly. If asked, I'll inform the undertaker that identification has been made and for reasons of—the grieving family's wishes, he should arrange the burial as soon as possible in a nice, quiet, respectable place as befits a lady who met a tragic and unexpected accident."

"Those people—they don't need to," Mrs. Everly blinked rapidly, fingers twitching as if trying to pull the right words from the air, "to *bother* her, do they?"

Gill shuddered inside his woolen uniform. Mucking about with the stiffs was the worst part of his job, but you couldn't pay him to deal with the bodies, not for a thousand pounds. Unnatural, it was, the way these undertakers could devote their whole lives to flushing out "fluids" and other ghastly, nasty things he didn't want to think about.

He was spared an answer by the appearance of the brother, the fair-haired man from the photograph on top of the piano. He looked like he had a fresh, intelligent face—under normal circumstances. Right now, his longish bangs were flopping, his cheeks were sporting a pale growth of stubble, and his face seemed to be made of unset jelly, eyes blinking, mouth working, cheeks quivering.

"Mother! Constable? Oh, God, it's *true?*"

"Would I have sent for you if it wasn't? Oh, James. James, she's *gone.*"

Gill coughed and retreated into the hall.

He bumped into a pale, freckle-faced maid, hovering near the door. "I—I wanted to know if I should bring tea for Mr. James." Her pale skin turned a fish-belly white. "I didn't hear—I wasn't listening!"

Gills stared at her. If there was ever a clear signal of guilt, that was one. Still, not his bother. "I'm sure you weren't. I wouldn't interrupt just now." He dropped his voice. "In my opinion, 'Mr. James' could do with a very large whiskey." *And after seeing what was done to that poor girl, I could, too.*

****

James raked his hands through his hair. His mother must be mistaken. Everyone involved was utterly mistaken. This was implausible, no, impossible. "But… Mother, darling, that makes no sense, none at all. Even if she did suddenly develop a fit or take to sleepwalking"—both options huffily suggested by his mother—"she wouldn't have made it all the way clear to the Thames."

"She did!" His mother fretfully pushed from his outstretched arms and fussed with porcelain ornaments on the mantel. "She wasn't herself. Moody and asking strange questions. A sudden bout of brain fever must have overtaken her last night."

James froze. "Last night?"

"Yes. Last night. She must've slipped on the ice and fallen in. No one was there to see her, naturally, but one can only assume." Mrs. Everly recited the tale in a tight voice.

Blue, tear-filled eyes squinted in confusion. "The carriage was at my school first thing in the morning."

"I sent for you as soon as the police came to call. Thank heavens you didn't go to Oxford after all. You could get here quickly."

"No, Mother... how could they find her body, search the whole of the Thames for her that fast? Did you report her missing?"

"No. The police found her. They came to me. Oh, James. I can't bear it. I can't *bear* it. We mustn't talk of it anymore."

James didn't wish to upset his mother, but her words rolled off of him, more nonsense in a day that was straight out of Lear. "Lavinia couldn't possibly be near the Thames, and if she was, how could she have been found that quickly? How could they know who she was?"

"Her reticule had some papers in—" Mrs. Everly's voice shut off as if someone had snuffed it out.

He spun in a bewildered circle any moment expecting to encounter Lavinia's smirking face, her slender hands catching his arm as if this were all some mad game. "Her bag? She was in some mad, fevered sleepwalking state and she had her bag with her? The police were onto it that fast and you sent for me that quickly?"

"Why are you questioning me? What are you implying?"

"This isn't right! This doesn't add up."

"If you're saying that I've done something—"

"Not you, Mother, no. Of course not." James hurriedly enfolded his shaking mother in his arms, kissing her graying curls. She was still a handsome woman, but grief and ill-health were starting to harden the lines in her face.

"Then, James, please. *Please,* I beg of you, leave it alone. It's done. Nothing we can say or do will bring her back. It's best to leave it all to the police."

James nodded. Yes. Yes, that was true, and his mother must be suffering so. She had been home with Vinnie for these past few years, presumably growing much closer, while he and his sister had drifted apart as his studies consumed him and he stayed in the halls of residence for months at a time, even though he could have come home on any given weekend. "Of course. I'll do whatever you want me to do. I'll send a wire to Uncle Jeremy and Aunt Penelope. The vicar. The vicar will have some idea of when we can—"

His mother went from trembling like a willow in a windstorm to standing as stiff and unshakeable as the hardest oak. "No."

"No?" James looked perplexed.

"You'll not tell anyone."

"Mother, surely—"

"You'll not tell anyone until I tell you to do so, James. That is my wish. I want the funeral to be private. The—the undertaker is a man well-suited to his task and he'll select a nice, peaceful resting spot with a competent vicar to perform the services. No need to trouble ours."

It was his turn to stand rigid.

"Stop looking at me like that," Mrs. Everly finally whispered, sliding back into the darkness left by the draperies yet to be drawn, servants barred from their duties, the entire house holding its breath.

James exhaled slowly. His mother was mad. Hysteria had clouded her brain and sent her into some sort of grief-induced madness where Lavinia's death could—for lack of a better word—remain hidden. Or go unnoticed. His voice was gentle as he approached her, much like cornering a nervous rabbit in a hutch. "Mother, dear. People will notice Lavinia is gone." The word caught in his throat. Dead. *Can't be. Mustn't be. Healthy! Delicate, but still, lively, full of life, merry, playful*... Those words described Vinnie. Not dead.

She swallowed convulsively. "I'm very tired, James."

Ah. The quintessential end to the unpleasant conversation.

Normally. "You can rest in a moment. First, we have things to address."

"The constable in the hall will give you the address. Now… Now, I should like her to have a spot in one of these new resting places, they're rather like parks, only one wouldn't go to them for enjoyment, I suppose, but still. One of those places. No need to bother with flowers or a grand procession. I don't want anything that will attract undue attention."

"Lavinia loved attention. She loved flowers, Mother."

"Yes. She did."

****

Mrs. Everly turned away from her only son. She couldn't comfort him as he grieved for his sister. She could hardly figure out how to grieve for her. Stupid, stupid girl. Loved attention. Attention-seeking, thrill-seeking, out like a common trollop, probably searching the streets for the unsuitable suitor who dared to write her, searching for that nasty, common Jack. Maybe he left her wandering alone, poor little flower. She would have trustingly asked for help, probably lost in the dark. Then... well, it was quick. She was sure it must have been quick.

Lavinia had paid for her mistakes. She would not force the rest of the family to pay any further. "I need to lie down. Tell Cook I don't need breakfast. I want my sleeping powders, and I'll see you for supper, James."

Without another word, she swept past him, past the startled Gill who jumped to attention, abandoning his position of leaning against the elegant wallpaper in the foyer. "Sadie will show you out once you give my son the address. Good day."

"Good day, ma'am," Gill called after her.

****

The police constable turned his attention to the seething young man in the doorway. The pictures made him look like he was taller. He wasn't short, mind you, but not a big strapping fellow. He would have come a good head and shoulders above his little sister, but then again, she was a thin, waif-like little thing. The sheet holding her body felt so light, more like moving a sack of clothing than a body.

"The address?" Dr. Everly's tones were clipped, but they rapidly changed as his eyes focused on the constable in front of him. "Constable—?"

"Gill, sir. Bad business about your sister. Er. Drowning. Sudden-like."

"Yes. Yes. Where was the body found?"

"Down Whitechapel area, about—" Gill coughed suddenly. "I mean, sir, the Thames does move along. Who's to say that's where she went in?"

"What was she wearing?"

Gill winced. Her pretty frock was a horrible mess,

blood spilling down, blood flowing out… "A dress, sir."

"A nightdress?"

"I'm not big on women's fashion. Not married, y'see."

****

James had studied enough cases to know when the patient was avoiding an outright truth, whether it be admitting to a single glass of claret and omitting the fact that it was a single glass *every* night or whether it be faithfully swearing that they had gone riding every day and hadn't bothered to mention that the ride concluded with a three-pie meal at the club.

Gill was lying. Why?

"Will that be all, sir?"

"Yes, I supposed we'd best be going."

"Going?"

"You're to take me to the undertaker who's in charge of my sister's—arrangements."

"Oh. Oh, yes. I could just give you the address." The constable didn't meet his eye.

James had the distinct impression that the constable wanted to be out of this house, out of this incident.

James wanted to continue to talk to the man to see if his answers were a matter of misinformation or mere lack of information. "Well… have the police already declared this a simple accident? What about the inquest?"

"James!"

He jumped at the sound of his mother's shrill voice.

She marched down the stairs, hair cascading untidily as she stomped toward him with an outstretched envelope. "James, stop pestering the constable. He has rounds to attend to. Here, Constable, please take this as

58

a gesture of my gratitude." She thrust the small white packet into Gill's hand. "You've made a hellish day bearable by your discretion and understanding. If only *some people* would follow your example."

"Mother, I say! That's unfair. I'm only asking a few simple questions." James followed her as she fled back up the stairs.

"What good will questions do? Leave her alone. Let the matter lie, James." His mother gave him one last furious look, then fled, sobbing.

What in the world had happened while he was away? His mother gone mad, his sister wandering about in the dead of night, and constables on the doorstep at dawn. "This can't be."

"It feels that way, sir. I can see what your mother means, sir, if you'll pardon me mentioning it. She wants to remember the girl as she was, alive, healthy, and happy. Death isn't pretty to my mind."

"It's simply a state of inanimation. Life-force removed," James replied hollowly. He'd seen his fair share of bodies in the medical field. They began to blur in his mind, the ones that stopped moving, reduced to post-mortem diagnoses made by looking at skin and sags, bulges, and muscles. He blinked. Yes. So much could be learned by a proper post-mortem, the ones that the police surgeons would carry out. "Will there be a post-mortem?"

Gill jumped. "No, sir, no need. No need to drag this out, a simple accident, tragic, but simple. That's all. The undertaker will have this sorted out in a day or two at most. My superior says he's got the operation shipshape and Bristol fashion, this fellow who runs Harkness and Sons."

Chapter Four

Charlotte returned with ham and potatoes in one basket, ten yards of white cotton in the other. They needed more, but that was about all she could carry today. They needed a bulk order shipped to them directly. It would save time. It would likely save money. Why hadn't Father thought of that in all these years? Or had that been done in the past and proved too impractical for some other reason? If he'd treat her like a son about to take over the business, then she might know the answer.

"Father? I have a question about our yard goods."

"Oh, Charlotte, good. I'm glad you're back. I've had the most curious wire. Nothing to concern you, only I must take receipt of a body for a troubled family. The mother is in delicate health. It's her daughter who is the dearly departed."

"Oh! Oh, the poor lamb!" Charlotte rushed to hug her father's arm. He leaned his head warmly to hers, and she felt the fear and anger of the morning melt away. "I hate it when children die before their parents."

"I know, I know. Well, goodness." He looked heavenward, slightly rounded chin bobbing as he thought. "I don't know if I have a coffin that small and the coffin-makers probably can't fit me in until tomorrow morning." It was already late afternoon.

Charlotte thought quickly. Her father could fit one

together in a pinch, but he preferred to buy them already assembled. Still, if it was so urgent, they must adapt. "We could use that one that lost the foot board to the damp? Fit another piece on, a few feet in?"

"Good thinking, my dear. I must see the body for measurements, first. It could be an infant for all we know."

"Oh, no. I hope not. Surely not. The little ones should be kept at home with their mothers." Most of their clientele were still laid out at home, with embalming being the exception, not the norm.

Her father paused. "Grief does odd things to the mind," he remarked gravely. He patted her arm once and headed to prepare the embalming room.

True, Charlotte agreed silently, hurrying to put the cotton with her sewing machine. Oh, dear. A shroud for a little one. It wouldn't take long to sew, but she hated making them the most.

****

Charlotte's active mind dulled pleasantly with the usual chores, the baking, sewing, and putting the ham in the oven to roast. She realized she'd better make another loaf of bread if she were going to have the Parson boys calling sometime soon.

The sound of hooves and creaking wheels, not one set but two, made her pause as she measured out flour. Head cocked and the bowl under her arm, she moved to the back door that connected the kitchen to the back garden. Curious. Normally, clients came in the front door and only people in the trade knew to go round the side. That was where Bartlesby and her father always met to put coffins in carriages or carry in a new "customer." Now, she observed a hired cab following another one, a type of carriage or coach she couldn't place at first. It was long and low. A person could never sit in that. When the driver hopped down, she saw the hat and uniform.

Police. Curious, indeed. Not the first time the police had called, oh, no. But they didn't usually arrive in *that*.

Her father hurrying out to meet them, jamming his hat on his head.

She really must work on steaming the brim, one side was still drooping.

Mundane musings ended abruptly.

No!

Charlotte dropped the bowl, sliding down the kitchen wall as if someone had slammed her into it and pushed her down.

Heat, anger, terror… She was going to be sick.

"No, please. Please! He—" The scream in her head cut off abruptly.

"Where are you?" Charlotte gasped, trying to make her eyes focus. They wouldn't work. Everything was black and red, hot then cold. *I'm dying.*

No. She's *dying. The little girl, the child.*

With her head feeling as if it were on fire, she pulled herself up to the window in time to see her father take one end of a bier and the helmeted driver take the other. The body they carried, wrapped in stained sheets, was not child-sized.

"No!"

The wave came back as the scream in her head echoed.

A masculine voice joined it, a dark laugh. *"You wanted to see me. It was so urgent. Well, here I am, my darling. Your "Jack" was a faithful hound, to your beck and call…"*

"No, please. Please! He—"

"Stop. Stop, I can't help if you scream!" Charlotte hissed, clutching her temples, falling to her knees. "Oh!" She landed on a piece of jagged crockery, point sinking into her skin and tearing her dress. The bowl had broken and flour was everywhere. Her shoes and dress were caked in white powder.

"No!"

Oh, God. Not again. She'd go mad like this. What had her mother said? Practice not listening. "Stop," Charlotte groaned, louder this time. "I'm here. I'm here but stop and talk to me. I can hear you."

But no one spoke.

She waited for the horrible scene to start again, her stomach heaving. This wasn't right. This wasn't normal.

I was never normal, she conceded in her head. But this? No, spirits spoke *to* her, as if they were there, making conversation. This wasn't a conversation.

Charlotte flexed her bloodless hands, trying to steady her breathing. Her heart was hitting her ribs so hard she feared something would break.

A hammering heart. Like when she'd relived the memories of her father's anger and disappointment in her.

A memory.

Sucking in a harsh gasp, she nodded to herself. *It's a memory from that girl.*

The girl the police brought here.

The girl that was murdered by the man who panted in her ear, the man who called her darling.

Charlotte's fists curled tight. "Don't worry. I'll help you."

****

James leapt out of the coach and ran forward. His eyes were drawn to the sheet, rusty red pooling and streaking on it. "People who drown don't bleed!" he snarled, half to himself.

Unfortunately, half to himself meant half aloud. Constable Gill, who'd been surprisingly easy to persuade into joining him, overheard. Gill ran to catch up, grasping his arm. "Easy now, sir. Easy. It's just that the prison laundry isn't the best. Probably stained. Sadly, not all the bodies we get called to see to are in perfect condition."

James slowed, shoulders heaving. Just a stained sheet. That was all. He nodded jerkily, eyes full. Maybe he wanted to make more of this than there was. The circumstances were odd, but that was London for you. That was Lavinia for you. Dear, sweet, silly little sister. Always up to some lark. Maybe she thought a November dip in the chilly Thames would cool her down. People in the grip of fever did have their delusions. Probably experienced hypothermia.

"Come now, sir. Let's leave these good men to their work. I'll take you 'round the front and have a word with Mr. Harkness, then you can fix the date and place of burial. He works with a nice class of person. He'll know just the place to suit your mother."

James nodded again, this time with a grim chuckle. "She's very difficult to please when it's something she can't control. She could never control Vinnie. She certainly can't control death."

"Ah, sir, which of us can?" Gill tutted.

****

Gill relaxed and waxed philosophical as he comforted the stricken doctor. This strange day of deception was almost done, and he could go back to proper police work. What's more, Mrs. Everly hadn't specifically said where the twenty pounds was supposed to go. Gill knew full well that the chief inspector shouldn't be hushing up this case and burying the file as well as the body. If the chief brought up the matter of twenty pounds, he could bring up the matter of saying a young girl was washed up from the Thames instead of found in a dank little room in Goulston Yard, deep in the heart of the worst of Whitechapel.

"I'm becoming a surgeon, you know." Everly was making idle conversation.

Gill's relaxed air fled. This young fellow was too clever by half. He'd tried pinning Gill down about specific details on the ride to Harkness and Sons, but Gill gave stolid, empty answers that would be a credit to any of her Majesty's Police.

Who found her?

Poor beggar, sir.

Wasn't it too dark to see?

Must've tripped over her, sir. Washed up.

How did you come to identify her, then?

Did you want to enter the police force when you were a boy, sir?

Mother said she had papers in her reticule. Wasn't the ink too wet to read?

She hadn't been in for that long, sir. Don't take much for a person to drown. Was your sister a good swimmer, sir?

That was just it. Vinnie couldn't swim a stroke. She wouldn't have gone for a swim. Unless the fever made her think she could.

Gill stayed tense, knowing Dr. Everly wasn't done

with him yet. Tension turned to irritation. Why had that silly little bird been mucking about where she didn't belong instead of staying in her nice safe house? Why should the whole force drop everything and dash about because a daughter of a fine family had gotten done over when no end of poor girls met the same fate and only a few well-meaning churchgoers made a noise? Why should *she* be deserving of police time to track her killer when there were thousands of heads bashed in or throats cut in the city every year, thousands of cases unsolved, especially down in the East End slums?

Gill knew the chief inspector shouldn't have let a fat contribution from some old dowager sway the course of justice, but... Gill let his conscience sulk. The chief inspector was simply giving the much-maligned, severely overworked force a bit of breathing room, giving them one less case to tackle.

****

"I'm becoming a surgeon." *But right now, I'm still a physician. Why didn't Mother call me if she was so ill? Did she have a fever, truly? Mother is no doctor.*

Gill looked at the man cautiously. "You said, sir. Just now."

"I was going to be simply a physician. 'Doctor' sounds so much better than mister, at least to my mother. I suppose 'chief inspector' sounds better to your mother than a mere police constable?"

"She passed when I was a little lad, sir, but I suppose you're right."

"My father died suddenly. They called for the physician when he was in severe distress, pain in the stomach or the bowels, Mother said. I was at college at the time. The Royal College of Physicians."

Gill frowned, doubtless wondering where this line of chatter was leading. "An excellent profession."

"The fool told him to take an emetic. He ruptured something and died in the morning, after suffering all night. My mother hasn't been quite right since. That's when I decided I'd rather be a surgeon. We can do so much more."

"I've heard that. Shame you don't get to be called 'doctor.' Maybe one day, sir."

"Perhaps. The point is… I like to know what causes things. Even deaths."

Gill coughed. "Drowning is pretty self-explanatory to my mind."

James let out a long sigh. "I suppose it is. I just can't possibly imagine why she was there—" He looked around the crowded, bustling street and the neat but sooty brick building he was standing in front of. "Or what in the world I'm doing here. This isn't our part of London. Not to pull class on you, Constable Gill, but my mother is the daughter of a baronet. She married my father who didn't have a title but had an extremely profitable business and had some distant relatives in the landed gentry, all of that. I can't fathom why you've chosen this particular undertaker, who clearly caters to the—hrm—respectable lower and middle classes."

Gill's tongue was unguarded, perhaps slightly rankled by this James' mention of class, his money, and his schooling. Perhaps the constable thought he was picking on good, honest, hardworking folk. "Likely 'cause your mother's too much of a fine lady to want it all 'round London that her daughter drowned in strange circumstances. This is hardly the hub of elegant society, is it?" Gill snapped.

"Strange circumstances? So, you admit, you *agree*, they're strange? Ought to be looked into further?"

"Bollocks," Gill huffed under his breath. "Not my place to say, sir."

"Why don't the police think they—" A horrible thought struck him. *She drowned herself. Oh, God.* Suicide! *No wonder it must be kept quiet. Those papers… Was it a note? Why? What was so wrong that she couldn't bear it?* Despair silenced him.

"Come on, sir. Wait inside." Gill spoke quietly, gesturing to the front door.

James merely nodded and allowed himself to be led in out of the cold November air.

****

Reginald Harkness had seen his fair share of horrible things.

Lavinia Everly was going to top his list.

He had clucked at the state of the linens, assuming the police had used some other victim's old sheet to carelessly wrap the body of Lavinia Everly. "You can take these back with you," he'd said, carefully unwinding the sheet.

His hand froze.

His heart froze.

The middle-aged police officer who'd come in with him made a weak retching sound and quickly looked away.

"She… What's going on?" Harkness demanded. The wire had said the daughter was a victim of a tragic accident. Tragic, assuredly. Accident? Obviously not.

"Hush, sir. We know the truth, but we're tryin' to spare the family the worst of it. Mother's ill, that's what I've been told."

"She's been murdered. Slaughtered." There was a deep cut on her throat. It wasn't the only one. He hastily tucked the sheets back around her. Slaughtered was a very appropriate word. He'd seen carcasses in the butcher's window split like that.

"Poor girl. She don't deserve to suffer further scandal and indignity, that's what the chief inspector said."

"True, true." His paternal heart was tying itself in knots. This girl looked to be only a few years younger than Charlotte. To meet such a horrible fate… "Have the police finished their examination?"

There was a momentary flicker of hesitation before the policeman replied, "They have. Handed over to your tender mercies, sir."

Yes. Yes, it would be more merciful to let the lady rest with quiet dignity, rather than give the vultures who filled the scandal sheets something else to feast upon. Harkness felt protectiveness stir in him. He would shield this poor thing. He would treat her passing with the grace and dignity Charlotte so often claimed the dead inherently possessed. "Thank you, Constable. Your trust is not misplaced. I have an arrangement with the vicar at St. Clementia. Also with Mr. Pottsgrove, the property manager at Kensley Green."

The uniformed man gave him a relieved smile, nodding heartily. "The chief said you were the one to handle this!"

Even in the midst of tragic circumstances (which he met so often), Harkness plumped with pride. "Very kind of him. Yes, I'll handle everything." He warmed to the task. His timely action would have multiple benefits; sparing the grief-stricken mother the horrors of dealing with the sordid and foul circumstances, letting the police perform an investigation unmolested, and giving this beautiful young lady a gentle and quiet burial, clearly the opposite of her last moments. "Yes, indeed. I'll see to it. Of course, I need some input from the family. I must arrange a suitable date. But—in her state, I do believe the burial must be sooner, rather than later." It wasn't often that he failed to repress a shudder, but now his shoulders convulsed under his long dark coat. "The body will have to be embalmed immediately or buried immediately. Decay will set in rapidly when the body is in such a state. I'll go meet the gentleman. Her brother, was it?"

"Yes, her brother. Young lad, well-to-do, one of those 'a scholar and a gentleman' sorts. My superiors would prefer him not to meddle in this affair. He probably doesn't know the first thing about the harsh realities we see, and I'm sure he'll be grateful that you're taking charge."

****

"Mr. Harkness?" Dr. Everly sprang forward as soon as the undertaker opened the door to the cozy office.

"Dr. Everly. Constable—"

"Gill."

"Greetings, gentlemen. A sad occasion, but rest assured, at Harkness and Sons, every comfort shall be rendered for both the recently bereaved and the dearly departed."

"Thank you." James wrung the older man's hand, finding his eyes were the first truly sympathetic ones he'd found since hearing the terrible news. His mother's were tormented, too full of her own pain to make room for his. The police constable avoided his eyes or kept them downcast, the picture of grave reflection. "I must see her."

"Oh. Oh, sir. There will be time, of course. Please allow me time to do my work and make the necessary preparations."

"I'm a surgeon—nearly. I can handle it."

"I'm certain you could, Dr. Everly. Or should it be Mr. Everly?"

"I'm currently a physician, but I am—I was to qualify in the spring. I suppose... Well, that's not important. I've seen the dead, I've dissected them, I can withstand—I want to see her." James sat down hard. Yes, he'd seen many dead bodies, dissected a few. In those times, he kept his head while sweating, surgical precision and skill on display as the senior surgeons and anatomists watched and critiqued. The thought of Lavinia, cold and unmoving, bloated from the water... never to move again... He became hot and dizzy. He clung to the arms of the wingback chair to stop the room from swaying.

"We'll have her ready for you soon, Dr. Everly. It's part of the services," Harkness said firmly.

"That's right, sir. Make her look like she's only sleeping, isn't that right, Mr. Harkness?"

"Yes, to awake with the angels. Now, I'm sure that your mother's health and state of mind would be better if this was all put to rest, in the past, so that you can reflect on the happy memories. I'm almost positive that we can get the vicar of St. Clementia's to do a short service and place her to rest at Kensley Green tomorrow or the day after."

James nodded as if he understood, but the words were nothing but nonsense in his head. *Clementia's? Kensley Green? Mother's state of mind, that one hit its mark.* His mother was in a terrible state, something beyond grief and anger, but he couldn't place it. *Well, of course not. I've never lost a child. I've lost a parent. A sibling. My sister.* "Please. I want to see her before I leave. I don't care, Mr. Harkness, how horrid she looks."

Mr. Harkness caught Gill making a firm, deliberate shake of his head. He hesitated. "Well… I suppose it won't hurt see her for one moment. If the police have no objections?

"Really, Dr. Everly, no good can come of it!"

"But you don't forbid it."

"No, sir."

Harkness nodded. "I'll just need a few moments. In the meantime, shall we take care of all the other business first? Charlotte! Tea?"

****

Charlotte felt like something was pressing down on her neck. She tried talking, experimentally opening her mouth to call out the customary, "Coming, Father!" Her voice was much louder than she expected.

Pushing herself toward the cupboard to collect the good china cups, she muttered to the empty air, to the unseen presence. "Come on, lamb. I can hear you. I'll help the best I can. I'm sorry about what happened. If you don't want to talk, I understand."

She'd never done this before, not to anyone but her mother. She didn't entreat the departed to speak. If ghosts decided to speak to her, so be it. She didn't pop into the laying-out room or the embalming room, encouraging the corpses to start chatting. She didn't go out and rap on coffin lids like she was paying a call. She knew her place, and formerly, the dead had known theirs.

This girl was something else.

Another sudden sharp pain around her throat, a rush of heat, then cold soaking through her skin, penetrating her bones.

"Speak plainly or leave me alone."

"Please! He—"

Charlotte knew she was supposed to be getting the tea things together, but she stopped at the range, motionless. Yes, it was a memory from the girl. Her death. A memory wasn't terribly helpful, and yet, perhaps it was the girl's way of speaking.

"Help? I'll help you. I said I would. But you have to be patient."

****

Everly wondered if his jaw was cracking. His molars must surely be ground to powder now. No matter what Harkness said as they worked out the funeral details, James nodded quickly, eager to get to the part where he could see his sister. His stomach was a ball of dread, yet somehow his mind was insisting. If he could see Vinnie, this would all be a dream. He'd wake up. Lavinia would sit up, laughing lightly, declaring herself the mastermind of impossible jokes.

He'd smack her for it, woman or no.

Then he'd fall on her neck, weeping and beg her never to do it again.

Why didn't I take better care of them? Father would have expected me to take over the business, move back home, look after Mother and Lavinia, and what did I do? Stop home for a few weeks, talk things over with Uncle Jeremy, and sign up for another long stint of study.

"Will you need time for family to be informed?"

"Hm?" James found nodding wouldn't suffice this

time. He jerked his head up, startled. "I'm sorry. No. No, family to account for."

"Well, then. The fees for the necessary services, of which I then allocate a portion of for the vicar and the property manager of Kensley Green…" Mr. Harkness finished tallying the bill and slid it over, discreetly folded to conceal the total. "Please note, this doesn't include the headstone. However, Mr. Pottsgrove, the manager of Kensley Green will be happy to supply you with one in a variety of styles, and he'll have it engraved and placed within a few weeks."

Headstone. Lavinia doesn't require one of those.

"Angel, cross, or a simple stone with rounded edges? You could do a square or an obelisk of course, but for a young lady of such tender years…" Reginald Harkness paused significantly.

"Angel. An angel." James reached out and signed the papers presented to him, then pocketed the bill. "I'll pay promptly."

"Of course, sir."

"I'd like to see my sister now."

"Presently, Dr. Everly. Let me get that tea for you," Harkness stalled.

"I don't care for tea at present," Dr. Everly said firmly. "Police Constable Gill, you may go. You've done your duty. The b—my sister has been received by the proper authorities."

Gill rose, then sat back down slowly. "I'll wait with you, sir."

James Everly knew that Constable Gill didn't trust him. It was mutual.

****

Of all the times for Charlotte to be dithering about,

probably writing invitations out to the Parson family. Or would it be Danvers? Never mind who, the one time he could have used her sunny disposition, her charming smile, her sweet voice, and her way of turning one cup of tea into three—she stubbornly remained absent.

Mr. Harkness could have used Charlotte's youth and her speed. He had to dash around, binding up the lower half of the body more tightly, tucking the stained sheets over her torn, bloody dress, tucking fresh, white sheets over them as best he could so that nothing showed but her face. Her cold, still face. Even in death, she didn't look peaceful. She looked quiet, waiting.

He shuddered again as he tucked the linens in, right up to her chin, hiding her neck.

Charlotte wouldn't have been unnerved. She possessed a gift for this, calmly regarding the human remains as empty houses of which she was the caretaker, looking after them in the owner's absence.

Yes. The more she absented herself from his side (as he'd often told her to do), the more obvious it was that he relied on her.

That would never do. He couldn't dwell on it now, however.

Mr. Harkness washed his hands and opened a bottle of oil of camphor and placed it under the table upon which the girl rested. With a tug on his suddenly too-tight collar, he opened the door.

"Come in, Dr. Everly."

****

James marched in, steeling himself for the worst. Jaw set, eyes hard, like a soldier into battle, ready to put this hellish day in order.

The day spun him and kicked his knees out, left him

75

staggering suddenly into the woolen shoulder of the annoyingly present Gill.

"Steady on, sir." The man grasped his arm. "Perhaps it'd be better if you didn't—"

"Lavinia?" James gasped, pushing himself upright.

Of course, she didn't answer.

Mustn't make a fool of myself in front of them, James internally scolded. Fists tight to his sides, he walked forward and looked at the beautiful, still face, a perfect oval of light and dark, dark brown curls peeping from the white cloth at her cheeks, long dark lashes, lips still holding the tiniest trace of pink.

Indicating death has happened less than 24 hours ago, closer to twelve.

And the skin.

The tone and position of the skin and the muscles— James' eyes widened, and his arm shot out.

Gill snagged him back. "What are you doin'?" he hissed.

Harkness intervened in a more gentlemanly fashion, stepping between the deceased and her brother with his hands clasped apologetically. "Please, sir, do not touch the dearly departed at this stage. The body is—"

"She didn't drown!"

Harkness backed up, blinking. "Drown?"

"Mother said she drowned! You said she was found in the Thames!" James whirled angrily to face Gill, shaking the man's hand off his shoulder.

"She did. Was!" Gill barked automatically.

"That is *no*t a victim of drowning." James made to move forward.

"She must've been pulled out bloody fast." Gill growled and pulled him back yet again. "Interfering with the deceased is a crime, Dr. Everly. You can settle down or I can escort you out of Mr. Harkness' establishment and into a nice cell."

Exhaling a steadying breath, James attempted to compose himself. "I apologize. I'm sorry, Mr. Harkness, I had no intention of disturbing the deceased. But she is my sister, and I suspect that there is more to her death than meets the eye. I'd like to look at her hands, please. Or feet."

This time there was no mistaking the frown and shaking head from the huffy police constable. "I'm afraid the feet are impossible, sir. Her shoes are on, and I haven't—"

"Hands, then. If she was submerged in the water for any length of time, the skin is going to be swollen and wrinkled."

****

"Uh—" Reginald couldn't mistake the glare Gill was sending him. How to go about this without telling a lie? And why must he? Well, it wasn't the first time strange circumstances surrounding a death had caused him to err on the side of discretion. "Well... I will attest that she didn't have those telltale signs. I've been unfortunate enough to attend to victims who've been recovered from the Thames after a time and it's very unpleasant. Indeed, it's a mercy—in a way—that your sister must've been seen quickly. I'm only sorry no one saw her before it was too late." Reginald soothed, silently wondering how in the world the police would investigate such a crime without the family at least knowing there had been a murder. Perhaps they would tell the boy when his mother's state had improved? Yes, that must be it. They feared he would run home and tell the poor, grieving mother and send her irretrievably into madness. Losing one's child already placed you on the threshold.

****

Thoughts sped through James' mind. He was being a fool, an irrational fool. If his sister had died by her own hand, no wonder his mother wanted it kept quiet. And while he did know a few things about cadavers, he was not an expert. He supposed these men were correct, drowning and retrieval of the body could have occurred very quickly. Something the constable had said earlier wriggled in the back of his mind but slipped away before he could grasp it.

Did women throw themselves into the Thames while clutching their reticules?

He supposed if she'd been retrieved very quickly, that would allow for the legible documents found inside the bag, which led the police to finding her family.

You want to dissect this problem, analyze the symptoms, then cure it. That's what the medical man in you does, that's why your professors praise you. Top marks in diagnosis, surgical technique, and bone-setting.

And no matter how clearly you cut this problem apart, you won't solve a bloody thing. Lavinia is dead. She's going to stay that way. Knowing why won't really matter. Having every question answered won't really matter.

"I apologize, Mr. Harkness. I'm a medical man. I'm always trying to investigate the signs and symptoms. I realize there's no cure here. Still… I'd like to hold her hand. One last time?"

****

Hold her hand? An unusual request in these times, especially when the body had left the home. Death in London was so common—and it could be caught and spread. Harkness realized that was another card stacked against Charlotte. So many regarded undertakers as a step up from ghoulish grave-digging fiends. No family would want an undertaker's daughter for their son. Unless of course, their family was also in the trade.

Thinking of two different young women, both touched by death in inescapable ways, Harkness nodded silently. Only after he'd given his assent was he aware of the bullfrog-like noise coming from the constable. Clearly, he believed this to be a mistake.

Oh, blast! Evidence. But wait… no evidence could be gathered once the body was presented for burial, anyway. Things didn't add up, but the distracted undertaker barely gave them a second thought, mind full of other matters. "Please, Dr. Everly, let me work with the shroud. The bodies of the dearly departed are rather fragile, as I'm sure you know."

****

James watched the man in charcoal-black gently move his sister's wrappings about. The arm moved easily. *Rigor had passed. Definitely dead last night.*

Dead.

No matter how many mathematical and scientific properties he applied to this situation, he couldn't avoid the final outcome.

He was an only child now.

"My God, Vinnie!" he whispered, weeping, moving forward before he was bidden.

"Just the hand, now," cautioned Gill in a stricken voice.

Tears dripped down his cheeks onto his sister's pallid face. When his father passed, he'd grieved. He'd shed a few tears in private. He and his father had not seen each other much in the few years before his death, but when they did, they were at ease, happy. His father was always there, solid and reliable, knowing exactly what to do, and of course, obeying Mother's "suggestions" when it came to the house. His mother and father were quite devoted to one another. Still, even with the suddenness of the loss, James had coped. One knows, even if it is sudden, that one's parents will likely die before oneself.

One's little sister?

His mind couldn't organize it so neatly. He let out a string of incomprehensible apologies and words of brotherly affection, using her name over and over as if after this he'd never speak it again.

It felt final and wrongly so. *Mother intends to hide all of this. Will your pictures be down when I get home? Will your room be locked, and your dresses given to the mission barrels?* "Oh, Vinnie… You should have told me you needed me. What were you thinking? What's in that pretty little head of yours?" he murmured thickly. His hand reached down and clasped the untucked fingers, cold and limp.

And bloody.

****

James froze, the shaking grief temporarily iced over. He tugged gently. Pulled harder. Vinnie's head sagged to the side.

"Gill. I'd like a word with your Chief Inspector. Or the detective on this case, please." James spoke very softly.

"Of course, sir. You can come to the Whitechapel

branch any time you've a mind to."

"There's blood."

"Where?" Harkness sprang forward.

"On her fingers."

"Must be a scrape. Thames is full of stones, sir."

"True. Still…" More and more bits of the equation presented themselves and even though James knew the end result would be the absence of Lavinia from this world, he didn't like this missing bit in the middle. "Mr. Harkness, please don't continue with the embalming until a post-mortem has been ordered. I'm sure a police surgeon will be—"

"No." Gill asserted himself. "No, sir. Post-mortems are not done in these cases. Case of accidental drowning." James watched as Gill turned hard eyes on the undertaker, who was giving him a confused stare. "You *will* be cooperating with the police, won't you, Mr. Harkness?"

"Cooperate? Of course. If the police need to come in—"

"They do not. And failure to properly handle the deceased can give you quite a hefty fine."

The undertaker bridled. "My facility is absolutely state of the art. Why, just listen to this excerpt from the advance copy of—oh, it's in the office. But as you can see, no one is better able to—"

James had had enough lecturing and evading.

"Stop him!" Gill suddenly bellowed, and Harkness' huffy defense was cut short.

James dove for the table and yanked at the shroud which was tightly wrapped over and under the body, determination in every muscle. Hands were on his arm but he ignored them, which had the unfortunate effect of making Harkness join in with his softer hands and calmer voice.

"Leave off, I need to examine her. Leave off!" James snapped.

"Doctor, there's no good you can do once they've passed," Harkness pleaded.

In the scuffle, the table tipped, the camphor knocked over, and a jar of embalming spirits fell from the counter with a thud. The contents trickled from a crack in the glass.

"Out. Out, please. Those chemicals are quite dangerous to the skin," Harkness yelped, rushing to open a window.

"Get out. Get out, right now!" Gill ordered, dragging James away. "Dr. Everly, you are forbidden from entering these premises. Wait outside."

"She's my sister."

"And sorry as I am to say it, sir, she's dead and you've got to come to grips with it." Gill took him by the collar and the elbow and marched him from the room. "Making such a scene!"

Had he made a scene? What had he done? "She's on the ground." James gave him a stricken glance. *With those chemicals? She could get hurt. But… Oh.*

"Yes, thanks to you!"

"I… I can help…"

"You've done quite enough for one day. Your mother sent you along to make arrangements not play at being bloody Dupin! Disturbin' the body like that. God knows what you've knocked about. Not to mention all that foul-smelling stuff."

"But something isn't *right*!" James finally shrugged free, coat and collar rumpled, hair hanging wildly.

Gill's face softened. "None of it is, sir. It's a fallen world. Sometimes I think the East End fell a bit harder than the rest. Beautiful girls shouldn't die, no matter what takes 'em off. Rich bodies shouldn't matter more than poor bodies, and everyone oughta have a nice place in Kensley Green or whatever it is, instead of being stacked like kindling outside opium dens and in the worst yards. Kids in among the old biddies and the murderers and drunks. How's any of that right, sir?"

James was bewildered. He'd never thought of such things. He never expected Gill to have so many words to string together. The day was full of unfortunate surprises. "It isn't right."

Gill nodded sagely, maneuvering him out the front door until they were standing outside of Harkness and Sons. "So, you do your best to take care of what you can take care of. Me? I'm goin' on patrol now, try to get the bad 'uns off the streets. You go take care of your mother and when you pay your bill, maybe bung on a few extra pounds to make up for whatever you spilled in there. Right, then." He walked toward the waiting cab that had delivered them. "Your coach, Dr. Everly."

"I—no, thank you. I'll walk a bit. Clear my head."

"Well… be careful. Keep to the main streets and don't go botherin' hardworking people," Gill warned firmly. With a final searching look at the drained, miserable face, he bobbed his hat firmly on his head. "Good day, sir." He walked away, shoulders squared.

****

Everly stared around him. The cab's driver shouted something at him, and he waved him away, making an inarticulate noise.

His eyes were stinging from the smoke and soot of

the city and the foul chemical odors he'd unwittingly inhaled. He needed to clear his eyes *and* his head.

Something didn't set properly with him, and yet he was sure that if he appealed to the police for help, they'd give him a pitying stare. Poor deluded boy, he can't accept that his sister died suddenly. Or if they did investigate and found it to be a case of suicide, his mother would never survive the shame. His own soundness of mind would be called into question, which would ruin his career. No respectable clients would come to a surgeon who might be insane.

And none of those sensible reasons were louder than the howling in his gut that even if he'd failed Lavinia in life, he would not fail her in death. He could not rest until he knew what had happened to her, or at least until he'd done everything possible to uncover the truth.

Which meant getting back inside and getting a look at the—the body.

Lavinia was gone, no matter what he did.

His eyes closed and he stumbled forward, catching himself against the brick wall. For a moment, he didn't care if passersby stared at him. He clutched his hat in one hand and let his forehead rest against the gritty exterior of Harkness and Sons.

"What am I to do?" he whispered.

"Psst. Hello?"

James jumped. A voice from above? Well, he assuredly *needed* divine assistance, but he hadn't expected the Almighty to answer so quickly. Or to sound so much like a girl. "Hello?" he asked cautiously.

"Up here!"

James looked up and over. One of the front windows of the house was pushed open. Through the gloom of the damp air, a fair face appeared, hair a tumble of wheat-colored curls and pins, backlit by the warm glow of the fire and lamplight in the room.

"I can help you. Come to the door," she hissed.

"Help me?" James inquired, already in motion.

The face left the window, but appeared seconds later, greeting him in the doorway.

"How do you know I need help?" James demanded, trotting over.

In answer, she gave a roll of her eyes, pink lips pursed. "I know quite a few things. Hurry, inside."

Inside Harkness and Sons once again, James wasn't being shown a cozy office, he was being pulled pell-mell down a narrow hall, into the kitchen. "Wait! Who are you?" he demanded, shaking off her tugging hand.

****

Charlotte turned, shutting the kitchen door behind them. Good. She'd helped put the cloth-bound body back in the laying-out room, but her father was still busy cleaning up. He hadn't noticed. "That's all right, then," she breathed.

It was then that she noticed the young man was staring at her, baffled.

"Oh, pardon me." She extended her hand and fumbled a half curtsey, unsure exactly how one was supposed to greet a guest that one had just dragged into the kitchen in secret. "I'm Charlotte. The undertaker's daughter."

Part Two:

Doubly Detected

Chapter Five

James Everly stared at the figure in front of him. Charlotte Harkness, the undertaker's daughter, was wearing a simple red dress with a tiny check pattern on it, the toes of polished black boots peeping from underneath her long skirts. A brown apron with flowers tatted around the edge completed her ensemble. These things stood out to him for two reasons. One, he'd been working on his skills of observation for his medical training. Two, they were covered in flour. Come to think of it, one of his sleeves was also covered in the same after her unorthodox introduction.

"Tea?" Charlotte offered.

"*What*?" James blurted.

"Manners!" The girl gave him an affronted stare.

James' jaw fell open and stayed, hanging open.

****

Charlotte realized she shouldn't snap at the poor man, so clearly bewildered. But even when one is beset by the voices of the deceased, one still attempts to preserve decorum. She probably should have considered that before yanking him down the hallway and forcing him into the kitchen.

He blinked. "Do forgive my manners. No tea for me, thank you, Miss Harkness."

"All right." Hm. How to start without having the man run screaming from the house? Or getting herself

89

shunted off to an asylum? "I believe you have some concerns about the manner of your sister's death."

His eyes narrowed, surveying her uncertainly. He nodded in silence.

"I share your concerns."

"Ha!" The laugh escaped him, a single harsh explosion.

"Shh. My father's clearing up in the embalming room, and then he's heading straight off to St. Clementia's to talk with the vicar about her funeral service. I figure by half past he should be out of the house, and you can see what she wants."

The narrow eyes widened, gratitude flashing in them before confusion took over. "See what who wants?"

"Your sister. I… Don't you feel that the dead sometimes want the living to look after them?" Oh, dear. This was much harder than she'd thought. It had seemed so simple when she saw him leaning helplessly against the building. Here was a man who was grieving for his sister, who'd been quite vocal in his protests that something wasn't right.

Without speaking directly to Lavinia, she'd understood that the poor soul wanted someone to help her. Her suspicious brother seemed like the logical choice.

But one can't go about saying, "Your sister was murdered, and she's very persistent about sharing her last memory. I'd like you to resolve the matter so I can stop reliving that particular horror, thank you so very much."

James regarded her dubiously. "Do I feel the dead want…? The dead are *dead*."

"Well, I can't argue with that. Do you ever feel that

you must help those who are not able to help themselves?" Charlotte sighed and tried again.

Now, *that* he seemed to understand. "Yes. I'm a doctor. A surgeon—almost."

"I share your concern that something isn't right. I don't think this was an accident." *I know certainly it was not.*

"Yes, exactly! There are so many little things that I can't put my finger on, but I *feel* they're off." He put a hand over his heart, fingers digging into the stiff cotton shirt. "They claim my sister was found in the Thames, near Whitechapel, which is miles from our home. They claim the Thames must've moved her down this way, yet that constable also put forth she must've been retrieved very quickly from the water. She has no outward signs of death by drowning, which would back up his second claim, not his first." He hesitated. "Miss Harkness, I know the police are satisfied, and I'm sure your father has not had a chance to examine the body—nor would he perform an examination in his duties—but I would feel better if I made even a cursory examination to determine the cause of death. Everyone says she drowned."

Charlotte tilted her head. "Father was told it was an accident and that your mother's health was very poor. I presume, if he's withheld any knowledge, he's acting with a kind heart, trying to spare her pain or follow police directives."

"You and your father are both most kind and sympathetic." James gave her a weak smile. "I don't doubt that he acted out of good motives. I may be deluding myself, grasping at straws when the simple answer is that my feverish little sister acted foolishly, fell, and somehow drowned. A poor beggar may have pulled her from the river's edge and ran off once he discovered he was too late, and then another vagrant tripped upon her remains." He shuddered. "It's a terrible ending to a short story."

Charlotte bit her lip. The real ending was far worse. Was she acting in his best interests by telling him? Would Lavinia want her brother to suffer with this tragedy?

The sound exploded in Charlotte's head, terror that wasn't truly her own washing over her.

No!

"No, please. Please! He—"

James reached for her arm as she winced, her features screwed up in pain, a hand to her temple. "Are you all right?"

"I… I think you may regret finding out the truth. It hurts, sometimes," she managed to speak calmly, even though blackness was engulfing her.

"I would rather have a painful truth than an easy lie."

Their eyes met.

"All right. She's moved to the laying-out room. I believe he may have given up on the idea of embalming, considering the urgency and the need to bury her quickly. When my father leaves, I'll help you with your examination."

"Oh, no! Please. That sort of thing is no job for a woman." Dr. Everly looked horrified.

Charlotte's smile was forced. "I'm not your typical woman."

Before Dr. Everly could inquire as to what was so abnormal about her, a flustered shout echoed through the still house.

"Charlotte?"

With a gasp, Charlotte looked over her shoulder. With a determined frown, she grabbed Everly by the shoulders. "Wait here!"

"See here!" he sputtered as he was unceremoniously shoved backward, out the kitchen door, half stumbling into a tiny strip of garden.

"Hush. Keep quiet and wait here. Yes, Father?" Charlotte left Everly standing open-mouthed outside the door and shut it softly in his face. She whirled to face the sound of her father's voice.

Mr. Harkness marched into the room, his collar and tie undone, his hat off. He seldom appeared in anything less than his full, fastidious "uniform" of dark tailcoat, dark suit, and black or gray waistcoat. He was obviously upset and distracted. If he thought it was odd that she was panting and wide-eyed, her back plastered somewhat guiltily against the kitchen's back door, he gave no indication.

"What is it, Father?"

Her father collected himself with an effort. Charlotte was used to being his confidante, his accidental apprentice, so to speak, and it was clear he needed to unburden himself.

"I must go and collect more embalming spirits from the apothecary in the High Street. You must not enter the embalming room just now. Nasty stuff."

"Of course, Father. The dearly departed, she's in the laying-out room, isn't she?"

"Yes, and don't go paying a call!" he said peevishly. "Poor girl deserves peace and quiet."

Charlotte smothered a smirk. Her father certainly seemed to be taking a page out of her book. The dead had needs, did they? "Do you have measurements for her coffin and shroud?"

"I haven't had a moment! A standard medium should do nicely. Bother, I shall have to call at St. Clementia's and stop at the post office as well. I must wire Mr. Pottsgrove. I'll have to eat late tonight. Dash it all, where's my coat, Charlotte?" He looked around, suddenly lost in his own establishment.

"Which one?"

"Both." He sounded almost pitiful as he looked around, lost.

Charlotte wanted her father to get on his way, but she also felt a surge of sympathy for him. "Whatever is the matter? I'm sorry about the tea." She gave him a contrite hug, helping him with his tie and fastening his collar.

"Oh, my dear, no. The tea wouldn't have served us well. Dr. Everly, the brother of the deceased, was in such a state. That poor girl…Horrible. Shocking."

"What was?" Charlotte fussed over his collar, hoping he'd divulge more if he thought she was only half listening.

"N-nothing. Well, the death itself. The mother is in delicate health. This loss was a shock to her," he amended.

"The mother? I didn't see her."

"The police and the brother attended to the unpleasant, yet sacred duty." He patted at his waistcoat pockets.

"Police?"

Harkness continued patting himself down, muttering, "We'll stay out of it. Yes, that'll be it. Keep it quiet. Give them space to work without the papers poking their noses in—where *is* my pocket watch?"

"Who?" Charlotte inquired, fishing out the errant watch as her father stilled.

"What?"

"Give who space to work?"

"The—never you mind. My, that ham is starting to smell nice."

Charlotte shook her head. Her father was more adroit in handling bodies than changes of subject. "What should I do?"

"Nothing. Absolutely nothing," Mr. Harkness said firmly. "I must be off, and I want you to worry about other matters and leave Miss Everly to me, please. Hangment! Where *is* my coat?"

****

James shivered in the creeping cold, hiding in the shadows and trying not to be put off by what he saw around him. The tiny strip of garden opened into a sort of makeshift courtyard with several small outbuildings. Carriage tracks had worn a path between the street and the largest of them. A stable, perhaps? He tilted his head, straining to hear what Mr. Harkness was saying about his sister as well as trying to see around him.

One shed was probably a privy or perhaps some sort of storehouse. He squinted his eyes and managed to see lines and stacks of wooden boxes.

No. Coffins.

His skin gave an unpleasant twitch as if trying to rearrange itself.

Just as he was seriously contemplating leaving and fetching the police himself, the door silently opened, and the peculiar girl greeted him again.

"Well, don't just stand there! Get in before he sees

you." Charlotte Harkness reached into the frosty air.

For the second time that day, he was yanked into an unfamiliar kitchen.

"Miss Harkness, not that I'm not grateful for your help," he said in a rather priggish voice that he instantly loathed himself for, "but I could do with less tugging and pushing. I'm not a dog on a lead."

"I wouldn't need to tug you if you were a dog," Charlotte retorted with a toss of her head. "Dogs are good judges of character, and they implicitly trust helpful people."

James opened his mouth, then closed it. "Well, I do need your help. I suppose you want paying for—" He patted his trouser pocket in sudden dismay. The only bill he had on him was the one presented by Mr. Harkness.

Charlotte looked at him coldly. "I'm doing this to help your sister. You can pay my father whatever you owe him after the funeral is completed. He typically has the accounts settled after the burial. He's a conscientious man, my father, and likes to ensure satisfaction is complete before he accepts a penny," she concluded proudly.

Dr. Everly was oddly annoyed and grateful at the same time. Impatience and curiosity won out. "How do you surmise this helps Lavinia?" He swallowed painfully, her name like a sticking pin in his throat.

The girl seemed unable to explain, staring at him vacantly for a moment. She covered the pause by leading him through the kitchen and down a narrow hall, keeping well in front of him. "My father has seen more strange things than you can imagine, Mr. Everly."

"Doctor. For now." He followed her as closely as he dared.

She continued as if he hadn't spoken. "Whatever he's hiding from you has upset him terribly."

"He *shouldn't* be hiding it."

"Death is a very discreet business that has a very public reflection. No one dares speak ill of the dead. Everyone knows when one has passed. Why, I've seen families starve themselves to pay for a burial rather than let the body go to the flesh merchants who take corpses to hospitals and surgeons' colleges. The whole street will chip in a penny or two. Rather starvation than shame." She warmed to her subject, eyes flashing.

He winced. Yes, his college chums were quite cavalier when it came to getting bodies in, a rowdy groan going up in the halls of residence as they talked about particularly nasty dissections, occasionally making complaints about the scarcity of bodies to practice on.

"Yet that shame can hang with the family long after the dearly departed leaves this mortal coil. Harkness and Sons tries to make sure that's never the case." She stopped abruptly, both walking and speaking. "This is the laying-out room."

"How long will he be gone?" Cold sweat pooled on his brow and palms. After he went through that door, he'd know the truth. If it was anything aside from drowning, he'd know that everyone around him had lied. His mother, the police, even sympathetic Mr. Harkness.

"A few hours. Are you going to perform an actual post-mortem?" Charlotte twisted her hands together anxiously. "That would make quite a mess. I doubt I could hide that from Father."

"I hope I don't need to. I can't, I haven't got my surgical instruments with me. Anyway, I don't want to… I don't want to disturb her more than necessary."

"Good. She's suffered enough."

James gave his hostess a questioning stare, then turned his back to her and moved into the room.

He noticed the sickly-sweet odor that comes at the beginning of decomposition. That struck him as odd. The weather was cold. This room was very cold as well. He surveyed the table where the sheet-wrapped bundle lay and saw that the top was metal. Unlike the cozy furnishings of the undertaker's office, this room was plain and antiseptic, similar to the embalming room.

"You spilled the oil of camphor." Charlotte moved past him, over to a cabinet, and took out another large, square jar. "We have another one. Don't!" Her harsh cry stopped him as he hovered near the body. The girl's face was now concealed as well.

"Why bring me in if I can't complete an examination?" James asked, voice equally harsh.

"*I* will handle the dearly departed. You observe. If you're asked any questions, this way you can say you never touched a thing."

Retort stemmed by the image of a glowering Constable Gill, James nodded. "That's wise, I suppose."

"I try to think of all eventualities. Bearing that in mind"—Charlotte gave him a fleeting smile—"are you sure you wish to do this? You might be more at peace simply realizing your sister is gone and laying her to rest."

"The manner of her death doesn't matter?" He'd had that thought earlier, that even if he knew every detail, it wouldn't change anything.

"It's horrible, not being at peace. I know." Charlotte unstoppered the camphor and placed it on the counter behind her. The strong, familiar scent caused both living occupants of the room to blink their stinging eyes.

"We use that in my line of work, too. Well, during anatomy clinics. Too much can make you light-headed." *Like grief. Why am I exchanging idle words with this strange girl?*

Charlotte nodded, waiting by the cloth-wrapped figure.

James' jaw flexed a few times. "No. It's no good, I *must* know."

"Right." Charlotte moved forward.

****

Charlotte hesitated by Lavinia's head. If James had said he would be content to simply lay his sister to rest without further investigation, she could figure out a way to comfort Lavinia's spirit, help her move on. She'd never have to tell another living soul about her "peculiarity." But Everly wanted to know what secrets the body held… and she had a feeling Lavinia's secrets would soon expose her own.

"Ready?"

"As I can be." Everly nodded.

She'd never seen Lavinia's face, only heard her voice and the voice of her attacker, mere impressions. Undoing the winding sheet carefully, she smothered a gasp.

Everly cursed and bit back a cry.

"How they could say this was drowning…"

"That's why." Charlotte's soft voice held a note of realization. *Poor lamb. Can't speak. Throat's slit. God have mercy on her soul.* She bowed her head a moment, eyes closed.

****

James was not given to peaceful contemplation.

There was nothing about this horrific sight that brought him any closure, any sense of understanding. No, his head was filling with more questions, and they had no outlet. *Did she die by her own hand? Slit her throat? Slit her throat, then throw herself into the river? Why would she do such a thing? Does Mother know? Surely, it must be by her own hand, and that's why Mother won't allow the police to have an inquest.*

"I don't know what happened." The words tore from him, tortured. "I don't know why she did this."

"She?"

"My sister." James gestured impatiently. Daft girl, this undertaker's daughter, not Lavinia.

"Surely a woman wouldn't have done that, at least not on her own neck. Look how deep the wound is." Charlotte shook her head.

James blinked, struggling to look closely at this— this corpse. This body with his sister's face.

And blood on her hands.

Well, yes, from the wound she inflicted, the blood would of course be on the blade, on her hand. Wait a moment. "Let me see her hands, please."

Charlotte obeyed his request, gently, tenderly unwrapping the sheet and wincing as more stained cloth was revealed.

James stared at the rusty splotches on cotton. Was it simply stained cloth from a previous police case? Was it from her dress, which was soaked with blood at the collar and down the front? At last, his eyes focused on her exposed hands.

"Blood on both hands."

"Yes. Well, there's a good bit of it on her." Charlotte covered the form back up.

"Can I see the whole… Can I see all of her, please?"

Charlotte's mouth popped open. "Oh. Surely there's no need for that?"

"Do you think my sister did herself in?" James demanded without knowing why. How in the world would this stranger know a thing about his sister? Even if she believed so, this girl's thoughts were of no consequence. He was surprised by the careful nature of her answer.

"No. No, Dr. Everly, I don't believe she did. I don't know much about her, but just from what I can observe"—Charlotte thought quickly—"she's well-off and well-loved. Even if she was so sorely grieved, I can't imagine her hurting herself in such a violent manner. She doesn't look very strong if you'll pardon my saying so. That cut is long and deep. It had force behind it, wouldn't you say?"

"Murder?"

"Yes, sir."

"Then why would the police say she drowned?"

****

Charlotte looked at her shoes. She had hoped her comment would lead him on the right path. Perhaps he'd develop an inkling on his own take himself off, get the police to open an investigation, and the soul would settle down. She could go back to worrying about how much coal they should order and where she had put the nice blue writing paper Auntie Molly gave her, now that she had to write out invitations to tea. She wouldn't have to reveal her own dark secret. Funny, until right now, she'd never considered it particularly problematic.

The doctor was waiting for an answer. At last, she said, "Well-off and well-loved. I imagine your mother might think there's more value on a lady's *reputation* than there is on her life, at least once it can't be saved." Charlotte wondered if he could hear the bitterness in her tone.

Dr. Everly looked up from the stained sheet across the torso of the body. "Why, what would you know about reputation?"

"I'm an undertaker's daughter, sir. Haven't you already decided *exactly* what sort of a person I am? Or haven't you already put me in some neat file inside your mind, a woman, the weaker sex, the fairer sex?"

"Bold and outspoken, more like."

"My father worries more for my reputation than I do. I worry more for the girl on this table. All right. Let's see." Charlotte expected stab wounds to meet her eyes. She set her jaw and silently focused on other things, things not in this room. *A service. I'm doing the Lord's work, justice, mercy, helping... Oh, ruddy hell.*

Charlotte's silent prayer ended with an internal curse as the sheet was finally removed and the remnants of dresses and petticoats were put on display. Her cheeks were hot, and her head swam, not for the lack of modesty she was observing, but for something much worse.

****

James Everly, the strong, educated medical man in the situation found his head suddenly level with the table. His knees had given out, and his palms were leaving wet streaks on the clean-swept wooden boards on the floor. "Oh, God. Oh... Father in heaven."

Dress, corset, petticoat, torn asunder and split.

Skin split, too. Neat line. Clear down from the breastbone to where legs met the body, a single incision followed by something vicious that one daren't speak of.

Doctors might, perhaps.

"What madman did such a thing?" Miss Harkness breathed out, voice whipped away in horror.

James didn't answer. He was going to be sick if he parted his lips an inch. He was grateful when the strange girl with her outspoken ways and her dress speckled with flour covered the body up. She came around to him.

"I'll fetch some water. Stay down. You stand up, and you'll probably knock down this table as well."

Calling on all his resolve, he rose unsteadily, swallowing the sour bile in his throat. "No. That won't be necessary."

"Shall I ring for a doctor? Or the police?"

"I'll handle the police. I'll also…" James paused in his stilted speech, head tilting quizzically. Before she could warn him off, he exposed the chest wound again. "That's a surgeon's incision. That's the incision one makes to begin a cadaver's dissection, thoracic cavity to pelvic region. Oh, I beg your pardon, Miss Harkness."

"I think I'm beyond begging pardons now. This was done *after* she died?"

"Mercifully, I believe the throat wound killed her. I can't see anything being so—neat, if not. If there was a struggle—" The room blackened on the edges. He appreciated the steadying hand on his elbow. "I don't like to say such things before a lady, but this was no ordinary madman. This was a man with some medical knowledge. This was a man with a very sinister purpose." His eyes trailed lower.

The pompous, booming voice of Dean Lawrence abruptly replayed in James' mind as he surveyed her skin. Of course, right now he couldn't recall the words of the dull lecture on "female troubles," but he pulled some facts from his keen mind. In the 1840s, Charles Clay was the first to claim a patient to survive an abdominal hysterectomy. Then, more recently, there was an American surgeon, in the Boston area, he believed, who had further perfected the technique and reduced the mortality rate.

But Lavinia was far too young to ever need such an operation surely. This was murder, not a medical procedure. *Why...?*

Of course, there were back street butchers who would perform certain sinful operations on a young woman who wanted to end a pregnancy.

This was *not* their methodology.

No, this was murder and something more, but he couldn't figure it out.

"Hysterectomy?" He shook his head, confounded.

"Pardon?"

"Hystere— I do beg your pardon again, Miss Harkness. A medical term that you wouldn't be familiar with. I was only—"

"The surgical removal of the female organs of—of childbearing."

James gazed at her, his confoundedness doubled. "How in the world did you know that? It's a fairly new surgical technique."

****

Charlotte shrugged, even though Auntie Molly had often told her that shrugging was for the unintelligent and insolent. How in heaven's name did she end up in this mess? Her mother must be turning in her grave— and she'd hear about it later. Her father would have fainted clean away if he could see her now, and she'd be on the next train north.

She didn't feel like mincing words, nor justifying herself. "I read the medical and embalming manuals my father purchases. I know a fair bit, not that I'm allowed to use it, being a *woman*."

"You could be a nurse, a sister at any hospital with a constitution like yours."

Bitterness turned to melancholy. "I suppose I could." *Why should I?*

Well, yes, it would be a fine idea, to help those riddled with illness and suffering. But there are hundreds of doctors and nurses and ward sisters. Stubbornness was one of her besetting sins, Auntie Molly had also lamented. *I want to stay with my father. I want to carry on our family trade. I'm good at it—or I would be.*

She became brisk and businesslike to hide the sadness mounting in her, the idea that her father would push her away or only accept her help if it suited her husband, a husband who must also be in the trade. She would always be kept on the edges. "Are you quite done? Lavinia's suffered enough, and now that you've seen what must be done, there's no need for further indignities, is there?"

"No. Only…" Dr. Everly winced and looked around the room. "Will you fetch that water after all? And soap and a towel?"

"Of course. Father already keeps a stack of clean linens and plenty of soap in this room and the embalming room. Why do you need it?" Charlotte's eyes narrowed. "You mustn't make a mess in here!"

"I won't! I'm simply going to palpate the abdomen to see—never you mind. I've a reason."

"This is my establishment, and you are my guest. You said you wouldn't touch the body in case you were questioned!"

"This is a murder, and your father is covering it up. Let there be questioning!"

"Didn't the police tell you that you were not to set foot on these premises? Do you think they'll listen to you if you start off admitting that you've gone against their orders?" Charlotte countered.

Stalemated, he sighed. "Look here, I must work quickly before further decay set in. The blood is already settling. You can tell by the brownish-red discoloration in her hands and at her ankles. The damage done to the— the body is going to cause putrefaction to set in fast. I fear anything the police could find useful will be gone soon. I'm going to palpate the abdomen because the way she was att-attacked makes me wonder what else—" he broke off. He couldn't talk about his sister as if she were simply another body, not even another patient.

Charlotte's voice surprised him. It had gone from challenging to comforting. "I'll tell the police I insisted you come in and examine the body after I came to attend it. *If* they ask."

"Thank you." He shrugged out of his coat and rolled up his sleeves.

"She needs your help, Dr. Everly. This is all you can do for her now. I'll get fresh hot water for the basin."

****

With Miss Harkness gone, he allowed himself to stop and take a few deep breaths, then hold them. Later, in private, he might collapse, sobbing. He might rant and throw things, causing his mother to put him out of the house—if not for the scandal that would cause. For right now, he must remain steady. This part would be unpleasant, but necessary. He quickly pressed along the

106

wound with its gory, dark-tinged edges. He allowed himself a sigh of relief, for the most part. The thoracic cavity, while incised, was not opened. More of a preliminary incision than operational. Lower, his throat tightened again.

His hand sank.

Hollowed. Some tissue had been removed with the force of the attack.

The wound was deeper there, a plunge and drag of a sharp, thin blade.

He started, hands lifting off the body with shock. *He used a scalpel. The bastard was one of us. A surgeon.*

Somehow that made everything much worse. Fury replaced grief.

Clean, neat work along the midline of her torso, splitting the fabric of her dress became more like butchery below. *The beast meant to tear her open—but hadn't. Maybe he'd been content that she was already dead?*

"What sort of evil… When I find him…"

"When *you* find him?" Charlotte swept furtively into the room, a tall white pitcher of hot water in her hands. "Surely the police will handle that."

"Yes. Yes, of course. I merely meant—" James stopped, hastily covering up the ruined body. He hesitated and laid his hand, clean knuckles to his sister's silent, cold brow. "I don't know what I meant, Miss Harkness." No, he knew exactly what he meant. He would not rest until they caught the fiend who did this, until he was hung and buried. If he could put the rope around the murderer's neck, he wouldn't even flinch.

"Vengeance is mine, sayeth the Lord," Charlotte told no one in particular.

"And I'm sure the Bible also says something about women being silent?"

Charlotte chuckled drily. "Not like you mean." With a second's hesitation, she also laid a hand to the messy dark hair fanning around the girl's head. "I'll tidy her up. The soap and towels are by the basin."

****

"Goodbye and thank you, Miss Harkness. I'm afraid I'll be back with the local constabulary before long. Naturally, I'll make sure that your father is kept out of this as much as I can."

"Thank you, Dr. Everly. My sincere condolences. I'll make sure that Harkness and Sons use the utmost discretion." Charlotte dropped another clumsy curtsey as the fair-haired, somber-faced man bent over her wrist and kissed the air above it. She admitted to herself that such a gentlemanly farewell was a rarity, and it made her feel strangely, pleasantly anxious.

"I'm certain my mother will appreciate that. It was her doing, I'm all but positive, that led to the police delivering the body here in such a state with such a poorly thought-out story. To think that no one would find out." He shook his head in wonder.

Charlotte held her tongue. He was from a different world, only a few miles away. There, justice was always served, injustices were never overlooked. No one starved in doorways rather than go to the almshouse, no one drank or drugged themselves to death. The police turned a blind eye every day to dozens of deaths, were likely never even called to investigate a majority of ones that Dr. Everly and his ilk would find suspicious. The majority of the police constables she saw were harassed and harried, trying to help the living. A blind eye wasn't a failing, it was almost a necessity to survive. "I'm sure she was ill-prepared to handle such shocking news." Charlotte withdrew her hand with a fleeting smile. "One could never expect to—"

"What a stroke of luck, to find the vicar picking up his wife's rheumatism liniment at the apothecary when I was picking up the arsenic for the embalming spirits. He's able to see to Miss Everly tomorrow at three. I sent the wire to Mr. Pottsgrove, and we'll wait to see what he says."

Charlotte exchanged a panicked glance with Dr. Everly. Had they been occupied for so long or had Harkness simply been very quick about his errands? Charlotte couldn't very well drag her secret guest to the kitchen now, they were just inside the narrow front hall. As soon as her father took off his overcoat and put down all the parcels in his arms, he'd see the man who should have left ages ago.

James coughed gently. "Mr. Harkness?" He strode forward, hand outstretched.

Reginald Harkness jumped as though he'd trodden on a snake. "Dr. Everly? But—But you left before I did!"

"I came, sir, to humbly apologize for my behavior and to insist that you let me pay for the chemicals I inadvertently spilled." James hastily reached inside his pocket and presented the bill that Harkness had presented earlier. "Would you please add them to the total?"

"Oh. Oh, no, I couldn't do that." Mr. Harkness appeared mollified. "I do understand, sir. The mind and heart in their grief...." He trailed off significantly.

"Well, I insist on making a donation to your fine establishment, to cover a funeral for one less fortunate." James gave a deep, deferential nod to the flustered undertaker.

Mr. Harkness beamed at him. Charlotte's smile was smaller, sedate and appreciative.

"That's very kind of you, sir. That I won't object to. I'll mention it to the vicar of St. Clementia's. The parish is establishing a funeral fund for the needy of the parish. I hope Charlotte looked after you in my absence?"

"He just arrived not long ago," Charlotte quickly told the truth—depending on how one measured time.

Unfortunately, James declared, "Admirably, sir, she was a most gracious hostess," at the same time.

"Well, for the time, brief as it was." Charlotte reached for the parcels her father had set on the small table in the hall. "Let me take that for you, Father. Good evening, Dr. Everly."

"Good evening, Miss Harkness. Mr. Harkness."

****

Charlotte busied herself in the kitchen, speaking softly, hopeful her father wouldn't overhear or question. "There, lamb. Your brother knows. Justice will be done. You can go now."

A surprisingly petulant voice answered, *"No. Shan't."*

"So, you can speak?"

"It was good enough for you the last time. Out of the carriage or back home you go, without me."

Charlotte almost lost the last of their milk this time, her fingers suddenly frozen as a smooth, low voice invaded the conversation. A man's.

"Lavinia?" Charlotte whispered, looking around, breath starting to quicken.

"Please! He—"

"Oh no." Back to that again. "The others talk

properly," she complained as she firmly set the milk well out of range.

"Others aren't so confused, life robbed so abruptly away. She can't rest, she can't speak."

"Mama!"

"She's sharing memories?"

"Can you talk to her?"

"No, my little bird. She's not even here, not properly."

"She sends me sounds. No images. If I could see this man's face, I'd be able to help the police so much better."

Silence.

"Oh. They wouldn't believe me, would they?"

"Don't worry, my sparrow. One day, you'll find the one who listens."

"I have you." Charlotte smiled, warmth and comfort wrapping around her as her mother's presence lingered.

Again, silence.

"Mama? Don't I have you?"

A weariness couldn't be hidden. *"Of course, my darling."*

****

"You're trying to tell me that the good forces of the Whitechapel branch covered up a murder an' evisceration?"

Dr. Everly twisted his hat 'round and 'round as the sergeant sitting across from him gave him an openly dubious stare. "Yes. Only not a full evisceration."

"If I could beg your pardon, Dr. Everly, but why not go back to Whitechapel and have them sort it out then? This is out of the Westminster district. We've enough to do without mucking in our brethren's affairs."

"Yes, but you see—"

111

"If your sister's death was such a horrible crime, I'm fairly certain they wouldn't miss those telltale signs, sir." The sharp-eyed sergeant noticed the hands circling on the hat in Everly's lap, including the telltale twitching in his fingers and the strong medicinal odor coming from him. "Have you been drowning your sorrows, sir? Not that I would blame you."

"No. I—I haven't eaten yet today. It's been a shock! But that doesn't mean I'm lying or wrong. I saw the body, Sergeant. Her throat was cut."

The sergeant paused. "And how did the Whitechapel fellows claim she passed, sir?"

James blinked. "Drowning. In the Thames."

"Ah."

"What do you mean, 'Ah'?"

Sergeant Evesham didn't think of himself as a cruel man. He wasn't trying to break down this young boy who clearly thought he knew more about policing than did Her Majesty's Metropolitan. He cleared his throat and spoke quietly, "Sir, perhaps an accident is a kinder way to put what has the same end result. Sounds more like an accident than saying she slipped on a razor, doesn't it?"

James went white to the lips. "It wasn't suicide. I'm fairly certain the injuries on the rest of her body were made after death and that—"

"Oh, a coroner are you? Police surgeon? Detective?"

"I'm a surgeon, yes. Or I will be soon. Please listen. She'd been stabbed and injured below the waist." White cheeks were replaced with red. "I will pay for the force's time if you'd simply send your police surgeon to the undertaker to confirm my suspicions. *Please*."

Evesham sighed and rose. "One moment, sir. I must

run this past the chief inspector."

****

As Evesham left, James sank back in his chair. No one should have to say such things, and if one did, one shouldn't be disbelieved simply because someone else in power claimed it wasn't so.

James ignored the curious stares of the police and their charges as they passed Evesham's desk. He'd be right and they'd be wrong. More important, Lavinia's killer wouldn't walk free. He'd make sure to praise Mr. Harkness and his daughter to the police, saying they helped catch the miscarriage of justice that was about to occur. Mother would lock herself in her room for a few months, living on digestive biscuits and sherry, but eventually, she'd forgive him, and her true friends wouldn't care about the scandal.

Does Mother have *any true friends?*

He couldn't recall any coming over after Father died. Was that customary for widows? He hadn't been home much to find out.

****

When Evesham returned after what seemed to be hours, he was followed by a very tall, imposing man with shoulders that all but filled the doorway.

Yes! James cast an appraising eye over the newcomer. *Here* was the right sort of policeman, here was the sort who got things done. Hope surged.

"What rot are you talking, sir?"

Hope plummeted and met a painful death.

"Chief Inspector?" James rose and extended his hand.

It was ignored. "That's right. I've been in communication with my counterpart at Whitechapel. See here, lad, just because they're not as 'upper crust' as you doesn't mean you get to call into question their methods."

James floundered out a protest. "What? No! That has nothing to do with it."

"Would you like to see the telegrams, sir? Apparently, Whitechapel's already had its fill of you for one day. Hysteria, disturbing the dead, knocking about dangerous chemicals. You were told not to set foot on the premises by one P.C. Gill. When did you 'see' these injuries you claim your sister suffered?"

"Well—I—The undertaker's daughter told me I—"

Ringing laughter cut off his stumbling protest. He didn't want to implicate Charlotte, but he must make them believe.

Sergeant Evesham chortled. "A woman? A little girl, sir? Bless you, sir, and what would she know about anything?"

"A woman, an educated woman, who could tell the difference between someone who was murdered and someone who had drowned."

"Oh, an *educated* woman. So, the two of you educated types know more than Chief Inspector Briggs at Whitechapel, a man with fifteen years in Her Majesty's services? Been alive longer than both of you put together, I'd wager. He says your mother requested all discretion and here you are, breaking the poor woman's heart over again. Shame on you, sir. Go attend to the living!" The chief inspector's voice rolled like thunder.

The interior of the precinct went very still for a moment. One of the drunken forms waiting on the wooden bench near the doorway belched loudly and startled everyone back into their mundane actions, filing papers, hauling human refuse in and out of the corridor that led to the cells, shouting for this and that.

James didn't move. "She's to be buried tomorrow afternoon. I don't want to upset my mother. I don't for a moment think the police lied to her, Chief Inspector—"

"Ainsley."

He spoke through his teeth, trying to sound polite and deferential while he screamed inside. "Chief Inspector Ainsley, I don't believe the police lied or could be faulted in their methods. I believe that out of compassion for my mother, who I'm sure they correctly informed about the nature of my sister's death, they agreed to classify it as an accident. They sought to kindly spare my mother the scandal of a murder investigation and trial. It would be very sordid. Lavinia looked as though she'd been horribly interfered with. In the female areas." He ended, face feeling hot with anger and embarrassment. He shouldn't have to say these things.

Ainsley and Evesham exchanged a glance. "All the more reason, sir, that I don't think this could be the case. Could it have been, sir, that she went to a quack doctor to perform some... surgery? It was unsuccessful but accidental?"

Yes, the thought of Lavinia having sought an abortion had briefly crossed his mind. Too many things went against that. "One doesn't anesthetize one's patients by slitting their throats."

"Could she have done it herself afterward? Or put herself in the river? Might have had some bout of hysteria, afterward?"

"Why don't you come and look?" James ground out.

Evesham and Ainsley seem to waver. "It's not our

jurisdiction…." Evesham muttered. "Likely as not by her own hand."

"River may have been where she ended up after she took such an action," Ainsley muttered back as though James wasn't standing a few feet away. "I'm sure Briggs and his men left it phrased as gently as possible," Ainsley tutted before refocusing his hard eyes on the young annoyance before them. "All right, sir. I'll get in touch with the Whitechapel branch again and see if they'd like our assistance in the matter. I warn you, though, an investigation that turns up a verdict of suicide won't do well for the Everly family. The family forfeits whatever property the victim claimed, and the girl might be refused a Christian burial."

James gritted teeth were suddenly free from pressure as his jaw swung open. "I'm telling you, it's not a suicide. Nor an accident. If you weren't so blind and corrupt you'd—"

"*Corrupt*? Corrupt, did you say, sir?" Evesham looked personally and mortally offended, his black whiskers puffing up with indignation like a spooked cat's fur.

The image of his swollen-eyed and bedraggled mother stuffing an envelope into Gill's hand with a significant look and the face of his dean waking him with the words, "Your mother is a very generous benefactor to our school," suddenly connected unpleasantly in his brain. His mother, for whatever reason, was using the family wealth to manipulate things. Why?

"Why?" he echoed aloud.

"That's what I'd like to know, sir! What business have you calling anyone corrupt? The chief's already said he'll offer to help."

"But Briggs and Gill have already been bribed by my mother to keep this quiet and report it as an accident," James gasped, unwilling to believe it was true, but seeing no other logical solution. "You can't wire him and offer to help. He'll tell you no. It's a lie. It's all lies, and I don't know why in the world..." He broke off helplessly.

"Evesham, go get Selkirk. He's a lay preacher. Boy needs consoling. And tea. Get him tea." It was clear Ainsley was reaching the end of his patience, but he was not utterly lacking in compassion. "You see, Dr. Everly? It's a hard truth, but there it is. She's died in an unpleasant way, and you can't come to grips with it yet. I understand. A hot cup of tea and a few words with P.C. Selkirk will give you a good bolstering. You'll stop thinking these wild thoughts."

James shrugged off the paternal smile and the offer of tea with a flare of temper. "No, thank you. This is not some wild story, it's true, and all you've got to do is come and look at the body!"

"I'll thank you not to tell me how to do my job, sir. You're already pushing my patience past its—"

"I'll thank you to actually do your job, you pig-headed, pompous..." James searched for another word that began with a P as the chief inspector swelled like a balloon and Evesham halted, no longer in search of tea and comfort. "Prig! Why is this so difficult? Any sane person would—"

"That's enough out of you, sir! You'll go sit quietly up at the front while the chief makes inquiries." Evesham grabbed James by his collar.

It was the second time he'd been marched out of the room like a naughty child instead of being commended for preventing a lapse of justice and seeing his sister's murder properly investigated.

Everly snapped. He split his jacket tearing free of it as he rounded on the surprised sergeant, his fist already flying through the air.

He'd never punched anyone before.

He didn't realize it would hurt so much. His fist exploded in pain as it connected with Evesham's burly, bearded jaw.

The next thing he knew, he was being grabbed by a handful of shouting men, and a metal door in a foul-smelling room was clanging shut behind him.

"Dr. James Everly, you're hereby charged with striking an officer of the law."

Chapter Six

Charlotte had a restless night. The feeling of terror was persistently growing worse each time she woke up to screams, the feeling of pressure against her throat, a rush of heat, and then cold washing over her body. In between the bouts of sleepless shared memories, she listened for the hooves of a police ambulance or the authoritative pounding on the door, the police come to right the wrongs.

No one came.

****

"Charlotte!"

Charlotte sat up with a gasp. Sunlight streamed in. Her father hadn't had to wake her since she was a child, she was always up before he was, hurrying to make breakfast and lay the fires.

"Coming, Father."

"I can't find the flowers for Miss Everly."

"I haven't made them up yet."

"What? The service is in a few hours!"

"A few hours?" She struggled out of her nightdress and into her underthings, pulling one of her three clean dresses from the wardrobe.

"Well, at three, but of course we must leave at noon to get to Kensley Green. I'll pick up the vicar on the way."

But the police haven't come. She couldn't very well

say that out loud.

A roar of rage followed by mocking laughter echoed in the room, but her father was still speaking normally. He couldn't hear it, of course. The sounds and emotions that struck her like a physical blow were unseen and unheard by anyone else.

Lavinia's rapid breathing, the feel of her turning frantically away, only to be pushed back. Little screams that caught in her throat, a much louder, much angrier voice, the owner's madness evident even without being able to make out words.

Charlotte sank down, hands clasped.

This was madness.

This would crush her.

"Father, help me," she prayed, speaking to her heavenly father, not the one now cheerfully whistling down the steps.

But it was her mother who answered, a feeling of warmth and a whisper that cut through her panic. *"He will, my little sparrow. You've fallen to your knees, but you'd best get up. You're running out of time."*

Out of time? Charlotte pushed herself up with an effort. Lavinia Everly was already dead. Who was left to save?

****

He walked past the house.

No carriage from Jay's of Regent Street pulling up to deliver mourning clothes for the bereaved mother.

No. Of course, no need. The Everlys had suffered a death only two years ago, that of the late Mr. Everly, notable in Debrett's and a respected figure around St. James. By rights, at least according to *Queen and Cassell's*, Lavinia and her old trout of a mother should have both been in full mourning, nothing but black, this whole time.

Not so. The stupid girl wouldn't be put off of her first Season, and the mother, doubtless eager to secure her daughter's future, had allowed it.

Won't see a second one.

But... surely there should have been something in the papers by this morning? More frantic activity?

What if no one had found her? He'd silenced her quick enough once she was done her whining and blaming.

Truth be told, he didn't know what had come over him, not entirely. He knew he hated women, but he still considered aspects of them attractive.

Playing with them.

Like they played with him, had played with him his whole life.

Lavinia's letter reached him, and he managed to contact her and arranged for her to meet him at the crossroads. He picked her up at the corner of her street. She was silent in the cab, darting fearful eyes toward the front, as if thinking the driver could hear or would care to listen to her sniveling little voice.

But she told her pitiful the tale once he took her into the dank little room buried in the dark corner of Goulston Yard, a house so foul and filthy that there were more empty rooms than full.

A stroke of luck. For him, if not for her.

Such a babbling, blithering collection of questions and fears, all delivered in a half-sobbing voice. The sound of her whinging mewls instantly begged for silencing.

What   she   managed   to   convey   was

incomprehensible, literally inconceivable, proving she knew nothing at all about basic anatomy. He was torn between amusement and disgust as he listened to her cries about how their kisses must have "infected" her with a horrible disease, pregnancy. Not that she used such a coarse common word.

She wouldn't believe him when he explained, annoyed and mocking at first, that women couldn't come to expect in that manner. She called him a liar, she demanded he should take care of her. Her petulance turned to waspishness, the tone he imagined he might use with a servant who'd failed to lay out her dress properly. "Make it better! I'm still ill. Fix it!"

"Lavinia, there's nothing that we've done which could—"

"Prove it."

"You ignorant girl. The proof is in your own body. If you had any sort of knowledge or experience—"

"As if a lady would." Her eyes, so recently tearful and pleading, were full of anger. "Mother was right about you." She smacked him.

Mother.

The word and the sting of her hand against his cheek were enough to start the blackness flowing, no longer contented to lurk and creep in the back of his mind. It coated his senses and cloaked his body as if slipping on a second skin.

He hit her back. Then, with a laugh, muttering in a voice he didn't even really recognize, he was talking, no, *ranting*, hissing in the shadows as he reveled in her terrified eyes, providing a graphic, gory description of the female anatomy and how pregnancy occurred. He offered to show her firsthand, and she shrank back, babbling about how he'd be caught and hung, how he was the lowest class of common criminal, a base deceiver…

Only last week, he'd been marriage material. Simply because he told her the truth, suddenly "Mama" was right.

Mother.

Motherhood turned them all, foul and fickle, bearing a son and casting it off, turning fathers against sons and sons against fathers. Wives and mothers destroyed more than any raiding army ever had, a quiet canker, rotting men from within.

When she began to scream in earnest, his hand slashed forward.

He was never without his little black case these days, containing a syringe, scalpel, dressings, and more. When had his hand slid into his pocket? When had his fingers pushed the clasp of the leather case open and gripped the shining metal handle of his surgeon's knife?

No matter.

Her screaming stopped as the blade cut off her sounds.

It wasn't enough. There was so much more that ought to be cut off, cut out.

Feverish and feeling chilled at the same time, he started off neat and rapidly turned sloppy, shaking in hatred and excitement.

A loud, raucous laugh behind him sent him whirling, bloodied blade out.

Only drunks from the room directly behind him, their laughter carrying through cheap walls. It was growing late. More desperate fools would be seeking lodging in this pestilent quarter. Blood was seeping across the floor, dotting the soles of his shoes, staining his trousers and cuffs. He'd have to walk miles back to his lodgings and dispose of the clothes.

He'd have to dispose of the body, too.

Lavinia Everly lay mercifully silent for once in their brief association.

He rather liked the juxtaposition of the girl in all her finery, down to her pretty hat and the delicate bag flung behind her head, sprawled in the dirt where she belonged.

No one would ever connect the two of them.

As the blood crept toward his shoes yet again, the door rattled.

Just a stumbling drunkard or opium fiend colliding with doors and walls on his lurching way to an unoccupied room. Still, each second was a close call and since his own odious mother had cut off his allowance for the time being, he couldn't replace his shoes. His clothes, yes.

He gave a last look at Lavinia, a jolt of shock and horror slowly replaced with relief and satisfaction.

One less cancer in the world.

After all, he was a medical man. He should be doing mankind such services.

He fled.

****

The Everly house stayed silent. He dared not linger long. Walking quickly away, with his hat pulled low over his forehead, casting a shadow over his eyes, he alternated between sinking dread and buoyant relief. He hadn't been caught.

The rush of power was more intoxicating than any liquor he'd ever imbibed. He smothered a laugh. Wasn't he a clever boy? So much more than his mother and her disgusting husband gave him credit for. Cleverer than his professors, sharper than the police, who obviously hadn't a clue about what had happened.

Maybe... maybe he could do it again.

He just had to find a woman worthy of his attentions.

****

"The magistrate will hear your case, Dr. Everly."

James looked up, hair unkempt, face haggard.

He'd been in the lock-up overnight. His mother must be worried sick. She'd taken sleeping powders. Everly wondered if she'd slept through his absence. Cook might wonder about his absence when his breakfast went uneaten, but she might blame grief for a lack of appetite. If only they'd kept old Perkins on, his father's valet, but Perkins didn't relish waiting at home for James to finish his final qualifying exams, surrounded by Mother, Lavinia, Cook, Sadie, and the other female staff. Perkins had retired, and James hadn't bothered to employ a valet of his own for the few weeks of the year he spent at home.

It was purely ridiculous that no one would miss him, after being out overnight.

"What time is it?" he asked, his mouth dry and throat parched. There was a bucket and dipper for water, but he refused to drink it, not after watching several other inhabitants of the lock-up do so. They didn't look (nor smell) too healthy.

"It's ten in the morning."

"My sister's funeral is set for today," James gasped.

"Then you'd better hope the magistrate is feeling merciful," said the constable who opened the door. It wasn't Evesham. No, of course not. Those men went home last night, unlike him.

James was ushered from the crowded cell to a long hall where large windows let in the sparse late-November daylight. After so long in dimness, he blinked as if just waking up. He was so disoriented that before he knew it, he was stumbling into a wooden box and a Bible was being shoved under his hand.

"Are you James Everly?"

"Yes, I am he." It occurred to him after the words left his mouth that this would be in the papers. He couldn't use a false name now, not when he'd come in stating his name and his family relationships. He couldn't claim to be called Harry Smith or some other alias, as some of his school acquaintances had after being pinched for minor crimes. His mother would kill him.

The irony made him want to vomit.

The magistrate peered at him over half-moon spectacles. "It says you struck a police officer."

"I did, sir. I'm sorry, sir."

"Why?"

"My sister had died, sir. They were not looking into the matter."

"Excuse me, your worship!" a voice piped up to James' left.

James turned.

There was Evesham, the left side of his face swollen around the jaw. "The matter was ruled an accident. Not in our jurisdiction. Whitechapel branch. We've done our duty, sir, followed up with Whitechapel. They've formed their conclusions. Death was questionable, but to give the lady the *benefit of the doubt*... accidental."

"Ah. *Yes*."

James, tired, thirsty, hungry, and more than a bit grimy, felt all his own discomforts flee. The exchange between the man in the gallery and the man behind the bench made his blood boil. The tones and looks were knowing. The terms they used were hiding nothing.

"My sister did not kill herself!" he spat.

The magistrate gave him a sour, grave look. "An excellent thing to hear, young man, as suicide is a crime, against the laws of God and man."

"So is murder!"

"You're clearly distraught. Perhaps a stint in a facility where you can have rest and quiet is in order."

James eyes widened and his color drained. A madhouse? An asylum? For telling the truth? "I'm not unwell, sir."

"Do you claim grief caused you a momentary aberration? Striking a member of Her Majesty's Police is serious. And... do I have it here that you're a physician?"

The color left him utterly. The insinuation was obvious. He could tell by the magistrate's concerned face that this was not merely a matter of personal retaliation. He was genuinely incredulous that a man in whom others would trust their lives and health should go around flinging his fists about—at another man, responsible for the same things.

Defeat settled on his shoulders. Lavinia's life was worth his. If he could save her, he would sacrifice himself, no question. But... Her life had ended, all too soon. His might end now, in a different way, in this cold, impersonal room with strangers staring at him.

I'll have to find another way.

"It was a momentary lapse of common sense, Your

Worship. I was deeply grieved. I am certain Sergeant Evesham is a fine, upstanding man who was only doing his duty." *Something else, someone else is rotten here. No. In Whitechapel. I shall find them, alone if I must.*

Unbidden, the image of Charlotte's face swam before his blurring eyes.

Or perhaps, with a bit of help.

"The charges are dropped. Time served. Consider your actions more carefully, Dr. Everly. My sympathies on your loss." The gavel banged on the wood, echoing in the room that was somehow silent.

The silence burst, and the world had noises again, bustling people, shuffling paper, swishing fabric. James was thrust outside after a brief, bewildered walk back through the corridors through which he'd come, shivering with the sudden change of temperature.

He had to get home.

****

Sadie greeted him, dressed from head to foot in black. "Mr. James! Oh, sir! Your mother is ill with worry."

"And so she ought to be," he muttered. "Thank you, Sadie, let me wash and change. Has that undertaker been? Or the police?"

"No, sir. A telegram, sir. Kensley Green at three. Mr. Harkness is sending the coach." Sadie's voice shook. Her hand trembled as she held out the telegram, already opened and presumably read by his mother.

"That's... probably part of his services." James distractedly patted his pockets. The bill with an itemized list was on him somewhere. Unless he'd lost it in jail.

In jail.

He might faint. Shakiness and exhaustion were

rapidly pushing the boundaries of what he could stand.

Hunger wasn't helping. He was famished, having forgone eating yesterday when he heard the news, then heading straight to Harkness and Sons. "Sadie, ask Cook for some sandwiches, please. Leave them on the table in the dining room, I'll be down as soon as I can."

"Yes, Mr.—"

"James." His mother's cold, imperious voice interrupted Sadie's mild one. "Where *have* you been?"

"Attending to things, Mother." Food could wait. Bathing could wait. As he came close to his mother, her nose wrinkled. "Do I smell of unpleasant things, Mother?"

"In a word, yes. Have you gone back to your school? I specifically instructed your dean to—"

"Ah. *You instructed* a dean of the Royal College of Surgeons on what to do with his pupil. That's impressive, Mother. Did money also help give the orders? Did you use it for anything else?" His tone was acidic.

"How dare you speak to me like that? I'll tell him I'd like my donation back if he lets you come and go as you please when I *specifically* told him you were to return home for the term immediately!"

"I've not been to school. I've been to the undertaker's. I've been to see Lavinia."

"What?" she gasped.

James rushed forward as her eyes fluttered shut and she seemed to sway. "Mother! Sit down. Sadie!"

"Smelling salts, Mr. James!" Sadie rummaged in the pocket of her dark apron and produced a small vial.

As he helped his mother to a chair, he waved the strong-smelling salt ammoniac under her nose.

"Leave us, Sadie." As soon as her eyelids had stopped their tremors, Mrs. Everly waved her hand, feebly shooing the girl from the room.

Just as well. "Mother. I examined the body."

"Lavinia. The—the police used photographs and her papers to identify her. Surely you didn't need to do such a thing." His mother's lips quivered.

"I'm happy that I did, in a way." He swallowed hard, forcing himself to continue. "She didn't drown, Mother."

She was silent, refusing to meet his eye.

"But you knew that, didn't you?"

"Hush."

"No, I will not. I went to the police, Mother, to try to tell them that they'd somehow missed a shocking amount of evidence. No sane person could consider those injuries a result of drowning."

"Stop. I will not hear of this." With surprising strength, she pushed past her much younger, fitter son and headed up the stairs, only to stop in the doorway, realizing she'd have to face him soon, a captive audience riding to Lavinia's final resting in their shared funeral carriage.

James didn't move. He'd realized the same thing. "Funny how the police in Whitechapel were so adamant that they'd completed their investigation and discovered it was an accident. What girl accidentally cuts her own throat, Mother?" he asked softly, all out of patience. His words hung in the air, black powder drifting down, waiting for the spark.

Combustion.

"Stop it! Your father would give you such a hiding if he ever heard you say such disgusting things."

"Father always struck me as very honest, Mother."

"Well, Father didn't have to look after you two alone with every tongue in London tipped with poison and sharper than a sword! Lavinia made a foolish mistake."

James rolled his eyes. "No! It wasn't suicide."

"Suicide?" Her face registered shock, then carefully went blank.

Ah. So, she knows that much as well. "How did you do it?"

"What?"

"Make the police call this an accident? How?"

Resignation cloaked her. "I paid them, dear. I paid them a very great deal to say it was an accident. I will not have her shamed."

"But, Mother, her killer is going free!"

"I'm sure he'll make a mistake at some point. It's in God's hands, James. The wicked will not prosper. The Lord will see to it."

"You cannot speak to me of justice while perverting it! You cannot invoke the Lord's will while breaking His commandments, Mother."

Her eyes were cold, glassy, and blank. Rather like Lavinia's must have been when they found her body, bleeding and mutilated.

"You'd be very surprised what a woman can do, James. What she'll sacrifice to ensure that she protects what she has left." Her eyes lingered on a portrait of her late husband, then drifted to a photograph of James and Lavinia taken only months ago. "You always were the cleverest one, James. I know you want answers, but some bring more harm than good. I'm going to wait in my room until the carriage arrives."

131

Chapter Seven

"Father, I should like to come. May I?" Charlotte wore a stately, simple black dress. She silently thought of it as her "working dress" even though when she wore it, she wasn't engaged in any sort of domestic chore.

"Oh… I'm pushing the time as it is. You'd have to— Oh. I see you're ready. Well, dear, if you come, who will be here to greet clients?"

"I thought you didn't want me to deal with the business so much?" Charlotte countered.

Mr. Harkness paused, pursed lips and laughing eyes directed at his daughter as she stood behind him, looking at her reflection in the glass as he adjusted his tie and smoothed out the long dark tails of his coat. "Well, this is one aspect I don't mind so much. Of course, if you're saying you'd rather give up this silly notion of staying on in the family business, then by all means."

"Oh, go on then. I'll have supper waiting when you get back." She gave him a peck on the cheek as she shooed him on his way. For the first time ever, she felt uneasy being left alone. Although Lavinia's body would leave the establishment, her spirit wouldn't necessarily follow. What if the terrible memories never left her?

And where in the world were the police? What was Dr. Everly playing at?

"Charlotte? I said, 'Did you deliver those invitations?' "

"What? No. No, I didn't." She started guiltily. "I'll do it tomorrow." In truth, she hadn't even finished writing the invitations, asking the various mortuary families with eligible sons around for tea.

"Well, don't leave it too long. That much ham is simply not good for my waistline." Mr. Harkness patted his waistcoat's straining lower buttons with a sigh.

****

Mrs. Everly let out a long, shuddering sigh as the coffin was lowered into the ground by two appropriately dressed men in long dark coats.

It was done.

James would forgive her in time. He'd have to. He was all she had left.

Under her heavy veil, she turned ever so slightly, looking at his face. Lost. Hopeless. Angry.

Forgiveness might be slow to come.

"Mrs. Everly. I am so truly sorry." Mr. Harkness bowed low to the lady draped in swathes of black parramatta silk before pivoting to address her son. "Dr. Everly. My deepest sympathies on the loss of your sister. She is with the angels now."

James seemed to be struggling to keep something inside, jaw flexing as if he were afraid a yawn would suddenly escape. But words escaped instead. "Did the police contact you? Whitechapel or Westminster branches?"

"About your sister? No, sir. Should they have?"

Mrs. Everly gripped her son's arm in an iron grasp. "No, Mr. Harkness. They are to leave my daughter in peace. Should they—or anyone else—poke about and attempt to stir up salacious scandal, I want you to give me your solemn word that you contact me."

Mr. Harkness nodded gravely. "Harkness and Sons prides itself on discretion and respecting the privacy of the bereaved, Mrs. Everly."

"I've no doubt. Still." Under her veil, her eyes bored holes into James' earnest, pale face. "Any questions, from *anyone*, and I expect to be contacted. Is that understood?"

"Absolutely. Of course." A puzzled frown etched itself between the undertaker's graying eyebrows. It suddenly cleared as he gave a gentle cough and turned his eyes from the grieving mother to her son. "Oh. The police. Is this about the matter with Constable Gill, Dr. Everly? I assure you I made no complaints."

"No, Mr. Harkness. Not about that. About the matter of—Mother!"

"I'm overcome. It's simply too much!" Mrs. Everly indeed felt those sentiments. She also chose to act upon them at that exact moment, pitching backward into her son's startled arms. "Take me home, James. I must lie down. I feel faint."

****

James supported his mother away, into the carriage that had brought them. Mr. Harkness and the vicar were shaking hands with the property manager from Kensley Green. They, as well as the drivers and grave diggers, had been the only other souls in attendance for the funeral. Frustration prickled him and stirred his tongue, but his mother was sobbing now, shoulders wracked.

Was it his imagination… or did the sighs in between her bouts of tears sound relieved?

****

"Go to bed, James. You look utterly exhausted. You'll catch your death next."

"I'm fine," he answered woodenly.

Mrs. Everly wanted to pretend this entire ordeal had never happened. True, it had been a trying year with Lavinia, but her maternal heart was still broken. Protecting her daughter's memory and good name would be her last act for her child. Too little, too late, but it was all she had.

If James wouldn't interfere. "What did Mr. Harkness mean?"

"He seems a very sincere person. I imagine he meant everything he said Mother." He wouldn't look at her.

Mrs. Everly breathed out through her nose. James had always been a clever boy and when he'd been in a fretful mood, his answers were sharp digs. Not much had changed. "About the police?"

"Ha. Funny you should mention that, Mother. Do you want to know where I spent the night?"

Her tongue was fixed to the roof of her mouth. A strangled noise bypassed it, and James took it for agreement.

"In the Westminster lock-up for punching a sergeant in the jaw."

This time, her legs did give out. She collapsed inelegantly at the foot of the stairs, lading with a thump on the bottom step. "What? Why? Did anyone see you?"

"A great many people, Mother. None you'd concern yourself with. A number of opium fiends, vagrants, drunkards, cut-purses, and other disorderly sorts."

"The charge! Oh, my heavens! The papers. The *papers*, James. Word of this will get back to the college, to your uncles." She wrung her hands.

"Does that matter so much?"

"Yes! Our family's reputation is everything! You'll

135

ruin it, just like your sister seemed to be trying to do."

"What do you mean? What was she doing?"

"Oh, the usual things, looking for attention, never happy unless she was at the center of everything. This second year in mourning hadn't been good to her. Too few calls, too few excursions, and of course, without your father I didn't feel that we could travel…" Another spastic tightening of her hands, her color changing from pale to dark plum.

"Mother. You don't look well." James rushed to her side in alarm.

She let out a hysterical bark of laughter. "I should say not! Your father dead, your sister at the center of some scandal I've had to keep quiet, and my son imprisoned!"

"I'm not imprisoned, I wasn't even charged. They let me off with a warning and a night in the dock."

"Don't use that common language in this house."

"Mother, you mustn't let yourself get further excited. Your coloring is very—"

"No, *you* mustn't. You mustn't interfere again, not one single question, not one toe out of line, James." With an effort, she pulled herself to her feet and eyed him haughtily, standing a few steps above him on the staircase to emphasize her position, to look down on him imperiously. "If you do anything I even consider remotely suspicious… I shall cut off your allowance and your school fees. I'll tell Uncle Jeremy to put your shares of the business back in my name. I'll turn you out of this house."

****

James stared up at his mother in shock. It wasn't shocking to think that she'd use money against him. It was shocking that she meant it.

More shocking to think that she believed such threats would work on him.

He would earn his way if he had to. A physician could earn his keep and he could pay for his final term if he must. But his mother getting in his way and using her money to cause obstructions? That could be a difficulty. Her heart didn't seem well-equipped to take any further strain. "I will keep everything quiet, Mother," he murmured.

"Oh, James. Thank you, dear boy." She swept down to embrace him, pressing a relieved kiss to his unruly sandy mop of hair. "It's best this way, don't you see?"

Best not to alarm her and have her interfere? "Indeed, Mother."

****

James lay awake for a very long time, replaying horrible images and horrible arguments over and over in his head.

How in God's name could he solve this crime when the police didn't believe a crime had even been committed?

No, that's not true. At least one or two policemen knew. They were willing to keep quiet, probably under threats of his mother using her influence as much as for the money, maybe even with the misguided belief that Lavinia's death was some sort of back-alley butchery gone horribly wrong. Without seeing what he'd seen, without examining what he'd examined… it could look like suicide.

As far as he knew, there was only one other person who shared his knowledge and believed him.

The undertaker's daughter.

****

"Dr. Everly!" Charlotte Harkness looked like she'd been awake for three days straight. The man who greeted her looked no better, perhaps worse. "Do come in. My father's out collecting one of the dearly departed, but I'll be happy to settle the accounts."

"Accounts?"

Charlotte held the door wide and beckoned the young man in. Today, although he appeared worse for wear in his features, he was much more neatly and presentably dressed in a black frock coat with a black top hat clutched in one hand, neat gray-on-black pinstripe trousers visible beneath it. "Aren't you here for that?" She hoped he'd see what a perfect, plausible excuse she'd presented for his visit.

"Oh. Yes. Of course." He nodded slowly.

Charlotte led him to her father's office and made the customary offer of tea.

The young physician hesitated. "Yes, please. Thank you, Miss Harkness. Would you like me to go over the figures with you?"

Charlotte gave him an amused smile. "My maths are sufficient, thank you. I'll be back in a moment, the kettle's just boiled."

He turned to go with her. "I could come with you. I've already seen the kitchen, if you recall."

"Yes. Dr. Everly…" She hesitated. Lavinia's unquiet spirit had been giving her no peace. Why hadn't the police come? She wanted to express how urgently she wished this matter resolved without telling him her secret.

"Miss Harkness?" James Everly was regarding her with a quizzical expression.

"The police never came," she blurted. "The funeral happened, as I'm sure you know. Father said you were in attendance, but whatever are we to do? The police should surely have collected the body or at least sent 'round a detective!"

James let out a rush of air as if releasing a pound of lead from his lungs. "Miss Harkness, it was terrible. I tried to get the police to come, but no one believed me. They threatened—no, that's not quite the right word, they *led* me to believe that Lavinia's death could be called a suicide if I persisted in trying to get them to investigate, meaning a refusal of a Christian burial and the loss of my sister's inheritance, a large portion of my father's property, to the crown."

"That's horrible. God wouldn't punish those poor souls that took their lives in madness or grief. That's silliness. He would have wanted them to trust in Him, surely, but He made us. He knows we're weak." *I'm weak. So weak. I cannot keep this burden, Father.*

"I'm surprised to hear you speak so passionately on the matter, Miss Harkness."

"In my father's business, I have seen any number of deaths that would be considered suspicious," she said.

"Men in my line of business will as well, I should imagine. Still, I couldn't take that risk. My temper got the better of me, I confess. I struck a police officer."

Charlotte gasped, one hand over her mouth as the other pulled the hot kettle from the hob. "Oh, no, sir."

"I regret it. I spent the night in jail and only managed to make it home an hour before the funeral carriage came. My mother…" He met her eyes. "Miss Harkness, I don't have anyone else I can take into my confidence."

Her skin flushed. To be treated like an equal, a

person worthy of confiding in, was very gratifying. She quickly poured out a second cup, one for herself. "You may trust me, Dr. Everly."

He managed a brief smile at her serious tone. "I suppose I must. We've already shared one horrible secret. I must reveal another."

Charlotte tensed, her breath catching in her throat.

"My mother knew it was murder. She would rather the killer walk free than expose the details of Lavinia's sordid death to the papers and gossipmongers. Our family reputation is all she's living for. It's become a sort of mania, brought on by my father's death and my desire to eschew the family business and turn to medicine instead. That, and Lavinia missing most of her first Season, failing to make a match… I can make all the excuses I want, but the bald truth remains. My mother used her money and influence to bribe the police to rule this death as an accident. I imagine they might be grateful. I don't know where the murder occurred, but perhaps there were few clues, no leads. More work for them if they must investigate"—he shrugged helplessly — "but I've nothing but time until the end of term. I've been told I mustn't go back, must stay home, in mourning. And I *do* mourn her, Miss Harkness, but I also mourn that the beast that killed her will go free. Without the police to help, I have no clues, no idea what to do or where to turn." He looked helplessly into the steaming brown liquid before him. "I won't give up, though. I'll find him. And you—perhaps you'd be willing to bear witness to what I saw?" He swallowed. "I know it's shameful to ask a lady to recount such gruesome things. I don't know where else to begin."

Charlotte studied him, her own cup untouched.

"You obviously trust me."

Dr. Everly pulled the cup and saucer to him and took a long sip. "Ahh. Thank you for this, Miss Harkness. Hot tea and solid conversation have done more for my spirits than I would have believed possible. In reply to your remark, I do trust you. You helped me once, insisted upon it, in fact."

She bit her lip. "Do you know what it feels like when no one believes you?"

"I do now. Intimately," he chuckled bitterly.

"Some people…" She paused, knowing she had to tread carefully. "…think that simply because they haven't seen a thing, it can't be so."

"Exactly, but you *have* seen it!" He seized upon this point eagerly.

Not so much a matter of seeing, but of hearing, she thought woefully. "I'd like to tell you something. You must promise to hear me out. I'd like you to believe me, as I believe you."

Puzzled, he nodded.

"I can help you. I may have the lead that you need, something even the police don't know."

"What? You do? How?" James leaned forward and grasped her hand, so grateful that he forgot all sense of propriety.

Charlotte jumped when his fingers locked around hers, but she merely removed them and folded her hands in her lap. She would speak plainly and calmly, as a sane individual, not a madwoman. "The man who did this to your sister? His name is Jack, and Lavinia knew him well, well enough to have seen him before that night, anyway."

James stared for several seconds, unable to say

anything. "But... but this is incredible. My Lord, the name of the murderer! Oh, Miss Harkness, I cannot thank you enough. Tell me, how did you find this out?"

She tried not to wince. Her father might have her on the next train north. Dr. Everly—oh dear. He was a doctor, wasn't he? He might use his powers to get her put in some horrible madhouse.

"Miss Harkness? Please, you've got to tell me," James begged desperately.

"I heard it, Dr. Everly. From beyond the grave. Lavinia's spirit allowed me to hear her final moments."

Chapter Eight

Dr. Everly deflated like an India rubber ball with a puncture. "Oh. I see."

"You don't believe me. I realize that. Well, you can pay your bill and go." Charlotte knew she had no right to get angry at the young man. Her story was too fantastical. Still, she'd been willing to sneak him in, to avoid telling her father what had transpired, to get involved in something no respectable lady should ever even think of. *Perhaps I am mad. Perhaps I'm not truly a gentlewoman.*

James shifted as her voice take on a tired, yet defiant note. Perhaps he had been given to such tones himself, lately. At last he said, "It seems far too incredible."

"I know." She did, all too well. "You could find out where she died. It wasn't the Thames, that much is sure. If the Whitechapel police handled it instead of the police in your part of the city, then you can reason it happened down this way." Charlotte knew her "supernatural" information would be doubted, but she still wanted this crime solved.

Everly nodded thoughtfully. "Yes, I'd assumed so. My mother has seen that the police will never speak a word about the matter to me, unfortunately."

"Well, no. Not if you march into the desk sergeant and declare yourself to be Dr. Everly, brother of the murdered woman."

"What would you suggest I do? Read their minds?"

Charlotte's eyes flickered dangerously. "Don't say who you are. Get into conversation with a constable walking on the streets. 'Terrible business about that girl. You know, the rich one they found murdered in Whitechapel. What in the world was a fine young lady doing down in the yards at that time of night?' " she mimicked his deeper voice but sounded distinctly "common."

He smothered a smile. "Lose my well-bred tones, Miss Harkness?"

"It'll help if you don't sound out of place. Not that you would, not in this nice part of town. However, the deeper you go… if you go past St. Clementia's, for example."

"What's past there?"

"Yards, grotty little places full of filth and lice. Houses of Common Lodging." When her companion didn't appear to comprehend, she elaborated. "Anyone can stay there for just a few pennies a night. That means drunkards, those who've stayed too long in the opium dens, and—and women of ill repute with their customers will go there. They can afford it, and they won't get caught by the police on the streets." She flushed and fell silent.

"How do you know all this?"

"I have ears and eyes. I don't only hear those that have passed on, Dr. Everly."

"Well, I'm a medical man, I've gone to the Royal College of Physicians, and I'm now at the Royal College of Surgeons. I know a fair few things, but I didn't know *that*."

****

James was indignant that he should be so sheltered and Miss Harkness should have to educate him about such unseemly things. Women should be more delicate in their knowledge. Of course, if she was, she'd be little help. And if Lavinia hadn't been so refined, maybe she wouldn't have been killed. How in the world could she have been led astray, led alone in the middle of the night to Whitechapel? She didn't seem to have been kidnapped, that much he could tell from a quick search of her room and the windows and doors of the house.

Miss Harkness said Lavinia knew the man, not that he could take her seriously. Right now, she didn't seem to take herself too seriously, either, looking at him with her lips quirking up ever so slightly.

"I imagine you know much more about medicine than I do, but I doubt you've ever gone down Whitechapel's High Street or over to the market stalls. I know the area a bit better than you do, and I know that a crime like this"—she shuddered—"wouldn't have gone unnoticed in the 'respectable' parts of town. Someone knows something, but they may not realize it. Someone had to report the incident, Dr. Everly."

"I know that!"

"And if it were anyone of any consequence, the police couldn't simply pass this off as an accident. If it were in any respectable area, there would have been an outcry. But down in those dark corners"—her eyes turned from his and looked away as if visualizing the paths a woman must never venture down, the places gentlewomen would fear to tread—"there's so much death and sin. So much violence and poverty. A dead girl in an alley or a back room won't mean much to them." Her eyes met his again. "Even if she meant everything to

145

you."

James had to swallow several times. The tea was a good cover. Gill had said the same thing.

He and his fellow surgeons had even been a party to this cavalier way of thinking, hadn't they? When bodies were brought in, dumped like the dirty linens for collection, they were one and all the dregs of society, those that were unnoticed and never missed. No family members clamored for their return and burial.

"Sugar?" Charlotte covered the awkward silence that was lingering.

"No, thank you. And thank you. For the tip on how to proceed. I shall indeed make my way into the darker heart of Whitechapel."

"Be careful."

"I shall endeavor to do so."

"You stand out, that's all."

He looked at his clothes. He was in deepest mourning. He'd only just gotten out of it at the end of summer, the time to honor his father in other ways having taken precedence over black clothing. "I don't think this is too eye-catching."

"The cut and the quality are what thieves notice. Wear something older, walk quickly, talk like you know things, not like you're asking things."

"Oh?"

She shook her head. "Not like that."

"I mean, yes. Naturally." He made his voice sound much more authoritative. "How did you—"

"I'm a woman in a very difficult position." She shrugged.

"Ah." *Hearing voices. Well, this profession could surely drive you mad.*

"I'm not an undertaker, like my father, but I do assist him. I have to talk to clients, and I have to manage this house. If a woman doesn't want to be taken advantage of, she'll use her wits and her words wisely."

"Very true." His own mother certainly seemed to do so. Not so for Vinnie. She'd always been able to say anything, do anything, to the constant grief of poor old Miss Potts, the governess. Lavinia had been his father's spoiled darling and his mother's pet project, to mold into the belle of the year.

All hopes and all works dashed.

"It wouldn't have been so bad if it had been an accident," he mused aloud. "Accidents happen, most unfortunately, but they happen. Illness, too. One knows how to deal with that. But this? A murder, and no one seeming to care…"

"*I* care. For one thing, whether you believe me or not, I do not want to hear her horrible last moments over and over, and for a second, I want her to be at peace. She's not peaceful now. We must help her."

"Thank you. I hope that you'll hear good news from me soon, Miss Harkness."

"Please do keep me informed." Miss Harkness rose as he did.

"Oh. My account. Here, let me see." James produced Mr. Harkness' statement and began counting out the money he owed.

"No. No, you've overpaid by three pounds."

"That is for the embalming spirits."

"My father said—"

"To use it as a donation, remember?"

"All right." She gave him a genuine smile.

What a very beautiful smile, James noticed. He was

bound to notice something beautiful in a world that had become so horribly ugly lately. "I'd like to do more." He put out another few bills. "I cannot thank you enough for your offer of help and for letting me in the other day."

"Please, that's not a service. I was only helping as one should do."

"Yes, but—" James stopped speaking as a door banged in the rear of the house.

"Lift your end, Mr. Bartlesby."

"Heavy fellow, Reginald."

"His widow said he boxed."

"Poor chap."

"My father's here," Charlotte said needlessly.

Panic rose and receded easily. Mr. Harkness would find no objection to his being here—he was simply here to pay a bill. Many clients must deal with Miss Harkness if her father was out.

His mother, on the other hand? Panic flourished. "My mother wants me to make no more inquiries into the matter. She's threatened to cut off my allowance and the tuition for my education. I can make my own way, Miss Harkness," he hissed, "but I'm almost done with my qualifications. I'd hate to be pipped at the post, so to speak."

"Did she tell you *not* to pay a bill?"

Relief filled him. "Wit and words, indeed."

That beautiful smile came back, pink cheeks lightening tired blue eyes. He was caught smiling back, a little voice buried deep inside reminded him that London was a lonely city for a man of his station, one who had a desire to do something more than manage his estate or take on the family business, one who was losing his family, bit by bit to deaths of bodies or deaths of souls.

Also, James found his idle curiosity of the other day satisfied. The girl did indeed have good teeth, excellent ones, in fact, nestled between her lips just so, the whiteness of them making her blue eyes sparkle all the more.

"Charlotte must be out, Mr. Bartlesby. Do you have time to stop for a cup?"

"No, no. Must pick up Miss Minier and take her to a churchyard over in Gosvenor Way."

"Was she one of ours?"

"Old family friend."

As the casual chatter continued, fear left James and his hostess. Charlotte extended a bit of paper. "Your receipt, Dr. Everly. Please let me know how you get on."

He hesitated. He shouldn't be seen here, not if he wanted to appease his mother. The excuse of paying a bill was gone. "I'll write to you, Miss Harkness, and let you know how things progress." He stopped short of asking for her to do the same. He didn't need to hear about her ghostly visions. He was a man of science. Ghosts did not exist outside of an imbalance of the mind, perhaps with a sound and reasonable explanation. Perhaps the girl had been exposed to too many chemicals. Mercury was used in embalming once, wasn't it? Too much could turn one's mind.

"Good afternoon. And good luck." Charlotte nodded to him, and he tipped his hat to her before he slid through the office door and out the front of the building.

****

"Charlotte! There you are. I thought you were out." Her father and Mr. Bartlesby appeared from the embalming room. "Tea, dear?"

"Of course, Father. Oh, and Dr. Everly has paid his bill. I wrote him a receipt and left everything on the ledger in the office."

"Clever girl."

Charlotte beamed.

"Make someone a fine wife soon, Harkness." Mr. Bartlesby smiled his broken-toothed grin.

Charlotte's smile faded, hidden under a cloud of expectation.

****

James changed at home, choosing a blue-gray coat that was faded and a little too worn at the cuffs for his mother's liking. Brown calfskin shoes that needed polishing, last worn over three years ago. He found a large, checked scarf that Uncle Jeremy had once sent his father as a joke and put it on, wrapping up well around his chin.

Yes. He looked less "polished" now. Tomorrow, he'd go back to Whitechapel.

"Sir? Will you take tea with your mother?"

Sadie's timid voice caught his ear. Quickly shoving everything under the pillows at the head of his bed, he smoothed back his hair and tugged down his dark waistcoat. "Coming! Is she waiting?"

"No, sir."

James opened the door to see the girl shrinking away from him, her eyes still pink and puffy underneath, her pallor making her uneven freckles stand out all the more. "Is something wrong?"

"Madame isn't well, sir. She didn't eat her breakfast today or supper last night. She's sleeping an awful lot and I—" She swallowed hard, eyes darting.

"You what?"

"Cook says an awful lot of spirits've been moved from the shelves. I didn't do it, sir!"

"No, of course you didn't."

"She doesn't like to say otherwise, sir. I don't want to be put out for drink, sir. I never touch it."

Oh, wonderful. Alcohol on top of nervous disposition, dyspepsia, hysteria, and heaven only knows what else. "I'll see that she doesn't, Sadie."

"Thank you, sir." Sadie hesitated at the end of the hall.

"Was there something else?" he asked, in a hurry to get away, to think things through and figure out ways of getting around both the police and his mother.

"I—I'm so sorry about Miss Lavinia, sir."

His hurry melted. "I'm sorry, too." Hmm. Sadie was a housemaid. But Simmons, Vinnie's lady's maid, had married in the late summer. Something so seemingly unimportant to him might actually be rather important indeed. "Sadie? Were you attending to my sister after Simmons left?"

"Yes, sir. I'd hoped that if I pleased Miss Lavinia that perhaps I—well, I'm not as good at arranging hair as Simmons was and I'm not experienced like Bannet is." She nodded her head toward the attic rooms, where his mother's lady's maid, Bannet, normally resided.

"But you hoped to take on the position?"

"Yes, Mr. James. I was helping both your mother and sister while Miss Bannet is away with her niece and the new babies. Twins."

"Ah." It hadn't even occurred to him to wonder why the fiercely loyal woman wasn't supporting his mother in her hour of grief. They'd been near inseparable after this father passed.

He briefly imagined that Charlotte would scold him for such obvious lapses in his "detective" work. "How long has she been gone?"

"A fortnight, sir. She'll be back after Christmas. Your mother gave her leave until then. Of course, she didn't know that Miss Vinnie would be—"

"Would be?" One eyebrow arched.

"Would—would meet with an accident, sir. I must go, Mr. James. Cook is awful particular just now." Sadie gave him a frightened look and turned hurriedly from him.

"I imagine my mother and Lavinia were most grateful for your help." He easily caught up to her, following her down the back staircase.

"I hope so, sir."

"Mother said she was ill."

"Miss Lavinia? Oh. Yes. She was very ill." Sadie nodded eagerly.

"Ill in what way?"

"Not eating. Crying. Not sleeping much at night, sleeping a lot during the day."

Nerves. What did she have to be nervous about? "Had the doctor been?"

"I don't think so, sir, but I'm not in the house all the time. I run the errands for Cook and the other housemaid when we switch off."

James noticed that after her last remark, her color, which had returned, fled again. "That must have worried my mother."

"She was ever so put out."

"Put out?" Now, that surprised him. His mother being upset or anxious for her health, yes, but put out? Angry at Lavinia for her illness? That didn't make sense.

His mother had tended to treat frail, waif-like Vinnie like a hothouse plant, careful of her always, a jewel in the family crown.

Until Father died, anyway. He knew things had changed, but he was shocked to hear his mother's devotion to her only daughter was one of them.

Could that have something to do with this insistence on Lavinia's death being called a tragic accident? Was Mother enraged at her for something? Was she blaming herself, blaming Vinnie? "Something is off," James muttered.

"I have to go, sir, really, sir!" Sadie gave him a look of utter panic and fled, slamming through the kitchen door.

James heard Cook's querulous voice telling the unfortunate girl about her shocking lack of manners, slamming and banging in a house of mourning. He knew he'd best keep out of everyone's way for a while.

Which was problematic, because he knew next to nothing and he now wondered what Sadie, what Cook, what his mother might know about Lavinia's last few weeks on earth.

The dead leave clues to what they did while they were living, his most recent anatomy professor had boomed, pacing behind them as they dissected limbs, camphor stinging their eyes, congealed grime on fingers holding the scalpels. "What did this poor wretch die from, gentlemen?"

"A knife in the neck is pretty obvious," he told the phantom of his memory. "But other than leaving clues as to how they met their end, the dead have little to say."

Unless, of course, you're Charlotte Harkness.

****

"I'm dead, then?"

"I'm afraid so. Bother. I just had that inkwell." Charlotte looked around the kitchen.

"To your left, ducks."

"Thank you, Mr. Watkins." Charlotte was polite to the rough, garbled voice in her head.

"Are you sure *I'm dead? I can see things, you know. Wouldn't I have my eyes closed if I were dead?"*

"Does your soul have eyes, Mr. Watkins?" Charlotte sighed.

"Hm. Oh. That's a trick question, duckie."

She disliked being called a waterfowl, but Mr. Watkins wasn't to know that.

"Why'm I talking to you, then? Is this heaven? Not that I object to following a pretty girl around, but I have a missus. Muriel."

"Muriel is going to join you eventually. You'll have to look out for her patiently. Do you have family who might be waiting for you already, Mr. Watkins?"

"I do. Oh, blimey, I do. My boys, Georgie and Nels. Nels died in his cot. Georgie was a conductor on the Edinburgh line. Accident at stuck points." Mr. Watkins' *voice assumed an urgency.* "What'm I doin' wastin' time here? I suspect I must want to talk to Muriel."

"Would she be afraid of a ghostly visitation?"

"Bless you, miss, yes. She'd burn the house down, running like her skirts were on fire."

"Then I suggest you let me tell her you send your love and you'll be off to meet Georgie and Nels."

"Where's the door, then?"

"Mr. Watkins…"

"Right. Forget me own head next."

Charlotte waited.

Silence.

"Glad your head is attached," she murmured to herself, finishing the last note, an invitation to Peter Danvers. She'd put it in the post later. "Nels and Georgie." She must remember the names to tell Muriel Watkins—if her father weren't listening. Because if he was, he would ask questions about how she came to know such things. In her experience, the grief-stricken widow wouldn't ask, she'd just be grateful for the assurance that her husband was safely on his way heavenward.

Safely heaven bound. She felt as though she'd helped another soul on his way.

Which only created a dark, gnawing pain in her breast when she pictured the torn body of Miss Everly and her frantic screams. No peace there. "Oh, Lord." She folded her hands and put her forehead to her knuckles. "You've got to help her. You've got to help me. Please… could you help Dr. Everly? I don't think he'll ever let me tell him what I know or how I know it. You'll have to show him some other way."

Chapter Nine

"Tragedy about that poor girl," James said the words for the tenth time. Each repetition drove emptiness and dread deeper into his bones until they physically hurt.

Or perhaps it was the biting cold and the steady rain, the lack of light, and the horrid stench that always seemed to linger around the dark, uneven nooks and crannies in Whitechapel.

This particular place smelled of sewage and smoke.

The young man who sold him a newspaper looked at him curiously. "What girl?"

"That girl. Done in." His voice and mouth were carefully muffled by the large scarf which seemed oddly ineffectual at keeping both the stench and the cold out.

"Maisie? The girl on the turn?"

On the turn. His mind clicked and he pictured his mother's utter shock and outrage if she could overhear this conversation.

"Maisie?"

"Done in, wasn't she? Feller put the knife into her."

His heart jumped. But Lavinia wasn't Maisie, and his sister was most assuredly not turning anything. "Horrible."

"He was a nasty bit of work. He'll swing for it. If you ask me, she should've quit once he found out. Wouldn't stand for my missus doing that sort of thing, don't care how poor we were."

James dropped a coin on purpose as he hurried away. To sell oneself was poor indeed.

Another few blocks and he'd have to turn back. It was getting darker and colder. He had his wits and fists about him, but he knew he had the physique of a man who spent more time in study than in sport. Best not to encounter a gang of cutpurses or worse.

"Horrible about that girl they found in the yard, wasn't it?" James leaned against the door of a small public house that had guttering lights and smelled of beer, smoke, and urine.

He was going to have to burn these shoes or bury them in the garden.

Now who's mad?

"What girl? What yard?"

"Pretty girl. Dark hair. Throat cut." *I'm helping my sister. I have to say these things coldly, dispassionately. Pretend I'm not picturing the way her hair caught the light when she came gliding down the stairs the day she was presented at court. How beautiful she was when she smiled. The way mother's pearls rested on her neck, and suddenly my annoying little sister was a lady, a consort fit for a king....*

"You mean old Peggy? Wasn't her throat cut, was her wrists. Did her old man first. Caught him with the lodger again. Stupid thing. Her with a head full of rotted teeth, too."

Peggy or the lodger? James wasn't sure what her teeth had to do with it, but he clucked in the right places.

"Buy us a pint?"

"Hm? Oh." He didn't want to drink in this place. Who knew what he'd catch? He quickly flipped a penny toward the raggedy man.

It was a mistake. The half-lidded eyes opened hungrily, greedily noticing the stranger's dress and the easy way he handled money. "Pint's a bit more than that, sir. An' it's not just me that's thirsty. Jack! Tim! This fella is feeling generous."

Jack?

Charlotte Harkness told him the name. It was utter nonsense.

Still, his heart thudded hard as he turned to see two burly men emerge from the shadows just inside the pub's door. "Which one is Jack?"

"Me." The word came from a mouth full of yellow teeth clamped around a worn pipestem.

James balled his fists. There must be a million Jacks in England, thousands in London. The idea that Lavinia would "tell" the name of her murderer to the undertaker's daughter was preposterous. "Isn't it terrible what happened here the other night?" James heard the tremor in his voice. The others did, too, laughing and nodding amongst themselves.

"You mean about that young toff, lost his coin and that fancy scarf?" Jack's companion menaced.

"Now, now, Tim, that's what happened tonight—'less the boy makes a donation to a worthy cause."

"Worthy cause?" Why was his voice so much higher than normal?

"To the maimed and wounded, boy."

Something hit him squarely in the ribs.

An arm. The stump of an arm, no hand on its end.

Highly unlikely that a one-handed man could have held Lavinia down and attacked her, made such neat, clean incisions, and—James forced the awful images from his mind, swinging both arms out hard and clapping them against the sides of the man's head.

"Ow! What the devilment?"

James fled as Jack clutched his head, temporarily stunned by the blow that would put tremendous pressure on the ear canals. Jack staggered into the smaller, slighter Tim, and both went down in a yowling heap.

I've got to do better tomorrow.

I should start with Sadie.

Only, she seems so terrified of me. He was still trotting away, making for the High Street and his mental marker of St. Clementia's. Every few seconds he looked back over his shoulder, but he hadn't been followed yet.

Better to terrify than be terrified, he reasoned. At the same time, he called himself a weakling and a coward, so easily scared off when Lavinia's terror must have far outstripped his own.

And terrified people don't hang about to talk, they flee. It certainly was true of his own case.

He had no idea how to talk to a woman in service, or really, any women outside of his family and the hand-picked circle of his parents' friends. Even so, the daughters of such friends usually peeled off in a giggling, glittering pack while the men retired to another area of the house, completely separate.

His aunt and his cousins were in their country home for the winter, hardly likely to understand a telegram that asked for advice on how to put a maid at ease. They might take that quite the wrong way, in fact. He couldn't ask Lavinia, for obvious reasons. His mother would never provide any useful advice on the subject and seemed to take anything and everything he said in the wrong way lately. He couldn't very well go bother the charwoman at the Halls of Residence.

The only working-class woman he even had the slightest acquaintance with was... Charlotte Harkness.

"I find it very peculiar that you keep leading me back to where I'm clearly *not* supposed to be," he grumbled to the Almighty.

At that moment, he turned and found himself eyeing the brave little cross of St. Clementia's, barely visible in the dark but standing out in relief against the smoky backdrop of gray, glistening buildings.

"Fine, then." He sighed into the darkness. "I'm going."

****

Only belatedly did it occur to James that he had no earthly excuse for going to pay a call on the Harkness' establishment. He'd paid the bill. He lived miles away. It was quite late at night.

He wished it had occurred to him *before* he knocked and was supporting himself against the wall.

"Oh, dear." As he stood, staring transfixed by a lone gaslight on the street, he realized his errors.

Which meant that a flustered Reginald Harkness was opening the door as he was scrambling away from it. "Dr. Everly?" the graying man asked, squinting into the gloom.

"Mr. Harkness. I'm so sorry. It's far too late to pay a call." James inclined his head, lost his grip on his hat, and stammered.

"What's the matter, sir? Oh, surely not another death in your family?" Mr. Harkness stared, bewildered by the nervous young man's sudden appearance.

"No, thank the Lord."

The bewilderment grew. "Your bill is settled, more than settled. Thank you for your donation. I mentioned it to the vicar."

"I... I'm here to pay a call on..."

"Who is it, Father?" Charlotte appeared behind her father in the entryway. She wore a long pale blue dress. Her hair hung in loose curls that had apparently escaped the coil on the back of her head. When she recognized James, her mouth popped open in a wide O, matching her eyes.

Her appearance, as it had been only a few dreadful days ago, was a beacon of hope and help.

Not to mention the only plausible excuse his desperate mind could think of. "Mr. Harkness, I know it's very late, but I simply couldn't stop thinking about it."

"What?" The older man suddenly seemed uneasy.

James wondered if Harkness feared he would press him for information about the "accident".

"When I met your daughter the other day, when she handled the bill for Lavinia's final expenses—" He broke off with a cough. "Well, if you will pardon my boldness, Mr. Harkness... Miss Harkness, may I call upon you sometime?" James concluded in a rush.

No one answered him. Charlotte, safely behind her father, gave him a quizzical, disbelieving stare and mouthed, "What are you playing at?"

No woman he'd ever met at his mother's carefully orchestrated attempts to push him toward courtship had said anything like that. They mainly hid behind fans, opening and shutting them in some secret semaphore he'd never learned, batting their eyelashes enough to make him wonder about fatigue of the orbicularis oculi muscles. He couldn't help but smile.

****

"I… Dr. Everly…" Reginald Harkness was shocked. Stunned. Dr. Everly was clearly a class above their own modest means. For such a man to court Charlotte would never end successfully. The boy would be lowering his own rank and social position if it did, marrying beneath himself. Charlotte must be protected from such foolishness. "That's a very kind offer, but we must refuse."

"What?" Charlotte squawked. "Excuse me, Dr. Everly." With a firm tug, she pulled Mr. Harkness from the door, which she shut in James' face.

"Charlotte, that man is—"

"A surgeon in training and a very devoted brother. I see no harm in him paying a call."

"But—but…" But what? He wanted Charlotte distracted. Any distraction would do, as long as it was safe. She was a beautiful, clever, sympathetic girl. Nearly everyone commented on her brilliant future as a wife.

And you don't get to be a wife without at least courting. The *right* sort of courting. Mr. Harkness regretfully shook his head.

"That man, nice as he is, is quite a bit above your station. I don't think this will go far and it will sully your reputation. No, no. You'd best stick to nice boys in the trade, like one of Mr. Parson's sons or Peter Danvers."

Charlotte's surprised look of a few moments hence was nothing compared to the utterly horrified, shocked look she gave her father now. "I'm not good enough for him?"

"I didn't say that."

"You did."

"Charlotte, my angel, consider—"

"Consider the fact that nothing I do ever pleases you."

"That's not true!"

"You don't want me to help in the business, you don't want me to see a wealthy, generous doctor, you don't want me to live here!" Tortured accusations came steaming out as she marched back to the front door.

"A lady's reputation—"

"What reputation will I have as the madwoman of Whitechapel, Father? I find Dr. Everly kind and sincere."

****

Charlotte realized her arguments were true. Moreover, she realized she definitely wanted to see the good physician, not for a fancy to his looks or the wry smile that she found oddly captivating.

She wanted to aid him in laying Lavinia's spirit to rest. If he didn't solve this murder, she'd be headed to Yorkshire in a matter of days or Bedlam in a matter of weeks.

Her father reached out and touched her cheek with tentative fingertips. "You look so much like her mother when you're fierce about something." He let out a long sigh. "Your mother would have wanted to see you happy. I do, too. Promise you'll not get your hopes up? I'll end things with this young man if I see him toying with your affections."

"I'll end it myself if that's the case." Charlotte tossed her head.

Mr. Harkness groaned. "Yes, I believe you will."

****

James shivered miserably, waiting for the verdict. This was a horrible plan. It wasn't even a plan. It was an accident of an exhausted brain. Worse, he genuinely felt

163

bad for putting Miss Harkness in such an awkward position. Unmarried women had to be so much more careful about appearances than eligible bachelors, didn't they?

"Dr. Everly." Mr. Harkness was suddenly back in the open doorway, making his guest rear back with a gasp.

"I'm so sorry. I was terribly forward. I must beg your forgiveness for my—"

"It is entirely too late to pay a call to a respectable young lady."

"Oh, yes, I know. I was working up my nerve all day. If I'd been braver, I would have been here much sooner, Mr. Harkness." He hoped that struck an appropriate balance between interest and deference.

Mr. Harkness looked quite mollified. "You may come at noon tomorrow. Charlotte's making a ham and leek pie."

"Oh. Oh! Thank you, sir. Thank Miss Harkness, too. I'll see you on the morrow."

Tomorrow. Another coach ride. Another day when he should be studying. Another day of avoiding his mother's bleary eyes. Another night without answers.

After an exchange of farewells, the door shut and he stepped back, gathering his bearings and wondering where he'd find a cab the most expediently.

A rectangle of light from the top floor of the house caught his attention.

Charlotte stood framed in the yellow glow, a dark, featureless silhouette, moving gracefully backward and forward. He hovered on the pavement, a moth trapped by the lure of a candle's flame.

Something fluttered down to him.

Feeling rather like one of the gallant knights he'd read about as a boy, he bent to retrieve it, his heart beating quickly. A handkerchief for his lance point, a lady's favor for her noble challenger.

Not that this is a true courtship, mind you.

Still, his fingers curled around the folded piece of stiff card, damp from the spitting mist.

A message.

His foolish, lonely heart sped up a little more as he opened it.

He took a moment to make out the message, the ink smudged and blotted from its hasty composition scrawled across the paper.

No tender sentiment here. Charlotte was clearly on the same track as he. He stared at the words, mouthing them silently.

She knew him before that night.

How?

Lavinia knew her killer before that night. No supernatural intervention needed to suss that out. If she hadn't known the fellow, she wouldn't have let him persuade her to come to such a loathsome part of the city.

She must have known him quite well. A lady would never spend time alone with a man unless they were married or engaged.

Engaged?

Hm. Mother never mentioned anyone. Vinnie never mentioned anyone in her infrequent notes or during my rare visits home.

Must be someone she'd met recently, but trusted implicitly. A secret engagement?

Vinnie had always been far too trusting. She saw only her own version of the world and events, which made it easy to slip something unexpected past her.

He looked back up at the window, nodding slowly. He made a show of deliberately putting the paper in his pocket.

Charlotte closed the shutters, leaving him in the dark—and illuminating him at the same time.

I think I need to go through Lavinia's correspondence.

Chapter Ten

"What are you doing in your sister's rooms?" Mrs. Everly stood in the doorway, a shadow of her former self. Her eyes were underlined with pouches and her normally fashionable hair rolled untidily across her shoulders.

"I'm looking for the notes I sent her." James kept his head bent over the desk. That was partially true.

"James, have you eaten?"

"I had an early breakfast."

"Cook hates it when she makes kippers and you don't eat them. They used to be your favorite."

"We don't get kippers very often at school, Mother. I've lost my appetite for them."

"I told Sadie to tidy up the desk. Burn any papers."

"What?" James whirled, shock on his face. "Mother, why?"

"It's the decent thing to do. A lady's thoughts are her own, after all." His mother turned away, seemingly resigned and satisfied all at once.

James thundered past her, down the back stairs, ignoring her cries. He skidded to a stop as he saw Sadie through one of the windows, beating a rug in the back garden.

"Don't trouble the servants." Mrs. Everly's voice was a harsh, strained bark.

"I shan't," James called back. "Let me help you, Sadie." He ran over to her. He plucked the ornate beater from her hand and started slapping at the rug, clouds of dust falling to the frost-tipped grass.

"Oh! Mr. James, stop, you'll get all dirty." Sadie stared at him, aghast.

"James Everly! Get inside this instant," his mother's voice shrilled from the house.

"Just a moment," James caroled back cheerfully as though nothing were wrong. "Sadie, I hope you'll be able to help me."

"Of course, sir. Only, please do as your mother says. She's not feeling well." The little housemaid held out her hand.

With a reluctant sigh, he returned the tool. "My mother says you burned all of Miss Lavinia's personal papers and correspondence."

"I—I burned the box of papers she gave me. She told me to, Mr. James!" Sadie's face, already in stark contrast to her dark dress, went positively ghostly.

"You've done nothing wrong. Honestly." His voice was gentle, soothing a nervous patient. "Only, I'd be so grateful to know if you noticed any unfamiliar names among the letters. Men's names."

Sadie swallowed twice, her tongue skirting her lips nervously. "Could be, sir."

"Ah. But you wouldn't know, as Miss Lavinia didn't take you into her confidence and you didn't look at the papers before disposing of them?" he hazarded.

"No, sir. I wouldn't know because I—I can't read." Sadie twisted her hands nervously, almost guiltily.

At first, James wondered if she were lying. Her eyes moved anxiously between him and the windows of his mother's parlor, which had a view of the back garden.

"Please, sir, not to say a word against her, but

Madame looks very unhappy. I daren't lose this job."

James would much rather have pushed the issue, but Charlotte's frown superimposed itself over his mother's scowling face, hidden behind a pane of glass. He backed away slowly. "You can't read? At all?"

Sadie looked at her shoes, shaking her head.

"That's a shame. Not at all?"

"I know some letters. I recognize my name and the names of the family so I can give Madame and Miss Lavinia their letters. I know the street signs, sir, but that's more from learning what they're called," she replied, her voice so faint that he had to strain to catch it.

"Thank you, Sadie. I'll leave you to your work." He turned, then wavered and faced her again. "Should you ever want something read to you, I'll do it, if I'm home."

"That's too kind, Mr. James! Cook can read a bit, she'll read me anything I get. Not that I get any letters, but she reads me a few things her sister and nieces send her. Even the ladies' magazines that Mrs. Everly wants put in the rubbish bins. We read the recipes before they go out."

Women are very strange creatures, James thought as he nodded, still retreating. It had never occurred to him until this moment that their lives were very sheltered, as a woman's life should be, but it also made them rather... helpless instead of protected. A girl like Sadie could be at the mercy of an angry employer. Jobs were lost if love was found. Or if matrimony was found, for he was sure that in some cases love didn't enter into it. He knew countless tales of people of his own class and higher marrying for wealth, property, or a title. It must be so much worse if you have nothing but yourself to offer.

Or would it be better, if it was only yourself? To be

loved, for oneself alone?

Loneliness draped its dark wings over his back. Mother was locking herself away. Father and Vinnie gone. Cut off from even his chums at the RC of S.

He suddenly turned and pulled the last of the late-blooming flowers out of his mother's border. Behind him, Sadie let out a protesting whimper.

Well, he was going courting this afternoon, wasn't he? He'd better make a good show of it. He was sure that a woman like Charlotte Harkness would.

****

"I've been talking to Mrs. Miggins. Her husband is the ironmonger."

"I know, Father." Charlotte fastened her mother's brooch on her collar. As if she wouldn't know everyone on this street after twenty-four years! Not that the children had befriended her growing up. Aside from the casual games children play like skipping rope, catch-as-catch-can, conkers, and the like, they avoided her. They didn't want to be around her, or her house. Too close to death.

It was much the same for her father, she suspected. All of his friends were somehow related to his business.

"Her eldest was married a month ago."

"That's right. She married the fishmonger's son?"

"Yes! She said you must have a lady chaperone in attendance at your courting events. Or at least an older, married relative or friend."

"I'm taking tea with him in the sitting room. You'll join us."

"Ah, but I can't. Mr. Watkins needs seeing to and there could be a call at any moment. You know how it is."

Yes, she did. In fact, she was counting on it. If her father would hang about, they'd never share any information.

"No, please. Please! He—"

****

Reginald Harkness watched a sudden spasm of pain twist his daughter's beautiful face, her blue eyes suddenly shut tight, and her lips pressed together. Poor thing. She was trying valiantly to please him, wasn't she? She hadn't brought up that nonsense about changing the name of the business again. She was at least (at last) *appearing* to give some thought to her future, to entertaining suitors. She hadn't had the advantages most girls would have had, a mother to dress them prettily, to find ways to make their marriageability known to the right sorts of eligible men. "Ah, well. I'll be in the house, quite nearby. I'll pop in when I can. If I must go out—"

"I'll see Dr. Everly on his way. We can walk to the market stalls. I have to buy more flowers."

"A woman shouldn't work while courting."

"Courting is work," Charlotte said heavily. "I should have finished the baking before I put on this dress. Where's Auntie Molly's big apron? The one you gave her all those Christmases ago? It's much wider than mine."

Mr. Harkness stared after his daughter as she went from pained, lovelorn girl to practical housekeeper-cook-assistant. Though he worried about her quite a bit, he privately thought no father in England could be prouder.

****

"Mother, I want to discuss something with you." James invaded the sanctum of her sitting room. The room was dark, the drapes closed, the air scented with heavy medicinal odors. Shutting others out indeed, physically and mentally. He sniffed again, catching a whiff of alcohol and fermentation amid the harsher, sharper tang of coal tar oils and emetics.

"I have something to discuss with you, as well. Your aunt has wired. She wants me to come to stay with her. She got my letter."

"Aunt Eleanor?"

"Yes."

"Are you going?"

"Of course we're going. We would have spent Christmas with her and then New Year's with Uncle Jeremy's family. Can you pack for an afternoon train tomorrow?"

"Pack? Me? No, Mother—"

"You will pack, and you will come." Her voice was iron.

Iron can be bent. His voice was carefully thoughtful. "Yes. Yes, I suppose it will be good to see Aunt Eleanor, Alice, and Bertram."

"Your Uncle Oliver has to come to the city for business. He'll meet the train tomorrow, and we'll take their coach. An exchange, if you will."

"Yes." He nodded, his mind whirring while his voice played for time. "Perhaps Alice will know."

"Alice? Know what?"

"Who Lavinia was meeting in secret."

His mother's blotchy complexion settled into an even shade of spoilt milk. "She wasn't meeting anyone, James. Do not let me hear such words pass your lips again. That's an enormous insult to her memory, to make her sound like a willful, rebellious harlot!" She ended with a strangled cry. "Stay in London if you wish, at least until you have such nonsense out of your system."

"It's not nonsense to want to see justice."

Silence.

"Mother?"

"You are my firstborn. The apple of my eye. I love you dearly, James."

The sudden change in her tone and demeanor shocked him. His face softened, and his words were sincere. "I know, Mother. And I, you."

"I loved my darling little girl like you cannot imagine. Perhaps one day you will have a little girl with big brown eyes and—" She stopped, swallowed, and pressed ahead. "I wanted what was best for her, always, in every way. She made mistakes. I wish I could have protected her from the evils of this world and her headstrong ways."

It was his turn to be silent, to nod and reach out to clasp her hand. He was surprised to find it so clammy, trembling unsteadily, the pulse thready and fast under his fingertips.

"As much as I love you, I will not let you make a scandal of her good name, her virtue."

"I never—"

"No. You never can understand, never *will* understand what it is like for a woman to have to protect her reputation and her family's reputation! Every indiscretion that attaches itself to a lady harms not only her own future chances but the chances of all her relatives, her entire family's standing. Your sister was young, foolish, and not thinking clearly. Selfishly." His mother suddenly snatched her fingers back, curling them tightly into her fists, the nails digging into her skin in anger. "I long for the day when I can stop clearing up after mistakes. I wish I could have been firmer... I never should have let her buy that dress."

"Dress?" James cocked his head.

His mother didn't appear to have heard, now clinking a decanter to glass, dark, fruity-smelling liquid tippling into the glass, followed by a small paper envelope of powder. "Mother, what are you taking?"

"The doctor prescribed it for my nerves."

Before he could blink, she'd thrown the glass back and drained it to the dregs. It seemed to bolster her resolve as well as heighten her color. "Better?"

She laughed. "As if I could ever be better! I've lost my husband of over twenty years, I've lost my daughter before her twentieth birthday, and my son is determined to burn what's left of our good name down around our ears, throwing his own future on the flames to boot." Another hearty splash into the dainty glass, another unladylike gulp.

James caught her as she staggered and fell onto her chaise lounge. "Mother, you'll make yourself ill."

"The world has made me ill, I *am* ill. I'm ill and there is no cure," she moaned softly, eyes closed.

He'd never seen her like this, almost insensible in a few moments. He supposed that the last few days had seen her go through rather a lot of sleeping powders and liquors on a delicate digestion. He sat with her while she rambled about a mother's burden and foolish girls. Within moments, the talk slurred, then slowed. Her pulse evened, and her color improved.

"I'm going to go out, Mother. I'm going to pay a call on a friend."

"Don't... don't be late. What are you wearing?" She

opened her eyes again, unfocused, cloudy eyes.

James rose. He was appropriately in mourning today, dark grays and blacks. "I think I look quite dashing," he teased gently, hoping to see a glimmer of a smile on her grieved features.

"Good, good. Not until the time has passed. Should have made her… wait." Her lids closed again.

His ears pricked up. "Made Lavinia wait? For what?"

"Winter dress. Green and sable. Elegant. So grown-up."

A green and sable dress? What in the world was so tragic about a green and sable dress? "Didn't you like it after all?" he asked softly, hoping he wouldn't rouse her suspicions and that she'd continue to talk peaceably as she drifted into a healing sleep.

"She turned back to look at that hat. Lovely hat, ostrich feather."

This was useless and fast becoming irritating.

His mother's voice became strained, almost tearful, even as she turned to bury her face in the silk cushion under her head. "She fell in love."

She fell in love. With the hat? Well, that sounded exactly like something Vinnie would do. She would likely mount a shrewish display of temper if she didn't get it. It must have been too gaudy or unrefined for his mother's tastes.

"Was it too much?" he chuckled as he rose, looking for the duvet to spread over her.

"Looked fine at first glance… too common."

"She wanted it anyway, didn't she? That would be Vinnie, wouldn't it? I bet you had a devil of a time dissuading her."

"The devil…" She heaved a broken sigh that turned into a snore.

****

"Mr. James? Are you going out? Should Cook expect you for tea?" Sadie caught Dr. Everly as he wrapped a damp bit of linen around the flowers he'd plucked earlier.

"No, I'll be dining out. Thank you, Sadie."

"Certainly, sir."

James walked away, suddenly to hear footsteps on the walk behind him. He turned to see Sadie trotting after him, breathlessly holding her cap onto her flyaway hair.

"Sir? I—" Sadie froze as he stepped toward her.

"What is it, Sadie?"

"I… Do you have your gloves?"

James looked down at his hands. No respectable gentleman paid a call without his gloves, especially in the winter. "I seem to, yes."

"Ah. Th-that's all, Dr. Everly. Have a good afternoon, sir."

Sadie dropped a scant, nervous curtsey and fairly flew back inside.

Women were strange creatures.

****

Charlotte's father was behaving oddly. "Whatever is the matter, Father?"

"Where are your gloves? You must have gloves. I know you have gloves."

"Of course I have gloves, but I've got to do the wreath for Mr. Watkins."

"Shouldn't you be… I don't know. What do ladies do before courting?"

"I've bathed, I've dressed, I've baked. All that's left

for me to do is to have a fan to wave in front of my face in a coy fashion."

"Good heavens. A fan?"

"I don't see the point of a fan, Father. He's seen my face. Why should I hide it?"

Reginald paused. "I've no idea, really. If he hadn't admired it, he never would have asked to pay you a call." He lightly ran his thumb over her cheek, lifting her head as she sat sorting greenery from the sparse flowers that remained.

Charlotte blushed. No, it wasn't that Dr. Everly liked her looks. He liked her usefulness. For that, she liked him all the more, and that made her blush harder. She mustn't develop any sort of feelings or attachment, simply because he was a kind, intelligent man who also happened to like her for her kindness and intelligence.

Her corset must be too tight. That's why she had this strange pressing feeling in her stomach.

****

"How do you do, Dr. Everly?"

"How do you do, Mr. Harkness?"

"I'm well, thank you. May I present my daughter, Charlotte?"

"It's a pleasure to meet you, Miss Harkness. Formally, that is."

"A pleasure to meet you, formally, Dr. Everly." *Although we've already examined a corpse together and we've argued and exchanged secret notes in the dark. But how nice to shake hands.* Charlotte laughed at the absurdity of all these unnecessary introductions, a fluting giggle that covered her unease nicely. Moreover, it seemed to relax her sweating father as well. "Do step this way. I have a little luncheon prepared."

"Charlotte is a wonderful cook," Mr. Harkness boasted.

"Thank you, Father."

"I'm sure she is." James nodded and smiled stiffly.

****

James thought he might choke to death if he ate. He was barely able to keep from blurting out, "Lavinia was murdered. You know it, she knows it, I know it. Let's find out who did it!"

Mr. Harkness took this for nerves, and why shouldn't he? He was still in mourning, and courting and mourning ought never to mix, let alone courting beneath one's station.

"How is your dear mother?" the undertaker asked.

"She's unwell. The loss. My father passed away only two years ago this autumn."

"Oh, I am sorry." Charlotte opened the sitting room door and revealed a lovely little table.

"My late wife's best tablecloth and the good china. A thoughtful touch with the spray of holly around the candle, Charlotte," Mr. Harkness said with forced cheer. "Festive."

Charlotte let out a strange little giggle.

James tilted his head. Yes. Yes, this girl must be quite insane. "Do share the joke?"

"Oh, no, I'm sorry. It's just I—I think the room looks so pretty and it delights me. We don't often have company. The house is a business, as well. As you know."

"And a very busy one, to your credit, sir." James inclined his head to Mr. Harkness.

"Well, I couldn't do it without Charlotte. She—hrm, manages the household affairs beautifully." Mr.

Harkness rocked from foot to foot, hands clasped behind his back.

****

Charlotte knew her father was in an agony of indecision. Should he boast about her usefulness with the funereal side of things? Would that put Dr. Everly off? Was he behaving in the same manner of the other patriarchs in Everly's upper crust circle? She tossed her father a pitying look and imagined that he would be eager to attend to the late Mr. Watkins as soon as possible, worried about ruining her chances with too much information.

"Let's all sit and not stand on ceremony," Mr. Harkness said in a bluff and hearty voice, a jovial smile replacing his nervous rocking.

James sat across from her with a relieved smile.

Mr. Harkness opened his mouth—

"Reginald! Guinevere's thrown her shoe!"

"Blast!" Mr. Harkness put down the soup tureen lid he'd just lifted, clattering the china bits together. "Bartlesby is in the back."

"I hear, Father." Charlotte smiled. "Go and help him with whatever it is he needs, although goodness knows you're not a blacksmith."

"Yes, yes. I suppose I'll have to unhitch her and see if we can't rush to Mr. Miggins. I'll be back in just a moment."

"Of course." Dr. Everly rose and bowed his host out. As soon as the door in the hall shut, he sighed. Charlotte did as well.

"Oh, thank heavens. Here, soup and pie." She rose and served them both hastily. "What did you find out?"

"That a lot of girls get killed in Whitechapel.

Probably other places, too," he began, viciously cutting into the flaky crust of the ham and leek pie. One bite made him close his eyes and moan. "I don't think I've tasted anything I've put in my mouth since it happened. This is delicious, Miss Harkness."

"Can you call me Charlotte if we're alone?"

"I think I may call you it in public as well, once we've 'courted' a bit longer. I'm most dreadfully sorry about this ruse."

"It's all right."

"I'll make sure you do the 'breaking off.' I think that's better for the woman in the situation?"

"I believe so. Let's not worry about that, yet. Surely you must've wanted to tell me something more than there are many deaths in this part of London. If anyone knows, it's the Harkness family." She gestured to the rooms around them.

"Quite. According to the maid, Sadie, Lavinia seemed unwell, yet no doctor was sent for. I went to her rooms—Lavinia's rooms, not the housemaid's. I was looking for letters, telegrams, anything, any proof that she'd met a stranger."

"A *ruthless* stranger."

"Ah! But that's the thing." James leaned closer, voice low. "My sister was presented at court last year, despite the fact that she should still have been in deepest mourning for my father. She could always badger my mother into getting her own way. Not that I blame her, now. She was so beautiful, so angelic looking. Such delicate features, such fine bones... my father used to call her his porcelain doll." James' voice thickened as he mused, a mixture of wistfulness and pain on his face.

Charlotte nodded, feeling as though she were

peeping in on someone else's secret life, a life far too different from her own.

"The point being, she would never have gone anywhere unescorted unless she was—well, to put it frankly, unless she was already engaged or planning to be, perhaps plotting an elopement. I'm ashamed to say it, but that's the sort of dramatic taste my sister had. She loved attention."

"And I imagine she had precious little of it while she was in mourning for your father. All social calls would have been kept to a minimum. But, as you say, she did persuade your mother to let her attend parties and the events of the Season."

"That's just it. She fell ill early in the Season, seriously ill within a few weeks, perhaps a month or so. Her hair fell out in great clumps as well, and then she wouldn't show herself to any but the household."

"Vain. Oh. I beg your pardon." Charlotte hurriedly sipped her cooling soup, vexed with herself for such a remark. One shouldn't speak ill of the dead—but it was very hard to recall that rule when the dead very often spoke to her and seemed to have no such compunction.

The dead were awfully fond of gossip, in fact.

His chin jutted in defiance for a second. "True. Vinnie was vain. Pampered. Spoiled. She had many faults. None worth dying over."

"Agreed." Her spoon rested on the bowl for a moment, head tilting thoughtfully. "Not to make you think on such awful memories, Dr. Everly, but when you saw the wounds on your sister's... torso, didn't you remark that the individual who made such marks must be a surgeon?"

"Yes. A wolf in sheep's clothing."

"Would your sister be wooed by an educated man such as yourself, a surgeon?"

"There are plenty of wealthy, landed gentry who send their third and fourth sons into the city to do something useful, the army, the church, even plumb the depths and try something as coarse as medicine. If she met such a man, with the right family and the right connections, she might."

"Well, then… Surely this isn't terribly difficult?"

"What?"

"Won't be a moment!"

Mr. Harkness' voice unexpectedly broke their intense discussion, making them spring apart. It was only then that both parties realized how close they'd been during their furtive conversation.

"I beg your pardon, but whatever do you mean? There must be a good thousand surgeons in England, many with some claim to wealth or a title."

Charlotte prevented her shoulders from shrugging with an effort, hearing Auntie Molly scolding from memory. "I'm certain there are, but one would have to be in London and of a suitable age and attractiveness to catch Lavinia's fancy. If he were a dreadfully wealthy old man in his seventies with gout and rheumatism, she wouldn't look at him."

James bit his lip to keep from laughing. "Gout and rheumatism describe a fair number of the professors at the Royal College of Surgeons. Lavinia wouldn't consider anyone who wasn't dashing and handsome worth a second look. Style over substance, I'm afraid."

"So surely it wouldn't be hard to find a young, handsome, wealthy surgeon in London that met your sister some time in her limited exposure to the world, what with her illness and in mourning…" Charlotte led. She was tempted to add, "And you have the name, you fool. I've given you that much."

"What would a wealthy surgeon be doing down in the worst yards of Whitechapel?"

"What would your sister be doing with him?"

James tugged at his collar as if it had suddenly become far too tight. His cheeks matched the holly berries on the table.

"Oh." Charlotte cursed herself and wished the tablecloth would kindly cover her as well, allowing her to die of mortification in peace.

"Perhaps." He drained his tumbler of water.

****

Mr. Harkness opened the door to find his daughter and her young suitor sitting stiffly apart, well back in their chairs, both cheeks aflame. He was barely able to keep from rubbing his hands in paternal glee. Prudence would be so proud of him. His daughter's first foray into courting was going beautifully. Both youngsters were blushing bright, clearly shy and smitten, as was proper.

****

"Mother burnt all her papers. Well, she had Sadie do it. I asked Sadie about the contents that were destroyed."

"No luck?"

"She can't read. She looked most dreadfully guilty, though. I wanted to ask her more, but she seems utterly terrified of me. I don't feel very imposing. To be honest, I'm not even very tall," the young physician admitted.

Charlotte cast an eye to her left. Dr. Everly was walking a proper eighteen inches apart as they braved the dreary afternoon to head to Gatti's Confections along the Whitechapel Road. It had been her father's suggestion, as Mr. Watkins had to be taken to his final resting place, and she and James still seemed to be inclined to linger over the last pot of tea.

James wasn't very tall, but he had one of those sweet earnest faces that made him stand out, made him seem quite upright and respectable among men. He was only a few inches taller than her, but already the phrase "look up to" sprang to mind.

It was an excellent thing for both of their reputations that no one knew what they were talking about.

"Are you given to breaking the servants' hearts?" Charlotte asked, pulling her blue cloak with its black velvet collar around her more tightly.

"Never!"

"Do you control the family's finances? Do you do the sacking and employing?"

"Goodness, no. Mother wouldn't have it."

Charlotte knew it was none of her business what the Everly family did. She knew that it was quite common for the matriarchs and widows to retain the running of their household affairs until their adult sons were wed and establishing the next generation, lifting the burdens of daily management from elderly shoulders. Still, she couldn't help but feel a little disappointed that James seemed so quick to yield the reins to his mother. Somehow it made her think of weakness.

Charlotte was inclined to dislike Mrs. Everly, with no just cause. She'd best stick to the topic at hand. "Then the maid, Sadie, is not afraid of you. She's afraid of something else. Or she's afraid of someone else finding her talking to you."

"My mother has threatened to cut me off without a cent if I pursue this. I don't care. I can earn a living.

There are thousands of sick and needy in London alone. I'll take a job in the madhouses or the plague hospitals, I'll do whatever it takes to keep body and soul together, only… only, I cannot bear this. This will rip body from soul, Miss Harkness. Her killer must be caught." James paused, giving her an agonized look.

Charlotte nodded. "And no peace of mind…" she whispered, thinking of her own dreadful burden, the first time a spirit had ever haunted her, been unwelcome. If only Lavinia could show her something else, something more useful. She waited, expectedly.

Nothing.

"Your sister was very stubborn, wasn't she?" Charlotte sighed.

James blinked. "How did you know?"

"I had an inkling. Shall we go in?"

****

"We don't have to buy anything," Charlotte hissed as they perused the rows of confections under glass. "But this way, we can tell Father we took his suggestion, and we can take our time about getting back."

"No, I insist. Your luncheon was delicious. You are a wonderful cook." It occurred to him suddenly, that his own mother very likely could not cook at all. Her family might have thought it abhorrent for a woman to know such things, not when she could pay to have someone else know them for her.

"Yes, everyone says that."

"You sound rather unhappy about it. It was a compliment."

"Oh, no, thank you, Dr. Everly. It's not that I dislike the kind words, it's that they are usually paired with, 'She'll make someone a fine wife.' As if I've nothing more to offer than a pretty face and a nice light hand with dough."

"Well. Your face *is* lovely."

"Thank you."

"May I help you? A sweet for your sweet, sir?"

"Ah. Two marzipan squares, please. And a bag of clove rocks." James hastily reached into his breast pocket.

"Those are my favorite." Charlotte's eyes lit up.

"Really? One of mine, too."

As the shop assistant dipped his metal scoop into the neat rows of candy to retrieve their clove rocks, James gestured to two of the elaborate wrought chairs with plump pink cushions. Charlotte nodded and sat. "In my circle, I daresay a woman being a good cook would be more of a shock than an expectation for matrimony."

"Our circles are not the same. If it weren't for death, they'd not connect at all."

"I wouldn't say that," James argued, unaccountably annoyed that she'd said it so factually, almost indifferently. "I help the ill, you help the grieving. Wealth cannot prevent death, nor illness. Poverty cannot, either."

When the assistant, resplendent in red and white striped waistcoat brought their confections to them, Charlotte took a clove rock daintily from the bag James proffered and held it up in a toast. "I like the way your mind works, Dr. Everly. To equality?"

"I do so like the way you put things, Miss Harkness." His lips twisted up at the corners. "In life and death.

Chapter Eleven

"Your mother must've feared something incriminating would present itself in Lavinia's correspondence."

"She mentioned a lady's indiscretions being used against her and her whole family, yes."

The light was lowering. Mr. Watkins, bless his kind soul, would have been laid to rest. Mr. Harkness, Mr. Bartlesby, and the vicar of St. Clementia's would all be traveling home together. Bartlesby would be driving the funeral carriage, and her father would be driving the other with the widow and surviving children inside. The vicar would be squeezed inside with them, or riding outside next to her father.

She had to get supper prepared. What if there had been a client, calling in need, while she'd been away? Her polished black boots with their string of buttons up the side took on a brisker pace. Still the appropriate distance apart, Dr. Everly matched her.

"There must be someone who knows something. Sadie doesn't have to read to know whom Lavinia would meet or speak of. Perhaps your sister's personal maid?"

"She hasn't had one for weeks. She married and left the service."

"A close friend? From school?" Charlotte imagined such a wealthy, fortunate woman as Lavinia Everly had been would surely have taken advantage of her position and attended some sort of institute for high-born ladies, a finishing school. Thank the Lord her father had never taken it into his head to try to press her into one of those places. Auntie Molly was thoroughly content for her to learn the domestic arts and any "book-learning" that could be squeezed from her father's well-stocked library. After his wife's death, Mr. Harkness's guilty pleasure had run to books, even though they were considered a luxury and somewhat expensive. He had no idea that his delight would be shared with his only child, who read everything he brought into the house.

****

James pondered Miss Harkness' question, but then shook his head regretfully. Around him, people pressed and pushed, carts and carriages rumbled, and smoke and fog were beginning to mingle as night came on. Soon the darkness would hide all the little looks and gestures that he was beginning to enjoy with his new companion. Somehow, they seemed to be piecing *something* together. He wasn't sure it was the identity of his sister's murderer, however. "Mother thought Vinnie was too delicate to go to any sort of school. She made sure she took art and music lessons from private tutors. We had a governess who was really there for Lavinia's benefit. I went away to school."

"Eton?"

"Westminster. Near to home, not that I stayed there. Except for holidays." He impatiently shook his head. Miss Harkness was confoundedly easy to talk to, but his education had nothing to do with Lavinia's death. "Lavinia was no shrinking violet. She could embroider and crochet, she could sing and play the pianoforte, speak passable French, and was rather too fond of giving dramatic recitations. Mother has scads of friends who have scads of daughters. They all do things like go from house to house in the country and Lady Lipton's charity gala here and Lady Peel's portrait unveiling there. Honestly, it seems like an excuse to buy dresses and see what dresses other girls are wearing. I don't think anyone much looked at Lady Peel's portrait. They were too busy looking at each other's frocks."

Charlotte burst out laughing. She tried to turn it into a demure giggle, but too late. Even in the shadows, she caught sight of his frown. "What is it?"

"Hm? Nothing, I suppose. Mother mentioned something about Vinnie fussing over some new dress or hat, that's all. Everything seems to remind me of her."

"The mind is funny. It tries to give us the best pieces it can, I find."

"What do you mean?"

****

What *did* she mean? That spirits who spoke to her left clues and her mind made impressions? She typically used such impressions to say just the right thing to the mourning loved ones left behind. In terms of Lavinia's murder, the spirit had given her a very good clue, a name.

Not that anyone would believe her.

Playing for time by adjusting her cloak and pretending she cared to navigate a puddle with the utmost daintiness, she answered, "Well, I suppose our brains store up the most important pieces of information to help us make sense of things. Whether that's the death of a loved one or finding a killer, the mind keeps track of the clues we're too busy to notice. If the dresses stuck in your mind, or your mother's mind, perhaps it's important."

"I think Sadie knows something important. Yes." James warmed to the subject, steps quickening so that Charlotte had to exert herself to keep up. "My mother received a visit from the police before I even arrived. That's how she knew that something was wrong, how she knew to send for me. Sadie, Bannet, and Cook are the only servants we have who take their lodging with us as part of their wages. The gardener never has and— well, it occurs to me that I don't know much else about the staff, not that it would interest you. Bannet, my mother's personal maid, is away. Sadie would have opened the door. She would have roused my mother. She must have heard or seen…" He broke off. "I don't know. I don't suppose my mother sat down to entertain the police with Sadie in the room."

Charlotte gave him a sidelong glance. "Do you think she might've listened in?"

"Even if she did, she wouldn't have been told the identity of the murderer."

"True. Do you think she might have overheard Lavinia talk about a person she planned to meet?"

"It can hardly have been a public meeting, one that Mother would allow. She didn't know Lavinina'd gone until the police came."

"So, someone educated, handsome, and in the right social circles… that your mother wouldn't approve of." Named Jack, Charlotte silently added.

"This is hopeless."

"It's not."

"I can't even see any correspondence or papers she…" James broke off.

"Have you thought of something?" Charlotte asked excitedly.

"My sister had a reticule with papers inside when she was recovered. It had something inside with her name or her address, something that led them to identify her and contact Mother. Mother ordered Sadie to burn the letters from Vinnie's desk, but I wonder what became of the papers that were found upon her person?"

Charlotte slowed her steps as the shape of Harkness and Sons, sitting apart on its corner, came into view. Instinctively, Dr. Everly matched her, moving a bit closer as they came to a stretch of pavement temporarily devoid of other people. "Do the police have the bag? Or does your mother?"

"I don't know, but I'd like to find out. I—Miss Harkness?" James sprang forward and caught her elbow as she stumbled.

Charlotte's head swam as someone else's memory was forced into it.

"There you are." A masculine voice, full of curiosity and mirth. "For God's sake, what was so urgent?"

A frantic hiss. "Don't swear! We mustn't talk here. What if Mama or the servants should wake up and look out into the street?"

"Then let's away quickly. I told the cab to wait."

The breathless feminine voice turned imploring. "Take me... take me to one of those little places we went before. A place that's nicer and cleaner, though."

"Nicer, cleaner places don't exist in secret for people like us."

"Then take me where you must, only I must have a word alone, please!"

"Of course, as my lady commands." The man's

voice turned mocking, bitter.

Charlotte was aware of Dr. Everly's hand under her elbow, a gesture that polite society would consider improper, had she not been fainting.

"Are you ill?" he demanded, concern in his blue eyes, earnest face full of sudden worry.

"No. I... I'm sorry. I tripped."

"Did you injure yourself?" He surveyed her with a professional eye.

Charlotte managed to stand upright, knowing her cheeks were flushed and her eyes were roving uneasily. "I don't... I don't care if you don't believe me. Lavinia sent me a memory, that's how I knew her killer was called Jack. They met near your house. He had a cab waiting. She asked him to take her back to the place they went before so they could speak privately. I don't know what he looks like or anything more than that, Dr. Everly." She took her elbow from his grasp and marched forward, head down.

"What?" James stood rooted to the spot, even as she moved forward, about to be swallowed up by a throng of people.

Charlotte turned and met his eyes in the pool of light a freshly lit gas lamp sent over the street. They were large and mournful.

It had been nice, having a friend for an afternoon.

James hurried to catch up to her. "I... I don't see how you could know that, Miss Everly."

"Nor do I." Charlotte sighed in resignation.

"It would seem an excellent deduction, though."

"Down to the name?" she pressed.

He had no answer.

****

James said goodbye to her with gentlemanly grace, a soft, melancholy smile, and a promise to let her know if he found out anything.

He didn't believe her. He seemed genuinely regretful about it, too.

Her father arrived home just in time to see Charlotte receive a courtly bow from her suitor. Charlotte knew she ought to be wreathed in smiles, giddy with excitement after an evening with a handsome gentleman.

She couldn't force herself to pretend. The disappointment of Dr. Everly's disbelief and Lavinia's memories weighed on her too heavily.

"Oh, no." Mr. Harkness came to kneel in front of her. "Oh, I should never have allowed him to pay a call. I should not have let you two go out alone, even if it was in a most respectable part of town. What did he do? What did he say?"

Charlotte blinked in surprise. "Why, nothing! Nothing wrong, Father. He bought me a bag of clove rocks." Charlotte held out the small bag of sweets. "Have one?"

"You—you love clove rocks. They're your favorite." He took one, puzzled.

"I know. They're Dr. Everly's favorite as well." Inexplicably, she was blinking back tears.

"Oh, Charlotte, tell me what happened. I never should have left!"

"Don't be silly. Mr. Watkins and his window needed you. Dr. Everly was a wonderful gentleman, Father, who did nothing wrong. We had a very good time." In fact, she had. The subject matter was tense and troubling, but their conversation never flagged, he didn't disparage her wits, and she was equal to his. For the first time, ever, she'd had a truly engaging conversation with someone near to her own age and intellect. The girls she knew from her area, the daughters of local merchants, were focused on matrimony and domestic needs. The men ignored her aside from mannerly greetings and brief business matters.

"I'm simply afraid it's not… it's not meant to be, Father, as you said. I imagine Dr. Everly will soon realize that he cannot pay calls on me anymore without ruining his future prospects."

"I can ask him not to visit again?"

"No, Father, I imagine he'd *like* to visit again, but… but perhaps we shall just part as acquaintances. I am quite tired. Do you mind having the cold pie for supper? I should like to go to bed."

"Of course, darling." He kissed her cheek and watched her walk away, uncertain what fatherly, comforting words to offer.

****

Charlotte didn't know what this odd feeling was. She was a very happy person, most of the time. She was always cheerful and busy, a shock to the neighborhood matrons who expected she'd turn into some weedy little ghoul, neglected without a mother's care, raised among coffins and shrouds. She took her role as unofficial assistant to her father both domestically and commercially very seriously, especially after Auntie Molly passed. She and her father were always good company for each other, not to mention she never lacked for conversation partners, albeit unseen ones. Life was not *exactly* what she wanted, not with her marriage prospects bleak (to some). Not to mention her dear father's lurking disapproval and his constant worry over her "peculiarities." Still, it was satisfactory.

Until she and Dr. Everly parted courteously, nay, cordially, on the threshold. She shut the door gently behind him—and opened the door to realizing that she was a busy, cheerful, peculiar, rather *lonely* person.

The voices of the dead didn't really linger. She was always "meeting" new people as her father dealt with new clients, but after a day or two, they were gone, and their voices left as well. Even when one guest of Harkness and Sons was chatty, they didn't want to talk about what Charlotte wanted to talk about, her frustrations with her father, her curiosity, her desire to have a career or at least a hobby aside from what women were "expected" to do.

"James." Charlotte tried letting his Christian name fall past her lips as her hair fell past her shoulders. It was time to brush it out and braid it before bed. It made it much more manageable in the morning, that's what Auntie Molly said.

Charlotte could have talked to Auntie Molly about this odd, empty feeling, about her aspirations. Her response would have been a dour and unshakeable, "As the Lord sees fit, Charlotte."

James would converse. He'd challenge her thoughts, wouldn't he? Perhaps that was only because they were jointly investigating this matter of Lavinia's death.

She wasn't doing much to help, was she?

But she could.

She knew roughly where Lavinia had been found. She knew the family's address. Mr. Bartlesby and her father were well known at the livery and stables at the Lion and Eagle yard. That's where most coaches and cabs that went anywhere in the Tower Hamlets came home to roost.

So… She paced as the stiff bristles worked from right to left, crown of head to tips of her softly curling blonde hair. So, it was a matter of purporting to go there on business, perhaps to look at a replacement horse that could be leased by the day in case of emergencies, like Guinevere's thrown shoe. Yes, she'd go there to get an idea of prices, and while she was there, she'd talk about how much ground the horses could cover and how quickly. Say… Westminster to Whitechapel, how long would it take in this weather, in the dark? Had any driver made such a trip recently?

If she could persuade Mr. Harris, the stable manager, to tell her who had driven such a route, perhaps that person would recall picking up an elegantly dressed lady and probably well-dressed man quite late at night from a very wealthy and respectable part of Westminster and bringing them to the worst areas of Whitechapel. Such a couple combined with those circumstances should have stuck in someone's mind. Not to mention the fact that although the police could be bribed to keep the matter quiet, Mrs. Everly hadn't been down in the depths of humanity, paying coppers to keep the person who *found* the body quiet. That meant that the person who found the body and all those who knew about it were the sorts of people who didn't want to talk to the press or the police, or who were too oblivious to notice.

The kind of people who saw murder and foul things all the time, buried in the backstreets and grimy alleyways.

She would go to the stables.

She would go past St. Clementia's.

"James." The name made her feel more alert, less

sad. Perhaps they would go together.

Perhaps that was folly.

Charlotte sank onto her bed, her fingers now deftly working three strands of smooth hair over and under into one long plait.

If this murder were solved, she and Dr. Everly would part ways. If it remained *unsolved*, eventually she'd be in the madhouse, or the Yorkshire Dales, and he'd be too sorrowful and disheartened to continue fruitless investigations.

"Either way, we part," she admitted softly, speaking to the empty room. It wasn't that her heart burned with some sudden infatuation for him. It was that she had enjoyed having a friend for the day. They barely knew each other and yet... "Silliness."

Charlotte put her feet firmly on the floor. With military precision, she laid out tomorrow's clothing and turned the wick down on the lamp. She would not waste any more time on such foolish notions that she and James could ever have a true, lasting friendship or anything more. That was not why she was filled with melancholia.

"It's that I've never had someone to converse with like that and I suppose I never will," she finally admitted as she closed her eyes.

Sleep usually came easily.

Tonight, it evaded her.

"Mama?"

For the first time ever, she didn't hear a response.

"Mama?" Charlotte lifted her head off the pillow, alarm flooding her.

"I'm here, my little bird." The voice was faint, far away, thinning like the point of toffee pulled, just before one piece became two.

"Will you sing to me?" Charlotte whispered in the darkness, swallowing the fear in her throat, but that only sent it pooling into her chest.

"Sleep, my child, and peace attend thee… All through the night.

Guardian angels God will send thee… All through the night."

****

"Where on earth have you been?" Mrs. Everly had thought and said this phrase far too often for any well-bred matriarch. Honestly, if she could find Miss Potts, she'd wring her twig-like neck. Obviously, the governess had failed in her duties.

"I've been to call upon a lady, Mother."

"What? You stayed out all this time?"

"No, I simply didn't feel like eating when I returned. You were still asleep, I imagine."

She had been sleeping a lot. When she was awake, the world seemed like a sickening nightmare. Her cordials and powders made sleep much more pleasant, devoid of dreams, good or bad. "Your sister is barely cold in her—" Mrs. Everly stopped. The expression was too horrid to use.

"I thought we were supposed to carry on?" James laughed bitterly as he stared into the last embers of the fire in the drawing room. He rose and took one of the fire irons and poked the ashes up, sending fresh life into the blaze. "You'll be off to visit Aunt Eleanor. I'll be staying here. I want to sit my exams for the term, Mother. I… find it a healthful distraction, study and revision."

She hesitated. "The boys at your residence…"

"I'll stay here. I'll only go to sit my exams. I'm sure the dean would allow it, for the son of such a *generous benefactor."*

Mrs. Everly met his eye, swallowing. She left his cold gaze to rally another protest. "Cook won't be here."

"I'll manage with whatever's in the larder. Maybe I'll scrounge a few meals at the Halls of Residence."

"James, you mustn't—"

"I promise you I'll come as soon as term ends. It's not long, barely a fortnight."

****

This was working out beautifully. Mother would be leaving. Sadie would go with her. Even Cook would depart and he'd have the house to himself, and he'd still sit his exams.

Carry on, indeed.

"But who is this girl? Surely, she must think it's unseemly for you to court her whilst mourning."

James swallowed. His mother would possibly die on the spot if he said the object of his manly affections was the undertaker's daughter. The connection to Lavinia's death, not to mention her being of a different class would send his mother crashing to the floor and him rushing for the smelling salts again. He brazened it out.

"Her name is Charlotte. She's beautiful and well-spoken. She's clever. She'd make a good wife for a surgeon." As he wove the story like a spider anxiously weaving a ladder of escape, he realized all the things he said were quite true. In fact, he could tell a few more truths that his mother would enjoy, without divulging the full truth of her identity. "She's the only daughter of a London business owner, most respected in his work, owned an establishment in the city for—" He cast his mind back to the swaying sign on Harkness and Sons. Bother it, he couldn't recall the dates, but it was from the

199

last century. "Oh, over a hundred years, I believe." Maybe it wasn't quite that long, but right now, it sounded favorable.

His mother sat and a basket of fancy work materialized from the side of the settee. "Is the business prosperous?"

"Enormously! Her poor father couldn't even sit through luncheon with us, he was called away by an associate."

"Hmm. Well, what's her surname? Where's her family from?"

"I haven't found out too much about her relations, Mother, but mainly they've lived in the city. I imagine one day her father will be given an honor for his services in business. Perhaps the Honorable Order of the Bath." *Well, I certainly think he ought to be given one. Civil service? There's no one more civil and kindly in this predatory city than Reginald Harkness.*

"Really? Charlotte?"

"Charlotte Harkness," he mumbled her last name as he clanged the poker a bit too boisterously back into its brass stand, making sure to speak while facing the freshly roaring fire. "She understands about mourning, very well. She knows… she knows I loved my sister and that this is torture to me. Yet, she's content to simply have a quiet meal with her father and me, then to stroll down to the sweet shop… Do you know, Mother, her favorite sweets are clove rocks."

The first genuine smile he'd seen in days crossed his mother's weary, woebegone face. "Imagine that. Well, of course, I shall have to meet her. I imagine her father has asked some questions about that, but I'm sure you've put him off for now?"

"Yes, yes… He's quite protective of Charlotte but she's—" Headstrong was the proper word, but his mother wouldn't like it. He thought perhaps Mr. Harkness didn't like it, either, but the fellow was likely used to it. "She's special."

The fancy work disappeared again, quickly as it had come out. His mother stole over to him, voice soft. "I'm glad, dear. Have you known her long?"

How long had he been in this nightmare? Less than a week, but this week seemed determined never to end. "It feels like forever." James sighed.

"Now I see why you're not quite so keen to leave London."

No, she didn't see at all. "I hope to see Charlotte again before I come up to Aunt Eleanor's." That was the truth.

"You're a good boy, James. All I have left." Her voice was tremulous.

He wrapped his arms around her suddenly shaking shoulders. "Oh, Mama. Of course."

****

"Mr. James? You're not going, are you?"

James surprised the housemaid as she struggled down the stairs with a trunk. She looked stunned and ill-at-ease to see him up so early.

"Going? Not yet. I'm seeing Mother off on the train."

"Very good, sir."

"Let me help you with your trunk." James bent before she could protest and picked up the small, battered trunk that she had been struggling with.

"Madame wants all the luggage to the front of the house. I'm to ride with her." Sadie seemed terrified by such a prospect.

James took a slight comfort in the fact that Sadie's near-perpetual look of fear wasn't solely caused by him. He took the girl's case to the front doors easily. It was scarcely bigger than one of the pillows at the head of his bed. His mother's case by comparison... Or Vinnie's. They would need a team of porters at the station. "You don't have much in here for a month."

"Well... I haven't ever taken the train before, sir. I've never stayed at a country house." Sadie's terrified look intensified. "Your mother might want some fancy hairstyle for Christmas. What if I can't do it?"

James lowered his voice. "My cousin, Alice, always looks like she stepped out of one of those women's fashion plates. Her maid must know *something*."

"That's just it! A real lady's maid will know I'm not a proper one. Oh, I wish I'd had more time."

"Before your debut?"

Sadie looked at him blankly. "My day of what, sir?"

"Before your big entrance into society?"

"Yes. Oh! We shouldn't be talking. That's not proper, either."

"It's perfectly proper. You are asking your employer questions, and he is giving you advice. Admittedly, I don't know much about dresses and hairstyles, but you've been helping Vinnie—" He paused, tried again. "You helped Vinnie, and she was more demanding and fashion-conscious than my mother is, not to mention a lot more helpless. You'll watch and learn. You'll do fine."

"Thank you, Mr. James." Sadie's voice dropped, as well as her eyes. "If I could have stayed awake that night... I'd have stopped her."

"I think those same thoughts. If I'd have been home, I'd have stopped her. I never knew my little sister had gotten so sneaky, leaving the house unnoticed. Lot of good it did her." His hands rand distractedly through his hair, undoing the time he'd spent in making himself look presentable. His bangs immediately flopped forward again.

The pale maid tugged anxiously on her long black dress, which trailed over the tips of her worn shoes.

James imagined part of the girl's worry was caused by the fact that not only was she a stranger to riding on trains, but that she was also unfamiliar with country house parties and playing the part of a "proper lady's maid." It would be easier if she looked the part. "Can you sew?" James asked suddenly.

"Yes, Mr. James. By hand. I don't know how to use those new sewing machines, but Cook thinks Madame will get one eventually. I suppose I'll have to learn."

"They come with manuals, I'm sure." James met her eyes. "Ah. Well, Cook and I will read them out to you. I was thinking, if you sew, I'm sure my aunt will have some fabric around the place. It's a big old estate and it's a few miles from the village. You could…" He gestured vaguely at the girl in front of him. "Smarten up some of those things you've got in your case. Maybe even make something new. Here, we've got plenty of time before the cab comes. I'll write a letter to Alice, telling her to give you a few minutes in Aunt Eleanor's stores."

"That's too kind."

"Oh, nonsense." James moved from the front door, down to the parlor. His mother must have some paper and ink in there, somewhere. They used to play charades, after all, acting out the words assigned, usually by

Lavinia, scribbled on bits of paper. He began to rummage in the little side table where the cribbage board and chess set sat.

"Mr. James?" Sadie's voice was a rustle behind him.

"Yes?" he replied, trying not to jump.

"I think your sister, not to speak ill of Miss Lavinia, God rest her soul, sir, was worried about something. She'd been giving me letters to post. It only just occurred to me lately that she wasn't sending them out with the regular post that your mother sent. Why would she do that?"

James' heart, which had felt lighter as he did a kindness for the young domestic, began to hammer. "Because she didn't want my mother to see them?"

"And she knew I couldn't read." Sadie blinked rapidly. "I'm so sorry, Mr. James. Please don't tell Madame!" She put both hands to her mouth, eyes wide above them.

"Shhh, shh, you weren't to know. I wouldn't have found it odd, either. Lavinia was always running late for things, wasn't she? I would've assumed she'd missed the morning post." He spoke soothingly, but inside he was agitated. Was she writing to the man she met? Was she writing to a killer? Wouldn't she have known the danger? Questions swarmed and the ink blurred as he scrawled an untidy note to Alice.

"M-maybe she worried so much she... she went walking by the river."

James' head turned sharply as he blinked away the moisture that clouded his vision. "Walking by the river?" he asked sharply.

"An accident in the Thames, I—I heard Madame

say." The girl began to back away. "I'm sorry, sir, I shouldn't have interrupted your writing. I don't need the note. I don't know what made me forget my place, Mr. James."

"I can see you're a bright one, Sadie. Of course, you would hear Mother say that. It's just that the way you said it gave me pause. You don't think she 'walked by the river,' do you?"

"It's what Madame said." Sadie seemed to shrink, almost out of the room now, voice so faint he could hardly catch it.

"My mother says an awful lot of things. Servants hear an awful lot of things." He strode over to her with quick, angry steps.

Sadie flinched, as if expecting him to shout or strike her. He didn't, instead pressing a note into her hand. "There," he said in a soothing voice, pushing his anger at his mother away. "Give that to my cousin Alice."

"I couldn't approach a lady like that, sir!"

"Well, pass it to her maid or the housekeeper. It's addressed to Alice, personally, so there should be no trouble about getting it to her. And if anyone loves a good lark and a fancy frock, it's Alice."

"Thank you, Mr. James." Sadie nodded, shoulders relaxing. She bit her lip.

"If you hear anything you think I should know, please tell me. It will be our secret, and Mother need not know of it. I will make sure that you don't lose your place, and I promise you... no one here will ever hurt you." James bowed to her, as he had bowed to Charlotte.

Sadie flushed and fled.

Dear me. I'm terrible at this. I can't talk to women.

Well, I can talk to Miss Harkness—Charlotte, when

we're alone, she said. I can talk to patients of the female persuasion, but that's quite different. Mother... Can I talk to her? Somewhat. I mainly listen *to her. She has this mystical ability to go conveniently deaf when she doesn't like what I say.* He let out a sigh. Mother would likely have his head, or at least his inheritance, if she found out he'd been writing notes advocating for the housemaid to be given run of Aunt Eleanor and Alice's fabric stores.

Another sigh. Very likely anything she'd found out about his behavior in the last week would give her pause.

He let himself be lost in gloomy thoughts about how December had arrived that morning, one of the most joyous times of the year, when all of London was soon to celebrate Christ's birth, yet he was consumed with thoughts of death and loneliness.

James was so mired in these sad reflections that he didn't hear Sadie's return until she spoke at his elbow, making him start violently.

The girl skittered away, mumbling an apology.

"No, no, Sadie." He tried to laugh. "I was just lost in my own gloomy thoughts, that's all. Is Mother awake? Shall I help with her trunks?"

"No, sir, Madame's not awakened yet. Anyway, she said to let the coachmen attend to the luggage. It's not seemly for a gentleman like you."

"My mother is terribly old-fashioned." He spoke with a snicker. If she'd seen just how ungentlemanly he'd been lately…. Perhaps they ought to hire a housekeeper or a butler again. It occurred to James that his mother had let vacancies go unfilled since his father passed. It seemed like she herself was rather empty, slowly filling herself up with pills and potions.

"I—I came to give you this, sir."

James frowned as Sadie held out a small silken bag, complete with a stiffly arched handle and a dainty silver clasp. "Thank you, Sadie, but I'd rather stick to my old bit of calfskin."

The girl managed to hold a smile to her lips for a few seconds before the look of perpetual unease came back. "It's not mine, nor yours, Mr. James. When the police came—" She swallowed hard, looking over her shoulder before finding his eyes again. "They gave this to Madame, that and a hat. Madame told me to burn them all."

James' heart thudded in his chest again. "You didn't?"

"Well, I burnt the rest, but this… Well, it's brand new! It's beautiful, real silk."

"Yes, yes, it is." He nodded as though he knew or gave a tuppence for it. It was Lavinia's, and it had been with her on the night she died. "You want me to take this?" His hand slowly extended, trembling.

Sadie hesitated. "I thought I might have it, but I think… I think you should. I could never use it, not while I'm in service here, anyway." She thrust it forward into his hand.

"Was it wet?"

"Pardon?"

"When the police came and you took it from Mother, was it wet at all? Even a little damp?"

"No! Not at all. Had a funny smell, though, but it's been airing out."

"What kind of smell?"

Sadie blushed. "Reminded me of when the waters don't agree with people."

Sewage, waste. Death, blood? Funny how to the layman, so many smells were simply unpleasant, but to a physician they were specific. He couldn't detect anything now. "Listen, Sadie, I'd rather keep this our secret."

"Oh, yes, sir." She nodded eagerly.

"But I doubt I'll need this for very long, and it would make Miss Vinnie happy if you were to have it. When you leave this house, if ever you do, I'll entrust it back to you."

Sadie curtsied, cheeks pink again. "Thank you, Mr. James."

"Now, you'd best go have a proper breakfast. The train ride takes most of the day. See that Cook packs a hamper for both of you."

"Very good, sir." She exited, calmer than James had seen her in days.

"Very good, indeed." James collapsed on the nearest chair, but only for a moment. He tucked the reticule under his jacket and slipped back to his room.

****

James locked the door behind him, feeling as though his body and his brain were no longer connected. Every step seemed to be taken on a marsh, uneven and wobbling. His head was floating above him while his throat was tight.

Don't be silly. Nothing's going to spring out at you.

They used this to find her address. There has to be some paper or other in here.

Mother most likely ordered them burnt.

Yes. She did, knowing the papers were in here, she ordered the entire bag burnt.

Yet, the bag is here. Not burnt.

208

He put the small bag with its flat bottom and ruched sides on the polished wood of his desk. He sat down slowly, gingerly in his chair, as if the weight in his chest would communicate itself to the wood and he'd soon end up sitting in a pile of elegant kindling.

Breathe, you fool. Fainting won't yield any information!

Hands still shaking like a man with the delirium tremens, his fingers found the little clasp and fumbled it. The bag tipped forward, delicate stitches on the sides popping as he pried it open too hastily, all his delicate surgical skill abandoning him. The contents spilled out.

Handkerchief.

A few coins.

A silver comb.

Elegantly printed calling cards, stiff pink card with her name and address in gilt-script, a little blue bird adorning each one. He smiled for a moment, turning one over in his hands. Something tucked in the recesses of the bag caught his eye.

Paper, folded and creased unevenly. As if taken and hidden in a hurry? James wondered as he plucked it loose from the fabric where it was nestled.

My Dearest Girl,

I got your letter, and I'm sure I can get away Sunday evening. I shall call for you at nine. The cab will be at the corner of your street, just like the last time. I wish you had explained yourself better in your last letter, but I expect that you're being coy.

Love, Jack

"Love… Jack. Jack." He mouthed the words, then let them pass his lips aloud, stunned. "Jack?"

Numb and unable to move for a moment, he simply

sat.

Charlotte was right.

How would she have known?

Science warred with superstition. She could have seen the letter—only, no, Sadie said the police brought it to the house when they came. He assumed she meant the first time and even if she had not, the police hadn't brought the bag along with Lavinia's body to Harkness and Sons.

Sunday night—he left the college on Monday morning, urgently summoned by his mother, urgently awakened by the dean.

The man who wrote this must have been her killer. There was no other likely explanation and it matched what Charlotte said.

Could she have known the man somehow, heard him boasting about the rich young lady he was after?

That was unlikely. He imagined that Lavinia wouldn't have associates traveling in the same social circles as Charlotte. He looked at the handwriting. It was in the precise, masculine, public school hand that looked similar to his own. A well-educated young man whose family could afford to send him to one of the finest schools in England, to secure his brilliant future and career.

Well, that capped it, didn't it? Charlotte was unlikely to have known the perpetrator. Young, handsome, wealthy surgeons weren't typically in the company of undertakers' daughters.

Present company excluded, he thought ruefully.

Logic failed him.

Logic could go hang. All that mattered was— Charlotte was right. Charlotte wouldn't coldly, callously toy with someone in their grief. She was too sincere. Furthermore, she was too clever. He could see that in only a few encounters. If Charlotte had lied about her knowledge, she'd be found out and he wouldn't show any mercy because of her sex. If she knew something through illicit means, she would never have been the one to approach him, to help him.

No, if Charlotte knew the name of Lavinia's killer, he was beginning to believe it was because Lavinia communicated it to her in some fashion, from beyond the grave. At the moment, James didn't care if that sounded ludicrous. This whole thing was absurd. Her murder was a sin, a folly, a tragedy. Why should the manner in which he found the name of her killer be anything else?

Death was no respecter of persons.

Nor did it have any sense of decorum.

The pealing of a bell knocked James sharply from his stupor. He shoved everything back in the bag and hid it in the bottom drawer of his desk. Mother was awake and summoning Sadie to attend to her.

He must keep calm and collected until they were safely away, off to the countryside.

Once they left the house, he'd follow, bound not for a pastoral retreat but for the darker heart of the city. He'd journey to see Charlotte Harkness, to ask her to do more than simply share information.

James caught sight of himself in the glass as he rose to rejoin the household. A near week of this torment had taken anything fresh and boyish from his features. He saw a haggard man with burning eyes, the proverbial "man possessed."

At this moment, he felt confident that the darkness in his gaze would send any woman running. Not

Charlotte. She'd shown him proof that Lavinia's death was murder.

"Now, will you help me catch him?" he whispered to his reflection, though all he could picture was the solemn face and knowing eyes of the undertaker's daughter.

Part Three:

Darkly Devoted

Chapter Twelve

Charlotte kissed her father's cheek. Saturday was such a busy day in their line of work.

"Dearest, are we still having tea with Mr. Parson and his sons? Or Peter Danvers? Or... perhaps you'd like to see if Dr. Everly wants to come 'round?" Mr. Harkness added the last option cautiously, unsure how it would be received.

"Oh, Father. I never did send out the invitations. Perhaps you could ask Mr. Bartlesby and the vicar?"

"I could, but they're hardly of an age to—"

"Father!" Charlotte actually managed a genuine smile. "Now, no more matchmaking from you. I'll make up my mind about a mid-week luncheon if Mr. Parson can spare any of his sons."

"See that you do. I have to meet Mr. Parson and the younger Messrs. Parson en masse at the Christmas pantomime planning meeting."

"Oh, no. You simply can't let the elder Mr. Parson be the Old Dame again. Don't you remember last year? He blew snuff into the pianist's face just as he started to sing along. The poor fellow fell into the sacramental wine under the stage. The vicar was ever so put out."

"Perhaps he'd be more amenable to one of his sons taking over the role over a nice bit of your plum pudding?"

"That reminds me, I must get the brandy for that."

"*I* will get the brandy for that." Mr. Harkness pursed his lips in mock severity.

"Very well." Charlotte hedged around her topic, keeping her hands busy and relieved that her father was also similarly engaged as he prepared to go out for the better portion of the day. "How's Guinevere?"

"Sound, very sound."

"You know, one day Mr. Miggins might not be able to set her right so quickly. Or she might go properly lame. You know how the roads get in the winter, especially now that you're going to be going to Kensley Green more often."

Mr. Harkness looked thoughtful as he buttoned up his long black tailcoat. "Well, Bartlesby has Samson."

"I know, Father, but you still need two horses or more if the burial is out at Kensley Green and you want to provide a coach for the family of the dearly departed. You're such good friends with the manager at the livery. Would they let us hire one for the day?"

"A horse?"

"Yes! A black one, one hopes."

"Hm. Whenever you speak about the business, I've learned it's wise to listen. It would do to find out, I suppose. It would be as well to have a plan in place. I'll have to stop in there on Monday."

"I could go today," Charlotte offered, her voice carefully devoid of eagerness.

"A woman, go to the livery alone? Saturday's a very busy day!"

"For every merchant, Father."

He hesitated. "I suppose you might, given that you're there on an errand for me. Here, I'll jot a note to Mr. Harris for you."

Charlotte rolled her eyes when her father wasn't looking. How silly that the woman who'd thought of the sensible idea couldn't make the inquiry herself. She went to the shops alone. That was a mercy, she supposed. She wondered if many a "high born" lady was forbidden from doing that. Yet, they probably sent their maids, who were women, likely to go alone. Did they have a fleet of errand boys stashed someplace? Maybe they never shopped. Was everything delivered? She could ask Dr. Everly—if he ever paid a call again.

Mr. Harkness passed her the note and put on his hat. "I'll be home late. It's two in a row, I'm afraid, one in Kensley Green and one right at St. Elizabeth's."

Charlotte nodded and ran after him as he went out the back door. "Sandwiches," she called, handing him a few hearty cuts of ham and cheddar on thick slices of bread, all wrapped in a clean kitchen towel.

"You're an angel. Thank you, dearest." Mr. Harkness put the sandwiches on the coach seat and climbed up behind Guinevere. A tip of his hat and he was off to collect the first of the day's dearly departed.

****

James did not see his mother to the station, though he saw her off from the front steps of their large home in Westminster. With all of her trunks and hat boxes, not to mention Sadie, the maid, there wasn't really room for him.

What a brilliant stroke of luck.

As soon as they turned the corner, he hurried back inside and collected his doctor's bag of stiff, polished leather, containing his physician's instruments and now including a tightly rolled up scarf, Lavinia's reticule, and its contents. James hesitated, then walked over to the

217

trunk he'd hastily packed when his mother had summoned him home on Monday morning. He hadn't even opened it yet. Now, he undid the brass latches and sifted through the chaos of clothing, books, and papers until his fingers closed around the hard leather case, slightly larger than a gentleman's shaving case. A gentle tug revealed its shining, sharp contents, silver gleaming in the dull light of his room.

He decided to pack his surgical instruments. Lavinia's murderer certainly had.

****

Charlotte hadn't meant to delay so long in setting out. It was after noon when she finally had the washing and sewing done. That was not to mention sweeping out the sawdust in the garden shed and trying to coax the potted flowers in the upstairs sitting room to stay alive by carrying them to a sunnier location. At last, she locked the front door and put the key in her pocket, along with the money for flowers and the note for Mr. Harris.

"You were right, Miss Harkness. His name was Jack."

Charlotte, still facing the door, swallowed hard, smothering the gasp instinctively rising. With a careful smile, she turned to greet the man who addressed her. "Good afternoon, Dr. Everly."

The man on the pavement tipped his hat, backlit by the timid December sunlight that managed to make its way to street level. Despite the courteousness of his manner, he did not return her smile. He fumbled inside his bag for a moment before holding out a folded piece of paper.

Charlotte closed the distance between them until she was an arm's length apart and able to grasp the missive.

Her eyes were drawn immediately to the words, "Love, Jack." "Jack!" she murmured. She looked up to meet his knowing eyes—and found only a black veil over her own.

"Make it better! Well, I'm still ill. Fix it!"

"Lavinia, there's nothing that we've done which could—

"Prove it."

"You ignorant girl. The proof is in your own body. If you had any sort of knowledge or experience—"

"As if a lady would. Mother was right about you."

The memory became incoherent, reduced to a jumble of screaming, hissing, and ranting, a torrent of heated language that played at high speed, chasing Charlotte down until she was panting as if she'd been running for hours.

"Come and sit?" Dr. Everly had her by the elbow as she stood stock-still.

"I... I see you found some proof," Charlotte wheezed through suddenly parched lips, breathing returning to normal with an effort. She shrugged his hand off gently.

"Yes. Odd as it sounds, I believe I'm looking at much more." His eyes locked on hers.

"What do you mean?" She backed away, almost retreating to the steps of Harkness and Sons.

"I mean that I believe you, that Lavinia showed you his name, told you his name."

Charlotte's hand went to the key under her cloak. She would not be dragged away. She was *not* insane.

She was simply... blessed or cursed? She'd sort it out later.

Dr. Everly followed her, still a respectable distance

apart, but his eyes entreating now. "Please, it's not enough to know his name. I must find him. I must... I must put this right. Will you help me? Please, Miss Harkness." He stood before her, pleading done, waiting for her to answer.

"You... Do you think me mad?"

"No. Well, yes, inasmuch that all this *world* is fallen, sinful, and mad. Justice must be one of the few redeeming qualities man has left—if one could see it done."

"I will help you all I can."

"I don't know where to start. I have some ideas."

"So have I. Come along to the Lion and Eagle."

"What are we doing? Is that a pub?"

"We're going to see a man about a horse."

****

"I've no idea how I'm going to explain this to your father," James murmured.

"What is to explain? You are clearly besotted, so much so that when you heard I was to run an errand alone, you thought it safer for a lady to have a gentleman escort her. Father will like that," Charlotte answered quickly, as if she'd thought it all out.

She had, in the few moments they'd been walking.

"How far is this place?"

"Not far."

"Do you walk everywhere? Do you take cabs?"

"No, heavens! Why would I need to?"

James gave a helpless shrug. "Lavinia and Mother always made use of our own coach or a cab in the city."

"My father's coach is for a different sort of passenger." She didn't quite catch the smirk before it danced across her lips.

God help them both, they laughed.

"You have quite a dark wit about you, Miss Harkness."

"You laughed. You must as well."

"Surgeons are quite proficient at laughing instead of crying. There would be a great many more drunkards among our number if we were not."

"The same amongst my father and our—his—associates," Charlotte stumbled over the words. She considered herself as much a part of the business as any son could claim to be, but Dr. Everly was already turning quite a few blind eyes.

"Speaking of the nature of your business—what is it that we are doing?"

Charlotte kept her voice carefully modulated, loud enough for him to hear over the shouts of the stall-dwellers, low enough not to attract attention from idly curious ears. "Your sister took a coach ride from your home to somewhere in Whitechapel, presumably one of the very worst areas the city has to offer. Most of the coaches and hackney cabs who finish up near Whitechapel late at night are stabled at the Lion and Eagle Livery. I shall inquire about the cost to hire a horse for the day, particularly one that can easily do the distance between Westminster and Whitechapel, even in the dark."

****

By George, she was brilliant. James stopped for a full second, goggling at her, before trotting to match her stride. "Won't they think that's odd, you asking such a thing?"

"No. Kensley Green is about an equal distance, perhaps a touch farther." Charlotte blushed as she caught his awestruck, admiring look. "It's only common sense."

Here was the tricky bit. James coughed a few times, partially because he'd just caught a whiff of some overripe eels and partially because he couldn't quite believe what he was going to say. "You deal with *uncommon* senses. A sixth sense, some might say?"

Charlotte's spine stiffened. "Yes, some might say," she responded shortly.

"Does she truly speak to you? Tell you things?" James heard the desperation in his voice, saw the desperation in his hand, suddenly pulling on her elbow, wanting to watch her face as she answered him.

"Some souls do speak to me. Lavinia does not, Dr. Everly. Instead, she lets me *overhear* her last memories, perhaps more than just the last. I hear the souls, I do not see them, nor see what they saw. If I did, our task would be so much easier, as I should know the face of her attacker."

James knew that a man should not lean upon a woman. It wasn't his fault that her words and the revelations they presented knocked his knees from under him. "You hear her... you hear it happen?" he asked weakly, all color draining from him.

****

Charlotte hesitated. All in black, his face so pale, he looked young, and noble, and weak, some knight without his armor, some hero that lay dying on the battlefield. It would be a mercy not to tell him.

Do lies ever do anyone a kindness, she pondered, steadying him. "I do. I hear him. Them. They argued as if they knew one another well. At least, I presume your sister would not speak so freely unless she had some long acquaintance with a man." Charlotte concluded her tale with a blush.

"A man with years of acquaintance?" James shook his head. "And a surgeon? No, it cannot be! There are no men in our circle who are surgeons."

"Well, you're not a fully qualified surgeon yet, but you knew enough to place the marks upon her as made by a surgeon's hand. What about someone in training? Like you?"

James bristled.

Ignoring the sudden angry flash in his eyes, Charlotte warmed to her topic. "A young man is surely more probable? A young man might be brash enough to escort her alone to such a place. Surely, if the suitor was older and more established, he would court her properly." Charlotte concluded in a rush. She felt very presumptuous talking about such things. She'd never been courted before and didn't spend much time talking to girls who had. Even this outing with Dr. Everly was merely a convenient sham.

"Court her?" James paused in the act of settling his hat back on his head.

They pushed through a particularly crowded corner, shoulders brushing together, squeezing through the throng. When they made their way to a clearing, Dr. Everly remained intimately close by her side, his hand in his breast pocket. As she watched his sinewy fingers fumble, he drew out a folded note and held it out to her.

My Dearest Girl,

I got your letter and I'm sure I can get away Sunday evening. I shall call for you at nine. The cab will be at the corner of your street, just like the last time. I wish you had explained yourself better in your last letter, but I expect that you're being coy.

Love, Jack

"You see?" Charlotte hissed. "Dearest girl? Last time? Being coy? Those are words of a man at ease with her, surely?"

"She snuck out before."

"Is nine so terribly late for wealthy persons? I thought there were revels and balls until all hours?" Charlotte asked before considering it was very ill-bred to bring up a person's financial status, even if it was no secret.

James smiled wanly. "Perhaps during the Season, or perhaps for other members of the *ton* society. Not for a family in mourning and not for a respectable widow and her daughter."

"What about you?" *What about him? You don't need to know anything personal about Dr. Everly.*

Everly didn't seem to mind divulging his habits. "For many of the lads at school, nine is the hour of escape. The Halls of Residence have rules about coming and going. You may certainly never bring a lady to visit you inside the dormitories, even one's sister or mother. No woman sets foot inside except the charwomen. If you're caught in such an act, you'll be expelled immediately. That's not to say many a man doesn't sneak out after we're supposed to have retired to our chambers."

The Lion and Eagle was still a few streets off. Charlotte hesitated before asking, "Are there many surgical colleges in London?"

"No, not many."

"Would it be likely that Lavinia knew this man through you? Not that you introduced them, but by the gentleman claiming to be an associate of yours? Perhaps meeting Lavinia during the Season last year, developing a friendship over time—though now one can see that the terms *gentleman* and *friendship* are sorely misused," Charlotte concluded with a scolding cluck of her tongue.

"I suppose it is possible. But... but why, Miss Harkness?" James' tone was desperate. Tears stole a march upon his eyes. "She had no money of her own, no property yet, whatever was to be hers would only have been released upon her marriage. She was not by nature a mean-spirited girl, though certainly foolish and willful at times. Why should any man use her so?"

Charlotte hesitated. "I don't know, James." His Christian name passed her lips before she could halt it, her gloved hand on his arm, consoling. "This man... he has poison in his soul. To claim to care for her and then to attack her... his voice rings with madness, but it slips, suddenly calm, then quite deranged, so fast I cannot make out the words. I suppose that means Lavinia could not, either, or perhaps her senses were too overcome with terror."

"If you heard his voice, would you know it?" James demanded suddenly.

Charlotte paused, uncertain.

"You ignorant girl. The proof is in your own body. If you had any sort of knowledge or experience—"

"As if a lady would." A sharp slapping sound. *"Mother was right about you."*

"Miss Everly? Charlotte!" It was James' turn to seize her as she was struck motionless. He steered her swiftly out of the path of a loaded wagon.

"I think I would know the voice. She will let me hear him." Charlotte nodded, shakily freeing herself once again and looking back at the wagon rattling past on uneven pavement. She would have been flattened, injured if not killed outright. "Thank you, Dr. Everly."

Another few yards in silence, the silence between them, but not around them.

"Do you come over funny like that whenever you are privy to such otherworldly speech?" Dr. Everly asked carefully.

Charlotte shook her head. "Absolutely not! Most souls who desire conversation are simply unsure about what has happened to them, and they are—they are taking stock of events before they depart this mortal coil. Lavinia is far different than anything I've ever known or experienced. When she allows me to overhear her memories, I'm frozen in terror or overwhelmed. A river washes over me, Dr. Everly, and I am pulled down in the flood. Therefore, I must thank you for the gallant rescue of a few moments ago. Father would never forgive himself for allowing me to make a business inquiry for him had I been killed going about it. The poor man already blames his profession for my peculiarity."

"Ah. He knows?"

"Yes. He does."

The conversation died, snipped off.

****

James was growing adroit at repairing wounds and saving lives. He hoped he could restore his conversation with Miss Harkness so easily. "My manners are terrible, once again. It was my pleasure to provide timely assistance. I'm so sorry you're made to endure such painful recollections. At the same time, I'm ever so grateful."

They paused now, facing one another as they drew abreast of the livery. The smell of horses, leather, and manure mingled with some truly excellent smells, roasting meats and ale. A chophouse for cabmen and the like was established across the way from the Lion and Eagle.

It was not a romantic setting. Nor was his interest in Charlotte Harkness in the least bit romantic. Yet, as he stood there, his heart was pounding in an unfamiliar way. He'd never thought that being darkly witty was an attractive thing in a woman before, but Charlotte's rather macabre humor had come as a welcome relief, and her sharp conversation gave his weary brain new strength.

James watched her drawn face slowly bloom into a tentative smile, her dark lashes modestly dwarfing the bright blue of her eyes as she nodded in acceptance of his thanks. This was a woman of courage and strength—in a very feminine package. Women were said to be weak and fair, in need of protecting, or broad and manly, unsuitable for a gentleman.

Charlotte Harkness seemed admirably suited.

****

"I appreciate your words," Charlotte finally managed to reply to his kind compliment. It was the first time anyone had ever seemed grateful for her abilities or even spoke of them without pity or fear. Emotion clogged her throat. All her life, she had known there was no better man in England than her father, but right now, with his earnestness and determination, his genuine gratitude, and simple acceptance of her odd powers, Dr. Everly was quickly rising to take second place.

"This is the place, Miss Harkness. Shall I accompany you inside?"

"Thank you, Dr. Everly. I say, have you a coach of your own?"

"We do, yes, but no longer a coachman and groom. Nor horses. They were Father's fancy, not Mother's."

"Hm. I believe you could help me with my inquiries." Charlotte looked around. No privacy anywhere. No help for it.

Dr. Everly swallowed a shout as she pulled him into the dark recesses of the wheelwright attached to the livery. "Miss Harkness! A word in my ear would suffice."

"That's exactly what I want, a word in your ear, where no one else can overhear us. Now. A ruse. You're in need of a horse for your coach. And your sister rather liked the look of the one that picked her up the other night…."

****

"What can I do for you, sir?" Mr. Harris greeted James as he stood before him. Charlotte stood behind him, the picture of patient waiting. He watched the stable manager cast an eye over both of them, perhaps wondering if they were a couple.

"Hello. Ah. Yes. A few days ago, no, just over a week ago," James stammered the beginnings of his act. This was Charlotte's idea. He was a terrible actor. He'd only ever managed to deliver one dramatic reading properly and he'd been so relieved to simply be in the chorus in his school's production of *The Light Brigade*. Behind him, Miss Harkness coughed discreetly. "The last Sunday in November, I believe one of your coachmen picked up my sister and her friend in Westminster, at the corner of Wedgwood Crescent and Garden Road? It would have been about nine in the evening." James smiled, trying to appear at ease.

Mr. Harris, a man with an elegantly curled mustache

and a short, round face with apple cheeks, was not at ease. He drew back, eyes narrowing, clearly expecting a complaint. "I see, sir. And what makes you think the coach was from our fine establishment? There are plenty of coaches and the like in Westminster."

"Ah, well, you see, the coach ended up here for the night. My sister was staying in Whitechapel for the evening. It would have dropped her off around..." Oh, blast it. What street name had Miss Harkness said to use? He gave her a desperate look over his shoulder.

Charlotte seemed to naturally adapt to any situation, quite the opposite of him. She stepped forward. "I believe you mentioned it was one of the Yards, Dr. Everly. Goulston, Darby, or perhaps the ones off Booth Street?"

Mr. Harris blinked in surprised recognition. "Heavens above, is that Reginald Harkness' little lass, all grown up?"

"Yes, Mr. Harris. When Dr. Everly is finished with his inquiry, I'd like to ask you about the cost of hiring a horse for the day, just in case Guinevere is ever lame."

"Of course. Right then, sir. Why do you—"

"My sister took quite a liking to the horse. Or horses. She's not terribly practical or specific, my sister, but as we've no horse, nor driver, for the family carriage, I did think of inquiring about the animal. Naturally, it wouldn't be for sale, but I would like to see the animal and talk to the driver, if possible. Perhaps he can advise me on what to look for in a suitable animal. I'd like to get one as close as possible to the one she took a fancy to, but I've never spent much time with horses, you see."

Charlotte held her breath as he finished out his far-fetched tale.

"Do you drive often, sir?"

"No! My mother and sister live a very quiet life at the moment." It was technically true. The dead didn't travel.

Although Lavinia's spirit was most assuredly *unquiet*.

"I do have a few older nags that could do with a new home. Not quite up to the pace of a full day and then some in bustling London. I'll see if we can't find one that'd please your sister. Let's see which horse she was so fond of. Shouldn't be too hard to find. Not many cabs here make runs from the posher points…" Mr. Harris looked at a leather-bound ledger on the sawdust and tobacco-strewn desk, shifting on the tall three-legged stool to grab his rather bent spectacles. "None of me regulars… ah. Wait, now. We have a few drivers who will put up for the night around here if it's too late or the weather's taken a turn for the worse. Put their horses and rigs here, room above the chophouse, or maybe down in those very yards you mention, sir. Cheap places, the Houses of Common Lodging. I don't suppose your sister caught the name of the driver."

"No, I'm afraid not."

"The color of the horse?"

James turned to Charlotte.

"It was very foggy and dark that night." She quickly stepped forward. "Perhaps the gentleman in question would have mentioned the unusual circumstance of taking a lady in all her finery to such a—a common abode. She was… involved in charitable pursuits."

"Yes, indeed, that would have caused most fellows to take notice."

"Even more so because the gentleman escorting her

was also well-dressed. A medical man."

Mr. Harris smoothed a hand thoughtfully over his face, careful not to unsettle the precariously clinging spectacles on his stubby nose or to flatten the precise curl of his mustache. "Ah. Charity work. Bless your sister and her friend, sir. The poor souls down in such places are sorely in need of aid. More of the sick end up sent Mr. Harkness' way than recover. If they can even afford the price of a shroud. Most likely end up in a less respectable establishment. Now, then—Doctor, was it?"

"Dr. Everly is a physician, also training to become a surgeon," Charlotte interjected, a note of proprietary pride in her voice. "Like his sister's escort for the evening."

Mr. Harris looked at the pair thoughtfully, then threw his head back and bellowed. "Noyse!"

James jumped back, clutching his hat to his head. Noise, indeed. Even the imperturbable Miss Harkness seemed startled.

"Edwin! Noyse, where are you?"

"Coming! Blimey, Father, you'll spook the mare in box twelve. I've only just settled her." A tall, thin man appeared, hustling from down the long line of noisy stalls and loose boxes that echoed with the whinnies and grunts of horses and the shouts of stable hands, grooms, and drivers.

"Edwin, my son-in-law, takes turns swapping Sundays with me. You were on the last Sunday of November, lad. See if you can help this gentleman while I assist Mr. Harkness' daughter."

James reluctantly left Charlotte's side to follow Edwin, whose surname must be Noyse, to a large slate board with names, dates, and figures covering every square inch. The board was nailed to the wall a short way off from the desk and the front doors where patrons came in, not the large back entrance where horses entered and exited.

"H'are you, sir?" Mr. Noyse doffed his flat cloth cap, his elbow threatening to pop through the tight, pinched joints of his worsted shirt.

"I'm well, Mr. Noyse. I'm looking for a particular driver, one who would have picked up an elegantly dressed young lady and handsomely dressed gentleman from the corner of Wedgwood Crescent and Garden Road in Westminster. About nine in the evening?"

"Begging your pardon, sir, but why not look at a livery in that neck of the woods?"

"They finished up down here, in one of the worst yards in Whitechapel. A medical affair." James told himself that indeed, it had become a medical affair, a death, a surgical procedure that was a mockery to all physicians and surgeons in the land. What's more, he hoped that his hastily concocted tale would not provide him with a false lead.

"Oh. Last Sunday in November? Just on a week, sir?"

"Yes! Yes, that's it." James watched the man's face cloud and clear, a sign of recollection, perhaps?

"Medical affair? Young couple from Westminster?"

"Unusual enough to be remarked upon, I'm sure." James laughed in what he prayed was a careless manner.

"Yes, well, that's what I'm thinking. Seem to vaguely recollect Barney Gibbs mentioning that he and his pair were too tired to go back to their home stables a bit south from St. James." Edwin's long, narrow fingers scratched under the back of his cap as if trying to nudge a thought from the back of his mind to the forefront. " 'Cause first they picked up a lad right 'round Portugal Street and thought they were only headed a little ways away, off to some posh villas. Didn't recall the street names, sir, not sure he mentioned them. Anyway, he was that put out that the man then wanted to go clear down to Whitechapel, down to Goulston Yard. No cabbie likes to go down there, even in the best of circumstances, a bright sunny day, let alone a cold, wet night. He came in here, mad as a wet hen, hadn't even been given a penny over the fare for his trouble. Cheap bas— Oh, beggin' your pardon, sir. He wasn't to know them two were on a medical mission of mercy. Charity society? Probably didn't have much to spare." Edwin peered at the slate, dabbing off numbers and dates from the week past with a damp cloth. "He put Belle and Blue here for the night and took a room at the chophouse down the road. I believe he drives for Salisbury Steeds. The livery at the Black Boar?"

James nodded. He'd been nodding emphatically the entire time Mr. Noyse spoke as if he understood every word.

In reality, only a few words filtered through.

Barney Gibbs.

Portugal Street.

Posh villas.

Goulston Yard.

Salisbury Steeds.

Portugal Street. Portugal Street.

It was this last that burst from his lips. "Portugal Street!"

"You know the place, sir?"

He nodded, throat too dry to speak. He should say

he did know it, indeed.

The main lecture halls and operating theaters of the Royal College of Surgeons were located on Portugal Street.

Chapter Thirteen

"Dr. Everly, you look white as a sheet."

"I must get to Salisbury Steeds. I must find a man named Barney Gibbs." James no longer cared for appearances. He put his arm behind Charlotte's shoulders without letting their bodies touch, herding her forward as he spoke in an urgent whisper.

"Why, what have you found out?" Charlotte paid no heed for the curious eyes upon them. She bent her head close to his to catch his words, far too close for decent society.

"There's too much of a coincidence, Miss Harkness, so much so that I cannot imagine any other—" He stopped, collecting his wits, and trying to tell his partner in detection what had transpired. "Mr. Noyse does recall a very irate 'cabbie' from the date in question. He was much put out because he believed the fare he picked up, rather late into his nightly runs, I would imagine, requested two stops on his journey. First, to an area near some 'posh villas' and then to Goulston Yard." He was positively trembling with nervous excitement now, not truly coming to grips with what this information would mean.

"Posh villas?" Charlotte tilted her head.

James waved the curiosity in her tone away. "He picked up the man first, then the lady, as I can make out. But the truly damning bit of evidence—oh! Forgive me.

The truly incriminating bit, at least to my mind, is that the man was picked up near Portugal Street." He looked at her significantly. Seeing only a furrowed brow above confused eyes, he explained. "The Royal College of Surgeons was moved to Portugal Street only a few years past. The Halls of Residence are in the immediate vicinity. The murderer was a surgeon and if he was indeed picked up by the RC of S, Miss Harkness, it means that he is very likely a student or a member of the faculty." He shook her arm in his exuberance and ended up clutching her hand. "We must go at once to see this Barney Gibbs and—"

"Dr. Everly, wait. You must use caution. The fiend must surely imagine the police are investigating. If you are indiscreet, you may well be the next victim. You must be careful, for if he is at school with you—you might know him."

****

Charlotte did not withdraw her hand from his. She needed it as much as he did. The thrum of her blood was pounding like a drum in her ears, every call and shout magnified about her as excitement gripped her. She clung to his arm for support as the world spun a little too sharply.

The Lord is kind and merciful. Or we're utterly on the wrong track. Either way, Dr. Everly could be in real danger. "If the man believes you are seeking him, you may be in danger. You will have to keep your investigations secret."

"I have the perfect cover." James would not be dissuaded. "I have you."

****

"The man will be out on his rounds, I suppose,

carting people about. People will want to go shopping. Lavinia… Well, she and Mother would have enjoyed Christmas shopping and all the dresses, and hats, and things that come with Christmas events. The city is at its best right now if you ask me. Her Majesty and Prince Albert make things so festive. All of London catches the spirit." To James, a solid course of action made the world look suddenly brighter, like a glint of starlight in an oppressively moonless sky. He could see the single white candles being placed in windows, yet unlit, though the night was swiftly drawing in. Garlands of pine boughs and holly were starting to adorn some of the shop windows they passed as they made their way back to the Whitechapel High Street.

****

Charlotte shared his relief and a heady rush of success, but she was not so easily beguiled by the pretty sights at present. "If only it was all wreaths and hot chestnuts. It also means that those without money for fuel will freeze in draughty bits of wood that can barely be called a shack, the almshouses will be overflowing, cold and consumption will run riot, and Father and the vicar of St. Clementia's will pray earnestly that no one needs to be buried on Boxing Day." Charlotte's eyes saw all the beauty and festivity surrounding them. She thought of the joys of the Christmas season, the silliness of the upcoming Christmas pantomime, the blessed peace of the Virgin Birth. She also saw the girls in ragged cloaks with blue-tipped fingers selling kindling, the emaciated boys selling hot chestnuts but not daring to eat any themselves, and the shuffling, stumbling figures who came into the church just to keep warm.

Her hand left the unaccustomed warmth and

friendliness of his. *We are from two different worlds, a scarcity of miles apart.*

"I'm sorry. I know that not everyone enjoys such bounties as those in my circle."

"No, *I'm* sorry. I do see the wonder of the season. I didn't mean to sound so harsh and joyless, Dr. Everly. My 'circle' will be celebrating the festivities of the holiday, as well. I love this idea of a 'Christmas tree.' We've had one for the past few years. I believe the bigger homes have large, elaborate ones with lots of decorations," Charlotte remarked as they stepped a few more inches apart.

Silence hung between them, even as noises of the city continued to cascade.

"This could put you in just as much danger as I," James informed her suddenly, eyes pointed forward, hat low over his forehead.

"What? Me?"

"Yes! You know what I know. If this *Jack* should find out"—he spat the name as though expelling poison— "you could—" He stopped speaking abruptly.

Charlotte knew he was picturing her meeting the same fate as his sister. "James, don't."

"I said you were a cover, and that was cowardice, Miss Harkness. I must not involve you further."

"What?" Charlotte cried, utterly faithless to Auntie Molly's teachings that a woman's voice should always be soft, gentle, and well-modulated. "You can't do that! I need to know it's sorted. I can help you so much more, Dr. Everly."

Her forthright outburst sparked one of his in return. "I believe you can. For one thing, you can hear his voice, I cannot! But I would not repay your kindness to me in such a wretched fashion as to endanger you, Miss Harkness."

A well-bred and respectable lady would not argue with a man of such short and tenuous acquaintance. Nor would she do it in public. Most assuredly, she would not argue with a gentleman so obviously above her station.

A well-bred woman probably doesn't read embalming manuals and chat with the dead, either....

"Rubbish," Charlotte huffed impatiently. "I was already on my way to the livery before you turned up. I had the idea about it being a fellow that might have attended your surgical college, or at least a young surgeon." She sniffed, partially because the damp chill was making her nose run after so long out of doors and partially out of annoyance. What right had this stranger to tell her to mind her place?

My own father can barely keep me in the place deemed appropriate for a woman.

Furthermore, stranger? What happened to friend? Her heart felt hard and small, yet so heavy.

Silence stretched, then dragged, taut until it snapped. "You'll do it anyway, won't you?" Everly finally asked.

"I must. All my life, I've been given the ability to converse with those who've passed away but not yet passed *on*. Lavinia is not able to be free. I do not believe she willingly chooses to stay. Other spirits seem mildly confused, transient. Lavinia doesn't even speak to me, she... transplants me into the thoughts that bind her here. Terrifying, miserable thoughts." Charlotte gave a desperate shudder, then steeled herself. "Dr. Everly, I want Lavinia and myself to find peace and some measure of freedom. I believe that solving her murder would help us both. If you wish to assist me in such an endeavor, I should be very grateful, but—" She took a deep breath. "—if not, I shall undertake the matter myself." She thrust her chin forward in determination, something her auntie Molly had also told her was unbecoming in a woman, either making them look willful or saucy.

****

James' eyes flickered to the side, catching the iron in her tone, hidden under quite delicate features, a small, shapely nose, and beautifully shaped lips that were thin and grim at the moment. "You're quite right," he admitted with a sigh.

Charlotte nearly fell over. "I am? That is, yes. I am. Although you made a good point, too. We shall have to be very discreet."

"I'm doing a very poor job of maintaining it. Miss Harkness, will you accompany me on a walk to see the sights of Westminster… by way of a carriage procured from Salisbury Steeds?"

She grinned. "I am grateful for the invitation. Oh! Bother. Invitations."

"I beg your pardon?"

"Invitations. I'm supposed to take a few invitations to the post office."

"I'm so sorry to have detained you. May I escort you to a pillarbox, if not the post office itself? Or, if the matter is urgent, allow me to pay for the cost of a telegram," Everly offered solicitously.

"Well, the ham will go off if I don't use it up in a day or two, that's the urgency. It's more than Father and I could handle in a week of nothing but ham three meals a day!" She laughed softly, but the laugh turned mournful. "I persuaded my father that I would invite a few young men in my—our—no, *his* line of work to share a fancy tea. I've written out the invitations to the sons of two other prosperous and revered undertakers, but I've yet to send them."

"Oh!" Well. This created a layer of confusion he didn't need. James instantly felt an unfamiliar sensation in his stomach, strong enough to make itself known under the tension and grief he already endured.

Was that jealousy? A mistaken sense of propriety? Charlotte Harkness was too fine a companion and too beautiful a woman to be shared, and how dare she play like those fan-waving ninnies of the Season, dashing from ball to ball—or in this case, investigation to tea—getting all the fellows' hopes up?

Silly thought. Courting is a cover. No wonder she sounds sad. Perhaps she truly fancies one of those fortunate young men. Perhaps she has to invite the sons of both lest some rivalry or bad blood spring up between Mr. Harkness and his brethren. Dear me, I suppose even death becomes political. Here I am, taking her away from the man she truly loves and botching Mr. Harkness' business into the bargain.

"Miss Harkness," James began gently, "I will gladly withdraw my suit, fictitious though it may be, in order to let you pursue your heart's desire." Charlotte looked at him with confusion, so he coughed and clarified, "The young man you wish to have tea with? I could hear the sadness in your voice. We will find a way to work together that doesn't blight your courtship with—"

Charlotte cut him off with a harsh laugh, quickly turning apologetic. "Oh, I'm so sorry, Dr. Everly." She dared extend her fingertips briefly, barely brushing his elbow. "That was a lovely, kind thought, but it is sorely incorrect. My heart's desire is to join my father in his business, even if it is only managing the affairs of the sewing and flowers, assisting with clients and the bereaved, things I already do. I wish to carry on my family's work, providing a respectful service to those called from this world, and to those they leave behind. The sadness in my voice is not for blighted courting, but rather for forcing it." Her cheeks flushed. "I know I shouldn't talk about such things, but I would not have you break off our partnership with kind but misguided intentions. My father knows of my peculiarity. He deems me harmless but knows no husband ever will. I cannot expect to marry for love and keep one foot in the business and both feet from the madhouse. I must make a pretense of courting and love of an undertaker's son to appease him and maintain the balance."

Relief didn't flood him, but it trickled through, warming him. *She's not in love with anyone else. Nor is she in love with me, naturally, but… Dash it, I can sort those thoughts out later.* "Ah. Still, if you wish me to make myself scarce?"

"I do not."

"Did you say you wish to join the business? Undertaking?"

"Yes," she replied, her chin raised in defiance again.

"Surely that's unseemly for a woman? Amongst other things, one would assume fifty percent of your clientele would be—well—male."

"And are fifty percent of your patients not female?"

"That's different."

"How? I should say mine are far safer. A dead man has never taken a liberty."

It was his turn to release a short bray of laughter. "I

should say you're quite right!"

"Besides, my father could help with any 'delicate' needs, or one would presume my future husband would attend to those matters."

They walked in thoughtful silence, seemingly unaware the other had stopped talking or feeling the need to fill it until James remarked, "There is a college for women, now."

"Yes. But they do not offer a degree in my chosen field."

"Wouldn't you be content to work in another?"

"No."

Her brief answer made him hide a smile. "Surely, if you marry and have children one day—"

"I do not wish to deprive my father of the running of his business, I only want to be allowed to continue assisting him in it. My mother helped him. I do not know if this is done in your circle, Dr. Everly, but very often tradespeople run things as a family affair. To be sure, the women must take more time away from the business to rear their children, but it's not long before the children help in some fashion or are off at school, if school can be afforded. Mr. Miggins, the ironmonger and smith, does all the heavy work, but his wife makes the bookings, and their two boys are in the family trade as well."

"But surely so funereal an atmosphere is not suitable for a child?"

Charlotte fixed him with a gimlet stare as they approached Harkness and Sons. "I wasn't left to crawl among the corpses, Dr. Everly, but was raised to respect human life and show compassion for those who mourn, to provide tea and comfort for the grieving, find flowers to brighten the darkness of death, and to sew a shroud for a final garment. I see that even the most foul are treated with reverence, for the soul is much more valuable than the shell. Perhaps that's why I can hear them. They know they will be given a chance."

"Such a speech," James murmured after a moment. His companion's color was high, her eyes ablaze. Clearly, she put her whole heart into everything she said, everything she cared for.

He had that startling thought that kissing Charlotte Harkness would be a splendid thing to do.

"I'm sorry," Charlotte mumbled suddenly, misinterpreting his unblinking gaze. "I must have seemed terribly ill-bred, ranting like that."

"Please don't apologize... for anything." James stepped closer to her as they came to a gradual halt in front of her father's establishment. "If you'll pardon my boldness, Miss Harkness, courting would be a far less terrifying prospect if a man could be sure to find someone so heart-whole as you, as plain spoken as you."

"Plain speaking is not such an admirable quality in a woman, so I've been told. Often." Charlotte winced at the memory.

"Who told you that?"

"Everyone who has ever mattered to me or cared for me," she confessed, a drooping smile on her lips.

Not everyone. I quite disagree. But I hardly suppose one could tell a lady such a thing at so early a stage. "I find it refreshing. Admirable. I—"

"Charlotte?" Mr. Harkness' voice cut through the gloom of the now-fallen night.

Charlotte started guiltily as Mr. Bartlesby and her father turned the elegant, open-sided funeral carriage into the small lane that led behind Harkness and Sons.

"Good evening, Father. Good evening, Mr. Bartlesby."

"Gor…" Bartlesby let out a low whistle through his uneven teeth, taking in the sight of Charlotte and her seemingly smitten suitor.

"Quiet," Mr. Harkness snapped, springing down. "I say, whatever are you— Oh. Dr. Everly?"

James swept his hat from his head with an almost theatrical bow. "Mr. Harkness. I forgot that a man such as yourself works all hours, supplying such a Christian service to a city in need. I have come to ask if Miss Harkness would care to accompany me on a carriage ride one afternoon, to see the city as it prepares for Christmas. With your permission, sir."

Reginald turned his head from the well-spoken young physician to his beaming, blushing daughter. "I… A carriage ride?"

"Yes, sir. Through the city. In daylight, naturally, and in a party of other suitable young ladies and gentlemen of good character." James hoped that Mr. Harkness didn't notice his fingers crossing, hidden as they were inside his hat.

****

Mr. Harkness hesitated, for longer this time. People out and about, enjoying a whirl of festive gaiety, people her own age? He must say yes, it would do her so much good. But propriety! This gentleman seemed all too keen to court his fair flower, his only child, peculiar though she was. Would he break her heart? "Charlotte, it's been a cold afternoon. Would you fetch Bartlesby a cup of hot tea with a strong dose of sugar to see him on his way?"

"Of course, Father. Good night, Dr. Everly. I hope to see you soon."

"I sincerely wish it as well. Good night, Miss

Harkness."

****

James stared at the trim figure, bustling inside the house, off to perform a simple and humble task that would bring comfort and show kindness. His mother would have rung for the servants to make the tea. He found it quite appealing that Charlotte seemed self-reliant. If only Lavinia had been so unfettered, perhaps….

"Dr. Everly?" Mr. Harkness' voice was low and cool, an unmistakable warning in it.

"Yes, Mr. Harkness?"

"You've come an awfully long way from Westminster at this hour of the night. Twice, now. Are you so besotted with my daughter that you cannot contain your impatience, or is it because you imagine that she is a woman of lower virtue, simply because she is of lesser means? Because I assure you"—a brass-topped walking stick suddenly pressed into James' ribs—"that such is not the case."

"Let me assure you"—James found his tone was equally fierce without any contrivance—"that I prize and value everything about Miss Harkness, her virtue, her plain speaking, her bright mind, and her quick wits. Her beauty and her cooking are wealth upon wealth, Mr. Harkness. Think me an improper young fool if you will, but I set little store by a lady's birth and all too much by what she makes of the years afterward."

The cane dropped away abruptly. A grin threatened to split the older man's face in half as a chuckle bubbled up. "Do come in for a cup of tea, Dr. Everly?"

"I would love to, Mr. Harkness."

****

"How did you manage this?" Charlotte asked as she took the teapot off the table. Her father had accompanied Mr. Bartlesby outside to see him on his way and would return in moments.

"I told your father that I esteem your virtue, wit, beauty, and cookery skills. He was much mollified."

"Well, yes, he would be," Charlotte conceded, "seeing as he's assumed such talents will go unnoticed forever."

"Why? Have the men in Whitechapel lost their sight in some localized plague of blindness while the rest of London remains unaffected?"

She blushed again, shaking her head. "He thinks you don't know about my particular habits of conversing with our clients," Charlotte explained. "I imagine that after a few more encounters, he'll advise me *not* to tell you about them."

"He seems a most forthright man. He would not encourage you to lie."

"No. He would encourage me not to speak of it, that's all. Very few people would demand to know if the dead speak to me, so the chance of my having to tell a lie is slim." But she did wonder about the truth of this, the truth of this charade. It was all for the best of reasons, but soon his pretty words would pierce her heart, make her believe them, make her believe that she could ever be loved for herself, simply the way she was. "It's very late, now. I do not like the idea of you traveling alone with a killer on the loose, perhaps wondering what you've discovered," Charlotte murmured, quickly bustling plates, cups, and saucers away.

"I'll be on my way. Would a Sunday afternoon carriage ride suit you, Miss Harkness?"

"What about the others you mentioned?"

"I'm certain we will find many suitable young people out and about in Westminster and the surrounding areas."

"But they will not accompany us in the coach?" Her throat was strangely tight. It was something that shouldn't be done, to ride alone with a man in an enclosed space, hidden from protective eyes, unless he were a very particular friend of the family, one's husband, or one's betrothed.

****

Why hadn't these rules ever made themselves such a nuisance before? Oh, yes. Because he would have gladly walked the length and breadth of England rather than be trapped alone in a carriage with Lavinia's giggling, simpering coquettes with their flounces and acres of crinolines and lace. From the moment the girls of his acquaintance were presented at Court, they no longer smiled at him and greeted him with friendly cordialness. They all took to looking at him like a prime cut of beef on a silver platter. A man of means and property with minor connections to a baronet here and a viscount there? If he hadn't been avoiding almost all society after his father's passing, he supposed he'd be stuffed and mounted on some debutante's wall, one husband, flushed out and bagged.

James cleared his throat. "Ah. I suppose I can handle the visit to the Black Boar alone."

"No! I want to hear exactly what he has to say, and without any intended offense, Dr. Everly, you can perform beautifully, or you can also do quite the opposite." Her back to him, the words flew out in a rush. "I wish to accompany you, however many occupants of

the carriage there may be. You mustn't lie to my father…
but kindly do not tell him, either."

"A lady's secrets are sacred," he reassured.

Something stirred in the back of his mind as he
clumsily grabbed a cup and saucer to bring along to the
kitchen. Now, what was it his mother had remarked
about a lady's secrets? Or was it indiscretions?

"Certain indiscretions…" he mused aloud.

"What?" Charlotte's cheeks rapidly darkened.

"Mother mentioned something to me, though she
wasn't in a rational frame of mind."

"And who could blame her?" Charlotte remarked.
"Your poor mother, I cannot imagine her distress."

"She seems far more distraught about whatever
Lavinia did that led to her death than about the death
itself."

"Surely she cannot blame the girl for—for what
horrors she suffered?" Charlotte's voice was a mere
rustle of silk.

"She said Lavinia's indiscretions could harm not
only her own reputation but that of our family. What's
more, she said such things are true of all women."

Charlotte's shoulders rose and fell delicately as she
gently placed the fine saucers and cups into the washing-
up basin. "Can you ride alone in a coach with a friend of
yours from school, Dr. Everly?"

"What? Of course!"

"And surely two men may lead each other into bad
habits? Gambling, drinking, philandering?"

"I daresay. In fact, it's all too common."

"But should a lady be alone with a man for any
length of time, it is assumed that she is not careful of her
virtue, that her conduct is shameful, and that she is a

woman of poor morals and character." Her eyes flickered to his, then back to the soapy water. "You'll notice far fewer assault the man's character for his presumed purloining of hers."

James nodded. He nodded harder and harder until he burst out, "Good heavens, Miss Harkness, where did you develop such a way with words?"

"By refusing to listen when other girls advised me to hold my tongue, lest I scare off potential husbands."

Over their sudden shared laughter, neither heard the soft creak of the door in the passage, a tired tread on the old wooden floorboards.

"I don't think your words are frightening. By Jove, they're inspiring. A man should marry a girl who makes him think."

"Oh, no. No, that is *far* from a popular opinion." Charlotte chuckled bitterly.

"Well, it is equally unpopular for well-off gentlemen with no need to earn an income to go about into the muck and gore of surgery, but it saves lives. One needs to exercise one's mental muscles if one is to be successful about it." His eyes held hers now, handing her the final saucer. "I… I find you very pleasant exercise indeed, Miss Harkness."

"Hr-rhm." Mr. Harkness cleared his throat and pointedly pushed into the kitchen. "What an excellent little treat you've graced us with, my dear. Charlotte, did you manage to send those invitations?"

"Oh. Father, I—"

"I was thinking that you should add Dr. Everly and his mother to the party if she is willing and able to move about in her grief."

"I will extend her the invitation," Dr. Everly said

quickly, pumping Mr. Harkness' hand. "I'll call for you tomorrow, Miss Harkness, after Sunday services. Good night to you both." Another bow, another moment where he stared at the girl as if he had more to say, and then he was gone, without waiting to be shown out.

****

"He's a rather odd sort of gentleman," Mr. Harkness remarked, staring after him.

"I think he's quite nice." Charlotte rinsed the dishes and put them in the wooden slats of the rack to dry. Perhaps she'd drunk her tea too quickly, for there was a scalded feeling in her chest.

A man should marry a girl who makes him think.

I find you very pleasant exercise indeed.

Alone in the city with him. Again.

My little indiscretion, though nothing untoward will happen. I wonder what Lavinia's was, exactly? I wonder what Mrs. Everly knew or suspected?

If only she could communicate with the girl more directly! If only she could reach out to the spirits lingering about on this mortal coil, instead of waiting for them to speak.

"—find that forward?"

Charlotte nearly dropped the saucer she was holding. "What, Father? Forward?"

"I happened to overhear his little remark about marrying a girl who makes him think." The older man's eyes narrowed quizzically. "To mention matrimony so soon—"

"Oh, he was merely remarking that he doesn't find my incessant conversation off-putting. Nor my desire to work in our business."

"Then he thinks little of you as a woman."

251

"But perhaps he thinks quite highly of me as an equal." Charlotte drew her head up and placed the last dish on the rack. "It's very late and you are to serve as usher tomorrow. We should retire shortly."

Mr. Harkness shook his head.

Charlotte radiated surety like a queen upon her throne, though she didn't give in to airs and graces like a lady of high birth, however. She felt her father's eyes upon her as she swept down the hall, moving from room to room, making sure things were in their proper places, lamps put out, grates clear.

"You are a hard and tireless worker, with quiet pride in every bit of work."

Charlotte turned in surprise. "Why, thank you, Father."

"Any man would be proud to have you look after him. Do you find him good company, Charlotte?" Mr. Harkness called softly. "Does Everly make you... happy?"

Charlotte paused, her fingers slowly turning the brass key of the small lamp in her father's study, turning the flame down until it winked from sight. "Yes."

"It's early days, of course."

"Yes."

"Far too soon to think of—er-hrm, a permanent state of affairs."

"Yes."

"Charlotte, whenever you're this agreeable, you're assuredly up to something."

"Why, Father, whatever could I be up to? You said it yourself. Dr. Everly is a fine young fellow from a fine family."

"Did I say that?" He scratched his head.

"Most definitely." Charlotte pecked his cheek. "Good night, Father."

"Oh. Yes. Good night, my darling."

****

A Saturday night saw a bunch of the fellows together, enjoying dinner in the city, then carousing at Juke and Peal's. Some of them split off for port and cigars at their fathers' clubs around St. James, those lucky few who had membership in good standing, who had records above reproach. A few, and he was one of them, had no such claims. They were heading after a different libation.

"Good old Franny. She's a nurse for the Butterfields. Do you know the Butterfields, the London Butterfields?" Bateson was leaning back in the carriage, eyes dancing as he dreamed of this girl, a girl he would sully but never marry.

"I'm sure my mother does." His mother was painfully aware of any and all social connections, studying every bloodline like she'd be called upon to recite them before the Queen.

"Where's your bit of sport, old man?"

He grimaced and mumbled something, but the other two occupants didn't mind that his answer wasn't particularly detailed. It couldn't be. His bit of sport was decently buried now, her mischievous brown eyes forever closed, her warmth concealed in layers of cold earth instead of the layers of lace and crinoline she encumbered herself in.

Served her right, the strumpet, nothing but a common whore, just like this girl, Franny. She could know with certainty that Bateson, who was the sixth son of an earl and therefore barely allowed to dabble in the common waters of medicine, would never marry her. Yet one assumed…

Bateson's roguish wink as he slipped from the cab was enough to make him feel quite ill. Not due to the lack of Bateson's character, but for lack of the girl's, yet again.

"You'll be careful?" he choked out suddenly.

Bateson nodded sagely. "Oh, I have my fun, but I'm dead careful about it. No scandals for me. That'd ruin everything. Mother's got it all fixed up. Lady Belinda Cheshire of Hampstead. Face like an oil painting, body like a dray horse."

He and McKinnon made noises of commiseration.

"No, no, I like 'em built that way. Franny… oooh, fellows. There's a girl made to keep a man warm on a wintry night! See you back at the halls."

"Good night, Batey."

"Night, Bates."

McKinnon pulled a silver flask from his coat. "Nice and heathery. A dram?"

"None for me. Clear head. Dissection in the morning."

"Ah, that'll be no good with a weak stomach. You'll stop off soon?"

As soon as you're gone and I have my fun, he thought longingly. He couldn't ask the cabbie to head to Whitechapel with a witness. "Where will you go?"

"My sister and her husband are near Garden Road. He's a good sort, fine cellar, fine cook." McKinnon put his flask away. "Mother's in a state, her wee baby girl married and moved to London, even if the fellow is rich as a lord and may well be one if his uncle dies without an heir."

At the mention of Garden Road, he'd started so violently that even the most ardent lover of spirits couldn't miss it.

McKinnon could drink them all under the table and cheerfully whistle his way through an amputation. His face transformed, sympathetic. "I'd heard about Everly's troubles. Wasn't in the papers, but the dean mentioned, discreetly of course. You'd heard?"

"No. No, I just... recalled that Everly lived near Garden Road, didn't he? Or was that Jaysworth?"

"No, Everly."

"Hm. What's wrong with him? Is he ill? I haven't seen him all week."

McKinnon frowned. "I thought you and Everly were thick as thieves."

He shuffled a silver pen from finger to finger, rolling it easily and quickly across knuckles and through digits, like a sleight of hand magician at Astley's. "Why? What's happened?" he pressed, hoping his voice didn't sound too sharp.

"His young sister, wee girl, barely nineteen, died suddenly."

"Died?" His shock was genuine. *Died? Not murdered?*

"Hush, man! Sir Lawrence himself said it's a shocking tragedy." McKinnon's voice lowered further, "Not to be confirmed, mind you, but I believe the rumor is she drowned. Ah, horrible. No warning. If Everly's mother fussed over her daughter like my mother fusses over Beatrice, it'll have near killed Mrs. Everly. James must have gone home to nurse her through her grief. I shouldn't wonder if he'll have to sit the term again."

"Shame."

****

"Drowned?" The words left his lips and echoed in the dark, empty cab.

"Where to, sir?" The cabbie called down.

His hunger burned, but his confusion was marring his appetite. "Portugal Street, please."

Whitechapel could wait until another night. He wasn't sure what games were being played. Perhaps he'd have to seek out young Everly and ask.

Or perhaps he'd best stay low and quiet, well-distanced from whatever trick the police must surely be playing.

The trick was on them. They'd soon be thanking him, every one, if he had his way. His pen rolled again, cold metal on his skin, comfortingly like the handle of his scalpel.

If he had his way, no heartless woman would be left standing, and as he could see it, all women were heartless, willing to sell something precious for their own gain.

Like his dear, devoted mother.

She sold his future out from under him when she married again, spread her legs again, bore a son again. Cast him off, not just in public with the laws of inheritance and succession, but also in private, inside his stepfather's home. He was the holdover, proof of his wife's youthful encounter and brief marriage before a fortuitous widowhood made her look at an aging codger like him.

The thought of what she must have done to bear him a son made him physically ill, and the sight of the odious little brute made him ill as well. Fair-haired and wide-eyed, he was fawned over as the long-awaited heir….

He should never have tried to push him into the millpond. Well, he should have, but he should have made sure none of the tenant farmers were about to rescue the brat. Ever since that day, his stepfather had never given him more than a passing glance. His mother, fearing to fall from the comfortable graces she'd ensconced herself in, spent hours doting on her second son, spoiling and cosseting him, having him educated by tutors from Oxford and Cambridge until he was nearly in the sixth form. Meanwhile, he, the unwanted stepson, was shipped off to public school as soon as possible. After that little incident with the rope and the stables, even his own mother refused to have him home unless absolutely necessary for appearance's sake.

Ink spattered his hand. He'd bent the nib clean off in his remembered fury. That was years ago, now. His half brother was three years younger and about a prince's ransom richer. Beyond that, his mother had angled a prime matrimonial alliance with some beautiful, virginal countess with a fortune of her own.

At his stepfather's insistence, his own son would have to be married off first and the new wife brought to the estate, and the "succession" secured before he considered allowing his wife to make any arrangements for her firstborn.

"And did she object?" he asked his blackened fingers. "No, no. Mustn't upset the lord and master. Mustn't let the throwaway son have any help, any love, just the education that's socially acceptable in public and in private, the crumbs that a 'poor relation' deserves." He sneered.

His mother, a woman of respectable birth made far more respectable by her second marriage, was worse than any courtesan. She sold herself for a lifetime of security. The bawdy slatterns on the street corners sold themselves for a few coppers and a single meal.

Was that better or worse?

It didn't matter, really. He had to start somewhere. Lavinia Everly had been somewhere in the middle, he imagined.

Caught in the middle. Just like me. He laughed again, the glimmer of insanity reflecting off the broken silver he slipped inside his pocket.

Chapter Fourteen

"Is this the fashion the young girls are wearing?" Her father stared at her critically as she tied her good church hat back on after luncheon.

"Father, I'm hardly a young girl. Besides, we were just at the Sunday service. Surely you must have seen some other ladies of my age."

"But you're courting now." He plucked at his tie fretfully. "Should I buy you a new dress? What about for Christmas? What if he asks you to a ball? What if—"

The bell clanged outside the front door.

"He's early. Is he early?"

"I always buy a new dress around Christmas, Father—if the old one is worn out." Charlotte kissed his cheek soothingly. "Would you feel better if you came with us?"

"I mustn't. The first Christmas pantomime meeting is this afternoon, heaven help me. Old Mr. Parson has gout."

"Well, that settles it. He can't be the Old Dame."

"The vicar approached me in the vestry when I helped count out the offering. He wants *me* to do it." Mr. Harkness closed his eyes, the picture of acute suffering.

"Oh. Oh, my." Charlotte put both hands over her mouth in an effort to stuff her laughter back inside. It was no good and it bubbled out. She left her father sighing and wearing a much put-upon expression to answer the door.

It was not Dr. Everly, but a rather wizened old man in a cloth cap that was too big for his narrow head. His gray whiskers were tobacco-stained, creeping up his cheeks, and flowing down his threadbare coat. Between the beard and the cap, all she could see were masses of wrinkles, squinting eyes, and a prominent nose. "I've come about my missus. She's… she's gone in the night."

"Oh, dear. Yes, please come in." Charlotte easily transitioned from "courting mode" to "working mode." She slid her hat back off as she led him to her father's office.

"I've a bit put by," he said, almost defensively.

Of course, he was defensive. To be poor, too poor to bury someone with dignity, was the worst shame. The Harkness family knew that. "I'm certain you have. Don't worry about that. Harkness and Sons has something for everyone, no matter their means."

The old man nodded, almost collapsing into a chair as soon as they reached the office. "It was a shock. She said she felt poorly last night, something she et didn't agree with her. This morning… cold, right beside me in the—beggin' your pardon, miss. It was sudden. She weren't even that old, not as old as me." He gave her a puzzled glance, eyes very bright.

"I'll fetch you a cup of tea, and my father will be with you directly."

As she hurried into the kitchen, Mr. Harkness was already changing from his dark blue woolen suit jacket that he wore to church into his black attire.

"He looks so lost. It was his wife. I am sure he hasn't eaten," Charlotte confided, eyes sorrowful.

"Cut some sandwiches down small and bring them out with the tea." Mr. Harkness patted her arm, eyes already moving past her. He always had a gentle manner with his clients, but bewildered widowers were his specialty. He could relate all too well to their suffering.

"I shall send Dr. Everly on if you wish, Father. I can stay and help."

"You've already helped, my dear. Serve up the tea and be on your way when he calls. I imagine you'll be busy tomorrow."

Yes, flowers and greenery to buy, another shroud to sew.

With a sigh, she started slicing bread.

****

James was sweating inside his collar, despite the December chill. How was he supposed to convince Mr. Harkness to allow Charlotte to accompany him alone in the carriage? What if the good gentleman asked for the names and addresses of their supposed chaperones or the members of their party? Nonetheless, he turned up before their establishment, steeling himself to tell a heap of necessary falsehoods on the Sabbath. His polished shoes crunched on the grit of the pavement as he walked to the front door.

Miss Everly sprang through it, tying a long blue ribbon under her chin, securing a blue and black affair with a simple cluster of cream flowers over her tilted bun. "Father is with a widower. I've fed them some tea and sandwiches. He gave me leave to depart." Charlotte swallowed and peered past him to the small cab in the street behind him. "So, we should go."

"Absolutely. At once." James proffered his hand to help her into the cab, his black-gloved fingers delicately resting under her dainty blue-covered ones. "You look lovely, Miss Harkness. Blue brings out your eyes."

Charlotte turned, apparently nonplussed by the compliment. It was unfortunate, as she'd just put one foot down on the swaying interior of the coach. "Thank you, Dr. Ever—ly." She fell unevenly inside, skirts bunched to the side, bonnet falling down her back.

James followed her inside, apologizing. "I'm sorry."

"You didn't have to compliment me, there was no one about to hear."

"I didn't say it for anyone else. I said it for you." James rapped on the side of the coach lightly and called out, "Driver, Salisbury Steeds at the Black Boar."

"What? I can take you anywhere in the city, sir." The driver was so startled by the request that he held onto the edge of his high seat and bent low to look at his passenger through the large rectangular window.

"I'm sure you can. We merely wish to pay a call to a gentleman at that establishment."

The driver sat back up with a sigh. "If you say so, sir."

****

"I've been thinking." Everly had been doing very little else. He didn't sleep but a few hours. He paced. He ate what was in the larder. He very nearly clubbed old Harmon when he came in through the back door to make sure all the windows were secured against burglars. Harmon was the day gardener who also acted as caretaker and night watchmen while the house was unoccupied. Or at least, *supposed* to be unoccupied.

****

"Do tell me your thoughts, Dr. Everly." Charlotte was busy trying to discreetly get her skirts back under her rear, instead of off to the side, making her sit sideways like an artful peacock. One loose cobble and she'd be thrown forward into Dr. Everly's arms. That sounded both mortifying and thrilling. *Concentrate on the issue at hand!*

"Jack. Very few people are christened 'Jack.' " Dr. Everly didn't notice her determined shifting and wriggling, his eyes burning with realization. "Certainly, very few men who can afford to attend the Royal College of Surgeons. For one thing, he must first have attended the Royal College of Physicians or another equally prestigious medical school, not to mention university."

"Well, even down our way, amongst the working families, Jack isn't a Christian name, it's a—a diminutive, like Lottie for Charlotte."

"Does anyone call you Lottie?" Dr. Everly was temporarily derailed. "For some reason, I cannot imagine anyone calling you that."

"No." She smiled. "I don't like it."

"I thought not. But you're quite right, the name Jack is a casual term for John. Or Jacob, or Jonathan. I've even a few lads in my time named Jason or James that have taken it on. To be calling himself Jack in the letters to my sister, he surely must have had an intimate association with her. To be sneaking out alone at night...? I believe my sister may have been secretly engaged to one of the young surgical students. I blame myself. I must be the connection between victim and killer."

He swallowed hard, head lowered, eyes filled with guilty, grieving tears.

Charlotte murmured sympathetically as she finally tugged her dress free. She pitched forward, bouncing into

Dr. Everly.

He mistook the accidental collision as a gesture of compassion. "Oh, Miss Harkness. You are too kind a friend."

She awkwardly pushed herself upright, his shoulder under one hand and his sandy locks brushed by the other. "I beg your pardon," she murmured.

Restored and resilient from her sympathy, he straightened up. "There's one issue."

"What is that?" She didn't correct him. *There were likely dozens, if not hundreds, but one at a time.*

"I haven't the precise records, but off the top of my head, I can think of about ten or twenty men at the RC of S who could use the name Jack. Sir John Harrington, Sir Jacob Glyne, John Middlesford." He ticked them off on his fingers, then stopped, hand curled into a fist. "Far too many to list, and there must be more."

"Well, surely if your sister was so intimately acquainted with this man, she must have had some opportunity to meet him in the appropriate setting. A ball? Some theater?"

"That's just it, Miss Harkness, the men at my institution are all quite respectable and travel in the same circles. I shun such society much of the time unless my mother or my friends insist. Lavinia could have met him at any number of functions."

"Ah, ah, but she was in mourning, yes?" Charlotte leaned forward eagerly. "I'm sure the list is short. All you need to do is find what events she went to, which ones would be deemed appropriate to attend whilst still in mourning."

"And she was ill during her first Season, and her second had not yet begun. If the man was met over a year ago, surely I'd have heard *something* about him by now. Wouldn't I? Dash it, I wasn't an attentive brother, nor son." Frustrated hands scrubbed at his brow.

"You are proving your steadfast love now when no one else seems interested. You must start somewhere." Charlotte bit her lip. "Although… I suppose it is likely that the gentlemen you mention will not have such abbreviated lists, nor would they be likely to share them with you."

"Not if they're the murderer, you mean?" He leaned back in his seat, lids half lowered, eyes fixed on her. "You could ask her, couldn't you?"

"What's that? Who?" Charlotte drew back, even though she knew precisely what he was referring to.

"Lavinia. Can't you… *ask* her?"

"No." Charlotte's tone was equal to the December air. "I'm not some necromancer, nor a practitioner of witchcraft. I don't 'call forth' the spirits."

"I know that." The impatience left his tone. "But surely when she shares her memories, you could ask her to share a different one, the one where she met him, the one where she says his full Christian name, a surname, something solid!"

Charlotte flinched as the excitement and desperation in his tone rose and filled the carriage. "I can try," she finally conceded. Her father would hate that. She never tried to force a deeper connection with the souls speaking to her, and Lavinia wasn't even talking properly. Would this open up a darker doorway, something wicked she couldn't escape? Or would it make her so-called madness more obvious, more undeniable?

"I'm sorry. I've been uneasy lately, running short on temper. I know what you do is not a parlor trick. Again, my apologies, Miss Harkness."

Charlotte let out a slow breath, the weight of words far more restrictive than her corset stays, which she always kept rather loose. "I must do all I can to help. There is a murderer on this earth, in our city, pretending to do God's work of healing, and instead he may well take a life! Who would know, in an operation, whether he was willful in his actions or merely made a mistake? No, I know I must help."

"You are helping, Miss Harkness, tremendously," James assured her.

The coach was silent now, the rattle and clamor of Sunday afternoon streets surrounding their island of gravity, mocking them with happy bustle.

"I fear that encouraging the souls to do more... to stay longer, rather than to depart swiftly for their final destination, will worsen my 'condition' to the point where my father feels he must take some action." She turned her head to stare out the window, eyes refusing to meet his. A man knows nothing of this. A man is a man when he is of age, a free citizen in London, no matter his race or wealth. An unmarried woman could work for wages in an ever-widening circle of jobs, but if her father should forbid it, she had no recourse unless she abandoned home and family completely. Should she be married, any property was instantly her husband's. And should either her father or her husband wish her put away? She swallowed, a cold fist of fear around her heart. Her father would never be so cruel.

He'd see her married first or sent to her aunt.

What might a husband do? Especially one who did not love her?

****

"I had no right to ask. It was a moment's desperation," James comforted. That was a lie in and of itself. A moment's desperation made it seem like there was a moment where he was not desperate. James watched her nod stiffly, keeping her eyes upon the passing sights.

Moments when I am with Miss Harkness—Charlotte—seem better.

"Do you think the driver will recall the man?" James tried again to break the silence. Before she could reply, he answered himself, "Of course he will. The man at the livery said he was much put out by all the traveling and lack of a gratuity for all his troubles. If even he remembers if the man were tall or short, fat or thin, mustachioed or bearded, if he remembers the lady who he picked up at Wedgewood Crescent and Garden Road—" James broke off, fist thumping his knee, impassioned. "There must be *something*."

****

Charlotte closed her eyes, lips thin. *Come on, lamb. For your brother, who mourns you so, for your family's name, for the sake of other girls he might deceive? Give me more. Another moment's conversation, a slip of his surname?*

Silence greeted her.

"You can get out here, Sir. Black Boar's just there, livery behind."

Had time flown so quickly?

James sprang down and offered a hand to his companion, who took it.

Charlotte stepped down lightly, surefooted and blinking into the brightness of the afternoon from the dim interior of the coach.

So why did she suddenly feel as though the world slipped unevenly away, making her tilt? She was falling backward. The sound of creaking wood and metal greeted her ears and echoed in the memory she was sharing.

A carriage.

Falling backward as she stepped into a carriage, uneven footing, horse not standing?

"Lavinia!" A shrill, matronly voice, well-bred even in its gasp.

"Oh!" A short, startled cry.

"Allow me. Is that better, Miss?"

"Oh, yes, thank you, sir." Lavinia's voice was breathless, instantly coquettish.

"Thank you, indeed. A thousand pardons for my daughter's clumsiness. Her eye was caught by that concoction in the window. I—why, don't I know you?"

"I do believe I have had the honor, Madame. Are you not the mother of Dr. James Everly?"

James paid the cabman and returned to find her frozen to the spot, eyes open but unseeing. "Miss Harkness? Charlotte?"

Charlotte blinked, looking around. Why was that memory significant? Was that the man? Was it a clue to something else? "I may have heard when she met Jack. Or I may have heard something entirely different. I'm sorry, I've no better answer."

"Then let us hope that this Barney Gibbs does. Salisbury Steeds awaits.

****

"I'm looking for Mr. Gibbs, Barney Gibbs." James greeted the manager of the livery, dressed in a much more refined style than his counterpart at the Lion and

268

Eagle.

"Mr. Gibbs? Why, may one inquire?" The man drew himself up.

"I wish to commend him for safely escorting my sister on a mission of mercy the other evening." James' tongue all but withered with the falsehood. Had that coachman only known. What could he have done? Was this Jack truly a madman, killing all and sundry? How could his crimes have been hidden for so long?

Or was Lavinia the first, the only?

"Ah." The manager's eyes drifted behind James to the simply dressed girl behind him. Fair. Pretty. Dressed sensibly but in good, serviceable quality. Must be in the missions. Nursing, perhaps? Hm. Barney hadn't mentioned taking any noble rescue.

"Dr. Everly wishes to pay him for his trouble, as his sister and her companion were unable to do so at the time. On her instructions, he was to pay it directly to his hand, with a personal message," Charlotte stepped in.

"Oh?" His eyes traveled between the two figures more earnestly now.

First "ah," then "oh." Fat lot of good that does us. James turned his head to see if Charlotte was also sharing his frustration, but he instead observed her face carefully closing over. The manager's eyes were roving up and down her, from her plain polished shoes to the cloak with its unadorned clasps. His mouth opened, and by the set of it, James could tell they were about to be put off. Clearly, the proprietor found a man of his station traveling alone with a woman of Charlotte's class suspicious.

He had to take care of that without delay. "My intended and I hope to make the gift on my sister's behalf

269

as she is otherwise engaged at this moment. If Mr. Gibbs is not about, would you please let us know when we can find him in? Or if you have the address of his lodgings, we could call upon him."

****

Charlotte, momentarily stunned by Dr. Everly's casual use of the word *intended*, was quite tired of single sounds as answers. "We should inquire about Mr. Gibbs' horses, dear. Remember? Lavinia was so fond of them."

"Yes! Belle and Blue," he recalled hastily.

"We are looking for a reliable pair of carriage horses of our own, or a driver who can take Dr. Everly to work. Wedgewood Crescent to Harley Street, James?" She tried to sound confident, one eye carefully peeping at the manager's face as she dropped what she hoped were the right names.

"Middlesex Hospital, darling." James threw himself into the charade, barely containing a gleeful smile.

The man behind the desk was nodding, his smile expanding.

"But of course, we must attend to our own matters after taking care of Lavinia's." Charlotte smiled sweetly.

"Well, it just so happens that Mr. Gibbs caught a dreadful cold. He's in his rooms over the livery. I let them out to my reliable drivers, and Barney is reliable as they come. Belle and Blue are a handsomely matched team. If you go round the west side entrance, sir, miss, you'll see the stairs. He's number six."

****

"You thawed him properly," James praised once they were out of earshot. "I thought we were stuck at 'ah' and 'oh.'"

"He's a businessman, even on the Sabbath. If he

won't do a good deed, he'll do his establishment a good turn. I hope I used the right street names."

"Well-to-do places, one and all. Brilliant." James beamed on her.

"You were marvelous as well. You… surprised me."

"I hope I have not offended you."

"No! No, although I'm afraid you are far above my station."

"I don't believe so. If I were just an ordinary surgeon and you were an ordinary daughter of a well-established businessman…"

"You're not, though, are you?"

He let out a long breath, watching it briefly crystallize in the cold air, sunlight glinting in the mist he made. "Miss Harkness? What did you mean, that your father would be forced to take some sort of action?"

"You know very well. Place me in some ward for the mentally unsound, the infirm."

James knew it was a liberty, but hadn't he already taken a fairly large one today? He put his arm through hers, tightening it until she stopped walking, pulled close to his side.

"A father's right does not supersede the husband's in the eyes of the law of England."

****

"N-no. But we are only pretending to court, and this pretended betrothal is even more of a farce."

"I—I would not see anything happen to a mind like yours. It is not infirm, nor unsound."

What did he mean? He would save her from the madhouse for the sake of her sound mind? Save her how, through elopement, matrimony, her father's approval granted or absent?

"You mustn't say such things," Charlotte cautioned.

"I must if they are true. I mean it, Charlotte. I will owe you a debt, a lifetime's debt, if you can help me bring Lavinia's murderer to justice."

A debt. Ah. Not for anything other than gratitude, his gratitude which was right, proper, and quite enough. "Thank you, Dr. Everly. It is an honor to assist you, and a debt I hope never to need repaid." She would not trap him in a loveless marriage, one beneath himself to boot.

"The offer stands, nonetheless."

****

He released her arm and began climbing the narrow exterior staircase to the second-story rooms. His heart was pounding, and not just from the fear that perhaps he'd suddenly fall through the rather thin wooden railings.

Charlotte had just rejected his suit. Not that it was truly made or made in any sort of acceptable way.

Once, as a boy, he'd snuck into the kitchen and tried to take a jam tart from Cook's tray. It had just come from the oven, and it singed his skin and made him howl, sending the whole kitchen into an uproar.

His heart felt rather similarly seared by her firm rejection.

"Number six." Charlotte pointed to the door ahead of them.

James knocked gently on the door and was greeted by a horrible catarrh-filled cough.

"Who is it?" the voice growled once the coughing had subsided.

"A grateful patron," Charlotte improvised when he stood mute.

For a moment, there was silence, then a wheezing

and shuffling could be heard from within, the sound of wood scraping on wood. At last, the door opened a few inches, enough to display a weather-reddened face and a mop of untidy graying hair over bulbous eyes and nose. The bleary eyes struggled to comprehend the sight of the well-dressed man in black and his demure companion in her blues and velveteen. "Who's that? Patron?"

"Mr. Gibbs?"

"That's me."

"You took my sister on a mission of mercy the other night. You picked her up from Garden Street and Wedgewood Crescent, Sunday last. She was with a man."

The eyes, a watery blue, sharpened. "Aye, I remember them. Why I'm so sick, innit? Over half the city in the night air. I wouldn't have picked them up if I'd known he'd want to stop off all the way down in Whitechapel, down to bloody Goulston Yard, them lice pits! Oh. Begging your pardon, sir, madame. Mission of mercy, was it?"

"Yes." Charlotte slid her hand into her cloak, down into the pocket sewn inside, and found a few copper coins. "We wish to pay you for the extra trouble you took."

James, spotting her hand on its journey toward Gibbs, quickly retrieved his own purse and took out a silver sixpence. "I have to tell you, Mr. Gibbs, that your action was invaluable." *Though not for reasons you might suspect...* "But I have another matter which I wish to ask you about."

"A confidential matter, that you'd be paid quite well for," Charlotte quickly interjected when she spotted the way the man's eyes lingered covetously on the silver coin.

"Well, if it's a ride you're wanting, it'll have to wait a bit. I've been in bed for three days now. Any money'd come in handy. Not earning while I'm laid up, y'see."

Without warning, James went from playacting the part of well-to-do busybody and fell into the comfort of his natural role of physician. "I heard your cough from the outside, Mr. Gibbs. It's heading into your chest. You mustn't play about with your health. You'll need a few more days in the warm before you head out into the damp and the cold again. You need a mustard plaster, several times a day, chest and back. Not only that, but also a course of garlic syrup and tincture of lobelia."

Mr. Gibbs' mouth dropped open. "Who'd you say you were?"

"Dr. Everly, a physician and surgeon," he replied matter-of-factly. "You can get all of that from the apothecary. Better yet, I will arrange to have it sent and I shall cover the cost. Before we're on our way, I'd like you to answer a few questions."

Charlotte hovered near the door, an expression of admiration on her face. James knew he was again putting her in a scandalous position. She was not supposed to be in a man's quarters, to say nothing of being there with two men and no other lady present. However, his heart was warmed in a whole new way when he caught her proud glance.

"All right, Doctor." Mr. Gibbs nodded. "This is your nurse?"

"Miss Harkness is indeed my assistant." James didn't pause, fully in command of this charade turned reality. He put his fingers on the man's neck to take his pulse. "Have you had any pain of the joints?"

"No, sir."

"Back?"

"Only when the rain's real bad."

"Hm. And the man you picked up at Portugal Street who then picked up a lady at Wedgewood Crescent and Garden Road, how would you describe him?"

"Beg pardon?"

"How would you describe him, his voice, face, height, build?"

"What's that got to do with—"

"Your faculties, Mr. Gibbs. Are you having trouble recalling? Miss Harkness, the patient seems confused."

"Yes, Dr. Everly," she answered instantly, equal to any assisting nurse.

"What? No! Ah, let me think now. He was a tall fellow, nice build, fine clothes, and hat like yours. Not over-generous, though."

"Whiskers? Clean-shaven? His voice? Could you tell where he was from?"

"Eh?" Mr. Gibbs cocked his head while James pulled back his matted hair and peered at his ears. "Clean-shaven, I think. Proper gentleman, sir, spoke as well as you do, not that he said much to me."

"Would you recognize him if you saw him again?"

"I don't 'spect I would, sir, no disrespect to your friend. It was dark, and he was bundled up in a hat and muffler. Not like the girl. She was dressed fine as you please, but not near warm enough to my way of thinking."

James made a contemplative sound, stalling. *Not short or fat, well-spoken, and well-dressed. He's described three-quarters of the Royal College of Surgeons.*

"What was the most memorable thing about him, Mr. Gibbs?" Charlotte asked.

"I s'pose it was where he wanted to go. Goulston Yard is no place to bring a respectable lady, sir, not even for charity, if you ask me." The man addressed Dr. Everly as if he had been the one to speak, head tilted back while the man prodded the sides of his neck. "He said it nice and low as if he was familiar with the place, which shocked me, I can tell you! Furthermore, the streets down that way can scarcely get a proper coach through 'em. People who live in that part of Whitechapel need every penny for food and lodging. Barely knew the way if you want the truth. Haven't ever had a passenger ask me to set them down there."

"Could you tell us what building they went to?" Again, it was Charlotte who asked, keeping her voice flat and unremarkable.

"No idea. Didn't stay long enough to look. Although…" Gibbs considered a moment, then nodded, "You know how you spot a House of Common Lodging?"

James nodded, even though he did not.

"I saw the big lantern down the little street they took as I turned my team around. Thought to myself—" Gibbs paused. His eyes suddenly fixed on Charlotte. "I thought they went there."

For an illicit liaison, James supplied the missing words inside his troubled brain. Charlotte had deduced that a death might not be much remarked upon there. Oh, someone would call the police most likely, but there would be little clamor for an investigation as the inhabitants dreaded the police's involvement in their lives.

"You are quite sound, mentally fit, Mr. Gibbs. The cold has not dulled your faculties. I will send up some hot luncheon from the Black Boar and those items from the apothecary. My sister and I thank you."

"But please do keep this quiet. Dr. Everly doesn't want notoriety for his charitable actions, and he cannot afford to pay for all his patients' care in this manner," Charlotte added, eyes suddenly severe.

"Oh! Right. Mum's the word." Mr. Gibbs tapped his nose. "If ever you want a ride, Doctor Everly…"

"As it so happens, one day in the future I may indeed be looking for a regular coach and driver for my rounds. I shall place you at the top of my list, Mr. Gibbs. My sincerest thanks." Another silver sixpence, a bow, and a quick flurry of motion concluded their visit.

****

Barney Gibbs sat in his nightshirt and pyjama trousers, staring at the two coins on his battered table.

"That must be the kindest doctor in all of England."

Chapter Fifteen

"You do realize—" Dr. Everly left the Back Boar with a throbbing head and collected Miss Harkness as she waited in front of a milliner's window. "—that he described half of the surgeons in England, if not more."

"Yes, but now you know that you're looking for a man named John, Jacob, or what have you, who is quite tall and well-built, who speaks like you."

James sighed. "Thinking of all the fellows I know, and I do know a great many of them, I believe I can eliminate John Rummock and Jason Jennings. They're both quite short. And John Islington. He's rather rotund."

"That's three."

"Out of a dozen more."

"If only he could hear the voice I hear. If only you could!" Charlotte groaned. "You'd doubtless know his voice, but I can't project those noises to you. Nor would I wish it upon you," she added softly.

James shuddered. He couldn't imagine having to listen to what Charlotte heard, a murder, the screams.... Did she cry? Did she call for him? He was shaking, not from the cold. "You must be famished."

"I'm fine, Dr. Everly."

"Please, as long as we're alone—and 'betrothed'— let us abandon the formality."

"James, I'm not hungry. I'm sorely vexed by the fact

that if you but heard the voice I hear you would—"

"If you heard it, you'd know," James gasped.

"I *do* hear it." Charlotte's brows twitched in annoyance.

"I mean if you should hear it again, from the man in question, in the flesh! I could introduce you to the men who fit our description."

"What, you could take me around the halls of the Royal College of Surgeons, where women are forbidden to enter, and waltz me up to all the men called John or Jacob?" She laughed.

James did not. "Waltz. Indeed, yes, a waltz. Charlotte, you've got to come to the end-of-term Christmas Ball with me. It's—" He thought hastily. "It's the week before the final examinations are made, a Friday night… Goodness. That's this coming Friday. It'll be perfect."

****

While her companion seemed to suddenly recover his spirits and his determination, Charlotte found herself shrinking. A ball? With dancing? With all the beautiful women in expensive gowns and jewels, and all the men laughing at James' choice? "I couldn't."

"Why? I promise, introductions will flow quite naturally!"

"I haven't anything to wear."

"I'll buy you a gown. You could wear one of—no, Lavinia was far shorter. I say, you could wear one of Mother's. She's away, she'll never miss it."

"No!" Charlotte drew back, offended. "You must never give a woman clothing, you know that. It implies… it implies she comes to you in poverty, with nothing."

"Nonsense! This isn't a true matter of dowries, Miss Harkness—"

"Dr. Everly." She bit off his name, reminding him of the formality they had so rapidly reinstated. "My father is not a rich man, but he is quite able to clothe me. I will not have my family made out to be so poor a match, even if the match is fictitious. I will... I will procure a dress of my own if you think this ball is a good idea. Only it will be a rather plain gown." There went all the savings she'd carefully garnered. She supposed when this was all over, she could ask James to repay her. It simply felt wrong. All of this was wrong, but it hadn't seemed uncomfortable until just now. It hadn't been a matter of *wealth* until just now. "I'll see to it."

They walked down St. Margaret's Way, listening to the sounds of a choir in the distance. Many businesses were closed, of course, being a Sunday. The businesses that were necessary, places with food and lodging, the apothecary, the livery, they were open. The rest had closed at the half day. Still, the displays in the large plate windows were pretty, catering to the Christmas-minded.

"Do I wear something like that?" Charlotte gestured to a couple that passed them on the other side of the street, the woman in a pink frock, the skirts wide and the waist tiny, not disguised by the sable-trimmed cloak over top of it.

"Possibly?"

"Oh, please, Dr. Everly, I must have *some* help. I haven't been to a ball, and I don't waste much time poring over magazines with the latest fashions."

"When I tell you I don't know, believe me. My mother and sister spent endless amounts of time shopping and sending servants shopping, spending lavishly, but I cannot tell you much about what they wore, nor much about what any of their companions wore. You see…" He coughed uncomfortably. "While my mother earnestly desires my career and prospects to be furthered by making a 'grand match,' I have no stomach for it. Everyone she has tried to foist upon me has seemed foolish and simpering. I cannot remember what they wore or said, only how glad I was to leave their sides. I am, to be blunt, a failure at courting and a double failure at being a gentleman of leisure. I'm too earnest and educated, much to my mother's chagrin, and I've little head for business, much to my father's sorrow."

"—holy night… Son of God, love's pure light. Radiant beams from Thy holy face, with the dawn of redeeming grace…"

The sounds of the choir grew closer, their notes still muted and misty. Charlotte spoke under them, heart softened. "I think you do it beautifully. I'm no judge, of course." She gave him a half smile. "I am twenty-four. I'm an old maid, a spinster. I've not been courted, and I've not even minded. If a gentleman did attempt to woo me, I imagine I shouldn't even be aware of it until he'd given up. I would scare him off, you know."

"Then all the men in your path must be cowards, for there is nothing but sweetness and brilliance about you. Or perhaps it is that you're so brave, they pale in comparison?"

"There is nothing brave about me. I simply have little to fear from death or those who already have entered their rest." She feared other things, quite enough other things. Abandonment, imprisonment…

"I did bring you flowers?" James offered.

"Clove rocks, as well."

"But I must never buy clothing?"

"No, no. That is the husband's job, but not the suitor's."

"Ah. See, you know more than me."

"Very little. I had a governess. She failed spectacularly at making me marriageable to someone of your place in society, but I've been told I'd be an admirable bride for someone who wants a wife to wash, cook, sew, and all of that."

"Don't they believe in marrying for love and beauty?"

"If the other factors are right. We're not all so blessed to be able to ignore the financial matters to wed and—" Charlotte stopped speaking as James guffawed. "I'm not jesting!"

"No, I know. I beg your pardon, Charlotte, but... but it's so ludicrous. You see, the wealthier you are and the more 'respectable' you are, the less likely you are to be allowed to wed whom you'd like. You must pick from a pool of carefully selected young ladies or young gentlemen who have enough money to be a good match or enough connections to make up for the money they lack, but the money mustn't be earned in a trade, or through dint and sweat, oh no. No, it must be the proper age, the money, just like the prospective bride or groom."

"It came upon a midnight clear..."

Eyes suddenly opened to one another's plight, their gait stiffened. The air was strained between them.

Charlotte whispered at last, "We're both terribly ill-mannered at this moment. Talking about such things."

"But murder and pretending to be a nurse? Or me pretending to be your intended? Those are signs of excellent breeding?"

He caught her eye.

Her lips twitched, then his.

It would be even worse to burst out laughing in front of the large cathedral where the clear notes of song swelled out, bathing the streets in holy music.

"Here! Cabbie!" James flung his arm upward and hustled Charlotte into the interior of a passing coach. As soon as he sprang in and secured the door, he lost his battle and laughter poured out of him, draining all the tension from his exhausted frame until he could barely lift his head.

"I hope we are forgiven," Charlotte gasped out once she recovered her breath, dabbing at her eyes.

"Doesn't the verse say that a merry heart doeth good like a medicine? Fitting for a doctor and his 'nurse.' " James leaned back, muscles loose, head lolling as he chortled. "You are incredibly fine company, for all those failings you claim."

"As are you."

I would very much like this to be real, Charlotte realized with a twist of her heart. *I would like this man's company. It is too fast and too unwise to think such things, and yet… if you can like a man at the lowest point of his life, is that not a good indication that you'd like him when things are going smoothly?*

****

James studied the girl across from him. Why did a woman need a fancy dress? To make up for flaws and imperfections, to flaunt her wealth? He had no need of further riches, and Charlotte had no imperfections, at least not to his keen eyes. "May I ask your father's permission to escort you to the RC of S Christmas Ball? It's certainly public and chock full of society's best. A lady would be safe there."

He didn't mention all the gentlemen and ladies who escaped the watchful eyes of the deans, out to the terrace or grounds to do a private bit of wooing or something else. Although, if he and Charlotte needed a private moment to compare notes and discuss evidence, they had a perfect cover.

Quite unexpectedly, James hoped and prayed to be interrupted. Pulling one's sweetheart into a passionate embrace under the mistletoe would surely allay anyone's suspicions.

"That's nearly a week away. We cannot let the grass grow under our feet. We have to go to Goulston Yard, and find the house Mr. Gibbs mentioned."

"That's no place for a lady. I shall go myself."

"But—"

"What did you think Mr. Gibbs was about to say when he described his surprise about Lavinia and her paramour traveling to such a low place of ill-repute?"

Charlotte flushed. "It would be unbecoming of a lady to say."

"Precisely. You must not accompany me. Your reputation would be ruined."

Charlotte must know he was right, but she was admittedly stubborn. "I am already quite ruined, having spent several afternoons alone in your company, public or not. Should anyone care to press the matter, I am on the slippery slope to being irredeemable."

"Not so! And even if it were, I would—"

"Please. Don't make grand offers. I cannot abide the idea of a heart so unrequited, such burdens to bear." Again, her eyes studied the outside world.

"I see." So unrequited. Burdensome. His offer was

not only unwanted, but she could already see he was becoming smitten. Very decent of her to let him see his folly now. Still, he needed her assistance, and this charade must continue, with or without his heart's consent.

"Don't fret. It is of little consequence, though I am most grateful for the thought." Charlotte gave him a warm smile. "Father will be very pleased about the ball, I imagine."

"Really?"

"He's been trying to get me away from *The Undertaker's Gazette* and into *Beeton's Englishwoman's Domestic Magazine* for the past five years. He'll find my sudden interest in dresses quite miraculous."

"Quite miraculous," James parroted. He wasn't thinking about the dress.

****

James promised to get in touch after he had been to Goulston Yard, and he had accepted a rather pleased and flustered invitation for a midweek tea from Mr. Harkness. What he did not tell Charlotte was that he intended to see her home and head straight over to the pestilent slum. After all, people had their routines. Was it possible that someone who had frequented this House of Common Lodging last week would be there tonight? He should have brought a photo of Lavinia with him. He should have been in his incognito outfit of older clothes and oversized scarf, not his Sunday best. He should have had his medical bag with him. He most likely looked like an easy mark. All of his common sense told him venturing down to Goulston Yard was folly.

Lavinia had been foolish, too.

"Let's hope I make it back to Mr. Harkness in better

condition," James murmured to himself, setting off into the twilight.

****

"Out by ten or pays again!"

James stifled a yelp as his heart hammered against his ribs.

His heart had been dancing a rapid minuet since darkness fell like a theatrical curtain and the moon stubbornly hid behind streaks of smoke.

Goulston Yard was enough to make a man despair.

Broken bottles and broken bodies lay in doorways, children with frightened eyes scuttled into dank openings in the walls while women and men emerged, switching places. The adults stared at a wealthy stranger with different kinds of hunger in their eyes. James told himself that most of them were simply less fortunate and he had nothing to fear.

"A fine gent looking for company?" One of the hungry-eyed women wrapped in a tight dress and moth-eaten shawl slithered out to him.

"I am not, thank you," he managed to keep his voice even with an effort.

"We don't want your sort around here," a belligerent voice growled at him from the shadows.

"Simply passing through." Best not to engage them.

That strategy didn't work. The chorus of voices enveloped him, mocking, snarling, and warning; a buzz that made him quicken his pace until he stood under a hanging lantern, flickering valiantly in the suffocating night. In the circle of wheezing light, the voices stopped.

Did they not dare follow him in for the conditions were so terrible?

"Out by ten or pays again."

Swallowing down the cry in his throat, James looked to the vicinity of his knees.

A little woman, a crone in a nest of soiled blankets held out her withered mummy's paw of a hand. "Tuppence."

"I'm not in need of accommodation, thank you."

"Out! Out, then!"

This must be why the rabble had stopped. They had no money to enter.

"I have tuppence for information, my good proprietress." James addressed her as he would a lady of noble birth, doffing his hat and bowing low, trying not to gag at the stench that assaulted his nostrils when he got closer. "I wish to know about a guest you may have had last Sunday evening."

Momentarily taken aback, the woman's mouth hung open, revealing stumps of teeth and rotted ones jostling for position. "You a policeman?"

"No."

"Had enough of them. Bad for business." She settled herself fretfully in her nest.

The police have been here? His interest quickened. *Steady, James. That could have been for anything. Heaven knows, there certainly seems to be enough work outside to keep Gill and all of his brethren busy for a month.*

"I'm not the police. My sister died here." He played his hunch boldly, voice firm, praying silently that he would get a definite reaction that would let him know if he were closing in on his quarry.

His prayers were answered.

"Ahhh!" she gasped, nodding vigorously. "Pretty girl, fine dress. Didn't belong down here. You don't, either."

"Tell me what I want to know, and I shall leave," he replied.

"I don't know anything. Police asked me the same and I told them to go. Not my affair what people get up to, I just rent the rooms!" her voice rose, a wild, fearful screech in her protests. "They said they'd be back. Now you've come. Tricky and sly, they are!"

Courtly manner gone, he knelt and glared, nostrils flared, and brows lowered. "Now you listen here, I am not the police but I will bring every detective from Westminster to Whitechapel down upon your head if you don't take my money in exchange for a few simple answers. It's either me or the police. What's it to be?"

She cowered back from his angry shout and James felt himself the worst kind of brute, intimidating poor old ladies. She was likely crippled or suffering from a wasting disease, which is why she sat down in her nest, why she didn't rise to tell him off.

"Answers," she finally muttered sulkily. "See the money first."

James was recklessly about to wave his purse before her eyes, but he could feel Charlotte's glare from streets away. He carefully showed her two copper pennies. Satisfied, the woman nodded, and he began. "Tell me about the man who was with her. What he looked like, sounded like, a name... anything. Tell me what happened that night, please."

"I don't look too close... but he was a fancy man, like you, all polished and neat. I saw him come in with the lady but didn't see him leave. Know why now. He must've nipped out another empty room, one with a window, after he stuck his knife in."

Hearing it spoken, almost with annoyance, made his temper flare. "Fair or dark? Thin? How tall?"

"I don't know, I only saw him for a blink of an eye. Slipped right past, on his way to his work, wasn't he?" the annoyance turned to downright petulance. "Made a mess of the floor. Had to mop it up when the police didn't come back. Was all sticky by then."

Oh, Lord. If he'd entertained the hope of seeing the crime scene, not that he wished to see it, but if it would yield him any clues... Well, that was a blighted hope now. *Thank you, Mother. You've made this nearly impossible, just as you wished.*

"Seen him before. Twice."

"You know that because you recognize him?"

A limp shrug. "Couldn't place him. Heard from the girls. Mad, he is."

"He killed two other women?" James hissed in shock.

"Nah, not them. Feared for their lives though. Paid for their company but didn't use it as they expected." Bright eyes in a seamed face gave him a knowing look.

Blood that had drained from his face rushed back, filling his cheeks. The man had been with prostitutes and terrified them. How? "Did he hurt them?"

"Bruises." Another limp shrug. It was apparent that bruising was to be expected.

"Well, surely they could report him! Battery and—"

Her cackle cut him off. "Lock the girls up, they would. Not legal to sell *their* wares."

James dropped a coin into her hand abruptly. "I have a few more questions. Can you tell me where those women are, or can you tell me what they said?"

The stubborn look shifted to raw hunger. "Bad for business, this has been."

"It's a common complaint," he muttered, thinking of Barney Gibbs.

"Why do men buy what the girls sell?" she asked abruptly.

"I—I — That is a man's own personal business and I do not wish to discuss it."

The crone rolled her eyes and shook her head. "Because they *want* it, boy. They love it, love the touch of a woman, the *feel* of a woman."

He was going to die and be carted off to Mr. Harkness after all, death by acute embarrassment.

"But not him. Took 'em into a room and never touched them but to push, shove, or slap! Ranting, ranting the whole time about their wickedness, the ways they trap men, hurt men. Ha. If that ain't a laugh. Ain't a woman born who hasn't been hurt by a man. He'd lunge at them, ready to do the deed, then push off, eyes like the devil, spitting, shaking. Poor Clara. She went off the game after he was done with her. Rather work herself to death in a factory than be alone ten minutes with that rat."

"Clara? Can I speak to her? She must know what he looked like. Or the other woman?"

Silence.

The jingling of purposeful coins.

Regret and mulishness cemented her refusal. "No. If I set you on them, they'll never take a gent here again."

Another coin dropped into the foul-smelling blankets. "Then tell me what you can, and I'll refrain from seeking out this Clara or any other of your customers."

"Dark. Dark hair. Strong. But what man isn't strong if the drink is in him, or the madness?" she countered, eagerly scooping up the coins and dropping them down the loose collar of her sagging blouse.

If James had any intention of asking for their return, it fled with all haste.

"Taller than me?"

"A bit. Or just about."

Dark, not fair. Tall as me or just a bit more. The pool of men was shrinking. "Is there anything else you can tell me that might help me find him?"

A thoughtful silence. "I keep it dark in here."

That much he could attest to. Everly imagined that was her way of saying she wasn't able to see clearly. But the women he accosted, perhaps they had seen more, and could describe him. "The girls he was with, surely he must have given them his name, surely they mentioned his description to you?"

"Ha, that's a larff. Only thing a girl looks at is the money 'cause the tackle is all the same."

His collar was going to start smoking soon, cheeks positively aflame. "A name?"

"All of 'em are Jacks and Johns, though that's not what their mothers named 'em."

Teetering between deflation and satisfaction, James sighed. "May I see the room where it happened?"

"Scrubbed the floors."

"I just... I wish to see it. I've paid my tuppence and I shall pay again, then be on my way. You'll have double the night's charge and still a room to let. It's good business." His tongue nearly disengaged from his head. To speak calmly and coldly about money when he was standing feet from where his sister's life was so cruelly snuffed out? It made him ill. It made him ill that human lives were being weighed against profits and inconvenience.

He'd never had to make hard choices before.

"All the way on the end, but one. Left. An' you'll not stop the night?"

"I will not." Another tuppence in her outstretched hand and he was away, deeper into the darkness.

****

The sounds around him were terrifying. The room had thin wooden walls, barely partitions. James could hear a pair of voices arguing loudly over who got the last drop in the bottle, the sound of smashing glass, and a scuffle. He shook his head to clear it, easing into the room slowly. Bed. Chamber pot. Three-legged stool.

Where had her body fallen? He was afraid to walk in further, lest he should step on such hallowed ground.

A volley of oaths and curses from another room removed any folly about the reverent state of the place. Shouting came from all sides, underlaid with distinctly female moans, and the scents of smoke and opium.

No wonder the inhabitants said nothing about a murder in their midst. James was wondering how many of the occupants would make it out alive. He wondered how many were breaking the law right now. To distract himself, he idly imagined the charges. Prostitution, solicitation, drunkenness, willful destruction, battery, and assault—he was sure the list could go on.

It was definitely hard to concentrate. The feminine sounds of satisfaction were assuredly distracting, leading his mind on unpleasant paths. Was that Vinnie's Jack in there with some unknowing woman? A married couple with no lodgings?

Was that why Lavinia had come here? Was she planning to elope with Jack, had she already done it, and this was the place that was to be her bridal bed and funeral pyre?

"I'm going mad. Mad." If word got out what he was doing, if his mother should hear, he'd be cut off. Sent away? Placed in an asylum?

Charlotte's fears merged with his own, and a sense of frustration for her helplessness and the unfairness of it all threatened to engulf him. Unwillingly, he sat, legs buckling.

As James sat in the poorly lit room, the only light coming through chinks in the walls, he could see that the floor under his feet was clean, unlike the dirt and grime on the rest.

The crude wooden bedstead? It had not received similar attention, either through ignorance or slovenliness, he didn't know. Even in the dark, he could see the drops, feel them with his shaking fingers as he lightly traced the legs.

Killed in this corner. Spattered.

Throat first.

He rose. Followed the clean track amidst the filth.

Blood flowed down and out. Pooled. Puddled. Made its way—his feet followed the path—*all the way to the door.*

The man must have had some blood on his clothing, yet he managed to escape detection, even once he left this area. Coming in quite late… Or terribly early. A smile quirked his lips as he pictured some of the fellows sneaking each other in the windows and back steps, respectable physicians one and all, but still men, playing at being boys all the same. Dear Lawrie Thompson,

Percy fforbes-Wellington, Milo Merelake, Kenneth McKinnon, and Charles Rutherford, all the good lads in his wing. He thought of abandoning this place of death and the empty home at Wedgewood Crescent to head to the friendly solace of the Halls.

But he couldn't. He couldn't look into those kind eyes without it all coming out, the ranting and raving about the injustice, the way her body looked, the crimes against their honorable profession, to use their tools to kill and butcher… Worst of all, to tell all of them that it was not just any surgeon, but one of their own.

I've broken bread with him. I've rubbed shoulders with him as we sat learning about resecting a muscle and the placement of nerves and arteries.

Have I been with him as we cut up a cold corpse, conversing idly while he planned to do the same to my sister?

James barely made it to the little pot in the corner before his lunch reappeared.

As he hastily staggered from the room, away from the mess, he realized that even if he did tell his trusted friends, no one would believe him. Nor could he implicate Charlotte.

Charlotte.

She'd had a lifetime of not being believed.

His throat burned with bile, and his heart burned with grief and something else.

I want to go to her. Be with her. I don't care if she doesn't "belong" in my class. Who in the world decides where your heart belongs based on your fortune, which can change in an instant? Lavinia's body was left in the filth in the worst kind of hellhole, while she spent her entire life cosseted in silks and satins.

How had an educated doctor of wealth and privilege ended up in these dank city corners by night and sitting in the hallowed halls of the Royal College of Surgeons by day? How had such a man come to be killing in private as he learned to save lives under watchful eyes?

There were all kinds of injustices lurking in London tonight.

****

"Father? You know that Dr. Everly has asked me to accompany him to the holiday ball at his college?"

Mr. Harkness had just finished attending to an embalming. He was scrubbing his arms vigorously while his daughter was making notes in the household accounts ledger. His Charlotte was so organized. But what had she said? "Should he be attending balls? Surely not while he is in mourning for his sister."

"You gave us leave to attend." Charlotte finished totting up the previous week's expenses for the household,

"Well, of course, it's a perfectly respectable entertainment and I was—I was flustered. You looked so happy. And a ball! A ball with such a distinguished gentleman."

Charlotte rolled her eyes as he practically swooned in delight. "Are you sure you wouldn't like to go in my place, Father?"

"What? Oh, hush. Such nonsense." He gave her a bemused smile. "I'm simply so pleased. When he asked to call upon you the first time, well, no discredit to you my dear, but I scarcely believed he would be such an ardent suitor. I suppose he wants to show you off to his friends and colleagues. I certainly would. I did with your mother."

Charlotte nodded. "Yes, James would like me to meet some of his friends."

"Oh ho! *James* already? But still—"

"Father, it's Christmas and the end of term. His heart is sorely troubled, and this brings him some relief. I doubt we'll stay long, nor cut a glittering swathe through society."

Reginald paused as he brought his own ledger out and set it across from his daughter's. "You seem to feel very keenly for his pain."

Suddenly fascinated by the cost of their groceries from the previous week, Charlotte blushed and re-totaled her figures. "You've always said I have a loving nature, Father."

His hand found her cheek and turned her face upward, grinning with paternal pride. "Indeed, you have. I could not wish for a more loving child. Child turned to woman. Hr-hrm." Mr. Harkness sat down and dipped his pen in the inkwell on the kitchen table. "My dear. You will be twenty-five next year."

Charlotte nodded. "I had remembered."

"Mm. Many a woman has settled down by now, into the routine of wife and mother."

"So they have." She gave him a wary glance.

"In Dr. Everly's class, I believe many of the young ladies marry even earlier. At twenty or so?"

"Yes, Father, I am most assuredly on my way to becoming a spinster."

"No! No. I simply was thinking that you seem willing to consider the possibility now. Obviously, any wife of the upper classes would not work apart from their domestic duties."

Charlotte swallowed. "It's far too early to think

about that."

"Then perhaps you should not go to the ball with him, Charlotte. If you care for him, don't let him envision a future you'll not be in." His eyes did not meet hers, fastened on a long column of numbers.

****

Charlotte forced a laugh, inwardly cursing her father's sudden attentiveness. "It's one ball, Father." *If we don't go to the ball, I can't meet the men he suspects, can't hear their voices. If his sister's unquiet spirit is to rest and his grieving heart is to have peace, we must proceed.* "As I was saying, I need a dress for the ball. I don't want to spend an excessive amount, Father. I want something I can wear again, as well."

"Practical," Mr. Harkness mused. "How much?"

Charlotte cast another eye over her figures. "I have a few pounds saved from the household expenses. I'll see what I—"

"No, my darling. You go and get the gown you want. Even if it is impractical and extravagant. After all, it may be just the one ball."

She had accompanied Dr. Everly to two different liveries and one spur of the moment examination-interrogation, and they'd looked at a murder victim together. They went for a walk and bought sweets simply so they could discuss how to handle their investigation. This ball might be the only time she would ever go someplace "nice" with James, do something that felt like real courting. And after things were solved, after he left…

Her heart shuddered under an unexpected weight of sadness. She couldn't say she'd never be courted again, for it could happen. But she wouldn't be courted by anyone like James.

Mr. Harkness let out a startled cry when Charlotte suddenly ensconced herself in his arms, head on his breast. "Why, my dearest, what on—"

"Nothing is the matter. I just wanted to thank you for the dress. I think I'll go look at the shops."

Her father nodded eagerly. "Absolutely! A young lady should—"

"I'll pick up something from the fishmongers on the way home, and I'll call into the stationers. You're running low on ink in the office. I'll be home to prepare a luncheon." She pecked his cheek and bustled away.

****

Charlotte's feet turned from her usual path, heading toward the more prosperous parts of Whitechapel. The farther she went, the more her simple, functional clothing stood out, as did the fact that she was unaccompanied. The majority of the women she saw without a gentleman were walking in pairs, white mob caps on their heads, black skirts rustling at their ankles, clearly servants for the wealthier among them.

" 'Three yards of the lilac lawn for Mrs. Pankhurst', I told Tilly. 'Whatever does she want lawn for' in this weather?' she says. 'She's already planning for Paris in April.' Of course, only Matilda will go with her."

"Lucky cow."

Charlotte followed behind two girls who appeared to be just a little younger than her, their arms already loaded with parcels.

"She's so particular. She wouldn't even let the shop deliver it. What's the point of those new bicycles with the big hampers on the back if you won't take delivery?"

"Tilly's surely not riding a bicycle. She's not

married!"

"No, Ernest, the shop boy."

"Riding him or the bicycle?"

"Gertie, you are wicked!" The two dissolved into laughter.

It'd be nice to have a friend like that. The one who laughs at all the foolish things you say, all the things that you oughtn't to say, at the slips of the tongue, and the clutter of your mind. Charlotte swallowed a sigh, her eyes momentarily closed. When she opened them, the pair of maids were gone, having turned down a tree-lined avenue graced by residences for the more fortunate.

Charlotte took note of the street names on the signpost. She was not going to her usual dressmaker this time but had followed the High Street until she reached the Apollo Concert Rooms which commandeered a large presence on the corner. Directly beside it was Clerkenwell's Fine Ladies' Apparel.

A wooden sign enticed its patrons, "All the rage in Paris. Inspired by Empress Eugenie of France! Gowns for all occasions."

Charlotte didn't believe they made a dress for dancing and interrogating, but she was willing to look. She told herself that she would not go over a certain price, even if it meant she had to sew the thing herself.

Entering the dress shop was like being forced headlong into a wall of textile confectionery. Pinks, purples, reds, and greens lined the walls, corsets and crinolines were proudly displayed, safe from public eyes due to the long white drapes covering the interior of the plate glass window.

"Can I help you, miss?" asked a young lady with a squint, probably from hours of sewing. She had the distinctly doubtful tone that implied she already knew the answer to the question.

"I need a suitable gown for a ball, but I don't want it to be too impractical to wear to church or the theater."

The squinting eyes widened. "We specialize in Paris styles at affordable prices."

"What do you consider affordable?" Charlotte arched one eyebrow.

"Well…"

"I have a certain number in mind, and that's what I shall spend. Not a penny more, preferably less," Charlotte said firmly.

"Mrs. Clerkenwell! Customer for *you*."

Charlotte sighed internally.

As if on cue, Mrs. Clerkenwell appeared, rather like the prow of a ship cutting through an ocean of taffeta, her large bosom bedecked with a measuring tape. "Good morning, madame. May we assist you?"

"Miss, and yes, thank you. I want a gown, nothing too extravagant. Suitable for a ball, simple enough for a church. Would you have such a garment?" Charlotte spoke firmly so she would not shrink before the woman's intimidating presence.

Appraising eyes wandered up and down Charlotte's body, mentally making improvements. "It's not our specialty, but I believe we can accommodate you. You'll want one of our Day/Evening specials. It comes with a bodice and skirt. The bodice can be altered by adding undersleeves to transform the gown. Let's see." Mrs. Clerkenwell whipped the tape measure from around her neck with a crack.

Charlotte swallowed.

The dead were far less terrifying than dress

shopping. No wonder ladies of status sent their servants on such perilous missions.

****

Nearly an hour later, Charlotte left the shop feeling hot and flushed, but triumphantly carrying a receipt. The dress would be delivered later that day or early the next, which would give her time to alter it before the ball. Overall, she was pleased.

Although Mrs. Clerkenwell had tried valiantly to stuff her into rich laces and brocades, Charlotte's eye was caught by something on the dressmaker's form.

It was a dark blue, almost black, with only one tier of lace along a low, gathered bosom. The skirt was long and full with tucks and gathers of cream lace. The more crinolines or petticoats she wore under it, the fuller it would be. She could wear the bare minimum of underskirts for an ordinary function and add layers for the upcoming ball. Adaptable. Simple. Elegant.

It was the finest dress she had ever seen—that would still allow her to look like Charlotte Harkness, not an actress in a costume.

"What about a hat?" Mrs. Clerkenwell followed Charlotte to the street, obviously feeling that her salesmanship was lacking. Charlotte had been stubbornly unswayed by her urging to try a dress with a lower neckline or a fuller skirt, something that would "make more" of her figure.

Charlotte turned back to assure the lady that no hat was wanted. Without warning, the world went spinning sideways. The outside world lost sound in favor of the memory rushing through her mind.

"Lavinia!" A shrill, matronly gasp.

"Oh!" A short, startled cry.

"Allow me. Is that better, miss?"

"Oh, yes, thank you, sir."

Charlotte shook her head to clear it and to block out Mrs. Clerkenwell's rather hectoring tones.

Wait? Is that voice... Have I heard that voice before? Is that Jack?

"I—why, don't I know you?"

"I do believe I have had the honor, madame. Are you not the mother of Dr. James Everly?"

"Oh, yes. Yes, of course. Are you not the son of Lord and Lady Silcroft?"

A pause. "Lady Silcroft is my mother, yes. You've met?"

"In passing. May I present my daughter, Lavinia?"

"Charmed."

"-evening shoes?"

"What?" Charlotte blinked as if waking up.

"You'll want dancing slippers or shoes for the evening, will you not?"

Charlotte hesitated. "No. No, thank you." Her dress would cover her feet if she didn't hem it beyond an inch or two. That wasn't the pressing matter. The memory was gone, but questions flooded in their place.

Who is Lady Silcroft?

Was that Jack's voice?

Lavinia? Charlotte aimed her thoughts toward the ether. "Lavinia?" Her eyes darted, wary of passersby catching her speaking to a ghost they couldn't hear or see. "Please, you've got to be clearer. Is that him? Is he the one who hurt you?"

Nothing.

"You're exceedingly difficult," Charlotte complained under her breath.

The male voice she heard in Lavinia's most oft-repeated memory was little more than a hissing, deranged whisper before the girl's terrified screams died with her and her memories were no more. There had been bits of other conversations, but the tones were low and loverlike or heated and seething. This man's voice was courtly and mellow. That wasn't to say that he couldn't be both a gentleman and a murderer, at least by all appearances. They already knew that was the case. However, this man might have some other bearing on the murder. Could he have been an old suitor? The one who introduced Lavinia to the wrong man? She couldn't be sure about what she'd heard, but if Lady Cynthia Silcroft, whoever that was, had a son named John or the like, that would cement things in her mind. The son of a titled family would surely have the means to attend any university he chose, not to mention the money to court, woo, and beguile.

But why kill?

Madness?

Even though the sun was bright, there was suddenly a shadow over her, a dark, clinging presence she couldn't escape.

Is this how it begins?

She shivered, but not from the cold.

Chapter Sixteen

Mr. Harkness noticed a change in Charlotte's manner. She finished all her tasks with a strained smile. Her excellent cooking remained on her plate, barely touched. She was a quiet, dutiful daughter, an admirable picture of womanhood—seen but not heard.

He hated it with a passion.

"Charlotte, my darling. It's no good pining for him. I'm sure he doesn't wish to appear too eager a suitor, but you'll see him tomorrow for luncheon. Cheer up, Dearest."

****

Charlotte pricked her finger as her father's voice broke into her thoughts. She hastily sucked her bleeding finger into her mouth, hurrying it away from the pristine white shroud she was finishing. "I'm not pining," she protested.

"You barely eat. You move about the house like a gh—like a mouse. You haven't argued with me about something in two days. I'm not sure what to do."

"Perhaps I've become resigned to a life of quiet domestic servitude?" Charlotte suggested, a pointed hint in her tone. "Isn't this what a man should want?"

"I—No! It isn't. A man should want you, as you are. Although... You haven't mentioned your past problems, have you?"

Wrapping her handkerchief firmly around her

finger, she returned to sewing. "We spend a great deal of time talking about his late sister. Father... don't you think it was suspicious? When you prepared the body for burial, did you—"

"I didn't embalm her after the police conveyed the mother's request to simply leave her as she was. I merely placed one of our shrouds around her. Why do you ask? Is Dr. Everly is concerned about something?"

"He does not believe it's as simple as the police make it out to be," Charlotte answered carefully, eyes on her sewing.

"I imagine that if there was something to worry about, the police are keeping it quiet so they can catch the fiend unaware, investigating without the press lapping up such a grisly tale—if such a tale there was. Or if there were anything to investigate. Not that there is. Or was. When will that shroud be ready?" Mr. Harkness ceased his incriminating speech with an abrupt change of subject.

"In about twelve stitches," Charlotte answered evenly.

"It's good you're getting his mind off such things. Erm. Charlotte? Miss Everly doesn't speak to you, does she?" he asked, his voice nonchalant while he idly rearranged the jars of jam and preserves on the narrow kitchen worktop.

Technically, no. Lavinia's ghost had never addressed Charlotte in words. Maybe her angst and terror would manifest to anyone who suffered with her particular "affliction." "She has never spoken to me, Father," Charlotte was able to answer honestly although her heart twinged warningly, reminding her that there are many forms of communication. The deception bowed her head farther into her sewing as the final stitches were finished and the thread was clipped.

At the counter, her father let out a relieved sigh.

"Is something troubling you?"

"Oh, no. No."

"You don't *sound* untroubled," Charlotte pressed.

"I recant my earlier statement about your habit of arguing with me." He gave her a lopsided smile.

"I can read you as well as any book, Father. What is it?"

"I know the man is in mourning. Perhaps… perhaps an association with an undertaker's daughter, with our family specifically, is more of a diversion for his grief than a 'genuine interest.' " Mr. Harkness put the phrase as delicately as he could, but he still winced.

Charlotte neatly folded the shroud she was working on and pulled another long strip of white cloth forward. "A woman as a diversion? I wouldn't be the first." Her father's words hovered dangerously near the truth. Dr. Everly would have no association with her if it were not for her confession, for their shared interest in the murder.

"What a horrid thing to say, Charlotte!"

"It's true. If I were to marry someone in the trade merely to stay with you, he would not love me, and I would not love him. We would merely be suitable. I am not suitable for Dr. Everly, Father, I know. I would be an inconvenience and likely a scandal, or at least a tasty bit of gossip for his mother and her society matrons. He could have a grand match. The fact that he continues with me may be exactly as you say, a tonic for his grieving heart, some sort of connection to what he's lost," Charlotte said the words without flinching. She had to hear them spoken, she had to remind herself that her ever-growing attachment to the handsome doctor couldn't lead anywhere.

"I didn't mean anything, my dearest. Idle musing, that's all." Mr. Harkness backpedaled after hearing her harsh truths.

"I'm always serving the grieving, Father. Whether it's tea and biscuits or a smile and a partner for a dance… I don't much mind." That last was a lie, but as she was only telling it to her own heart, it didn't count.

****

Reginald was at a loss for words, his paternal heart aching and his masculine mind beginning to feel pangs of feminine outrage. The women of the upper classes might be spoiled and pampered, but even a rung or two removed on the social ladder, they were cast into a very difficult plight. Still property, but with far fewer choices and compensations.

Women had a rum deal.

"The door, Father. The front." Charlotte rose and glided past him.

"It must be a client."

"You attend to them, and I'll get that dough rolled out." Charlotte traded places with him. "Ginger biscuits this time."

"Currants?"

"No currants. I'll get some next week."

Mr. Harkness hurried away.

****

Charlotte breathed a shaking sigh of relief. That conversation had cut quite close to the bone.

She scolded herself in a whisper, "James Everly doesn't love you or even fancy you. You are a convenience, a needed tool to solve a problem. Get any other ideas out of your head." *Especially the ones about the ball.*

They'd have to dance a bit, for appearances' sake.

He would say she looked beautiful. His eyes—a bright and piercing blue, would light up when he saw her. His face, a very grave, earnest face, would split into one of its rare smiles.

Blast it. She had started to like his looks. *Why couldn't he be an ugly but compassionate, intelligent man?*

That wouldn't help. I've begun to like the look of his heart, too.

"It's for you. Did you order gloves or a hat?" Mr. Harkness returned, looking quizzically at a large square box done up in brown paper and tied with twine. "It's from Wedgewood Crescent, Westminster. I wonder who—"

"James. I mean, Dr. Everly, Father." Charlotte took the parcel eagerly. It would surely be something related to the case. Or perhaps he'd failed to listen to her about clothing and gone ahead and bought her some garment. Although if it fit in such a box? He wouldn't be that foolish.

Would he?

"Let's open it, then." Mr. Harkness sidled up to her, a teasing glint in his eye. "Unless you think it's too private a gift?" he half teased.

"I'm sure it is not." *Please, please let me be right. If he's sent me a petticoat or something, Father will thrash him, and I'll assist!*

But she needn't have worried. She slit the twine with the shears she'd used while sewing, and her fingers scrabbled the sturdy brown paper down over a paper box made of corrugated material. Opening the lid, she revealed—a book. "*Buchan's Domestic Medicine*," Charlotte breathed, lifting the heavy book from its paper wrappings. "Oh, Father… it's a medical text. It's likely from his studies. Oh. Oh!" Charlotte clutched the book to her chest, eyes squeezed shut, enraptured. "He sent me a book. A scholarly book!"

"Good heavens. What an—unusual gift." Mr. Harkness frowned. "That's not at all appropriate for a lady!"

"But it's utterly perfect for *me*!" Charlotte swung away from him, book protectively out of his reach.

"There might be subject matter unbecoming to a woman's eyes."

"I've read every book in your office. If I can read about a dead body, I can read about a live one!" Charlotte crowed. "As soon as the biscuits are cut, I shall sit here and read a chapter."

Mr. Harkness fought down the smile tugging at his lips. "I wish to look over that book."

"As you wish. I'm sure smallpox over ginger biscuits will be just delightful," she giggled.

The bell at the front pealed again. "Ah, now that really *will* be a client," Mr. Harkness sighed.

Charlotte ran her hands lovingly down the sides of the book.

"Dr. Everly is a very *perceptive* suitor," her father remarked.

"Isn't he?" Charlotte murmured fondly.

****

Delighted as she was with the gift, she couldn't imagine it was purely a gesture of affection. As she caressingly opened the book and fanned through its pages, she found a sealed envelope in the first chapter. It bore her name. She tore it open and read the contents, heart beating quickly.

My Dear Miss Harkness,

I find you often in my thoughts. You know what an abysmal failure I am at courting, but I shall attempt to redeem myself with this offering. It's one of the first texts a physician consults, and I present it to your keen mind.

Perhaps your keen mind can help me with another small matter. If you should go out for a stroll at St. Mary's Park, Whitechapel, you will find me there in the afternoon, just around one.

I beg to remain yours, faithfully,

Dr. James Everly

Charlotte jammed the letter into the pocket of her apron.

Her father returned, his step hurried. "Three cups, Charlotte. It's Troy and Arlan Malone. Their father had an accident with the coal horse. He's a mangled mess, I'm afraid. Bartlesby will collect the body. I must go to the vicarage as soon as possible. But you'll be content, won't you, with your book?"

"Yes! I might even take it to the park and read."

"In this weather?"

"I'll wrap up well."

He kissed her curls in passing. "I never could sway you for long. Wrap up well, then." Mr. Harkness tried to look stern, but a broad smile blossomed on his face. "If I needed proof that Dr. Everly truly understands and admires you, Charlotte—you're holding it."

****

"Dr. Everly!"

"Miss Harkness!" James trotted toward her, bowing

over her hand when they were close enough. "Thank you so much for coming. I had hoped you'd find my letter today!"

"I'm glad I did. It was a near thing, though. You know how parents will often open letters addressed to their unwed daughters." Charlotte chuckled, eyes bright.

"Do they?" James blinked. "No, I didn't realize."

"*Especially* if it's from a suitor. He could be writing—indelicate things." Charlotte blushed. "Father was hesitant about this particular token of your esteem, but I pointed out that if I could read about dead bodies, I should be able to read about live ones."

James said nothing, blinking myopically in the December sunlight that managed to reach the center of the green haven in the midst of the city's bustling streets.

"He soon came around. He's not upset." Charlotte attempted to jar him from his silence.

"That's good," James said at last, breath puffing out in a great misty cloud. "Charlotte, is that common?"

"A woman who likes to read medical texts? Not very, I suppose."

"No, that mothers and fathers intercept letters from suitors?"

"It's something my governess spoke of, at any rate, especially if the suitor was not long established or... unsuitable." Charlotte's voice slowed, and her eyes widened.

"Come!" James seized her hand and pulled her behind him, running at a brisk pace.

"Dr. Everly. James!" Charlotte panted as she tried to keep up with him, finally getting him to loosen his grip on her fingers. "People are staring."

"Telegram! Come with me, where's the nearest

place to send a telegram?"

"To whom are we writing? What did you want to tell me about? I haven't even told you what I heard," Charlotte protested, still keeping pace with him even though her corset was making it hard to do so, pinching her lungs.

He stopped, nearly skidding on the ash and gravel that the park keeper had spread on the walks to prevent frequenters of St. Mary's from falling. "I'm being premature. But do you recall that my mother had our housemaid, Sadie, burn any papers she found in Lavinia's things?"

"Yes." Charlotte nodded.

"We found a letter hidden away in her reticule, but not the envelope. I'm sure that Lavinia must have sent at least one other letter to this beast. He may have written to her, as well. What if Mother intercepted it?"

"Proof," Charlotte gasped.

"At least something to lead us to him. Proof may be a stretch. What did you want to tell me? Some memory of Lavinia's?"

Pressing close to his side as they strolled to a far-distant corner of the park, Charlotte spoke in an undertone. "I went to buy a dress for the ball. As I was leaving, the proprietress came after me to inquire if I wanted to purchase something to go with the dress—a hat or shoes, I'm not sure just now, for all the sound of the waking world left my head and Lavinia's spirit impressed one of her memories upon me. I think it must be important, very much so, for she's let me hear it twice. The first time was when we were together. I heard Lavinia cry out, startled. Another lady, your mother, gasped out as well, but then a masculine voice inserted itself into the conversation. It sounded as if your sister had fallen but was prevented from hitting the pavement because of this man's timely action. The first time I had this memory, it was interrupted." Charlotte blinked, trying to explain. "I know Lavinia's voice. She seemed taken with this man, his looks or his courtliness, but the second voice, which must belong to your mother, is the one that is most telling. This is so hard to explain." Charlotte ceased, vexed with herself, trying to convey words and pictures that she herself had only partial knowledge of.

"You're doing beautifully." James reached over and gave her hand a little squeeze. "Beautifully, Charlotte. What did Mother say?"

She squeezed her eyes shut, willing Lavinia to share her message again.

It was like a prickling on her spine and a pulling in her muscles. Charlotte knew she was reaching for something, something just beyond her grasp that she'd always left alone, or never even knew existed.

"A thousand pardons for my daughter's clumsiness. Her eye was caught by that concoction in the window. I—why, don't I know you?"

"I do believe I have had the honor, Madame. Are you not the mother of Dr. James Everly?"

Charlotte let herself lean on James' strong arm, not bulky but steady and sure. "Lavinia had turned back to look at something—some concoction in a window. Shopping. They must have been shopping. When this man prevented her fall, your mother apologized for Lavinia's clumsiness and blamed it on the distraction in the window. Then, she asked if she knew him."

"And?" James rasped, voice hoarse.

Charlotte continued, shutting her eyes again as if straining to hear something far away or badly distorted.

"They *did* know each other. They had met somehow. He said—" she swallowed, voice reluctant, " 'Are you not the mother of Dr. James Everly?' "

It was his turn to stagger a little, to lean upon her. Reeling together, for different reasons, they made their way to a bench that was dwarfed by the shadows of the ornate Church of St. Mary and a cluster of bare trees. They were alone in a pool of gray, the sunlight just beyond them.

"He knew my mother. But he didn't say, 'Are you Mrs. Everly?' No. No, the association was somehow through me. Oh, God. What have I done?"

She kept her hand in his and held it tight, wishing she could comfort him. "You did not know the kind of man he was, and you are not the only link. Your mother then asked if he was the son of Lord and Lady Silcroft. He replied that he was indeed Lady Silcroft's son. If it is the man we need, we have a clue. A most excellent clue, James."

His head jerked like a marionette with a careless puppeteer but soon began to shake. "No. No, I... But I don't know the Silcroft family. I've heard of them, of course, a well-connected family in Kent, I believe. My family has no 'country estate.' We're definitely townies, Charlotte. The nearest thing we have to a country home is when we visit my aunts and uncles, my mother's sister in Hertfordshire, and my father's brothers out in Reading. Oh, Lord... they could have met at some house party, I suppose."

"But if the Silcrofts do have a son at your college, and if his name is John or Jacob, whatever it may be...."

Charlotte trailed off meaningfully.

Pain and guilt ebbed from his face.

"We've won. Then, we've won. Lavinia can rest, even if the rotten bas—pardon. Even if it is years until justice is truly served, she can rest."

"That's all that matters, that and that he is caught. He mustn't roam free, James."

"We'll see that he does not." Hope shone in his eyes, and she knew hers must match. "I could not have done this without you!" He took her gloved hand and pressed a fervent kiss to it. "Thank you, Charlotte. You have been my angel."

Tears danced on the edges of her lashes, silly things, coming unbidden. When she oft feared that others would think her cursed, possessing something of the devil about her, James saw her as a heavenly helper.

"This may not be the answer we need," Charlotte cautioned, though she was loathe to ruin the heartfelt silence they were sharing. "Lavinia shared this memory, but the name Jack was not mentioned, and I cannot tell if his voice is the one I hear across all the moments she has shared."

****

James didn't want to let go of his sudden elation, but he had to admit she was right. There were so many things that poked and prodded in his subconscious. He wondered if he would ever sort through them all. "You're quite right, Charlotte. There's more to learn." He would not call her Miss Harkness in private again, not until propriety demanded it. His heart would not allow it. "I made my own rather sordid voyage of discovery on Sunday evening after we parted company." His fingers wove themselves through hers again, easily this time, not caring if the touch was forbidden. "I found the place where it happened. The dank, vermin-infested pit he took her to, down in Goulston Yard. The landlady described him much as Mr. Gibbs did. About my height, well-dressed, well-built, fine clothes. In short, everything to make him stand out in a place such as that. The fact that he brought Lavinia was also quite noticeable." He cleared his throat uncomfortably. This next bit might indeed be significant, but he should not tell a woman such things.

Except that he felt he could tell Charlotte anything. "Was there something else?" Charlotte led, her frame tensing, no doubt steeling herself for vivid descriptions of the murder scene.

"Charlotte—" He licked his cold, dry lips. "—not to be coarse, but I ask you, if you can bear it, to imagine why a man might take a lady to those rooms."

Her eyes went blank, then dreamy. James wondered if she shared his fleeting thoughts, thoughts of being alone, held in his arms, pressing her lips to his…

She sounded breathless as she replied, "I can imagine it, yes."

"You would agree that it's likely the man and woman are on—" He coughed, strangled by having to discuss such things with a lady. "—on good terms?"

"Extremely." Charlotte shifted uncomfortably, but she clung to his hand.

"That's what I would expect. To be very blunt—"

"It would be much easier if you were."

"To be blunt, the landlady believed this man had called before, with women who sell their affections, but it was not their affections he returned. He threatened them, frightened them. Yet he did take the time to travel there, to buy their company. Why?"

"Why does a man want to be alone with a—a prostitute? That question has but one answer. He is a man of low morals who wants his carnal needs fulfilled outside of marriage. If he does not take advantage of what he's paid for? Then he must have gotten some other need met," Charlotte muttered, musing to herself.

"What was that?" He strained to hear her mumbled words.

"He didn't seek them out for physical comfort but sought them for something else." Charlotte couldn't meet his eye as she spoke, valiantly trying to explain. "A man buys a woman for his own purposes and needs, James. If not to—to have his way with her, then to do something else to her."

"To threaten and frighten? Why?"

"I suppose…" Charlotte's eyes cleared as she turned her face toward his. "I suppose he thought he could do what he liked with them. Women on the streets won't go to the police. They don't have rich families of noble status defending them. A Whitechapel harlot is likely to be one of the easiest women to oppress. What will she do about it?"

James nodded slowly, quite ill. "I'd never thought of that in that manner, but still, it begs the question, why? Why espouse such hatred of a woman? I cannot excuse it, but I can at least understand it if a man is a drunkard and beats his wife, or if he shouts and hits his wife for being unfaithful to him. The woman he hates is there, with him. This brute went out of his way, one assumes, to find a woman to berate and bully. He must be mad!"

"All madness has a root," Charlotte said simply. "If he would vent his spleen on total strangers, luckless

317

women forced to sell their wares, it seems possible he could not turn on the woman he truly despised. After all, can a young man, the son of a lord, go about London battering debutantes and dowagers? No, the scandal! The arrests!"

James rocketed to his feet, and Charlotte came with him. She had little choice, as her elbow had somehow become entwined with his. She yelped in surprise when ardently kissed her cheek.

"James!"

"You are brilliant. Brilliant, beautiful, and brave, my Charlotte." He could have swung her around in rapture if he were not urgently moving toward the edge of the park. "All the pieces are falling into place. This man has some hatred, some mania about women. He contained it in the confines of society, but in the darkness, he lets it out. Each time he got nearer to the edge until something with Lavinia sent him tumbling over. He attacked her physically. I don't know what it could've been, but—" James' joyous expression suddenly left. He was celebrating in a sort of madness himself, a heated hatred of an unknown that he would soon be able to identify, yet the misery and the senselessness of it all would always haunt him.

"We may know why, in time," Charlotte soothed. "But it begins here. Who were you about to wire?"

"My mother, staying with my aunt Eleanor. She told the police to look elsewhere, she told me to be silent, be content to watch the swine walk free, but I will not. She's holding answers like purse strings, done up tightly, keeping everyone in her control." Right then, his hatred became like the Hydra of old, sprouting another head just as he thought he'd cut one off. "Why? For the sake of appearances, scandal, our good name. What about his name? Does the Everly family sacrifice a daughter so the Silcroft family may save a son? No, I say, *no*, it will not come to pass!"

Charlotte slid her lips across his cheek as he finished his rant.

He gaped at her, blinking in shock.

"I—You are the hero of the story," she stammered suddenly. "I suppose that is when the fair maiden would have—not that I'm... Dear me, I'm in a muddle."

"You are not. If I am the hero, then you are the heroine. To Camelot?" James proffered his elbow. Engaged or not, in his mind their stories were well and truly connected and always would be.

"To Camelot."

Chapter Seventeen

Mrs. Everly was calm and content, forcing herself to look only at the fire in the hearth or the oranges studded with cloves lining the pine swag on the mantel. In the country, one was untroubled. Oh, the staffing problems followed (Sadie had suddenly become a much more confident little chit) and the entertainments were few, but that was perfectly suitable for a widow. In London, there was too much risk of running into someone, the odd conversation leading to old pains and new wounds. In the countryside, guests were invited for a week at a time; house parties were given with copious space and time to prepare everything just so.

You could pretend your children were safely on another part of the estate, watching after the farm cat and its new litter, making corn dollies in the back garden, wading in the little stream, picking daisies… In her mind, it was suddenly late summer and a brown-haired girl with her stockings rolled down kicked her feet in the water and giggled as a kitten crawled across her lap. Vinnie loved all those things. Vinnie was happy, untroubled.

If only she could keep her there, in that moment of remembered summer.

"More sherry, Mrs. Everly?"

"Thank you, yes." She nodded to her sister's butler as he appeared at her elbow.

Her eyes opened and the seasons changed, back to a dawning winter, with a glowing fire. The heating was a problem in these big country houses, but not if one had funds. Ample funds. A sizable (yet not immoderate) staff would be needed, no more economizing or taking jobbers and dailies.

The butler returned with a small glass, refilled to the brim, an envelope next to it. "Oh. The post?" And the post, one must ride down to collect it at the village, going once or twice a week if the weather was fine.

"A telegram from London."

Tranquility fled, followed by the sherry which went ahead like a scouting party, readying her nerves for the assault. London meant danger.

Or James.

Oh, thank heavens, yes, it *was* from James, she could tell straight away by the neatly printed box in the upper left corner, bearing his name, if not in his hand.

Her relief vanished as she read the three-word message:

Who is Jack?

"Madame? Madame, are you ill?"

Mrs. Everly met the horrified eyes of the butler from her slumped posture, hand clasped to her heaving bosom.

"Fetch my girl, send her to me. Is there a train to London on Thursday morning?"

"No, madame, I believe not. There is a goods train in the afternoon, and a passenger train on Friday morning. Shall I make further inquiries?"

"No, no. Just send my maid to my rooms. We must pack for a train Friday morning." Mrs. Everly rose, mustering as much dignity as she could.

"Is there any reply?" The imperturbable butler for once looked perturbed, shocked by the abrupt change in his honored guest's demeanor as well as her plans.

Mrs. Everly hesitated. She could reply in a few words or a great many, but the message would be the same. *Keep out of this, James.* However, it was apparent that he had already been digging in the muck. Heaven only knew how he had found out about Lavinia's sordid dalliance.

If he knew, others might soon know.

That would never do.

She must address the matter, but in person. After all, what was written could be read. "No. No reply."

****

"Another book for my daughter, Dr. Everly? Or a gift of plasters and dressings?" Mr. Harkness greeted him good-naturedly on Thursday afternoon.

"Ah, no, I often carry my medical bag. A force of habit." Dr. Everly shook Mr. Harkness' hand warmly, the other hand clutched tightly around the handle of his bag. It wasn't so much habit but the need for concealment that caused him to bring it to Thursday luncheon. "I do apologize about the parcel I sent. Charlotte mentioned it caused you some concern. Your daughter has such an intelligent mind. I didn't consider the impropriety of the gift, only that she would enjoy reading about the complex illnesses that befall the human body. How my trade may lead to yours, so to speak."

Mr. Harkness chuckled softly. "I understand. I'm pleased that you admire my daughter's mental faculties, as well as her other attributes."

"Indeed. Something smells heavenly." James closed his eyes and inhaled. The house had a comforting, spicy scent about it, although if one sniffed harder a certain medicinal, chemical tang was present.

"Ginger biscuits," Mr. Harkness said conspiratorially. "Lots of clove in them, too."

"I am very fond of clove. Clove rocks are my favorite boiled sweet. Charlotte's as well, I believe."

"So they are. Charlotte, hm?"

"Oh! That is to say, Miss Harkness. I am sorry, Mr. Harkness, for my forward manner." James, who had already taken off his hat, scrambled to tip it in apology. It instead looked as though he were reaching for an invisible cat perched upon his head, hand uselessly groping the air.

James knew he must look a fool, but it seemed to clear Mr. Harkness of any paternal reservations. His disapproving tone turned friendly. "I suppose that is the fashion these days, to call a young lady by her first name early on in the courtship?"

"No…" James answered helplessly. "I do not think it is. She is simply so—Miss Harkness puts me at ease with her kind manner and her ready wit. I confess I call her Charlotte in my head. At times it slips from my lips." Another grope for his absent hat and then a sigh. "I promise that I am not taking any other liberties, sir."

Which was untrue. He'd kissed her cheek, and she had kissed his. His whole body tingled in appreciation from the slightest touch from her, his sweet Charlotte, his clever Charlotte.

His was the operative word.

He had enough to be worthy of her, not in terms of money and property, but in terms of head and heart. She might not see it yet, but one day, when this was over, he would win her affection, court her for real.

It could not hurt to lay a little groundwork. "Mr. Harkness" —he spoke in grave tones—"it has only been a short time, but I would like you to know that—that my family is comfortably established and my career is not without promise."

"I see. Well, that is good to know."

James hesitated, then added, "My father's house is to be mine one day, but it is very large indeed, in a prominent location in Westminster. I would say that it could easily be converted to a surgery or some other form of business"—his eyes skirted the older man's reading the dawning surprise—"but it is a residential area and would not be ideal." James told himself to stop. He *implored* himself to stop.

He was apparently in a rebellious mood.

"That is not to say that a young man, a physician or surgeon, should not set up a home and office elsewhere. There are so many excellent locations between here and Westminster, don't you think? An easy carriage drive away, and I would naturally have a carriage. That is, we do, but I don't make use of it. We haven't any horses at the moment, but if needed—"

Mr. Harkness clasped the young man's shoulder firmly, softness in his smile. "I understand, Dr. Everly. You would have anything you needed to be successful in all your endeavors."

Again, his brain and his heart were loudly tugging on the reins, but James' tongue was galloping ahead. "It would appear so, but as I believe the Good Book so clearly shows, a man needs a 'helpmeet.' " *Oh, Lord. If you have any mercy, you will strike me dumb. Or do something else equally distracting.*

Mr. Harkness blinked rapidly, mouth opening and

closing as if trying to formulate the proper response, but at that moment, Charlotte came bustling down the passage, a broad smile on her face.

"Dr. Everly, how good of you to come. Shall we eat before it gets cold?" Charlotte gestured up the wooden stairs to where the luncheon was set out.

Both gentlemen sprang after her, all eagerness and babbling about the scent of ginger biscuits. Unbeknownst to the other, both men were simultaneously offering silent prayers of thanks for their deliverance from an awkward conversation.

****

James knew this feeling was sincerely wrong. Honestly, it was practically a theft. He felt as though he had no right to it. His father and sister were dead, untimely, erroneously dead through want of a skilled physician or one with any sort of sanity or scruples. His mother was sinking into a haze of patent medicines and mourning. He was on the hunt for a killer amongst England's finest young specimens.

He would gladly have handed over his inheritance, his education, and status, whatever they were worth, for this feeling of peace to remain.

A soft rain had begun to fall outside as Charlotte served up a fresh pot of tea and plate piled high with little round ginger biscuits. Mr. Harkness went and stirred up the fire until it blazed. In an unaccustomed show of intimacy, both father and suitor removed their jackets and sat in the glow of the blaze with Charlotte presiding over the table between them in long-sleeved, high-collared grace. Her hair stood out in a sort of frizzing halo, soft curls and wisps escaping as she laughed and fed them… and she laughed ever so much. As for the feeding! Her biscuits had the perfect crispy snap that delighted the ear and made his senses tingle for the clove, cinnamon, and ginger dancing over his tongue.

"I'll fetch the backgammon board," Mr. Harkness announced suddenly. "You two young folks play, and I shall challenge the winner."

"That would be me." Charlotte laughed again, rising to clear the table and make space for the board.

"She's a terror, Dr. Everly. I can count on one hand the times I've bested her in ten years."

"Do call me James, please, Mr. Harkness."

"I shall, sir, if you call me Reginald."

"Reginald it is." James beamed. He missed his father so terribly sometimes, but for a moment, the ache was lessened. All the aches were lessened.

Peace.

Happiness.

He shouldn't feel those things. They were wrong, not just for him, but for his esteemed host and hostess.

Death was below them. Death had furnished this house. By all rights, these two people should be the saddest and dourest in all the land, but they were loving and laughing, welcoming him into their midst.

It was for a charade, a worthy one, but...

I do not wish to let this game end, to let this act run its course. I want to keep it going. I want to make it real.

"Father, don't you have the pantomime committee this evening?"

"That's not for ages."

"I know. I was wondering if there was anything you needed to attend to since you'll be out until late."

"You are left alone here, Miss Harkness?" James lost the feeling of peace quite suddenly. "Mr. Harkness, shall I—shall I—" *Should you do what, you fool? Stay alone here, in the house with her?*

I've done it before, ever so briefly.

I didn't feel the way I do now.

"I'll be perfectly fine." Charlotte smiled reassuringly.

"It's a thoughtful notion, lad." Reginald pushed more biscuits onto both plates before Charlotte took the platter away. "I suppose I should make out the accounts for the parish funds. They helped cover the cost of Mr. Malone's final expenses, though his sons didn't like it. But young Troy, he has a wife and child, and another one on the way. His father wouldn't want bread taken from his grandsons' mouths."

"No, sir. If I can help—"

"You've helped enormously. Our last supply of lumber came from your donation. Now, I'll be in the office for a bit. Call me when she's trounced you." Mr. Harkness gave the younger man a friendly wink and went whistling down the stairs.

James laughed, both surprised and pleased. Once he heard voices below, he silently undid the catch on his bag and drew out the book he'd been looking for since yesterday.

"What's that?" Charlotte returned, peering at the book that now obscured the board.

"*Burke's Peerage*," James informed her, smile gone. "I knew Mother had a copy. There is not a matchmaking mama who does not possess this volume. Every year or so, a new edition must be bought, thumbed through, and crowed over to see who has passed, who has wed, and who has had an heir."

****

327

Charlotte had heard of the book, of course, but she had never owned a copy.

"This is from the year Lavinia was presented at Court. Naturally, Mother would want the most up-to-date guide for husband-hunting."

The loathing in his voice was unmistakable. Charlotte deftly pushed her pieces back to where they belonged, gently moving the book to the center of the board. "Surely, she did not know. If she believed Lady Silcroft's son was a worthy suitor, it is not her fault. You mustn't blame her too heartily, James."

His fair eyebrows kissed his hairline before arching down. "I don't hold Mother responsible for her death. I blame myself entirely. I, in all likelihood, had the opportunity to observe this man and never recognized him for the monster he was."

"Oh, you must not blame yourself, either." Charlotte pleaded, equally intense. "You seemed so happy a moment ago." It was true, and she had loved it. To see her dear father laughing and joking with James (who now occupied quite a sizeable space in her heart, however hard she tried to restrict his access) had given her a feeling of contentment that she hungered for. It was beyond pleasant or peaceful. It was a glimpse of a barely remembered dream, her mother, father, and grandfather, all in this room, laughing, eating, dandling her on their knees, passing her from one lap to the other.

Once, I was quite a normal girl, a happy little girl.

Could I be a happy woman once again, a happy woman… in love? With someone who loves me?

James' knuckles brushed hers as he moved his pieces to their starting marks. "The more I see of contrived matches based on pedigrees," he sneered at the book between them, "the more I feel like a bull to be offered for stud, and my sister was paraded as a willing broodmare."

"The upper classes sound quite animalistic," Charlotte said wryly.

"Oh, we are! They are! Bloodlines, good stock, the right family, it all must be obtained for the right price and in the right neighborhood. What folly. What rubbish. There may be a murderer wandering through St. James as we speak."

"Shhh." Charlotte hushed him, looking over her shoulder. "I'm glad you found the book, though I quite agree it cannot tell you the character of those it lists. Did you find him?"

"I had no time to look. I searched the library from top to bottom, followed by Father's study, and finally, it occurred to me that Mother was the one who would have read it most. I found a copy in her sitting room, but it took ages. By the time I located it, it was time to go and the light was too poor in the carriage. Besides—" He swallowed. "—you should be with me. I couldn't have come this far without you."

Charlotte lowered her head as his eyes stroked over her features, something beyond simple gratitude in them. "Silcroft?"

"Silcroft." James breathed, hands shaking as he found the page devoted to the titled family.

He had to read hurriedly through the history of the Silcroft title, conferred first in the 1500s. "How anyone could read this for pleasure…." he murmured darkly.

"Your mother seems to have taken a look, though I cannot say if it was for pleasure or business. See, the book is creased heavily here? She looked up this family, as well." Charlotte's scalp prickled, palms cold. Any second now they'd have an answer. Then what?

"Here. Arthur Edward Henry Drummond, the Ninth Earl of Silcroft, married Cynthia Drummond, nee Horton, issue…" James licked his lips as his eyes greedily reached the point they sought. "Christopher. Christopher?"

Charlotte rose and scurried behind him, bending low against his shoulder to read with him. "Christopher Arthur Edward Drummond. What year is this?" Charlotte seized the book out of his hand and flipped it to the cover and back. "This is the edition from two years ago."

"*Christopher*? Christopher Arthur Edward! There's no earthly way one could squeeze the moniker 'Jack' from that!" James put his head in his hands, angry tears suddenly blurring the mass of black and cream wood before him.

"He was only seventeen." Charlotte shook her head, bewildered. They'd been so sure. So very sure! "He can't possibly have entered the Royal College of Surgeons at nineteen, can he?"

"One must first be a fully qualified physician. Even if he was the most prodigious scholar, he would not be in surgical training yet, for the terms and coursework are paced at the Royal College of Physicians."

Silence. Charlotte idly rubbed his back as she would comfort a sobbing widower. James sat up, face turned toward her. Slowly, her hand traveled from back to shoulder. His fingers seized hers and held tight.

"Do you know anyone named Christopher?" she murmured finally.

"I do, several young men, but none of them are *that*

young, nor of that surname. I know no one with the surname of Drummond or Silcroft. Oh, Charlotte."

What use are my visions if they only led to dead ends? "I'm sorry, James."

You are not helping, Lavinia. Honestly, you are not. If you will not show me something a bit more useful, your brother and I will be left stumbling around for years while Jack goes off to murder some other helpless victim. Is that what you want?

She knew it was a mistake to take her frustrations out on one so helpless.

Lavinia seemed to think so, too.

The dreadful heat followed by the all-pervading cold washed over Charlotte as screams filled her head. They echoed and cut off with a blood-filled gurgle, leaving her gasping and falling forward, coming to land on James' knee, her head bowed to his as she struggled for air.

"Charlotte? My angel, what is it? Don't take on so, it isn't your fault. You've nothing to apologize for!" James lifted her head, lips to her shining hair as she shivered.

"She's angry, too. I can't speak to her, I try... She tries... I do not know what to do next. I've failed you, failed you both," Charlotte confessed, fatigued, frustrated tears escaping her eyes.

"You're making valiant efforts."

"It's not enough. She's back to immersing me in her final moments, the screams, the rush of blood, the cold seeping in." Charlotte clenched her fists and eyes tight. "I *must* help her. I cannot bear this!"

****

James experienced a surge of annoyance at his late sister. She had no right to torment Charlotte, yet that was

331

typical of Lavinia. Though she was gone and one must not speak ill of the dead, this was exactly the pattern of her behavior. Whenever she was unhappy, the entire household must know it and must suffer with her. Her tantrums and sulks were legendary. Frankly, it was no wonder his mother had been so determined to find her a match, for Lavinia's beauty didn't necessarily make up for her petulance and her foibles. So insistent was she about participating in the Season that Mother allowed her to break the established rules of mourning.

As he indulged these less than charitable thoughts, he was aware that he was indulging in something else. Charlotte was still clasped in his arms, her cheek resting to his mussed locks. If her father should walk in now and see the trembling, emotional woman in such an embrace, he'd be well within his rights to demand his immediate removal from the house or his prompt proposal. James didn't wish to place them in either position.

He rose with her and steadied her, both hands in his. "There will be another answer. We will not rest. The ball is tomorrow night. You'll meet some of the surgeons who—"

"But he said he was Silcroft's son!" Charlotte interrupted, pacing away from him. She passed her side of the board, idly rolled the dice, and moved accordingly.

"Perhaps he seized on what my mother said. After all, if he was a low cad, frequenting the likes of Goulston Yard and the women who entertain there, then he would hardly be likely to tell her the truth. I do not believe my mother has any connection to the Silcroft family, and one titled son is as good as the next when securing a match for a difficult, spoiled beauty like Lavinia."

"Oh, James, don't speak ill."

"The truth is best unvarnished." He paced as well, rolling and countering when she dropped the dice in his palm.

"But the truth would come out." Click, click, rattle. Their black and cream pieces parried on the old teak board.

"Perhaps that's what caused the row?" Pass, rattle, tap, tap, they moved the pieces as they paced and circled, neither sitting.

The logs snapped and crackled. Mr. Harkness shouted up something, and Charlotte shouted something back in reflexive reply.

"Mother knew him. Or rather, she believed she could place him, but he recognized her first. Is that right?"

"She recognized him. He used your name first. 'Are you not the mother of Dr. James Everly?' " Charlotte repeated the conversation.

"That could be any one of a hundred lads I went to school with."

"How many have followed your career and know you're now a doctor? How many are also surgeons?"

"A precious few, I should imagine."

"Far more likely to be someone of recent acquaintance, or else should she not know them and their family better?"

"Exactly." James blessed her again, his brilliant partner.

"Did you say women were not allowed at the college?"

"No, not to attend and most assuredly not as guests, not even wives and mothers. The exception to the fairer sex is the staff of charwomen."

Charlotte carelessly shoved her pips along the lines, advancing toward a win. "You began there after your father's death?"

"Yes."

"Not when you kept many social engagements?"

"What are you getting at?"

"Where in the world would your mother have met him, where would they have been face to face, not merely cognizant of one another's names?" Charlotte flung the dice down so hard that they bounced off the board and went skittering merrily along the floor. She scrambled down to retrieve one, going on her hands and knees under the table. "Where would they have seen each other and made the connection to you?" she demanded, her voice somewhat strained.

"I've no idea. I'm wracking my brains at this moment," James huffed, also crawling about in search of the missing dice, this time in the far reaches of the corner.

"What in the world sort of backgammon is this?" Mr. Harkness demanded upon entry, watching his daughter's flushed face and falling hair emerge from under the table.

"A heated game," James replied truthfully. "I've found it." He triumphantly held up the retrieved dice. "You were right, Mr. Harkness. She can't be beaten."

Mr. Harkness looked between him and the board. James followed his gaze and noticed that their pieces were nearly in identical positions. "Well. She may have met her match."

****

The afternoon passed pleasantly. James regretfully declined an invitation for supper, mindful of the fact that a gentleman should not call upon a lady's home after dark in most circumstances and he'd already done so. "I mustn't overstay my welcome," he bowed to his host.

"You are most welcome any time, James." Mr. Harkness clasped his hand and shook it firmly.

"I'll be here at five tomorrow evening to escort Miss Harkness to the ball. I'm sorry for the length of the carriage ride. If you should care to escort her to my home in Wedgewood Crescent, that would of course be an option."

Mr. Harkness clucked. "I expect I shall just be returning at five after a service at Kensley Green. But if that would suit you, Charlotte, you could come with Mr. Bartlesby and—"

"I think I'll wait for Dr. Everly. I may need every moment to get into that gown."

"I'm sure you'll look beautiful. You'll be the belle of the ball."

"I'm sure no such thing will be said. It's a simple gown," Charlotte hastened to remind him. "I have no fancy jewels, no frilly hat for the evening, no plans to paint my face…"

"A beautiful woman makes the gown stand out," James countered, smirking.

****

Mr. Harkness gave James an extra hard stare as he showed the boy out, particularly after catching the lad smirking at his daughter.

Inwardly, he was incredibly pleased. What a sensible boy. What a sensible boy with excellent taste, to appreciate the beer, not the bottle. It might be a tricky thing, courting between classes, but Mr. Harkness allowed himself a moment to fantasize about having his guest as a son-in-law, not simply a suitor for his daughter.

****

James found Old Harmon sitting at the side gate and eating a cheese and pickle sandwich when he arrived home.

"Good evening, Mr. James. Oh, beggin' your pardon, *Dr.* James."

"Good evening, Harmon. How are you? How's the leg?"

"Dodgy, sir, dodgy."

"Well, this cold can't help it. Come in, and I'll lay the fire. I'm going to have something from the larder. Will you join me?"

Harmon blinked. "Your mother wouldn't like it, sir."

"Well, Mother isn't here." James was both pleased and irritated by her absence. He couldn't demand answers as he'd like, but he also didn't have to contend with her threats and evasiveness.

"True enough, she isn't. Nor Cook, nor the maids. Never did hire on a new butler. I s'pose that'll be your lookout, sir?"

"I suppose. Don't you find that curious? Mother always insisted on a full complement of staff. I remember her and Father rowing about it."

"Ah, well. Widows. They've got to live a more modest life. I suspect she was keeping the place clear for Lavinia and her fancy bloke or you and your missus. Some people bring staff with them, don't they?"

"I suppose, although—pardon? Harmon, what fancy man?"

"Feller that Mrs. Everly didn't like." Harmon took

to the job of sorting out the fire in the drawing room while James hung up his coat and hat. "Poor Miss Lavinia. For once, she didn't get her way. 'Spect she wasn't too happy at home these past couple weeks. I'm right sorry, sir. She met a nasty accident, Sadie said?"

"Nasty indeed. Tell me about this man."

"Oh, sir." Harmon puffed out his cheeks and scratched his head. "Nothing much to tell. Few months ago, I remember hearing rattling and slamming fit to break the windows. Miss Lavinia was in a right state, but your mother... That's a woman of iron, sir. She wouldn't have him."

"Who?"

"Oh, I don't know his name. Only that he wasn't up to snuff."

"Jack? Christopher? Silcroft, Drummond?"

"Dearie me, sir, no. Not to my knowledge. Never heard that name bandied about."

James considered the sideboard for a long moment. "Will you have a drink, Harmon?"

"Well..."

"Put up here in the old butler's room for the night?"

"That's right generous, sir. To your health."

"To yours."

****

Plied with spirits though he was, Harmon yielded very little knowledge. Miss Lavinia had been courted and it had been broken off, but this was quite a while ago, in the early fall. She'd seemed in better spirits for a time, then had a week where the draperies in her room were always drawn, and she had the cook out in the garden lamenting over her lack of appetite.

James couldn't do too much with that, but it was

something to begin with, he supposed.

Spirits also made Old Harmon even chattier than he was normally. "Where have you been, sir? Why aren't you with the rest?"

"I'm studying for examinations." *Barely.*

"Ah. Still, couldn't you study in the country? Must be lonely for you here."

James leaned forward, his single drink still largely untouched. He took a small swallow. "I've got a friend in the city, Harmon. A beautiful girl."

"Ah! The missus will be pleased. What's her name?"

"Charlotte."

"Right regal sounding."

"She is not a princess. She is an angel. There's something calm and graceful about all she does... but her manner is plain and her mind is sharp. I can't think of anything else a man needs to be happy."

"I can." Harmon hiccupped.

"She's got a lovely face and figure." James gave the man a stern glare, but it melted. "Blonde hair that's soft and is always coming undone. Blue eyes. A fetching smile."

"Lor', makes me wish I was young again." Harmon drained his glass. "Of course, it'll be down to Mrs. Everly. Does she like your Charlotte?"

"I daresay she will."

"Gather she liked Miss Lavinia's lad up to a point. Must've done something wrong."

You've no idea, thought James. "Charlotte is beyond reproach." *Only no, she isn't. She's risking her reputation by being alone with me, over and over.* "I don't care what Mother says. If Miss Harkness and I continue as we have, I hope she'll receive my suit one day in the near future."

"Ah, that's the ticket, Dr. James! Let the young live and love while they can. Gather ye roses while ye may."

"Harmon, you old fraud. You're a poet."

"Know lots of verses about flowers." Harmon smiled tipsily. "Should take her a poem. Write her a flower."

James stifled a laugh. "I may try that the other way around, if you don't mind." Harmon nodded again, his eyes starting to take on a glassy look. "I'd best study and lay out my good suit for tomorrow night. It's the Royal College of Surgeons' Christmas do. I've asked Charlotte to go with me."

"Ahhh." Harmon nodded.

James waited but apparently, the deep, satisfied sigh was all the commentary the older man wished to share. "Come on. Up you get."

"Real kind of you, sir. Mrs. Everly might fuss, but the good Lord would be right proud. Made all men equal in the beginning, didn't He?"

James steadied the listing gardener-cum-watchman and took him toward the old butler's room. "Indeed. Doctors know we're all still the same. Undertakers, too. The rich might dress it up better, but everyone sickens, everyone dies."

"Don't let Madame hear you shay that, shir." Harmon put a wobbly finger to his slurring lips. "Woman's got to make a grand matsch."

"I hardly think Vinnie—"

"Not the only woman in the housh." Harmon tapped his nose knowingly, missed, and jabbed himself in the eye.

James blinked.

Mother? Making a match? "What's that, Harmon? Are you speaking of my mother? She's barely out of mourning for Father!"

"But out she is. No offense, sir. I don't think she's overeager. She's a young widow, all things conshidered."

James tipped Harmon into the room, where he promptly stumbled to the unaired, unmade bed and started snoring.

"We should all be so lucky," James mumbled. Any peace and joy left from his afternoon visit vanished. He didn't think he'd be sleeping much tonight, and he doubted his studying would go well. The exhausted surgeon-in-training realized something as he threw himself down at the desk in his room. Even though the time they spent together was far from a traditional courtship and the topics that occupied most of their conversation were far from pleasant, he was genuinely happy whenever he was in Charlotte's company.

"Living for the moments when I'm with you," he muttered, revising notes on dissection before him.

Chapter Eighteen

*"Little bird." Mama's voice distant and faint.
"Look at you. So grown up. Elegant."*

Charlotte gasped a word of thanks which quickly turned into a groan of frustration. "I've been dressing for this ball for nearly an hour." First the stockings and underthings, then the petticoat and corset, then the crinolines and the camisoles, and now the bodice and the skirt. The skirt tied in the back and the bodice cinched at the sides through tiny eyelets with fine blue-black woven thread which she feared to break.

"This is impossible. If I pull these any harder, the threads will break. If I leave them any looser, I shall be indecent. I'm already indecent!" Charlotte looked in horror at the snowy white mounds of skin pushed up by the corset and revealed by the dipping neckline of the dress. "Father will never let me out of the house, even if this is the style."

"Indeed he shall!" Mama laughed. "He will be too stunned to say a word. His little girl is a woman being wooed."

"Oh. I'm… I'm not, Mama."

"Oh, but you are. You have always been an honest child. Should womanhood make you a deceiver?"

"All of this is under pretense, Mama. Dr. Everly could not truly court me. Even if he did… it's very soon to think of such things. Barely a fortnight."

341

"And what of these society parties, groups of eligible young men and women, with their doting and scheming parents, spending fortnights in the countryside and returning home with a betrothal?"

"That's not for me! I wouldn't want it," Charlotte declared hotly. No, she didn't want to be set out like sweetmeats at a feast, waiting to catch some hungry eye. She didn't like the idea of husbands and wives being picked for wealth and pedigree, pairings made like matching socks.

"But you want him. *Do not lie, my sparrow."*

Wanting something. Like an ache in her chest and heat in her limbs. He'd kissed her and she'd kissed him back, chastely, but still. Perhaps in some wanton tropical climes such gestures were commonplace and unimportant, but not here, not in England. In a world where any kiss was an intimacy, they'd already started crossing lines. They'd been crossing lines since the beginning of this charade.

"I might. I want to help Father, too. I want to be here. More… I want to use this gift that God must have given me, to speak to souls, to help them on their way, or to help them with their unfinished earthly tasks. I'm the last hope. It's important, Mama. Is any man worth losing that?"

"The right man will not ask you to stop. He will find a way to help. You have helped him, have you not?"

"But—"

"Go, little bird. Your love waits below."

"Oh, Mama, honestly…" Charlotte rolled her eyes toward the heavens. Her mother didn't reply.

****

"Miss Harkness. Oh… Miss Harkness. Charlotte!

You're a picture, the very vision of loveliness."

"I'm entirely uncomfortable, but I thank you," Charlotte curtsied to him as gracefully as she could while worrying about her bust escaping its daring confines. "Father is changing into something warmer. He's been out all day, and he'll be out much longer, off with Bartlesby, the vicar, the Parsons, and all the crew of this year's pantomime. They're having a run-through and a supper made by the Church Ladies' Guild. At some point, someone will uncork the sacramental wine and I'll not see him until after midnight. Although not too much later, I hope. He and Bartlesby have a funeral in the afternoon, and they must take Guinevere to have her remaining three shoes replaced. The sound of the forge on a tender head is less than desirable, or so I imagine." She laughed lightly, tucking her key into the pocket of her cloak, and doing the final button on her high, dark gloves. Truly, they should have been higher, but she could not help that now and wouldn't indulge in more frivolous spending.

James looks stunned. "Mr. Harkness? Having a late night with a bunch of actors?"

"A bunch of devout churchmen, undertakers, a vicar, a few aldermen, the fishmonger, the ironmonger, and the SCADS."

"The what?"

"The St. Clementia's Amateur Dramatics Society. The vicar's wife, his rather stubborn daughters, their henpecked husbands, and a bunch of others. It's one or two nights a year that my father allows himself to drink a bit too much and laugh a bit too loudly. Typically, I accompany him, but not this year."

"I'm delighted to have won out over so lavish an

evening." James winked.

"You haven't lived until you've seen Mr. Bartlesby and Mr. Miggins singing 'Come Into the Garden, Maud' while doing a knees-up with linked elbows." She winked back.

"Goodness. I'm afraid this night will be terribly dull. Although, if McKinnon and fforbes-Wellington are in the mood, you might find yourself treated to a spectacular display of juggling and yodeling."

"Here I was worried that I would stand out. Will I?" Charlotte self-consciously fluffed the full skirts that shimmered and swished in the lamplight, a rippling ocean of blue catching sunset orange glints.

"Indeed, you shall, as the most beautiful girl there. Every gentleman will be after you."

Charlotte licked her lips. "That sounds… utterly dreadful."

*****

Dr. Everly considered the idea of every man in the room being as drawn to Charlotte as he was. Once the brighter of his associates engaged her in conversation, he'd never get her to himself again. What's more, once the fellows with baser inclinations caught sight of her swan's neck, her beautiful face—his gaze drifted slightly lower before pulling resolutely back to her smile—or any of her other fine attributes, he would be waiting in an interminable line for a dance. "It does sound rather awful," he was forced to admit.

"I don't dance very well. Of course, my governess, Auntie Molly, taught me to waltz and to do a few other socially required maneuvers around the floor, but—"

"—that's the least of our worries. I just hope it's not too noisy. You must be able to hear *his* voice."

The rosy dream of romance burst like a stretched bubble. Charlotte nodded gravely. "Perhaps it's a good thing that the other gentlemen will want a turn around the floor. I can hear them better that way."

"Perhaps." A mulish look had to be forcefully pushed down. Jealousy had no place in a murder investigation, and Charlotte was not his sweetheart. She was just a very convincing actress. Speaking of which... "Are you missing a rehearsal?"

"Oh, for the pantomime?"

"Yes, are you one of the SCADS?" James asked.

"I serve the dinner, help with the washing up, and sewing costumes. I'm not much for the stage."

"But you're such a fine actress!"

"Well, that's hardly acting, Dr. Everly. James." She finished tying on her hat for the evening, a small, scalloped affair of black lace.

"What about your performance at the livery? Or with Barney Gibbs?"

"It was simply a matter of falling into step with you, filling in lines, making sure I caught your cues. Hmm. We might dance very well together after all. Father! James is here."

"Coming, my darling." Mr. Harkness hurried down the stairs to wring James' hand and blink back proud tears from his eyes as he watched Charlotte depart, finally dressed in a fine gown and doted upon as she deserved.

****

Glasgow Hall was lit like a beacon and wrapped in garland and holly, an oversized Christmas package for some giant's child. The white pillars and columns supported a simple arch where carriages halted and glittering figures emerged, handed down by men in tail-coats, starched shirts, and elegant cravats.

Charlotte did her best to keep her jaw from flopping free as she surveyed the fine establishment. "This is where you learn all about amputation and treating wounds?"

"Here and Middlesex Hospital. The dissection lab isn't here in Glasgow Hall. It's in the operating theater, just there. There are the Halls of Residence, the Deans' quarters, and the main lecture hall. That's the gate where my coach was waiting to take me home to Mother, to hear the dreadful news." James pointed out the buildings as he spoke—"

"Which hall is yours?"

"The very first one, second floor, the East Wing."

****

Most women, at least in James' experience, would be too busy noticing the jewels and frocks of the other women, their so-called "competition." Not Charlotte. He puffed up with pride that she was on his arm, more than a pretty piece to show off, but a true partner.

"Do you see any of the possible suspects?" she breathed as their carriage halted.

James looked around. "No, not yet."

"Perhaps they're staying away. They must imagine you know something is amiss."

"One of them, yes. All of them, no. They must be inside already. Shall we?" He proudly offered her his arm and felt his collar tighten when she looked at him with steady eyes, slipping her arm through, her hand resting lightly on his. After a second, he brought his arm to his side, hers with it, his free hand coming to rest atop of hers as if he could somehow hold onto her if he only encircled her enough. "Thank you for being here with me," he whispered.

"It is I who should thank you, such a glamorous affair," Charlotte breathed back, head dipping to rest against his.

James knew they looked very loverlike and didn't care at the moment.

"*Looks* glamorous. What you and I do… it has nothing luxurious about it." He laughed, his normally open tones dark and harsh. She shivered against him. "Few women that I know would dare do what you do, even what you do every day as a matter of course… walk alone, work alone, take care of the dead's needs, listen to their voices." His feet halted before the entrance to the ball proper, hearing strains of strings drifting faintly in the cold night air.

"It's nothing. Simply a matter of devotion to what's right," Charlotte murmured modestly. "It's only how I am, naturally."

Naturally devoted. James gave their names to the attendant at the door and waved absently to a few men who hailed him, scarcely aware of anything but the woman in blue and black, gold and cream. *All the best of dark and light… and devoted. Not flitting from suitor to suitor or theater to ball in hopes of a better match or more attention.*

"Charlotte?" James' voice grew raspier still, as if the weight in his heart was pressing on his vocal cords.

"What?" Her head was still as her eyes roved, looking for danger in the sea of bright silks and velvets, brocades and laces, the men in dark suits, a rest for the eye in an onslaught of color.

"I know that you haven't known me long, but I must

tell you something." His fingers meshed with hers more tightly, making her turn her head to his. "I could be, no, I *would* be very devoted. To you. If you would consent to my calling upon you without false pretense, I promise you—"

"Dr. James Everly and Miss Charlotte Harkness!"

"Oh!" Charlotte nearly tripped as they both started, shaken from their intimate whispers by the bugle-like call of the steward.

James gritted his teeth. At the announcement of his name, there was a perceptible shift in the ballroom, heads turning, men rising from their seats and abandoning their partners. "Steady on. Here it comes. There's John Hayes with curly hair, and John Naysmith. That's Jacob Babcock."

"I'm listening," Charlotte replied under her breath. She went to step aside, out to arm's length as he took her hand at the wrist. They glided down the short set of stairs together. "James?"

"Yes?"

"I was listening. I can't imagine how we could ever—"

"Is not the twin of devotion determination?"

"I suppose."

"Then if you will not let me give you my devotion just yet, let me show you my determination."

****

Charlotte realized that she was out of place. She was the only woman not wearing jewels or carrying a fan. The styles around her spoke of wealth and class, the hair piled up in masses, stuck through with jeweled combs and circlets of gems. The length of the gloves and the number of buttons on them also were silent indicators, the higher up the arm the fabric traveled, the deeper the pockets.

She realized all of this within a few moments, but after that, she had no time to care. They had a mission to complete. James whisked her around the small tables that encircled the space left clear for dancing, stopping at each man whose Christian name began with J, no matter how unlikely the connection. In between this covert detection, James was set upon by dozens of his fellow collegiates, half of whom were curious about the cause of his sudden absence. The other half knew and wrung his hand in silent sympathy. The men nodded politely to her and greeted her cordially while a great many of their partners eyed her with everything from open disdain to quiet confusion.

Why would a man like James want to saddle himself with a woman like me?

"I can't take another moment's conversation, knowing one of them might be her killer even as he shakes my hand in sympathy." James abruptly pulled her to the center of the floor.

"I don't dance well," Charlotte reminded him in a hiss, acutely aware of the couples moving about them, dancing a chaste distance apart, palm to palm, full skirts swinging like ringing bells, effortlessly turning and swirling. "Just look at them…" she murmured in an undertone.

James did, briefly. "I would far rather dance with you. Dancing is not my forte, either. Come, we shall plan our attack to the strains of Strauss."

****

"His voice didn't sound the same across the memories, but… overall, low and husky, almost as if he didn't wish to be heard."

She hadn't found the owner of the voice yet, though James had contrived to introduce her to a dozen gentlemen fitting their limited description.

"He likely did not wish to draw attention. A secret romance, that much I've concluded, one that my mother likely forbade." James supplied her with the details he'd learned from Old Harmon, sparse as they were.

"But surely your mother has—"

"Mother has not bothered to wire in return. She may have written. Most likely she is ignoring the problem and hoping it goes away. She buried the evidence, paid it away." In his anger, James danced faster than the music allowed, arm like iron beside hers, commanding her across the floor.

Charlotte didn't seem to notice they were cutting a swathe through the dancers, her eyes intent on his troubled face. "She must have a reason, James."

"To avoid a scandal, as if that matters more than life!"

"Scandal, yes, but—" Charlotte stopped as the small orchestra brought the song to an end. Everyone paused to applaud, flushed with laughter, exertion, and sips of Christmas cheer.

It was at that moment that a stunning brunette with glossy curls piled high upon her head turned and nodded to them, then paused. "James!"

James blinked at the woman who addressed him. She was certainly what many would term eye-catching, with lily-white skin and delicate rose tinting her lips and cheeks. She wore a crimson dress that set off the stark contrast of her skin to her advantage. James recognized her as one of the girls from various musical evenings he'd been dragged to. In fact, wasn't this Vinnie's duet partner? The one who had constantly invaded his parlor to practice a quodlibet on the piano this spring? "Oh! Good evening, Miss—" James turned his head strategically and blessed the sound of the cello and violin striking up a gay and spirited tune. "May I present Miss Charlotte Harkness?"

Charlotte extended her hand with a curtsey. "It is a pleasure. I'm sorry, I didn't catch your name?"

"Lady Asquith. Catherine. James, of course you know your fellow surgeon-to-be. Theo Jackson." Catherine's eyes shone with possessive pride as she looked at the tall, dark-haired man beside her, blessed with naturally fine, striking features and expressive eyes. "Son of Admiral Jackson, First Lord of the Admiralty," she emphasized.

James extended his hand to the man. He must be in a different year. James was sure he'd seen him in passing. "Ah, yes. Theo."

The strapping man shook James' hand in a powerful grip and spoke in a deep husk of a voice. "Oh, gracious, man. Don't be stuffy. Call me Jack, all the fellows in my year do."

Charlotte's fingers dug deeply into his wrist.

Jack. Tall, well-built, rich, dark-haired, husky-voiced Jack.

"Oh, I do love this tune, it's a regular romp! Come on, James. Jack won't mind." Catherine suddenly tugged James away with a tinkling laugh and the air of a woman used to taking exactly what she likes.

"I shan't complain. I have my own distraction. Isn't that right, Miss Harkness?" Jack bowed over her hand and swept her across the floor to the rollicking music.

****

James was tempted to push the girl away from him, but her first words changed that. The glad light in her eyes dropped as if someone pulled a curtain. "It isn't true? It's a stunt, an exaggeration? Has she been disowned by your mother?"

James could barely keep his feet moving. By sheer force of habit, the noblesse oblige drilled into him since birth, he kept making the required pivots in time with his lovely partner. "What, Lady Asquith?"

"Lavinia! I heard… I heard she died. That she's buried. That can't be true."

"It is." James had no other words.

"But she only wrote to me a few weeks ago. She was so happy, on the verge of a proposal. Well, at least she hinted at such a thing. She always was hinting. Oh. Oh, no, James. How did it happen?"

James was relieved when the lady suddenly seemed unable to continue. She made a desperate shake of her head and allowed him to lead her to a nearby table. "Mother didn't want an inquest."

"Was she ill?"

"Not so ill that she should die," James said stiffly.

"Oh, dear! I'm being dreadful, aren't I? I'm so sorry for your loss, dear James." Her sad, stunned eyes overflowed. "I simply can't fathom—"

"Proposal, you say?"

"She hinted at one, yes." The dumbfounded eyes suddenly narrowed. "What in the world are you doing at a ball? If these rumors are true—"

"Shh. I'm here because I intend to finish the term this year, and I'll be moving back into the Halls of Residence shortly. Nothing more. Charlotte knows my grief and supports me in it. No finer wife could a man have."

"Oh. Oh, I'm sorry, I should have held my tongue. I didn't know of your engagement. Harkness? Would that be the Sussex branch of the Harkness family?"

"The London branch." He stepped back with a curt bow, sickened by how quickly grief could turn to social climbing and shaming. "Did she mention the name of her intended? Believe me, I will not divulge her confidence to another."

"Don't you know? She said he was a brilliant match, and she hoped to invite us to her 'country place' next summer."

"Good heavens. Really?"

"Well, that's not the first time she's said such a thing. Our first Season was peppered by Lavinia's letters, sure that she'd caught the eye of everyone from Prince Edward to the dustman."

Vain. Petty.

Sweet. Silly. Curious. Clever.

"When did she meet Jack?" He turned his head and his heart stopped for a moment. Where was Charlotte? Had he truly left her with a murderer? He sagged in relief when he caught sight of her waltzing past with the handsome brute, her head nodding gravely.

"Theo? I don't know if they've ever met."

"Then who was she engaged to?"

"Oh, don't be silly, James. A woman wouldn't put anything in writing unless he'd proposed officially and been accepted."

"You must know who she was referring to," he hissed. He would have shaken her if he thought it would help.

"Why? Does it matter? She's—she's gone!" Catherine's shoulders began to tremble.

"It may matter a great deal. If you know, please tell me."

"She didn't put it in her letter, but naturally I saw her at the Prince Consort's birthday concert at the Crystal Palace. She'd worked on your mother for ages to let her attend. Seeing as it was musical, she at last relented."

James blinked. That was an event? "Naturally."

"She mentioned a name, Thomas someone? I'm sorry, we were only together a moment at intermission, and it was dreadfully noisy and crowded."

Jack. John. Christopher. Thomas. Jackson? His head swam. "I must take my leave of you. Good night, Miss Asquith."

****

"How did you come to know Dr. Everly's family?" Charlotte wasted no time.

"I can't say that I do, but his father and mine were members of the same club," Jack murmured, his smile faintly amused. "Are you like every other woman here? Interested solely in a man's family and his properties?"

She bridled but suppressed her retort. This wasn't the time for a confrontation, not if she could handle things skillfully. "Everything about Dr. Everly is of interest to me," she replied demurely.

"Well. That's an evasive answer."

"And yours is patronizing."

He laughed suddenly, then winced as he rubbed his throat. "Oh, that smarts like the devil in hobnailed boots. Pardon my vulgarity, Miss Harkness."

"What?" Charlotte looked at him in confusion.

"Well, if you're a surgeon's companion, I expect

this won't make you faint. Have you heard of a tonsillectomy?"

"Briefly."

"I've had one two weeks ago. It's still dashed hard to talk, but Lady Asquith will not be done out of a ball, and you can see why." His fond eyes fastened to his partner as the dark-haired beauty circled the room with James. "I'd be jealous of your fellow if Catherine wasn't such good friends with his sister. Not to mention, he has quite a lovely damsel of his own."

Charlotte sliced through the complimentary twaddle and small talk. "Two weeks ago?"

"Dashed nuisance. Tonsils had swelled up to the size of eggs! It was done right here, last Friday of November it was. I remember thinking it was lucky it hadn't happened a month later or I wouldn't be able to make my way through Christmas dinner. I was a demonstration case for the Friday surgical clinic. Sir Henry, one of the deans, supervised a team of surgeons himself. Saved my life, even if it is confoundedly miserable."

"Are you telling me that you don't normally sound like this? Rather low and quiet?" Charlotte blinked. Since she met him, she'd been listening to him speak and trying to see if his tones matched the memories she'd overheard. They did not. She was waiting for a signal from Lavinia. Nothing.

"Quiet? There's a laugh! I have four older brothers and our entire family has been in the navy since before Napoleon's time. Not only that, but I was the coxswain for my crew at Cambridge. Quiet is the last word to describe me, Miss Harkness. Why do you ask?"

"I am naturally a curious woman," she answered truthfully.

"Oh, ho! I wouldn't let Dr. Everly find out. A curious wife is no end of trouble for her husband."

"I may hope that a husband of mine thinks differently. So, you do not know Lavinia Everly?"

Jack frowned, seemingly puzzled by her refusal to play along with his dashing wit. "I doubt it. I shun the company of society debs whenever I can. I'm afraid tonight I couldn't resist Lady Asquith's charms."

"Very bountiful they are, too. I'll let you attend to her." Charlotte clapped politely as the jubilant holiday tune came to an end.

"I'm sorry if I offended you, Miss Harkness."

"On the contrary, you relieve me." She curtsied and turned away hurriedly, letting out a deep sigh when she collided with James in the whirl of bodies.

"That's not him," they said as one.

James cursed under his breath. "Let's go out for some air. This place is stifling."

****

"That couldn't have been him. He was recovering from a tonsillectomy on the day she was killed, and that's not the voice. That's not even his normal tone of voice. It's the recovery after his surgery affecting him."

"Lady Asquith was a rather good friend of Vinnie's. Vinnie hinted that she was soon to be engaged. A man named Thomas, she believes."

Charlotte sat down on a small stone bench between two high shrubs. The air was biting, and she hadn't bothered to retrieve her shawl. She huddled farther into her dress, but she soon found a much warmer solution. James hesitated, then sat down next to her and placed his coat around her shoulders. He adjusted the garment tenderly before resting his arm around her back.

"May I take the liberty?" he asked.

"You may." She let her head droop to her shoulder. "James… I didn't meet anyone with a voice that sounds like the one Lavinia lets me hear."

"I don't know whether or not that's a blessing," James followed suit, his head against hers.

"I'm sorry."

"Do not be."

They sat in silence, keeping each other warm while a soft, yearning song drifted from inside.

"My sister should be here. She should be dancing to this, sitting like this, her head on someone's shoulder. I would have welcomed a brother-in-law in my profession."

"You would not welcome a man capable of murder."

"No. But why? I don't understand why… I need to find out who to know why. I sound quite mad."

"No, but the man who hisses through her memories sounds utterly mad. The man who said he was the son of Lady Silcroft, that voice is completely different. Then again, a quiet conversation *would* sound different than a murderous outburst." Charlotte swallowed. "There was a beggar by the stalls where I shop."

"Yes?"

Charlotte was nestled against James, uncaring for the eyes of any passersby, giving him a moment of comfort in his grief.

"Old Peg. She talked to herself, harmlessly. I would often give her an apple or pear. One day, I saw a constable try to move her away from the carts and barrows. She leapt at him, hissing and clawing, spitting out words I had never even heard." Charlotte blushed. "I could not have believed docile Old Peg was that hellion.

I'm beginning to wonder if I am hearing the voices of one man or two."

"I don't know, my love." James swallowed audibly. "Sometimes, I wonder if this is all madness, you, me, everything about us. This must be a fever dream that I cannot awaken from."

Charlotte lifted her head to take in his faraway face. "Yes. Must be." Why else would she be here, with a man's arm around her, a wonderful, intelligent, kind-hearted man? She should be at home, playing a quiet game of cribbage with Father, helping him polish the coffins dropped off by the cabinetmaker, or helping him knock together the wooden boxes for the very poorest who couldn't afford such a finely made final resting place.

"I think of how senseless and brutal this was—is. Do you know what I've just realized?"

"Tell me?"

"My sister was not a selfless person. Never was, I daresay never would have been. In her final acts on Earth, or rather hovering over it in some fashion, she's given me the best gift in the world. I want her back more than anything... which is hard for me to understand because—" He took a deep breath. "—because that's how much I want you, Charlotte. If everything else in my life goes wrong, I've met you." A head tipped back, blowing out a fog of breath in the night air. "Of course, that might all go wrong as well."

Charlotte sat frozen, but not from the cold temperatures. All of her felt hot, shot through with rushing blood and flushing skin. No, she had to be utterly still to keep up with her brain, which was clacking along at a rapid pace, throwing up objections and arguments.

All of them were overridden with a simple refrain. *He has no reason to lie. He can get no more out of me. I have failed in the one way I could aid him.*

"You can speak. Put a fellow down as nicely as possible." He separated from her, arm lifting regretfully from around her shoulders.

She grabbed his arm back, both arms in fact, as they turned on the bench. For once, she had no clever words, but her mouth was put to good use.

****

"Dr. Everly!"

James turned groggily toward the sharp voice. Charlotte was kissing him. *Had* been kissing him, although she was now blushing vividly and retreating into the shadows cast by the shrubbery. He hadn't known people kissed like that, desperately and silently, uncaring for manners or rules.

"Dean Lawrence!" The mental mist left abruptly at the sight of the imposing man in evening dress glowering down at them. "Ah. Sir Henry William Lawrence, the Dean of the Royal College of Surgeons, may I present Miss Charlotte Harkness?"

Charlotte rose and curtsied with a sweet, sincere smile. "Good evening, Sir Lawrence. This is a splendid function. Thank you for your hospitality."

Disarmed by her smile, the bewhiskered man harrumphed a few times. "A pleasure to meet you, Miss Harkness, and 'tis the pleasure of the college to share in the goodwill of the season. Ahem. May I have a word with you, Everly?"

James' stomach clenched, not in the pleasurable way of a moment ago, but this time with dread. His voice was light and his smile calm as he replied, "Certainly.

Charlotte?"

"I'll step inside. It's rather chilly out here." She managed to deposit James' coat into his hand and slid back inside the ballroom.

"I believed you would be out for the rest of the term. It's good to see you." Lawrence began, shaking James' hand. "How is your mother?"

"In the country with her sister."

"Ah. Sensible course of action. Change of scenery." The gray eyebrows rose approvingly, then fell. "Why aren't you with her?"

"I wish to finish my examinations, sir. I know I can do it. I've been studying and—"

"Everly, I have no doubt that you can sit your examinations and pass them on the spot. Shall we say.... Tuesday?"

That wouldn't leave much time for revision, but no matter. James nodded eagerly. "Thank you, sir. But the final dissection?"

"Hmm. Well. We should have fresh specimens overnight. I must reserve some for the first-year students." His head turned toward the gate where corpses were left overnight, deposited in a wicker basket by the flesh merchants who took those who no one would miss or who could not afford a proper burial.

"Of course."

"And I've set the final years' dissection examination for Thursday a week, but really, Everly. You ought to get out of the city and rejoin your mother. She's alone in the world now!"

"I will go, sir, promptly after I finish my examinations." James wasn't lying. He would journey out for Christmas with his mother and his aunt Eleanor's family. He would return swiftly to London. When he pictured Christmas festivities, he envisioned sitting in the humble pews of St. Clementia's, holding Charlotte's hand, and roaring with laughter at the sight of Mr. Harkness as the Old Dame in the panto. Frankly, at this moment, he would have preferred to be dissecting a cadaver rather than playing an interminable game of Shove, Piggy, Shove or charades with his aunt's houseguests.

Dean Lawrence sighed. "You are incorrigibly determined, Everly."

Is determination not the twin of devotion? A smile lit his eyes while his mouth remained serious. "Thank you, sir."

A dry chuckle split the dour lips. "Tomorrow morning, first thing."

"But it's a Saturday!"

"And it is quite an exception. I wouldn't offer it to just anyone." The piercing eyes warned the younger man not to seem ungrateful.

"Thank you, sir. I will be there, first thing."

"Well... not too early. Shall we say by nine thirty or ten? Come to the dissection theater and wait. Provided we have a fresh offering, I will personally oversee your examination."

James nodded his thanks once again. "I will be ready and waiting, sir."

"See that you are." The dean hesitated. "Everly, your circumstances, as well as your talent, have prompted my unusual offer. Another factor is *Mrs.* Everly's abundant generosity."

"Thank you, sir."

"Still, I prefer not to become overfamiliar with my

students lest it lead to cries of preference. So, I shall tell that your conduct with that young woman is frowned upon as you're still a student."

"I understand, sir. I'm sorry, sir."

"I shall be lenient this time, considering the situation. Do not let me catch you making such a public demonstration of affection again. If you'll take my advice, you'll not make such a display in private, either."

****

James swallowed down a hiss of anger at the rebuke. He and Charlotte had been rather carried away, but it wasn't shameful. He would kiss her before God and all of England if he could find a church big enough. His anger vanished and he smiled crookedly. "Sound advice, sir. If she accepts me, I hope you'll attend the ceremony."

****

Charlotte waited by the doorway, listening as discreetly as she could and not catching much. Was James in trouble because of her sudden exuberance, her utterly unladylike behavior?

What in the world had possessed her?

Love?

Did love feel like that, sudden and painfully all-consuming? Overwhelming enough to make you act on instinct, some sort of wild animal with the jungles in your blood instead of polite society manners?

Worst of all, as a lady, she should not have responded to him in that way. She should have told him his fears were needless. She should have told him to continue to court her properly and in due time...

"Dull as ditchwater. Not a bit of fun, if you know what I mean."

Charlotte was glad the music was loud and she was close to the aperture. She let out a harsh gasp the rang in her own head, quickly muffled by the sounds of Lavinia's screams and mocking, sadistic laughter.

That voice.

She *knew* that voice

"Not your sport, old man?"

"I like a bit of *hunting*. Nothing to bag in here."

"Plenty to bag. Diedre Powell is a right goer."

A sneering laugh cemented it.

Charlotte looked back toward the grounds and then into the ballroom. There was a positive sea of men circling past with partners and strolling past in groups. She rose unsteadily, still feeling weak from the violence of Lavinia's sudden intrusion into her mind.

"It's him, isn't it?" Charlotte cried to the unseen soul that forced the words into her ears.

Nothing, but then again, Lavinia couldn't speak, only replay old acts in this horrible tragedy. "Take me to him, help me find him."

Nothing. This moment hadn't happened in the dead girl's lifetime. She had no memory to share, no way to speak the future. Lavinia couldn't help.

James was outside. It was up to her.

Pushing her way through the crowd, she was blocked by wide skirts and cold eyes, by broad shoulders and polite grins. Charlotte wriggled her way through blindly, only knowing where the voice had come from, but not where it had gone.

"Gentlemen. Honored guests." A man stood before the small chamber orchestra now, a broad smile on his face. Everyone fell silent.

Blast, Charlotte thought. So much for following the

voice now.

"Let us welcome the esteemed Professor Emeritus of Human Anatomy, Member of the Court of Examiners… our esteemed President of the Royal College of Surgeons, Edward Arnott."

Tumultuous applause broke out, in which Charlotte reluctantly joined. Her eyes were moving through the crowded room.

"Before we get to the syllabub and mince pies, I have a few words I'd like to say."

Charlotte felt a sudden draft behind her. She turned her head as discreetly as she could, just in time to see a group of men exit the crowded hall. If anyone else noticed, they gave no sign, all eyes riveted to the revered speaker.

Walking backwards as slowly and smoothly as she dared, she made her way back to the outer ring of people, then worked her way back along the wall. James would surely see her if he was still outside. Better still, perhaps some of his friends would be among the fleeing group and they'd all be conversing together.

She slid out the door.

Into a solid chest.

Charlotte whirled, fire in her eyes and ready to scream and summon help.

"What's the matter?" James hissed, seeing her face cloud and then clear.

"Where are they?" Charlotte demanded, looking past him frantically.

"Who?"

"I heard him. I heard his voice, I'm sure this time!" Charlotte tugged desperately on his sleeve.

"Who? Where?" James easily outpaced her, turning

back, looking at her for direction.

"They went out that door, a group of them. The one, the one I've heard before, he said he wanted to go hunting and there wasn't anything to bag in here." Realization dawned on her face. "James, he's going to go after another girl!"

"Father in heaven!" James grabbed for her hand as she barely caught up to him. "They'll have to take a cab."

"What if they had a carriage waiting in front of the hall, waiting until the ball lets out?" Charlotte demanded breathlessly, still running, absolutely delighted now that she hadn't been pressured into buying any fancy dancing slippers.

"He mustn't get away."

****

He had gotten away. Coaches lined streets in all directions, waiting for their glittering occupants to return, cabs rattled past. The group of men had dispersed. According to one drowsing coachman, a half dozen fellows had emerged, some taking a carriage, some hailing cabs. Where to?

"How would I know that, sir? They didn't ask *me* to drive 'em anywhere. I'm only waiting for Lady Hawkins to return from her fancy do."

"We'll ask every coachman along the street," James said as their disappointing interview concluded. "One may have been close enough to overhear where they wanted to go."

"Yes. But which one?" Charlotte shivered. Her evening shawl and her cloak were still inside. "A half-dozen men, all fairly tall, all in evening dress? The only help I can give is the voice I heard that no one else can hear!"

James paused, panting and wild-eyed. "You're right. So close," he whispered, voice scraping out. "Are you sure?"

"I am as sure as I can be, which is not much comfort, I know." Charlotte eased closer to him. "James, can any man attend the ball?"

"Hm? Oh, no, only current students are invited."

"Then we do know his whereabouts—simply not his immediate ones. What's more, he daren't commit a murder in the company of witnesses, or while so many can claim to have seen him leaving. Either witnesses or a spoiled alibi, it is likely he is forestalled from his worst work."

There was hope, a glimmer of hope at least. "I'm going to move back into the Halls of Residence first thing tomorrow. I'll ferret about and find out who left early and we'll work from there. The dean has graciously agreed to let me sit my examinations on Tuesday and complete the final examination in dissection tomorrow. I will finish my qualifications."

"Wonderful. That is wonderful news in the midst of everything," Charlotte said fervently. She wished she could do something, anything to restore his spirits.

"I will no longer be Dr. Everly, physician, but Dr. Everly, FRCS. I intend to open my own practice."

Charlotte cocked her head. This was certainly a fine plan, but a mighty leap from their current problem. "I'm sure it will be a grand success."

"I hope so. I can use the capital left from my father's shares of the business that passed to me to purchase just the right sort of premises. Somewhere near Harkness and Sons would be ideal."

"Oh, dear. James, you ought to have a place more

prosperous."

"Fine. You can help me search for properties, tour what listings property agents suggest. Would you like to?" His head was forward, quizzical, chest rising and falling rapidly.

"Me? James, I'm not a surgeon!" Charlotte laughed, caught off-guard, though flattered.

In the street, under the gaslight that caught the shadows and highlights in the folds of her dress, he pulled her to him, the way no gentleman should ever grab a lady. "I know that. I know that you could surely be, if that's what you wanted. You could be an undertaker, an embalmer, a physician, a detective. Charlotte, you could be anything this world has to offer, were you of a different sex. But I'm glad you are exactly as you are. I must ask you. Out of all the things you could possibly be in this world... Would you like to be a surgeon's wife?"

Chapter Nineteen

James had always found the journey from Westminster to Whitechapel rather tedious, even if it truly wasn't very long.

That night, he did not. That night, he wished the road would stretch and stretch, that the moon would stand still overhead, leaving him and Charlotte alone forever.

"I would love to be your…." She bit back a gasp, overwhelmed and unsure. "I would not like to be *any* surgeon's wife, but if you were the surgeon—yes, James, I would love it, but I know that it's far too soon. People will talk."

"We needn't rush. I simply would like to know that it's not something you reject out of hand," he pleaded.

"Far from out of hand." She slid her fingers slowly over his shoulders until they danced in the soft hairs at the nape of his neck. "If my father will consent, you may have both of my hands, indeed."

This time he kissed her, ignorant of the whistles and japes from the cabbies and coaches along the street, the shocked gasps from couples exiting the ball for a breath of air.

"We have to stop that." Charlotte blushed.

"Ah, no. We have to do more. Much, much more of that," James disagreed. Courting suddenly made sense.

"Well… we should do it in private. After—after it's proper."

"Like an engaged couple?"

"I suppose—oh."

"Let's get your cloak and get you home."

****

"Harmon? Harmon, would you like to hear some truly splendid news?" James sang as he entered the house. The place was lit up and warm. "Rather extending yourself, old chap," he muttered, looking for the gardener.

"Good evening, James."

James dropped his coat and hat as he whirled. "Mother!"

****

She paced, still wearing her traveling dress, her spine and manner stiff, smile even stiffer. "What wonderful news do you have?"

"I've met my future wife, Mother."

The smile fell into open shock. "What? I haven't even met the girl! Or have I?" The shock transformed into something James could best define as calculation.

He snipped off the questions he imagined would follow. "Not that I'm aware of, but that's no concern to me. If you have any sense in you, you'll love her and embrace her to your bosom as a second daughter." James knew he was being cold. He didn't care. "Perhaps you'll do more for her than you did for your first one."

His mother's hand left a smarting sear across his cheek.

"You know nothing!" she spat, lips white and trembling.

"You *tell* me nothing!" James thundered back, sickened with himself for taking pleasure in watching her shrink back, momentarily cowed. "But that doesn't matter! I can find things out."

"I told you to leave it, James. I'll put you from the house, I'll—"

"Take the house. Take the money, and the property, and the investments, and hang the lot of them! I'll hang her murderer, Mother, and sleep a poor but peaceful man."

"You'll spoil everything." His mother collapsed onto the settee, clasping at her chest.

"What could be left to spoil? He slit her throat, Mother! Hacked her open, and you don't care!"

"Of course I care! Everyone in the city would care. Lavinia Everly was found down in the squalor of Whitechapel with her throat slit in some fit of passion or a robbery gone wrong!"

James was unable to do more than stare. "You... knew?"

"The police told me where she'd been found and that she—she died from knife wounds. A lady oughtn't to know such things, not that you care, parading such words in front of a poor widow. I knew going into medicine was a sinful folly, the waste of your father's hard work. It's made you callous and cruel, speaking of such things to a grieving mother."

"Callous? Cruel? Mother, if we don't catch this brute, he'll do it again! He's a surgeon, an educated man, he may inflict damage upon a trusting patient that—"

His mother made an impatient sound through her nose and rose, the pretense of a weak and feeble woman abruptly vanishing as she roughly seized a decanter. "Of course he wasn't. A common, nasty thing, her Jack. She did it to spite me, you know. She took off with the lower-class filth to—to do things a lady must never do. She cheapened herself, made herself easy pickings. He probably wanted money."

"Jack. You said Jack." James blinked, aghast at the way the name tumbled out with surety. "You know him?"

"I never met him."

"Then how—"

"Letters, you silly boy. What fools I've raised! She continued to write to him and he continued to write to her, even after I began intercepting the letters. Of course, some must have escaped my hands. Hm. That dull-witted girl, Sadie. As soon as Bannet is back, I'll sack her."

"If you do, then I shall hire her, promptly, for my new practice. I'll teach her to read, too. She's not a dull-wit. She's kind and helpful." James defended the timid maid.

"Oh, no. Not you, too. James, what have you done with her? What if the girl, Charlotte, should hear about your dalliances?" She poured a hefty measure of brandy into a sherry glass and brought it to her lips.

James yanked it from her hand and tossed it all into the fire, not caring for the explosion that made her scream as glass shattered and fragments flew across the hearth, scattering at their feet.

"I've never done anything with any woman but Charlotte, whom I have only kissed. Do you know why? I hate the way you shove them at me, down my throat, like pretty cakes for me to eat instead of a woman I might spend my life with!"

Silence.

Laughter. Wet, bewildered laughter.

"Don't laugh," James ground out, fists balling.

"I loved your father so dearly. Now, I'm his widow,

alone in London, unable to keep my wayward children in line. This is not the life I want, to be back in the marriage market again at my age."

Harmon was right, James thought silently, but that matter was neither here nor there. At this moment, he was a step away from being disowned, so what did it matter if his mother used her late husband's wealth and this house as a lure to catch a new husband? The cheapness of it all, wrapped in the richest trimmings, made him sick.

"What does it matter who killed her, a poor man or a rich one? We can find him. You have his letters, his address? There must be some clue as to his identity in his writing."

"I burned them, just like I burned every other piece of correspondence your sister took it into her foolish head to write. A lady must never pen her secrets. If it had been me, I would have refused all of his letters at once. Some of the things he suggested! Meeting alone, at night."

It was James' turn to sink down, hands supporting his head as it threatened to blow from the sheer volume of anger inside it. "She knew you didn't approve?"

His mother didn't answer. The only sound was the still snapping fire and the soft clink of glass to decanter as she attempted another drink.

"Mother. Lavinia was probably misled. She was foolish, I know, but that doesn't excuse letting her murderer walk free.'

She drained the glass and faced him, looking tired and beaten. Her words came out heavily. "I know. It's not the right thing to do. What I've done is terrible. Will it make you happy to hear me admit it?"

"Not very."

"James, do you know who Lord Sutterford is?"

"I don't."

"He is a neighbor of Aunt Eleanor's. He is a devout man, a member of the English Moral Return Movement. He is a peer who plans to run for Parliament."

"This neighbor is relevant, why?"

"He is desirous of a wife to quell rumors about his own morality. A man of near fifty, never wed... some claim it is his principles while others claim far worse. He is wealthy enough not to want this house as property, but he doesn't believe in keeping excessive staff. It looks too frivolous. I would likely only be able to bring my personal maid and possibly Cook."

The hints his mother dropped finally hit their mark. "You want to marry this man?"

"Want? I wouldn't put it quite like that."

"Do you love him?"

A brazen laugh, hollow and miserable underneath, burst from her lips. James was shocked. He'd never seen his mother display so much emotion, so much real, raw emotion, not even when her beloved husband died. She'd buried it all in a haze of pills and powders. She'd drowned her sorrows in a sea of sherry and spirits, but at last, she was wading ashore.

"I'm not a young widow, James, not a soldier's bride of twenty-something, or even a comely lass of thirty-something. I will be fifty in a few years. I could wait to find love, but it would not find me. It is not a luxury I have, shall we say. No, the best thing a woman of my age and status can hope for is a widower of similar means and property. Lord Sutterford is actually quite a catch, a bachelor too long, ready to yield himself to matrimony if the woman is suitably respectable and her family is beyond reproach."

"But Lavinia wasn't?"

She continued as if she hadn't heard him, walking around the room, her fingertips trailing over the furnishings and moldings on the wall. "He thinks London is quite a foul place, full of drink, debauchery, and devilment. He looked up your career, you know. You had no youthful indiscretions. Lavinia's illness and my quick thinking kept him from finding out about her follies. I'm confident the marriage shall take place within the year, likely in June. As I said, I will take Bannet, sack Sadie and Harmon... Cook may come if she likes, I haven't heard much praise for his table. The house will be yours if you stop this nonsense. Of course, should Lord Sutterford win his seat, we would expect your hospitality when he must come to the City."

"I... I haven't even met him, Mother."

"Then we are even. I haven't even met your 'future wife.' And you *have* met Lord Sutterford at Aunt Eleanor's Easter dinner. He has no family, you see." Her face softened. "He's a good man, James. He's strict and stern, but he's kind. He's charitable. A good woman could soften him up."

His head lost the war with gravity and collapsed, pulling his torso with it. Flung back against the couch, he gazed at his mother with wretched eyes. "Mother, you're not too old to find someone to love. Or if you do not wish it, why not stay here? Replenish the servants. I shall not be far, I plan for my practice to be in the city, a few moments away by coach, perhaps. Widowhood need hold no terror for someone as beloved in society as you."

In her sweep around the room, her hands now ran

along the wooden edge of the horsehair sofa, fingers gently brushing through his locks. "A widow is not a whole person in London society, James. Nor is a single woman. She is a burden who must be protected and escorted at each turn, but who adds little value to her surroundings unless she is incredibly wealthy or uniquely talented. I am neither. Wealthy, yes, but not wealthy enough to become a benefactress or patron of the arts. Thank God I have my reputation intact, for if I did not, I would only be fit for playboys, divorcees, and foreigners"—she gave a shudder—"and eventually I would be too old to attract even those sorts of men. If there was even the slightest whiff of scandal around us, I'd be forced to move in with relatives and be a burden on my sister and her husband. But if I were the wife of an M.P., the wife of one of the county set"— her eyes suddenly shone—"a country estate to manage and improve, the house to redecorate and furnish more stylishly, charities to coordinate, parties to host with my sister… yes. Yes, James, I will marry him when he asks. I don't love him, but I love what I shall gain from him, just as he loves what he shall gain from me. A perfect, seasoned wife and hostess with excellent connections and a fine stepson into the bargain. Of course, you won't be his heir."

"Far from it!" he cried. "But surely if you don't even love him—"

This laugh was wrapped in a bitter sigh. "Love? What a notion! Love does not end well, James. Look at your sister's tragic case. Had she not been besotted with that pretentious young lout, Thompson—"

James' head jerked sharply. "Thomas?" Yes, Lady Asquith had mentioned a Thomas.

Mrs. Everly shook her head stubbornly, the effects of brandy, grief, and exhaustion beginning to show. She pushed past him like a locomotive. "No! That upstart friend of yours, Thompson."

"Thompson? Lawrence Thompson?" The idea was laughable. "When in the world did the two of them even meet? I'm sure you must be mistaken."

"Oh, are you certain indeed?" she questioned mockingly.

"He never attends society functions. He strictly prefers to be with the lads in our year, always out with McKinnon, Bateson, and me, or down playing billiards in the common rooms."

The stubborn look became downright mulish. "She didn't meet him at a function. No, I met him at your birthday supper."

His birthday supper?

Last year had been a bleak time to celebrate, and his birthday came and went without a murmur. His family was in mourning. This year, Uncle Jeremy, his father's brother, had not let the occasion go unmarked, despite the fact that the two-year period of mourning was not over. His uncle was a jovial chap who believed the only cure for sadness was to chase it out with food, drink, and jokes. With that in mind, Uncle Jeremy had rounded up a half dozen of his closest friends from the college, his other uncles and his cousins who were of age, and they'd all gone round to Simpson's for steak, game pies, oysters, chocolate ice creams, and everything else that a human stomach could possibly hold. His mother hadn't been there. It was strictly an evening for the lads. "You didn't come, Mother. You had—" His words slowed as memories returned. "A recital for Lavinia."

She nodded knowingly, a sad smile on her lips, "Yes, indeed, and wasn't she ever so put out that Uncle Jeremy and her only brother were going to miss her performance?"

"It wasn't my idea, this party!"

"Did that matter to her? Not in the slightest. She was absolutely enraged that you would miss it and she didn't care tuppence for whether or not it was your birthday. I told her that I must stop in and say hello to my brothers-in-law and my nephews, as well as my son on his birthday. Your father's brothers did so much to help manage the business once he passed. It was Jeremy who thought of giving you that supper and finding out which of the gentlemen were your particular friends. Well, that didn't seem of any importance to your sister." She clicked her tongue angrily. "Lavinia was highly put out that Uncle Jeremy hadn't offered to host the party on a different night, and equally put out that you would choose 'your boring bookworms with their specs and whiskers than a night of the finest music in London.' " A flicker of fire lit in her eyes. "So selfish. We can see things clearly afterwards, can't we?"

"Not selfish, not only. She was probably missing Papa. He always made such a fuss over her talent. It was her first recital without him."

"Be that as it may, when I directed the coach to stop at Simpson's on the way, she flew into such a passion. She told the driver to head on without me, claiming that she must prepare and run her piece one more time through with Lady Asquith."

A sick sense of dread filled him. The pieces were beginning to knit themselves into one picture, but the picture made no sense. His mother was still talking, pausing only to pour herself another glass of strong, dark liquid.

"I came in to wish you many happy returns and found myself conversing with several of your friends, including Dr. Thompson. The encounter was brief, but I did recall his face."

"But *Lavinia* didn't even see him. She'd driven on." It made no sense at all. Anyway, Lavinia's paramour was called Jack, not Dr. Lawrence Thompson. There was no way one could possibly derive the nickname of Jack from *that*.

His mother fixed him with a gimlet stare. "No, of course she didn't see him that night. She never would have met him at all if…" Another gulping swallow. "I want to go upstairs, James. None of this matters now."

He gripped her arms as she tried to move past him, wincing with her when he saw the sudden flash of pain in her eyes that managed to penetrate the brandy-induced fog. "You're telling me that one of my very best friends courted my sister and never even told me about it?"

"It didn't last for long, I made sure of that. I found out his true nature in a few months."

"What do you mean, his true nature? When were they introduced? I certainly never—"

She shook his hand from her arm furiously, teeth bared. "Impatient. Selfish! Both of you."

"What happened? For God's sake, Mother, if you love me at all," he begged, voice breaking, "just tell me when they met and how. Please."

"It was my weakness as much as hers. I allowed her to persuade me that she should have a new dress made for the holiday balls. Several, in fact. She was so tired of being in black all the time, and it did nothing for her features, nor her figure. It made her look quite sickly and far too thin."

Dress?

Alarms clanged in the distance, fire horses and their wagons rumbling over the distant, uneven streets of his psyche.

"Green and sable?" James asked, mouth parched. Bits of a conversation from a week ago flitted through his brain, warring with the ever-increasing percussion in his temples.

"Winter dress. Green and sable. Elegant. So grown-up."

"Didn't you like it after all?"

"She turned back to look at that hat. Lovely hat, ostrich feather."

"She looked beautiful in the gown we chose, even though I forbade her to wear it until the appropriate time had passed. She was still pouting about the wait, despite getting everything she wanted. Do you know—even after all my concessions, she turned back to admire a new hat in the window of the shop? I'd already ordered her one to match her gown!"

"She turned back to see it?" James supplied, hardly able to hear his own voice, the dread moving up and settling into his throat.

"She fell in love."

"Was it too much?"

"Looked fine at first glance... too common."

"She wanted it anyway, didn't she? That would be Vinnie, wouldn't it? I bet you had a devil of a time dissuading her."

"The devil..."

"It was green with ostrich feathers. Clumsy girl, she

was already climbing into the carriage when she turned to give it one last glance."

"But Lawrence caught her?" *But... how? Why would he tell her he was some nobleman's son?*

"Why—yes! How did you know? He must've told you at some point."

"I have my ways," James groaned, rising and pacing.

Like players in a torturous tennis match, as he rose, she sank, unburdening herself of the frustrations she'd kept hidden.

"I knew he was Lady Silcroft's son, her eldest. Naturally, that meant he would be the heir, the next in succession." Her eyes narrowed in disgust. "She never made it known, of course. Why would she? It certainly ruined his prospects."

"What on earth are you talking about? Lawrence Thompson is—"

"Lady Silcroft's son, but not *Lord* Silcroft's son. Your father and I sat next to the Silcrofts at Ascot, right before he was taken ill. She introduced both boys, Lawrence and Christopher, but she conveniently neglected to mention the eldest was a product from her first marriage."

James swallowed. "Thompson is Lady Silcroft's son?"

"Yes, but again, not *Lord* Silcroft's. Imagine our shock when he began to make overtures to Lavinia and I thought I was setting my daughter up to be the wife of an earl. No, she would be the wife of a penniless soldier's son. Silcroft, for whatever reason, has settled all succession, wealth, and property on his own child. I understand the line must pass through him, but to leave the eldest nothing? A shock and a shame. There must be some reason, but of course, Lady Silcroft mentions none of it."

"Mother, how in the world can you find out all about a man's money and affairs of estate?"

"There's not a mother in society alive who cannot ferret such things out, you silly boy. Our daughters' marriages ensure their livelihoods! Naturally, we know. Once I found out that Thompson didn't even have his father's pension coming to him, I broke things off."

"You broke things off. Because he was not wealthy?"

"That, and he wasn't of good character. His letters were obscene. He wrote like an animal, suggesting they meet alone, saying he dreamt... of her. It was wiser to break it off. A man with such unbridled passion and limited means was not worthy of her."

Their cozy drawing room seemed to swell to furnace heat, or perhaps it was hellfire heating his heels. He loosened his cravat and threw it on the chair, rolling up his sleeves. "How did she take it?" he demanded, but he already knew. His sister took nothing that was not to her liking.

"Oh, she raged and sulked and wouldn't eat. Cried. Threw ornaments. But then, almost overnight, she settled. I should have known. She'd found a way to spite me, you know, to make me pay for making her unhappy. She believed—ha—that she loved that common boy, Thompson. I explained that he was simply a sow's ear disguised as a silk purse, using family connections that weren't truly his to claim."

"Mother, a surgeon is a respectable profession. He may have risen to great prominence and wealth through his own efforts."

"That's never certain! I will not have my daughter living in such a precarious state."

"No, now she's dead in a permanent one." James stamped his foot in fury. "As for passion and dreaming of being alone—what man in love doesn't dream of those things?"

"He doesn't tell the lady!"

"Maybe he should!"

"Not where her mother can read it."

"A woman should have the right to her own letters, Mother."

"You see? I shouldn't have let you go to such a school. You're coming back with your head full of funny ideas about class and rights for women! Did *you* fill your sister's head with such nonsense, that class didn't matter?" Her eyes glittered dangerously in the firelight.

"Whatever ideas were in Lavinia's head were always firmly, stubbornly her own, Mother. Whatever she did, she did it of her own accord."

The room was filled only with the sounds of labored breathing, two people normally placidly in control no longer having any reason to hold back.

Then his mother thought of one. "Shh! James, Sadie is in the attic rooms."

Poor Sadie. He didn't want her dragged into this, or sacked by his mother on the presumption that the girl would gossip. He lowered his voice, "Thompson never mentioned seeing Lavinia, not once."

"Another proof that he did not care for the girl as sincerely as she cared for him. I do not think he wanted to embrace hearth and home, James. He was a playboy at best, an outright cad at the worst."

If Lawrence was the man they had been hunting, she was right, indeed. But… Lawrence wasn't Jack and Jack was the killer. The picture in his head was very clear, and yet still like something out of a madman's drawings.

Was Lawrence mad? Did he call himself by two different names?

With a weary shake of her head, Mrs. Everly continued. "Not content to be saved, the chit went and threw herself into something much worse. She started seeing a man named Jack. I don't even know how she met him. I half suspect he was a butcher's boy or a dustman. They were writing to one another and arranging to meet. Of course, after the trouble with her last suitor, I kept a close eye on the post. Somehow… somehow she still contacted him." The tired eyes began to leak, a solitary drop from each. "She ran away from home that night, James. I believe she was going to meet him. A beautiful girl in a fine gown, walking alone in London at night? She must have been mad. Of course, thieves fell upon her. Or worse." The tears multiplied.

"Mother, if the police knew this, they could—"

"Disinter her? Run stories in the papers? 'Everly Girl Found Slain in the Gutter'? Lord Sutterford wouldn't give me another glance. No good woman would have you. I know that if your Charlotte's family found out about how shamefully your sister behaved, they'd have nothing to do with you."

"Charlotte knows exactly, Mother. She's the undertaker's daughter."

It was a good thing his mother was already sitting down. She didn't have far to fall when she fainted.

Chapter Twenty

As the pink fingers of dawn nudged the cold December darkness farther west, James collected his notes, books, and his medical bag. Freshly washed and dressed, with very little sleep, he departed the house, walking halfway to the college before catching a ride with a puzzled and amused iceman.

"Had a long night out, guv?" the driver asked.

He closed his eyes. "One could say that."

The matronly haranguing he'd endured had felt like several years instead of under an hour. Every objection she'd raised, he'd combated.

****

"She is beneath you."

"Father was a man who made his money in business. Mr. Harkness is very respected and successful, a pillar of the community and a member in good standing of St. Clementia's."

"She's too much of a commoner!"

"I have no title. I have no lands. I have money and so has she. I have a bit more. But when you disown me, I shall have what I earn and that, contrary to what you seem to think, is good enough if you love someone and are willing to work a bit. I've never met a woman who works as she does."

"You would have your wife work?" The smelling salts reappeared.

"*I would have her be happy. She is brilliant. I would have her do what makes her happy and I pray loving me is one of those things.*"

"*It is too soon.*"

"*That I agree with. I won't marry in haste, but I know what I've found.*"

"*I will cut you off, James!*"

"*As you wish, Mother. I will not cut* you *off. You will always be my flesh and blood. You could wish for no more loving and kind a daughter-in-law than Miss Harkness would make you. If your Lord Sutterford wants to boast of his 'family' then surely a respectably married surgeon is even better than a bachelor surgeon? Shall I start playing the rake, shun the comforts of a wife and family for the pleasures of gambling and drinking until all hours?*" James hinted, one eyebrow raised.

His mother was never beaten, but sometimes she changed her battlefields. "*You must not announce the engagement until after he proposes, James. He would not risk a breach of promise scandal.*"

His eyes rolled to the ceiling. "*It will be a quiet engagement, if an engagement at all. Her father must approve, of course.*"

His mother's smile was tremulous. "*He shall undoubtedly approve. On the spot.*"

"*Her father will not be swayed by wealth, Mother.*"

"*That doesn't matter,*" she said staunchly, coming over to him and shaking his elbow with a little shake. "*He will say yes because there is no finer boy in England. But, James, please leave Lavinia in peace.*"

****

That was exactly what he intended to do, which meant chasing down every possible clue and connection, or else her soul would never rest—and the woman he loved would never rest, either.

He would start with Lawrence. Lawrence couldn't possibly be the murderer.

All the evidence pointed to him, though. Lawrie Thompson was a talented surgeon, a final year student like him, and he'd courted Lavinia. He had likely been at the dance, and Charlotte must have overheard his voice. He was the one who Lavinia had met at the dress shop, which matched the memories Lavinia presented to Charlotte.

But the rest! The rest made no sense. Thompson wasn't mad. He was a bit of a rogue, having been caught sneaking into the Halls a few times, well after midnight or even early in the morning. He'd been known to turn up to lectures unshaven and reeking of alcohol, but even that wasn't unheard of.

Thompson was always ready to go with you anywhere, try any lark, study to all hours, and he valiantly tried to escape any society functions, which made him an ideal companion for a man in mourning.

Thompson was a thoroughly steady fellow.

A thoroughly steady fellow who couldn't really afford to mix with society debs and attend all the elegant balls of the Season. As soon as his prospects were known, he'd be dismissed, if not by the girls, by their parents. That must have made him angry. In fact, James often recalled that Thompson not only seemed eager to avoid most society functions but seemed downright spiteful about those who would be in attendance.

James sat up as the rickety wagon hit a pothole. Thoroughly steady fellows tell you they're courting your sister. They don't hide the fact.

What about this matter of his mother and stepfather? Why, any number of fellows had half brothers, stepsiblings, or some other fractured family situation. The majority seemed to unify and share their assets.

How come Thompson had never mentioned his family, in almost two years? Only once could James recall him making mention of his mother, a disgusted groan about having to head to the "blighted place of my youth to contend with my d—ed mother." James remembered laughing, the sort of stunned gasp of laughter one gave when one is too embarrassed and uncomfortable to make a proper response.

"College, guv."

"Thank you for the ride." James came out of his troubled reverie and tossed a few coins to the iceman as he sprang down.

"Cheers, mate! Good luck on cuttin' up them stiffs." With a cluck of his tongue and a slap of the worn leather reins, the horse plodded on.

Cutting up stiffs. Yes, in a manner of speaking, that's what he was here to do, though it would be several hours until time. In fact— James stopped in his tracks at what he saw.

A wagon with high sides pulled by two horses was stopping at the East Gate. Was it only two weeks ago that he'd been flung from his comfortable world of study and headlong into one of intrigue and mystery, carried there via a waiting carriage at that same gate?

This was no fine coach or even a cab. The horses were nags, grossly mismatched, a fleshy maneater of at least sixteen hands next to a swaybacked pony that was hardly fourteen. Two men hopped down from the buckboard seat and pulled a pin, lowering the wagon's wooden flap. Cursing and straining they tugged a huge wicker basket between them.

Laundry didn't weigh that much.

The body merchants had arrived. His "examination materials" were inside.

Once the basket was unloaded, the taller of the men tugged his cap down lower and lifted out a stone in the wall. His hand made a journey into his ragged cloth coat, then the stone was returned. Payment had apparently been left, and now they could do likewise.

James didn't know why he stood there for so long, but something seemed to be sticking his feet to the frosted patch of ground under the shadowy arches of the college's main entrance.

Just wait.

Wait for what?

This is a waste of time. I should make my way to my rooms, no, to Thompson's rooms. Perhaps that's why I'm standing here like a statue. I don't want *to go talk to my friend, I don't want to accuse him, I don't want it to be* him. *There must be some explanation. I'll simply wait for the porters to come and collect the bodies, and I'll follow them to the dissection theater.*

James settled himself against the cold archway, suddenly so tired that he could envision himself sleeping there, standing up, par-frozen. Although, if he just remembered last night, what happened only a few dozen yards away, he'd be warm as July.

Charlotte's warm mouth finding his, no timid little pecks this time, but sumptuous, desperate kisses that reached inside a man and stroked his soul. Like everything else she undertook, nothing was done by halves. When she lifted her head, her eyes locked on his and she mouthed his name…

A squeak made his eyes bolt open.

A figure was leaning over the body basket.

Grave-robbers? Or rather, corpse-robbers? How disgusting! James' mouth opened to give a warning shout, but the words died in his throat. The figure took out something from under his long frock coat and stuffed it in the basket, then ran.

What? Who leaves offerings for the unfortunate cadavers bound for dissection? Anyone who even dared to open the lid would be under no misapprehension of its contents. The figure was gone, but James followed its course, stopping at the tall basket.

Even from where he stood, the smell penetrated his nose and made him wince. Fresh bodies or not, they were obviously not in good condition. Holding his breath, James pried open the leather catches that held down the lid and revealed sheet-wrapped bodies.

Praying silently that no one would catch him, he wincingly reached inside and connected with heavy, yielding flesh. He shoved it aside to see—

Blood-stained cloth? James pulled on the edge of the fabric gingerly. Perhaps it was part of the sheets around the bodies, catching some seepage from a mortal wound?

The fabric pulled free with a single tug, revealing half of a tailored shirt, a gentleman's shirt just a bit bigger than the ones he'd wear. Why in the world would anyone dispose of clothing in such an unorthodox fashion?

Because the linens and clothes around the bodies are stripped off and discarded, burned in the furnace, or buried with the flesh in the back of Middlesex Hospital.

James kept the garment in his hand as he shut the lid

again. This blood wasn't fresh. It was old, a brownish color now, spattering up the front and soaking through the cuffs.

A spatter of an artery. Then soaking in blood that pooled.

Or soaking up blood as hands ran through it, dragging the scalpel down a torso, perhaps?

His feet took on a life of their own, running like the sparrow flies.

****

Charlotte woke in the dark. She smiled dreamily.

James loves me. I think I love him, too. Thank you, Lavinia. If only you would give me one last gift? Help me figure out how the man I overheard relates to your death! Was he simply an acquaintance who helped you into the cab? How did he know Jack? Did he introduce the two of you?

Charlotte rolled fitfully, waiting for an answer.

"Careful, little sparrow," her mother's voice held a note of warning. *"You're reaching past what the soul says to you, inviting it in."*

"I'm not, Mama. I only know that she cannot speak, so I must ask."

"Ask and ye shall receive."

Her mother's voice was replaced almost instantly with a bombardment of loud peevish tones, thickened with tears.

"I hate her. I hate her so!"

"Well, you're still meeting me, aren't you?" The masculine voice was bored.

"Mama will find your letters if you're not careful. Did you know she said she'd write to your mother?"

"My mother can do me no further harm." Boredom

turned bitter.

"She could remove your allowance."

"I'm fed and clothed by her husband's tight fist. My education is provided for—just. Anything else? That's why I have you, *my dear."*

Charlotte shuddered as if cold oil was pouring through her veins, slippery and chilling her through, despite the warm quilts she was nestled under and the flannel gown she wore.

"Don't talk nonsense, Lawrence. You do *love me, don't you? You wouldn't want us to be alone together unless…?"*

Charlotte could best describe Lavinia's tone as seductive. It made her twitch uncomfortably, knowing that the girl was tempting him, that she was offering herself. If you loved someone, did you need to lure them with bait? Shouldn't you simply trust that they felt the same?

"All right. Offering yourself up on a silver platter, aren't you?" The masculine voice lowered, something dark and hungry in its timbre.

"Stop it! What are we to do, since she has intercepted your letters? You mustn't write to me anymore. How will I see you? I'm still confined to this place for a few more months. Father's dead and buried. Why must I be entombed, too?" The sound of something wooden rocking and clattering. Lavinia must have kicked something hard enough to topple it.

"Hush, girl. Show respect for your dead betters and elders," the voice mocked. "Besides, your mother thinks I'm the sort of nancy boy that'll behave myself and listen. I'm not some scholarly swot like James."

They laughed together.

"What your mother doesn't know won't hurt her. Here, I know. I'll simply write to you under a different name."

"What name? Like Thom Lawrence?"

"Oh, don't be daft, that's far too close to Lawrence Thompson, she'd spot that in a moment. Don't forget that most women are far more clever than they let a man know. But I know. Oh, yes. I know."

The man's tone was so blatantly chilling, evening sinister, that Charlotte couldn't believe that Lavinia would want him to write to her ever again. However, the younger, more naive girl didn't seem to mind, based on what Charlotte heard next.

"How about Jack? Yes, tell her... tell her you've picked up some scruffy soldier, that'll make her realize an impoverished stepson-surgeon isn't so terrible."

"Jack? Why Jack?"

"Why, to be the knave for you, my queen!"

A giggle, a purr. "Oh, stop."

"Ah..." The murky tone deepened, his turn to seduce. "Wouldn't you like to know what us soldier boys get up to? A bit of rough? Plenty of capital, once we've overcome our parents' objections."

"Ohhh, Lawrence."

"Shhh, dear girl. It's 'Jack' as long as anyone might hear us."

Charlotte flung her feet to the floor. "Mama, I know who it is and he must be at the college! Mama, James is at the college!"

"Fly, little bird, fly."

"But how? They don't allow women inside."

"Any woman?"

****

She pulled on one simple petticoat, then her oldest dress, and torn stockings she hadn't mended. She abandoned her corset and chose last year's boots that needed to go to the cobbler. With a bucket and mop in hand and her hair under a crochet cap, she could pass for a charwoman quite easily. But how to get there? She didn't own a carriage and it was too early for most cabs to be out and about.

Well… I don't own a carriage of the conventional sort. Hm. I wonder if Guinevere is stabled here, ready for Mr. Miggins in the morning?

Charlotte left a note on her pillow, one she prayed her father would never read. He hadn't come in until after she had, so she imagined he'd sleep quite a bit longer. If only she were fast enough and if a bit of divine providence was on her side.

Today, divine providence looked like a horse peacefully munching on hay.

"Come on, Guinevere," Charlotte encouraged the black horse that stood in the small shed that served as a stable whenever Mr. Bartlesby left the horse and hearse overnight. "Today, you shall go to a college as well as a cemetery. Would you like that, girl?" She ran her hands over the arching neck and started to put on her harness. "You can go as fast as ever you like, far faster than if you were carrying the sacred dead. Shall we have a race, my girl?"

Guinevere whickered contentedly.

"I hope that means yes."

****

James raced after the figure, which veered off from the Halls of Residence, and headed toward the lecture halls and anatomy clinic rooms. The charwomen were already cleaning, and the porters were laying fires, stoking furnaces, and carrying hods of coal. They scarcely looked up as he skidded past.

"Lawrence!" James shouted. The man didn't even slow down. "Jack."

A scramble down the stone steps to the basement level, where the surgical instruments were boiled and sterilized, and operating gowns and linens were laundered. At such an early hour, the hall was still dark and the rooms were silent. The effect was like suddenly leaving the modern-day world and falling into the catacombs under some ancient city. James heard a door slam in the dark passage and made his way toward it.

Just as his fingers closed on the handle of a door, he heard a noise behind him.

"Hello, James."

He turned, and his head exploded. The world went murky black and dissolved as he made out the glinting eyes above him.

****

Charlotte wondered if the police would stop her. A speeding hearse traveling recklessly from Whitechapel to Westminster before sunup was a highly unlikely sight. What would she say? "I'm sorry, Constable, there's an emergency funeral?" Or, "If you don't move out of my way, there will *be* a funeral."

Would Lawrence Thompson know that James was a threat?

How in the world would she get to his rooms?

Should she simply wait at the dissection theater, where his exam was to be held this morning? She bit her lip as Guinevere thundered on, her whole body juddering and shaking. She'd never done more than drive the carriage from the side of the house to the back. Fortunately, the horse seemed to be enjoying its freedom to travel as fast as it liked, passing buildings and landmarks so fast that they were a blur. Charlotte conceded it might possibly be the cold wind making her eyes tear. Everything looked a bit of a blur, but the path was straight and falling away fast. In no time at all, she'd be there.

Then what?

****

James woke up within moments, his cheek wet and sticky. Blood was coating it from the cut above his eye. It was still dark, but he was able to see shapes. The legs of tables. He was no longer outside in the hall. He must've been moved. He could see a pair of legs in trousers.

"You were always very smart. Too much time with your head in a book instead of looking after a skirt."

"You evil, rotten spawn of Satan!" James pushed himself up and was surprised to find that he could. Had Lawrence been careless, or was there something more sinister waiting in the dark?

"I didn't think you'd wake up so quickly. You're a bit of a lightweight, but I suppose that's just with drink," Lawrence continued, almost companionably.

"You murdered my sister."

"Did I? How ever did you figure that out, James?"

"Don't toy with me!" James ran his hands along the shapes ahead of him. Table. Chair. A hook or two. What was this room?

"Don't toy with you? But all the Everlys seem to love playing games. Your sister was fond of urging a chap on, begging to get him alone, then pushing him away and hounding him about one thing or the next as soon as he tried to take what she was so plainly offering. 'Oh, Lawrence, take me somewhere, let's be alone,' " he breathed in an unflattering falsetto, "and then, 'Get away from me, you brute. Alas, Mama was right!' "

"She surely was."

"Your mother is as bad as your sister. I daresay as soon as she's out of her widow's weeds she'll be into a bridal bed. My mother surely was, and why? Not for love, no. For money. For control."

****

Lawrence moved silently toward his objective. James didn't know it, but he'd soon figure it out. They were in the furnace room. Once he was in front of the furnace, he'd wait until James charged him, then let him go in headfirst. A neat and tidy way to burn up the evidence. He really should have been down here earlier, but there were always porters and cleaners about during the term. Now that the year was winding down, there seemed to be fewer people milling. Even so, he daren't be caught sneaking around out of bounds.

News of his last few "excursions" that had brought him back in the wee hours had finally reached his stepfather's ears. Always looking for a way to put his unwanted relative down, the pillock cut off his allowance. The dean, the rotten old informer, not content with putting him on the outs with his stepfather also levied academic threats as well. One more toe out of line and he'd be expelled. Lawrence felt the sweat trickling down his eyes, not just from the heat of the sputtering furnace, but from the beginnings of panic. James had to die. James could expose him, hang him. But James had to die quickly and quietly. Even this "harmless" act of occupying the furnace room before dawn would count against him. Students weren't supposed to be in the lecture halls on this day or hour. Lawrence Thompson knew if he were caught returning to his rooms now, the dean would assume he'd been out all night, which was partially correct, and he'd be gone without his qualifications. A woman would not maneuver him out of his earnings like one had ruined his chance for inheritance. A qualified surgeon made more money than a physician if he knew his business.

He certainly knew his. "Let's settle this, Everly."

****

James heard the pop and hiss of a falling chunk of coal. Furnace. They were in the furnace room. That meant coal hods, scoops, and scuttles. "I'd love nothing more." He walked silently, back to the wall, one hand out as he felt for the door again. "Why did you do it?"

"No, James, the question is why don't we *all* do it? What good are they, these women?"

"Plenty of good. I know she was trying—"

"She was a bloody nuisance, but I blame myself. I've known what women are from the time I watched my mother throw me over, her own son, for a fat old codger with a fatter purse. She let him treat me like rubbish, and why? Money."

"Lavinia wasn't like that."

"Oh, dear deluded James. She was, she absolutely was. She believed I'd still get some sort of inheritance. She couldn't believe anyone would cut off a loveable charmer like myself without a penny."

"I can believe it now." James kept moving, able to see a bit better now. His foot hit something hard that clanked.

"Can you? Must have had something to do with trying to drown my mother's second mistake when he was a little nipper."

"You tried to kill your brother? Christopher?" James was truly shocked.

Lawrence must have been shocked as well. He gasped and moved away from the iron door of the great coke-guzzling beast behind him. "My God, you're thorough, aren't you? How did you... Ah. The letters?"

"Partially."

"Well, I'm no fool. I dispose of my evidence carefully."

"You left her lying there in that—that rat hole!"

"I admit that was dodgy." Lawrence sounded contemplative, a chess player reconsidering a tricky move. "I didn't want to, certainly, but then again... I hadn't planned to kill her. Oh, no. I thought, I really did, that perhaps she'd be the one for me. She was just needy enough to cling, so desperate for any and all attention, rough or smooth. I thought perhaps I could hurt her just a little. She was too ignorant to know the difference, you see."

James' blood was boiling, pumping out of the wound above his eyes. His hand latched around the heavy metal object at his foot just as his hip was jabbed by something hard. The door handle.

Escape? Or attack?

"Then why did you? Why not just let her be, if you hate women so much?"

"I tried, Everly, truly I did. I didn't write to her after the first time I took her down to Goulston Yard, only she wouldn't leave me alone. Hungry little thing, your sister. You see, she thought I'd gotten her pregnant."

James made a croaking sound, another boulder of grief crushing his heart. Had that been why she was so mutilated? He'd lost not only a sister but a tiny niece or nephew? A sudden anguished tear mixed with the blood under his eye. "You killed your own baby?" he rasped, hefting the weight in his hand, fingers curling tightly around the scalloped iron scuttle.

"No! I didn't even 'ruin' the girl. Hysterical pregnancy from a few rough kisses and me getting a good feel. Honestly, James, did you come to medical school just to learn whether or not the stork is what brings little bundles to good mummies and daddies?" Lawrence finished with a leering laugh.

"Hurgggh!" James hurled the scuttle with all of his might in Lawrence's direction. He heard a curse and clang as he fled the room. "Police! Police!" he hollered in the darkness. "Get the deans!" His feet scrabbled on the recently mopped stone floors as his fingertips searched for the staircase.

"I'll shut your mouth the way I shut hers!" Thompson growled, only a few feet behind.

****

Charlotte tethered Guinevere by the reins around one of the ornate hitching posts along the street. She breathlessly pulled her bucket and mop from the hearse and tugged her collar up and her cap down. Slightly jelly-legged from her wild ride and half numb with trepidation, she made her way to the main gate. "Father in heaven, you must help me find him, find a way in."

"Do you need help?

"I'm the one what needs help!"

"Miss! Miss, can you see me? Can you hear me?"

Oh, no. Charlotte bit her lip. This wasn't the time to

399

be bombarded by ghostly voices, but yet… "It's all right, everyone. I can hear you. Let me help you," she whispered.

"What happened?" one voice, very young, inquired.

"Your body is all done here, dear one. It's time to go to a better place, a final place."

"But I've got a sister t'look after."

"Have you? Where is she? I can help. I can help all of you, but I must help another first." Charlotte stood by a huge wicker basket in front of the gate. Her nose detected a familiar smell and wrinkled. "Some of you have been suffering for a long time. This is the end of that."

"Blimey!" One voice was assuredly irritated. "Sold me to the flesh merchants, did they? I'll not have it! I'll not be mucked about with. 'Tisn't Christian."

"Oh, but it is, sir. It's ever so noble of you." Charlotte used her most honeyed voice. "Think of how your brave sacrifice will save thousands, maybe tens of thousands. Each surgeon here who learns his trade through you will save hundreds of lives. They couldn't do it without you, sir."

"Well… but it's my body."

Charlotte dropped the sweetness from her voice. "Do be sensible, Mr.—?"

"Fuller."

"Do be sensible, Mr. Fuller. You're not using it anymore, are you? It will rot away or it will be used to teach others. What would you have?"

"I'd rather be helpful," said the young voice.

"There you are, Fuller, are you going to let a mere boy best you?" coaxed the third.

"Oh. Dash it all, I suppose. But I don't want no

ladies present."

"I promise not to look, Mr. Fuller. Only, I do need to get in and I—"

"On three, lads!"

Charlotte gasped as the gate swung open, its chain rattling back and slithering to the ground as if by magic. Divine magic. "Oh, thank you, sirs. Thank you! You may talk to me whenever you like, and I'll help however I can."

"Oi!" Four porters in identical blue cloth caps and thick leather gloves marched up to the open gate. "You're not supposed to open that, you old scrub!"

"Sorry. I thought—" Charlotte quickly muffled her voice, speaking down into her chest, "I thought the bodies were better brought in. It's getting light."

"You leave that work for us. No place for a woman. Here, there's a right mess after the ball. Get on with it, in the big room of Glasgow Hall." The leader of the porters ordered, barely looking at her. Like an army unit setting up tents, the four porters sprang into action, placing long wooden poles through the thick rope handles on the sides of the basket. Their leader grunted out a count of three and the foursome hoisted the poles onto their shoulders and set off.

Charlotte made as if she were going to Glasgow Hall, where the ball had been. Had she really been here last night, dressed like a fine lady of wealth and privilege? Was she truly here now, a handful of hours later, dressed like the lowliest charwoman?

Both for the same man, with the same man.

She doubled back and caught sight of the porters disappearing into a building across a patch of frosted green. Hiding in the shadows, she followed.

****

James knew his assailant was following him—for now. Thompson intended to kill him, certainly, but the timing had to be just right. If James found help first, Lawrence would simply flee, perhaps out of the country and justice would never be served.

At the top of the stairs, James pelted round the side and waited, waited for Lawrence to spring up and sprint after him.

He wouldn't have far to go.

James's eyes darted around. This floor was better lit by the gray filmy light coming in the windows, but the hall was still dark and deserted. It was Saturday. There must be fewer workers about as there were no classes to clean up after. Or perhaps it was the fact that it was not yet six in the morning.

What could be taking him so long? Had he gone back down the stairs? There was no way out through the basement. Chest heaving, James risked peeking 'round the stairs.

A hard hand came out and clutched his windpipe in a frenzy of strength.

The strength of a madman, James realized as the air left him, for that's what Thompson looked like now, his eyes wild and his teeth snarling. His forehead was streaked with black and blood from where the coal scuttle had made its mark.

"Like your sister," Thompson snarled, "you talk too much, prattling on and on. She wouldn't believe me, James, wouldn't believe me that I hadn't made her pregnant, wouldn't believe me that I was only after her money, that I had nothing to offer, no, no, no. Always about control, always about what they want, what they want to do to us."

James kicked his attacker's knees and used his elbows as best he could to break his grip, but it didn't work. Thompson was fueled by insanity and desperation. He pushed him back along the corridor to an empty classroom, still rambling.

****

Charlotte ran until there was a stitch in her side. She saw the porters leave, but there was no sign of James, or even of other students or workers. Everything was silent as the tomb. Even her ghostly friends had fled, at least for now.

But there was one that always came when she called.

"Mama? Mama, I don't know where he is!" Charlotte pushed the woolen cap from her head and stuffed it in her pocket, not caring for the sight of her long, uncoiled hair rippling in the light wind that blew.

Her mother's voice came, but from a great distance, sounding weak and worn. *"Hurry, little bird, to the right, the building on the right, down the winding stairs, you must go. But... I... Charlotte, I love you so, but I must make my peace. I must be helpful and go soon, my sparrow. Time is up. You no longer need me."*

Her thudding heart seemed to freeze, then explode in a thousand desperate beats. "Yes, Mama, I do. I must—I… please, please don't leave me alone."

"My love, you are not alone anymore. But you will be if you don't hurry. Go and help your husband, girl. I see the Lord's work at hand. You have to be brave as Rahab to aid the righteous, as ruthless as Jael, to fight."

She blinked at the lightening sky in confusion, trying to hold onto the ever-fading voice. "What? I must tell James that Lawrence Thompson used the alias Jack. I'll tell him to send for the police, that's all I need do."

"No! No, if you don't act quickly, the man you love will die. There is no time for anyone but you. Go and Godspeed."

Charlotte ran.

****

"Stubborn as she was." The madman squeezed and squeezed, but his quarry would not yield. "I don't need to do you down bloody, James. I've already lost a shirt and trousers, socks, and even my coat. Damn her, she was an expensive mess, wasn't she? D'you know, I hid the things in your room?" The tone was almost conversational, casual. "Funny, if you'd only come back earlier, you'd have had all the evidence you need, cut up in bits. Your little note, telling me to look after your room was heaven sent, a perfect place. Mind you, I've been disposing of the things here and there, but of course, I'd never leave them in *my* rooms, no. Maybe I *should* leave a few pieces scattered among your things? Hm? Make you out to be the murderer? It will explain your untimely disappearance. You didn't want to share with poor Lavinia, not even the tiny bit for her dowry. It's quite the perfect alibi, you know, covering my tracks not once, but twice." He laughed softly, a curling, creeping sound that would send demons themselves slithering away. "I'm smarter than people think. For one thing, I know what women truly are."

James eyes rolled up in his head as his fingers clawed at Lawrence's arms, tearing his skin but having no other impact. The man in the grip of madness wouldn't release him. As the world began to darken for the second time that day, he thought he caught a glimpse of his own personal angel, his Charlotte.

I will not *leave her.*

He arched his body forward with all of his might, catching Thompson's head with his own.

As his vision cleared, he saw a flash of metal.

A bucket.

A bucket swung full force by an avenging angel, indeed.

Lawrence crumpled to the floor as James slid down the wall, dizzy and breathless.

Charlotte knelt down next to him and put her arms around him.

"Hello, darling." James managed to gasp out through his swollen throat.

"Hello, my love." She kissed his bruised forehead.

****

Charlotte's breathing slowed as she surveyed the scene. James was alive. She'd found him. "You're hurt," she stated the obvious, her quick wits dulled by panic.

"Well. So is he."

"We need to send for the police."

"We need to get whatever he's left in my room and remove it!" James kicked the cur at his feet.

Shakily, they helped each other to stand. "We can't leave him alone here."

"I saw some porters a few moments ago. Shall I try to find someone?"

"I screamed for help, but there's no one nearby, or the thick walls and the noisy furnace muffled it all." James shook his head. "You go, fetch help."

"Are you sure?"

"I'm certain. How did you know that—"

"Lavinia helped. Mother helped. Three souls of the

men in the body basket helped. God helped. Oh, God, indeed!" She suddenly broke down, burying her head on his shoulder.

"Shhh. Shh, we're going to be fine." James caressingly stroked his fingers through her long hair. Women didn't wear their hair loose and free like this. As he lost himself in its silky texture, he thought they definitely should. At least Charlotte should. "My angel. Better still, my avenging angel."

James knew he was covered in soot, blood, and possibly some other nameless grime, but he didn't care and she didn't seem to mind. "We've got him."

"We've got him." Charlotte agreed as the reality of their achievement set in. They staggered a little together as he tilted up her face to kiss her. The kiss deepened as relief and exhaustion momentarily obscured the urgency of the situation.

"He's got *you*!" Thompson growled suddenly, his fingers shooting out and latching around Charlotte's ankle.

She screamed as she was jerked to the floor and dragged along the hard stone.

James didn't know what threat a woozy madman who'd suffered multiple blows to the head would be, but he knew that Thompson had killed one woman he loved. He would not harm another. James dragged the brute up and threw him back with a hoarse warning. That was all he intended to do, throw him off.

He'd neglected to account for the position of the stairs. Thompson reeled, arms waving wildly, hands clutching empty air before he disappeared down into the darkness.

Charlotte grunted as she struggled up, pulling

herself to her knees, and then crawling forward to the edge of the stairs.

Blood lined each step at the bottom, shining in the first light that illuminated the black stairwell.

At the bottom, Lawrence Thompson lay, his neck bent at a tortured angle and his eyes wide and glassy. A primal scream poured from silenced jaws.

"Oh, no. Oh, James…"

"I… I had to get him off of you. I didn't know… He's capable of such atrocities." James stared in horror at the sight below them. "Oh, Charlotte. I'm sorry. I'm so sorry."

She became suddenly brisk. "What are you sorry for?"

"I just killed a man!"

"You didn't. You saved a woman. He fell down the steps of his own accord, if you ask me."

"But he wouldn't have been in front of the steps if I—"

"If he hadn't been strangling you?" she challenged. "I need to fill this bucket."

"What?" James demanded, shaking his injured head.

"I'm the charwoman, I'm here to clean. I'm going to mop these stairs. You're going to fetch a sheet."

"What are we going to do?"

"Save the police and a jury a lot of time and effort."

Chapter Twenty-One

The fall down the stairs had scraped and contused much of "Jack's" face.

"Good," Charlotte said as she wrapped the sheet over and under his body while James, her savior and her partner in detection, watched in confusion. "He'll be harder to recognize."

"Recognize?"

"Take his shoulders and mind the steps. They're wet."

"Where are we taking him?"

"The basket."

James swallowed and met her unflinching eyes. "Charlotte—"

"He was a murderer who would've hung. I will not see my future husband imprisoned for tracking down the man that killed his sister and tried to harm me. I will *not*, James." She bowed her head. Was this right or wrong? The police had declared Lavinia's murder an accident at best and a suicide at worst. Mrs. Everly wanted nothing to do with it. What would the police say if James told them about tracking down a murderer for a murder they claimed never happened? How did one try such a case? "You must think me a very cold, strange woman."

"On the contrary." James shoved his hands under the still body. "I find you a brilliant and devoted one."

His head was ringing, and his throat hurt. His eyes

and throat stung. He found his lips irreverently threatening to smile. Charlotte had called him her future husband.

****

Are you going to faint?" James asked. His companion was white as the sheet they held and her face was glistening with sweat.

She shook her head, cheeks puffed out. "And leave you to carry this weight on your own? No."

A struggle in unison, a furtive glance, and then— "Stop, stop, put him down. The bodies are… not clothed when they're presented for dissection." James put the sheet-wrapped form down beside the basket.

Charlotte turned around while James grunted and tugged the fabric from the figure. The human body was such a thing of beauty, so intricate, so fearfully and wonderfully made. He was supposed to cure it, not harm it.

James felt bile rise in his swollen throat as he looked at the horrible bruising around the neck. He realized that he'd likely have similar bruises on his own throat by tea. He also realized again that Lavinia's neck wasn't even in one piece, throat severed, body torn apart, inside and out. He yanked the shirt off last and let the head fall to the stone floor with a sickening thud. He couldn't bring himself to care just then. He tucked the sheet firmly back over the bare flesh. "Ready?"

"Ready." Charlotte bent and lifted on James' count.

The body was dumped inside the basket at last. One final look revealed the victim's face was bloodied, bruised mass. The handsome charlatan who'd wooed Lavinia Everly was unrecognizable.

"I need to wash and change. Oh, Charlotte! He's

been storing his bloodied clothes and whatever other evidence may incriminate him in my room. I gave him leave to look after my things while I was gone... I'll explain later." James closed the lid and closed his eyes after, reeling.

"Where's the furnace in the Halls of Residence?" Charlotte asked, quickly gathering the discarded clothes.

"In the basement, I expect."

"Have you a fire in your room?" She shook the bucket meaningfully.

"Not in mine, no. The common room should have a fire laid soon, but charwomen don't do that."

"I'm not a very good charwoman. I expect I'll be sacked after today." She smiled grimly.

****

He found the items secreted in the bottom drawer of his desk. Charlotte took them in her now empty bucket. The first load had fed the fire she'd made in the common room.

"That's all I can find." James closed the final drawer.

Charlotte shook her head. "Your shirt. It has blood on it."

"Ah. Right." James hesitated, then began unbuttoning it. Charlotte turned around. "You've seen more than this in dead flesh, I imagine," he whispered, partially from necessity, partially because he didn't want to ruin whatever mood this was. Something desperate followed by something peaceful, something still waiting.

"True. And you, in both dead flesh and live."

"True." He coughed. "My mother knows about you now. She was home when I got there. I told her I met my future wife. How far in the future is up to you, of course."

She whirled around. "You told her?"

"Mmhm." James stepped closer, bare-chested, his shirt outstretched. Her fingers took it, brushing his. "She said a great many things that led me to figure out that Thompson was Lavinia's suitor, and possibly *Jack* as well, all of which I'll tell you later." He stepped nearer than was necessary for her to take the soiled shirt. "Additionally, she hopes your father doesn't object to my suit."

"Oh. He will not likely object. He may urge you to wait." Her hand delicately brushed his wrist, scratched and bruised. Bruises were appearing on his throat, his forehead, and chest. She set down the bucket so both hands could stroke up his arms, find their way to his smooth cheeks.

"I would rather not wait very long." James smiled crookedly, something almost playful in his eye. His hands pressed into her sides. They were different. Softer. "Are you all right? You seem… less armored."

She giggled into his shoulder. "I left my corset off. I was in a hurry—Oh! Guinevere and the hearse are outside! Father needs them this afternoon, and she's to be reshod."

"You'd better go then, you marvelous, wonderful girl." James kissed her fondly.

"I don't want to leave you until after your examination. What if the dean recognizes the body? What will you do?"

"Act very surprised and wait patiently while the police come. I shall say nothing about the matter, however. My mother told me not to. I'm a very obedient son." He winked with his less swollen eye.

Charlotte hoisted her bucket. "I'm off to do some washing and stoke the fire again. They say I'd make someone a fine wife someday." She leaned forward and kissed him once more, pulling away with an effort.

****

"Good heavens! Everly, what happened to you?" The dean gaped at his bruised face as he stood patiently in front of the dissection theater, his broad smile nearly lost in a puffy cheek.

"I had a nasty tumble, sir, but I'm keen to begin." James rolled up his sleeves and put on the leather apron over the protective gown.

"Excellent, excellent. I'm feeling just a mite delicate after last night's festivities, Everly. Would you mind if I sit back a few rows? I'll check your final product."

"That suits me fine, sir." James tied the camphor-soaked cloth around the lower half of his face.

"The body is laid out on the slab there. Standard midline incision to begin. That's the only help I'll give you as this is your final exam."

James knew by the size and the fresh blood on the sheet that it was Thompson. His friend of a hundred lectures and late nights, he of the rakish good looks and confident airs.

The liar and madman. The murderer. He yanked off the sheet and sunk the scalpel in nice and deep, leaving a long line in the flesh, just like the one the monster had left in his sister.

"Ironic, isn't it, Jack?" he hissed. The camphor made his eyes sting and leak. Or was it a confused tear for the man he'd thought he knew, a genuine tear for the sister he hadn't saved?

The flesh fell away in record time. James' face

remained as impassive as possible, aided by the rag as his features spasmed on occasion. Each piece he placed neatly on the clean sheet at his station was another piece closer to sending Lavinia homeward, to an eternal peace.

Although, his blade suddenly wavered, *Lavinia might be at peace.*

What will happen to Charlotte?

There was no more time for sentiment and reflection. This was flesh like any other flesh. What really mattered was the soul.

God was taking care of that bit. If it was cast into perdition, he didn't think he would mind.

But he would like the Lord above to send it there promptly without it tormenting his Charlotte.

****

"I took Guinevere to Mr. Miggins for you," Charlotte poured her father a cup of hot tea and handed him dry toast and two rashers of bacon, no egg. He couldn't tolerate an egg this morning.

"Thank you, Charlotte." He bit into the toast and winced as if the crispy sound was painful. "I didn't even get to ask you. How was your fancy ball with your fine gentleman? You know, I quite like him. I do. Level-headed. Steady."

"Devoted?" Charlotte tossed out, leaning against the sink for support.

"Exactly the word, the very word!" A bit of brightness returned to Mr. Harkness' eyes. "Was last night a success? Shall I be seeing more of the good doctor?"

Charlotte's breath caught, and something pulsed in the pit of her stomach. It was not... an unpleasant feeling. She'd certainly seen more of him this morning. Buttercream skin with fine sandy hairs, muscles and ridges that seemed so much more beautiful and captivating on living, warm flesh.

"Charlotte?"

"I think we'll see a great deal more of him, Father. He's… he's coming over today if things go as planned. He has an examination this morning."

"A patient?"

"No, his dissection exam. His final qualifying exam."

"Ah. Hm. Perhaps a celebration pudding is in order?"

"I was thinking of that."

"Excellent. If you could— Good heavens, Charlotte, you're letting me dawdle over breakfast when Mrs. Norton is to be buried at three!"

"I have the hearse already pulled around, waiting for the horse." Charlotte smiled and put an extra spoonful of sugar in his tea.

"You're a wonderful daughter."

Charlotte pecked his forehead in passing, singing, "And I shall make someone a wonderful wife!"

****

"I've never seen anything so complete and clean in such record time. Describe your findings. Cause of death. Ailments?" The dean looked over his work with a slightly green countenance and moved swiftly back to the observation seats.

James rattled them off, mind a careful blank as he blandly stated, "His neck is broken, most likely by a fall or accident, judging by the substantial bruising to the face and ribs." He waited for the dean to jot down his marks while trying to suppress the shudders that would soon overwhelm him. His friend, his enemy, was lying in chunks of flesh, the sheet waiting to be sewn up and buried in a pauper's grave. Thompson's mother wouldn't know where he was.

The way he'd spoken of his mother, perhaps that was better.

God forgive me. Am I a murderer or the instrument of Your justice? You know that I didn't mean to kill him, only to save my Charlotte. Protect her for me.

"The exam is at a conclusion."

Thank you, sir." James bowed. He turned from the watchful eyes and threaded a needle. "I'll sew the sheet up for the burial, shall I?"

"Yes, that'll do nicely. You pass, Dr. Everly. You pass with distinction in both dissection and anatomy. Of course, you'll still have to complete your written exam on Tuesday."

"I'll be here, sir. What time?"

"Ten in the morning. Ring for the porter, will you?"

"I will." James sewed the makeshift shroud hurriedly with many a little prayer, for himself, for Charlotte, for Lavinia, and even for the man who lay before him.

****

Guinevere pulled the hearse with a sedate and elegant tread, having already had the workout of her life earlier that day. Mr. Bartlesby and Mr. Harkness, with their delicate heads, didn't mind her slow, even pace. They wore their hats low to shield their eyes from the sun and held their bodies extra stiffly as if any sudden movement might prompt skulls to bound off for parts unknown. As she waved them on their way, Charlotte's broad smile faded.

How long does his examination take? He would want to wash and change afterward, I suppose. Perhaps the police were called. Perhaps he's fled. No, no, he wouldn't flee without seeing me first.

Her heart swelled with something she hadn't had in a very long time. Certainty.

James would not suddenly send her away or hint that she must be ill. He would never tell her she must pretend otherwise. Father was a dear, and Mama was a comfort. Her love and trust in the Heavenly Father were absolute, but He wasn't very conversational.

But James... James filled an empty place in her heart that she hadn't known existed.

She let out a contented sigh after her worried one. Whatever happened, she would stand by him as long as he wanted her to.

"A nice little piece he's picked, I will say that. I wouldn't have given him as much sense to look beyond a gilded cage and woo a woman like you."

Charlotte's steps faltered as she leaned against the side door, the voice recognizable, not only from that morning but from days of unwanted whispers.

"I have nothing to say to you. I hope for your sake that your soul is forgiven."

"I daresay it isn't. I think I'll stay here with you for a bit."

"Mr. Thompson—"

"Oh, no, girl. You'll call me Jack. And you'll do as Jack bids."

"That I shall *not* do. You can speak to me all you want, but you've no power over me."

"Are you quite certain?"

Charlotte jumped as the door banged hard, hitting her on the back of her head, jarring her spine.

She remained outwardly still while her mind raced. The three spirits who had undone the lock on the gate. Her entreaties to Lavinia that had brought results. Had her actions somehow caused a supernatural shift, made the otherworldly more present?

A mocking laugh filled her ears, and Charlotte knew she was helpless to block it out.

"All alone, are you? Time for us to play."

Another slamming, this time of the cupboard doors, followed the crash of crockery.

Charlotte turned her head a tiny bit but otherwise kept still. Fear was replaced by calm. "I have not bowed to a live man's dictates. I shall not bow to a dead one's. Go. Leave me."

"I don't see you as the bowing sort, girl."

A hard gust of air hit her torso, rocking her back on her heels, but she kept her feet with an effort, braced against the wall.

"I see you on your back. As far as I'm concerned, that's the only way a woman should be, as she is in death, so should she be in life." Another gust, harder, more violent.

"You can rattle and bang, but that is all you may do. I don't belong to you and never will. My Father says not one hair of my head shall fall… *His* hand may fell me, but yours shall not."

"You'll sing a different tune before long."

Charlotte was tempted to scream, but she wouldn't give him the satisfaction, the tormenting bully. Her voice dropped to a fierce whisper. "I don't answer to you. You *will* leave my home or I shall throw you *out*."

The laughter was louder, longer, bouncing inside her head, making her wince.

"How?"

"With help." As soon as she said it, she knew it was true. She could feel them ringing her, benevolent forces, a chorus of voices, two much stronger than the rest.

"Leave my daughter alone!"

"Mama?"

The next voice she didn't know, it was just a long banshee-like scream of rage and misery.

The air in front of her shimmered as she backed away, hidden behind a shield that she could feel, but not see.

"Steady, sparrow," her mother hushed.

Charlotte swallowed as something manifested from the opaque air, a silvery form, a woman's silhouette facing down a tarry misshapen mass that might once have been a man.

The wailing scream turned into fierce words. "Justice was served, you wretch!"

"Lavinia!" Charlotte gasped before she could stop herself.

"Do you need silencing again? I'll be more than happy to let the living wait."

Jack's crouching figure barreled toward the silvery maiden, only to find himself suspended.

"Vengeance is mine, sayeth the Lord."

Lavinia's voice has lost any traces of the petulance Charlotte had come to associate with her. This voice was calm and commanding.

"You... how are you doing this?" Jack's shout rose to a roar as something seemed to bind him, first pulling back his arms, then his legs.

"You will wait in a place of silence," Mama said solemnly. *"For it is written that men must die, and then be judged."*

"Then you can come along to hell with me!" he spat, fighting the invisible ropes.

"A place of silence.*" Lavinia swept her insubstantial arm forward, and Jack's voice died with a harsh curse.*

Charlotte watched as the blackness turned into wisps that slithered away, out the cracks in the doors and windows until there was nothing left of the murderous Jack. She expected more of a battle, but it occurred to her that she didn't know why. She'd never feared the dead before, none had ever tried to hurt her, only speak to her. She had only ever tried to help those she could hear.

Her trust seemed to have been repaid.

She felt the "shield" of benevolent voices surrounding her weakening, the little murmur of spirits vanishing, returning to their proper places beyond this mortal coil. At last, she was alone, a living woman with two ghosts.

Lavinia turned toward her, the brightness rapidly fading. "Well done, sister mine."

"I— Oh, please, can you wait? James will be here soon." Charlotte found herself at a loss. She had never seen a ghost before, only heard them. Was she having hysterics after this morning? Was she truly mad?

"No, I must leave. He couldn't hear me, anyway. This is your gift, dear Charlotte. Thank you for hearing me, for giving me back my voice. But you may rest assured, I shall watch over you both, and Mama, too." Lavinia's voice drifted sadly, "Tell her... I love her. I'm sorry. Tell James he's the best brother in the world."

"I will. I will, of course." Not that Mrs. Everly would take kindly to such a revelation, but she would find a way, someday.

"Papa calls for me. Dear Prudence, will you journey with me?" Lavinia's voice sounded small and scared, all her confidence evaporating along with her shimmering presence. *"It seems... a rather long way."*

Charlotte turned and gasped at what she saw. Her mother stood behind her, not merely a voice, but a golden mist in a female form, so radiant it hurt her eyes.

"My sparrow. No longer so little, but always my own dear babe."

"Mama. Mama..." Charlotte swallowed hard. "You must show Lavinia the way. She wouldn't wish to go alone. It seems—" She hastily wiped her eyes and cleared her throat. "It seems you're practically related."

Silver threads wrapped through gold, an ornate tapestry that was slowly fading.

"I love you so, my Charlotte."

Twin hints of warmth were on either side of her, filling her and then slowly gliding up. Heavenward.

"I love you, too."

"It's only a short time until we meet, then eternity on the far distant shores will bring us all together again. You will have ever such a warm welcome, sweet sparrow. There are so many you've helped on their way home."

"I know. I know, Mama."

She bit her lip hard to stop the coward's words. No. Stay. Please don't go.

"I love you so. I love you so, Charlotte." The voice was fading with each word until silence filled the room.

Silence.

Charlotte sank to her knees, her head in her hands as she wept a mixture of joyful tears and mournful ones. "I know. I love you, too."

Chapter Twenty-Two

"James!" Charlotte flew to him and kissed him as he stood on the doorstep.

James hastily backed away, though not through lack of desire. "Charlotte. Is your father at home?"

"Not yet." Charlotte pulled a shawl over her shoulders and joined James outside.

"Thank God you're safe," he breathed. "I realized too late that the blaggard might bother you still, though he would not trouble this world again."

Charlotte hesitated. "Well... he tried. But Mama and Lavinia sorted him."

James used the brick wall of Harkness and Sons to support his suddenly weak knees. "Pardon? Lavinia?"

"Her voice is restored, but she didn't linger here. She wishes me to say you are the best brother in all the world." Charlotte clutched his hand. "She didn't go alone. My mother... my mother has been with me since she passed. I began to hear her voice when I was just a little girl, James." Charlotte spoke in a rush. "I never confided that to anyone but Father."

"Oh, Charlotte."

Her smile was a mere flicker as she pushed on. "She has taken the journey to Heaven's shores. We shall meet again. But right now, I feel alone, all over again."

James nodded, throat aching inside and out. He drew her to his chest, not caring for the curious stares of those who passed on the other side of the street. "You'll always have me by your side."

"Thank you. Did you pass your examination? Did anyone say—anything?" Charlotte mumbled into his shoulder.

"All is well. His mortal remains will be consecrated to a pauper's grave in the grounds of the hospital, which is an ending too good for a fiend like him."

"Agreed. Are you hungry?"

James laughed hoarsely. "I doubt I can swallow much, but… yes. Come to think of it, my appetite has returned." His eyes held hers. "All of my appetites awaken around you."

She lifted her chin, preparing to kiss him once again, but stopped. "I need to go to the stalls. Flowers, holly, and greens for the upcoming funerals."

"They never stop, do they?"

"No, they never stop. I must fetch my list and the market basket."

"I'll accompany you. I can carry the heavy parcels," James offered quickly.

"I can carry everything perfectly well on my own," she reminded him.

"Well do I know that." His bruised smile was crooked and suddenly playful. "Is there a bookseller in your market?"

Charlotte's eyes lit up. "Not that I know of… but if we venture a bit further afield, we may find one. I'll be right back. Oh, and I must leave a note for Father!"

James chuckled as she dashed inside, leaving him to stand in a shaft of warm sunlight that graced the pavement. She swiftly returned with a large basket over one arm, her long blue cloak with its black collar done up under her chin.

"Shall we, Miss Harkness?" He offered his arm.

"We shall, Dr. Everly." Her arm slid securely through his. "You know, Father was saying that you must come 'round for some sort of celebratory pudding once your exams are done."

"Wednesday evening?"

"Perfect."

He sighed. It was far from what anyone else would consider perfect, but it was peaceful. Happy. She made him so happy that even all the grief and horror he'd witnessed couldn't mute his joy. "Charlotte?"

"Hm?"

"Maybe in a month—or two—we could tell your Father, officially? You could come with me to my aunt Eleanor's place, or my uncle Jeremy's. They have little house parties in the spring, and of course, we would be safe from the matchmaking matrons." Words rushed over themselves. "My mother... oh, she'll love you too, I'm quite certain, but there's —"

"James?" Charlotte cut him off with a soft squeeze on his elbow. "There will be plenty to celebrate. As long as I have you—"

"You do!" He whipped around to stand before her, taking both of her hands in his. "One day, I will ask you properly, with a ring, and a carriage, and all the fine things a woman ought to have. But for right now... Charlotte? Would you do me the great honor of consenting to be my bride?"

"I believe you have to ask Father before you—"

"No. I will ask him second, because my Charlotte does what she wants, with whom she wants, and who dares to argue with such brilliance and beauty?

Therefore, I ask again, will you marry me?"

"Absolutely." Charlotte sparkled and slid back beside him with a kiss on his cheek. "Now, let's hurry along. I want you to meet Bob and Mary."

"Bob and Mary?"

"They sell fruit and flowers."

"We must find the bookseller."

"Bob and Mary will know where one is if anyone does."

"What sort of celebratory pudding are you making?"

"That's up to you, Dr. Everly," she teased, nudging him gently. "Whatever you like."

"I like Miss Harkness. No, I *love* Miss Harkness! I love Charlotte. Isn't there a cake filled with cream called a Charlotte?"

"Oh, James." She gave a tired laugh.

"I want that. I want a Charlotte." He nudged her in return, laughing softly.

"Of course, my dear."

Epilogue

Christmas Eve

Mr. Harkness mopped his brow. The white paint wouldn't stick to his face unless it was quite dry, but he was sweating in layers of padding and acres of cotton petticoats.

"Reginald?" James ducked his head under the low wooden door frame in the back of St. Clementia's.

"Oh, Lord. James, it's good of you to come! I don't know how the women do this." Mr. Harkness batted his offending skirts down and abandoned the jar of paint. "I didn't expect you to come to the dressing rooms, such as they are."

"I'll go and sit with Charlotte in the pews directly."

****

James, already divested of his hat, twisted it nervously in his hands as he surveyed his potential father-in-law with a critical eye.

The normally somber and refined undertaker was in a white and pink gown, festooned and befurbelowed with lace and ribbons. A white horsehair wig in a comical tower of curls rested on a wooden hobby horse behind him. From under the edge of the gown peeped the toes of wide black boots. As his clever love had predicted, James' courage increased exponentially at the sight of Mr. Harkness in such a fashion.

426

"Mr. Harkness, I have something I wish to ask you." James knew that it was too soon to wed, even too soon to ask for permission to wed, but the thought of waiting a month or two to be alone together or even share an "allowable" kiss was becoming unbearable.

Another day was too long to wait to confess that he wished Charlotte to be his wife. A month after their fateful meeting, he stood before her father and prayed for the right words—and the ability to contain his laughter.

****

Mr. Harkness' face softened at the sight of the anxious surgeon. He knew exactly what was coming and his answer would be a resounding yes, despite the brevity of their courtship. Of course, he would have preferred the lad wait to ask him until he *wasn't* in his Old Dame costume.

"Mr. Harkness… Mr. Harkness, I love Charlotte."

"I know you do, James."

"I would like to ask for her hand in marriage. Not that we would marry soon," he hastily added. "I promise to make sure she never wants for anything in my power to give her. I know that courting while mourning is unseemly and arranging a wedding while mourning is more unseemly still. Notwithstanding those objections, I desire to make my intentions known before another moment passes. Life is all too easily cut short as we among the dead and dying know."

"A truer word was never spoken. You have my blessing, dear boy. Ask her and welcome. Of course, I imagine your family may not desire such a match. I will not have you follow your heart to wrack and ruin without due consideration," he concluded gravely.

"My mother consents, though I'm sure she'll avoid

telling her society matrons the specifics of Charlotte's 'fortune.' " The young surgeon's warm voice momentarily grew frosty. "If she would measure a lady by acres and gold instead of love and wit, let her. I shall use a different scale. At any rate, my mother intends to wed again and won't be living in London after the fact. We'll keep the house in Wedgewood Crescent if Charlotte fancies it. If not, my cousin Nathaniel and his young bride may want it. It'll stay in the family, just as my father's business has. As for a new home... I could look perhaps somewhere in Blackfriars, near St. Paul's? There would be ample patrons for a surgeon and physician, and plenty of properties that would house both a residence and a surgery. Best of all, it's near enough to journey easily to your establishment each day." James let the phrase dangle as a thread before a reluctant old tom.

Mr. Harkness cleared his throat. "Oh. Well, that's not necessary."

"It most assuredly is. Charlotte won't be happy unless you're in her life. She wants to help with the family business. Moreover, she has a gift. Souls speak to her. She helps send them homeward."

Eyes wide, Reginald demanded, "Charlotte told you about her—"

"Gift. Her *God-given* gift." James' eyes glinted dangerously, daring him to disagree.

Drawing himself up to his full flounced and bustled height, Mr. Harkness stared him down. "Be that as it may, I do not want Charlotte to mess about with embalming and things of that nature!"

The challenge in the younger man's eyes fled and was replaced with pleading. "Well... would you take me on, then? Surely a son-in-law can carry on with Harkness and Sons?" James hurried ahead before Mr. Harkness could speak, "Surely his wife can still help in the business in *some* fashion, as she has done, and maybe a bit more when you retire?"

Mr. Harkness' eyebrows slowly rose. "You're a surgeon. You've just finished your final examinations."

"I know that, Reginald."

"You'd give that up to learn our trade?"

"*If* you consent to allow Charlotte to assist you as she has been, or perhaps take on other duties. Not embalming. Well, not yet."

Reginald chewed his words thoughtfully before setting them free. "No… No, I don't think so, James."

"Fine." Everly masked his disappointment with a stiff manner. "I will take my leave and let you prepare. I thank you for your blessing."

Reginald smothered a smile as his future son-in-law turned to leave. "No, I don't wish you to give up your career in surgery. If you're as passionate about your trade as Charlotte is about ours, then it would be an unkindness on my part. I would value your assistance in some things, of course. Perhaps moving coffins if Bartlesby does his back in again, or picking up embalming spirits at the apothecary if you'll be going there in your capacity as a physician."

****

James turned slowly, ducking again under the low wooden beams. He caught the half smile Mr. Harkness set free. "And Charlotte?"

"I think she can help us both. A surgeon's wife and an undertaker's daughter. I'd like her to be happy and— and odd as it is, that's what makes her so."

"Oh, yes, indeed it does!" James sprang forward and

wrung the older man's hand. "Thank you, sir. She'll be so pleased that matrimony doesn't force her from your door or your business."

"She's found herself a treasure in you, James, honestly. Not many a man can see just how wonderful she is."

"Father! The vicar is growing impatient, and the pews are filling up. Aren't you ready yet?" Charlotte rushed through the door. She stopped at the sight of her father and her intended with their hands clasped in a heartfelt handshake. "What are you two doing? James, you're delaying Father."

"He was—just going to help me on with this wig. It's a monstrosity, isn't it?" Mr. Harkness hastily thrust the wig into James' hands.

Charlotte put her hands on her hips, radiating suspicion. "*And*?"

"I was down here asking your father about the particulars of your line of work. I thought I might give it a try, you know. Now that I'm to be a son of the family."

Charlotte's hands flew over her mouth in a happy gasp. "Oh, James! You asked him?" The joy was marred, tinged with puzzlement. "Our line of work? You can't give up being a surgeon. You've worked so hard for it."

"Precisely what I said, my dear." Mr. Harkness shuddered into his wig and squared his shoulders, which nearly split the seams of his dress. "No, no. That's for you to continue. Perhaps one day, when I'm ready to take things at a leisurely pace, James can take over—under your direction. Perhaps you'll have a son who fancies following in your footsteps."

"Or a daughter," Charlotte said pointedly, beaming.

Mr. Harkness let out a long sigh. "You will never let

me have the last word, will you, my dear?"

"Rarely." Charlotte laughed, putting one arm through her father's and one arm through James' outstretched elbow.

"Do you see what you are getting into, Dr. Everly? Are you quite sure you wish to enter into the holiest estate of marriage with such a stubborn girl?" Mr. Harkness' voice was rich with mock exasperation, but his eyes were wet around the edges.

"I assuredly am certain. There is no other woman for me," James answered staunchly.

****

Charlotte didn't know a heart could be so light and not lift her feet from the floor. Or perhaps it would if I were not so well-anchored, she mused, supported on either side by her two dearest friends, her father and her beloved.

"Reginald! Hurry and get your face on!" Mr. Bartlesby suddenly stuck his panicked, pop-eyed countenance down the back stairs. "The crowd is getting rowdy and runnin' out of patience with Christmas songs. There's a call for the pianist to strike up 'A London Lassie's Folly.' "

"Oh, heavens! The vicar will have my head." Skirts billowing and wig tilting precariously, Mr. Harkness rushed to his powder and paint.

"Evenin', Miss Harkness. Doctor!" Bartlesby also fled.

Charlotte tugged James' arm. "We'd better hurry to our seats and let Father prepare."

"Indeed. I wouldn't want to miss this." James trotted along, his hand in hers.

****

"Quite different from the operas and balls you're used to, isn't it?" Charlotte asked as they struggled through the clamoring crowd. Everyone who caught sight of her with her handsome beau nodded and greeted them warmly.

"It is. It admittedly has a different aroma than the powdered and perfumed parties Mother forced me to attend in my youth. Would you like to know something, my love?" James whispered as they inched and scooted their way into a crowded, overheated pew in the back.

"What's that?" Charlotte asked, finally taking a seat.

"I prefer this. Especially the company." He laid his arm possessively around her waist.

As no one could see them as the lights faded, Charlotte snuggled into his side and rested her head on his shoulder.

A month ago, she had seen his haggard face through a crack in the door. Now, she saw his handsome countenance everywhere, most especially in her thoughts. "Especially the company," she agreed, clasping his hand tightly as the bedsheet curtains rose and the show began.

Mr. Harkness' Favorite Shortbreads

Ingredients:
2 cups of flour
1 cup of cubed butter
½ cup of granulated sugar
Extra sugar for sprinkling
1 tsp of vanilla or the zest of one lemon (optional)

Directions:

Preheat oven to 300° F.

Cream butter and sugar together.

Add flour and mix till it forms a semi-firm ball of dough.

Using a parchment-lined 13x9 pan, press the dough into the pan with your fingers until the dough is evenly distributed.

Use a fork to prick the dough all over. You can make patterns, if you wish.

Sprinkle sugar evenly over the top.

Bake for 40-45 minutes until lightly golden.

Take out and let cool on the pan for about half an hour before slicing into squares.

Mr. Harkness recommends two large squares with a cup of tea at least once per day. If you have a stubborn daughter, a visit from the police, or a difficult client, repeat as necessary.

Charlotte's Chewy Ginger Biscuits (Modernized)

Ingredients:
6 tablespoons butter, softened
½ cup white granulated sugar
1/4 cup of applesauce OR 1 egg
2 tablespoons brown sugar
2 tablespoons molasses
1 ½ cup of flour
1 teaspoon baking soda
2 teaspoons ground ginger
½ teaspoon ground cinnamon
½ teaspoon ground nutmeg
½ teaspoon ground cloves
¼ tsp. salt
3 tablespoons white sugar (set aside for sprinkling)

Directions:
Cream butter and sugar together until fluffy.
Beat in applesauce, molasses, and brown sugar.
Add in flour, salt, baking soda, and spices, a little at a time until incorporated.
Dough should be shapeable but not too wet. Add more flour if needed.
Form dough into a ball and chill in the refrigerator for 20 minutes.
While dough is chilling, preheat oven to 350° F.
Pour 3 tablespoons of the white granulated sugar into a small bowl.
Remove chilled dough and shape into balls the size of large marbles or small golf balls.
Roll balls in sugar.

Place on parchment lined baking sheet and flatten with the bottom of a glass.

Bake for 8-10 minutes until edges are crisp and lightly browned. Remove cookies from tray and set on a cooling rack straight away.

Miss Harkness recommends these with a strong cup of tea and a good scholarly book. Or if you should have a gentleman call upon you, these are sure to warm his stomach—and his heart.

Ham and Leek Pie

(Also known as "What shall we do with the leftover ham before it goes off?" pie.)

Pie crust:
Ingredients:
1 1/4 cups all-purpose flour
1/4 teaspoon salt
1/2 cup butter, chilled and diced
1/4 cup ice water

This makes ONE 9-inch pie crust.

Directions:
>In a large bowl, combine flour and salt.
>Cut in butter until mixture resembles coarse crumbs.
>Stir in water, a tablespoon at a time, until mixture forms a ball.
>Wrap in plastic and refrigerate for 4 hours or overnight.

Ham and Leek Filling:

Ingredients:
1-2 cups of chopped ham (leftovers from a roast ham work beautifully)
3 cups of thinly sliced leeks (white portion only)
1 cup of thinly sliced peeled potatoes
¼ cup of cubed butter
½ cup of flour
1 ¼ cup of milk or nondairy milk
1 ¼ cup of vegetable or chicken broth
Freshly ground black pepper

Sprinkle of rosemary, parsley, and thyme to taste

Directions:

Heat butter in a large saucepan.

Add leeks and potatoes and cook until they begin to soften (Note: This is an ideal time to get out the pie crust you made earlier.)

Stir in flour until blended.

Gradually stir in milk and broth.

Bring to a boil over medium heat, stirring constantly until the mixture has thickened.

Remove from heat and stir in ham, ground pepper, and herbs to your liking.

Preheat your oven to 400° F.

Pour your mixture into a greased/buttered glass baking dish.

Roll out your pie crust between two pieces of parchment paper until it is very thin and will cover your pie dish.

Prick the top of the pie crust three-four times.

Bake for about 20-25 minutes until you have golden brown crust and a bubbly filling.

A word about the author...

Bestselling author M. Culler can't stick to just one genre. She writes fantasy, mystery, and all flavors of romance. M. Culler lives in historic Chester County, Pennsylvania, where potentially haunted battlegrounds and eighteenth-century buildings serve as never-ending inspiration. M. Culler lives for her two brilliant children (mini-bookworms), her gorgeous husband (who must hold the world's record for patience), her endlessly entertaining students, and her wonderful friends and family. If she's not hunched over a laptop, you'll find her baking up a storm in the kitchen, playing board games, or watching Brit Coms. Soli Deo Gloria.

mcullerauthor@gmail.com
Website and Newsletter:
https://ghostsintheink.wixsite.com/mculler
Facebook
https://www.facebook.com/MCullerGhostsintheink
Amazon:
https://www.amazon.com/M.-
Culler/e/B07MZ7KP6S%3Fref=dbs_a_mng_rwt_scns_
share
Bookbub:
https://www.bookbub.com/profile/m-culler
https://ghostsintheink.wixsite.com/mculler